The Power of Love
The One

Ross J. Kinnaird

ISBN: 978-1-7394634-1-0

For more info on The Power of Love Series®
www.thepowerofloveseries.com

Second edition: June 2024

First Print: June 2024

Edited by Imogen Howson

Cover by Ardel Media

DEDICATIONS

To Noel, who has shown me the power and magic of true love. Over the years, as events have unfolded, you have become the most important part of my life. You have healed old wounds and replaced painful memories with new, beautiful ones.

Always & Forever.

To Ketty, who I will always see as the one who guided me through life without ever failing me. There, where I had a hole in my heart, you filled it unconditionally, becoming the mother I had never had.

To Stefania, who inspired a good part of this story. As we turned our friendship in a forever bond, I look at you as the one who came in my life to stay. May you read these pages and find yourself in it, proud in how I see you through the eyes of Love.

Last but not least, to Rita-Louise. Writing the pages about you made my heart move at the speed of light. It's incomprehensible how a human being, a simple soul, could make the difference between light and darkness, pain and happiness. I can only wish to be to someone else what you have been for me, one day.

CONTENTS

Chapter One

Once Upon A Dream

∞

What would I have said, what would I have done if I had known the real me? If I had owned the power of my own brother, would I have gone back and warned the Daniel I once was? Would I have told my young self that nothing can be done, nothing can be changed once your heart suddenly starts beating with a new, strange sound? What should I have done when it had become clear that the man I was with was not the one? The thousands of thoughts, words, feelings I had brought with me, were they part of a Daniel that wanted to stay or were they part of me who wanted to move forward?

It all began, or so I believed, when I started to question my own true feelings. The truth is, nothing ever started or ended. It was a circle of coming to life and coming to an end, a search for something greater, a hunt for the real power of love. Something didn't feel right. For a long time, something held me back, like I was meant to move further, beyond what I long believed were my dreams.

For a long while, I thought I felt the wrong type of love, a love that could seem strange to many, a love that didn't quite fit the picture. After all, I could only compare it with the love I had seen around me, on TV or who knows where and when.

When I met John it wasn't special, it wasn't like I felt something new for the first time, but it was definitely strong. I was twenty-seven, during one of my trips from Italy back to the land of magic, how I loved to call it. I had ended up waiting at the airport for five never-ending hours because the flight was delayed. There, right in front of me, lost amongst hundreds of empty chairs, John was drawing something on a large book, completely taken by a silent spell, with his sad look hidden within his own body, like a cat that tries to hide its form before falling asleep. His hair falling over his skinny face looked like wet sand storming against the pale colour of his cheeks. The moment I looked over was the moment I got trapped in his magic movements. Between his hands and his book, there I was, wondering what he was drawing, thinking, feeling. My emotions formed for the first time, as he could draw them with the bare power of his pencil. I felt the weird impulse to ask there and then what was he up to, and before I could realize it, I stood right next to him.

'I wish I could do something like that,' I said. 'I think it would make this awful waiting a bit more bearable,' I added quickly, in the attempt to sound less of an intruder.

'It's not that difficult,' he replied, without even turning his head up to me. It was like he was about to save the world and I was just a breeze moving through. Well, that wasn't it.

'I imagine you are waiting for the same flight, back to Ireland. It seems we are the only people left,' I added.

'There are few down there,' he replied with a flat tone, at which point I was ready to raise the whitest flag of all the casual conversations. 'But yes, me, you and those folks over there are going the same way.' And then he looked at me with such a small smile that I almost believed I'd imagined it.

'*Those folks.*' How was it that I could see only him? We managed to put few more sentences together before he engaged in a more appealing conversation, but there we were, after thirty minutes, telling our stories, attempting a laugh, meeting each other in a strange, invisible middle ground. On a half-empty plane, we decided to defy the steward's instructions and sat together to continue our mutual digging into each other's lives. I didn't know he was into me and I didn't know I was into him. It was just the pure pleasure of sharing thoughts. Almost three years later, we had a lot to say still and a lot of life to live together. At least, this is what I thought.

Things didn't change from a day to another. For a long while, I thought I truly loved him and that he was the right man for me. John never failed in being a beautiful human being, in making me feel loved. To this day, after the magic, the losses we had to endure, the tears we shed, he is still one of the purest souls who has ever walked on this Earth. Whether I had chosen him or I had been moved by other

15

hands, like a marionette bound to its strings, it didn't matter. It felt right, it felt like my heart wanted it.

The unknown will behind every move I made, every corner I turned, had been there since the beginning of my time, with me and within me. It had been hiding for a very long time, silencing the fact that I had been moved like a pawn, moves and countermoves, by many, and furthermore by someone that had the power to own me completely. Initially, I struggled in letting go the idea I could fight that unknown power. I tried to stay by John's side even when it became clear I was meant to be giving it all up. Nothing worked. I could not move either way, I could not have him and I could not let him go.

Somewhere in my troubled mind, I still remember when the first signs of my awakening began. They were subtle, concealed in small, scattered pieces of dreams I had at night. If I had been asked then, I would have said I couldn't make sense of anything at all. Certainly, I would have never been able to understand that what I was actually witnessing was my first calling.

At first, I started waking up to a strange feeling of sadness. I didn't know why; I could not recall anything I had seen in my long oneiric walks. My days were filled with a sense of oppression and urgency, as if I was pushed out of my own body, my mind trying to have a life of its own. Then came the fog and its sense of oppression. Shortly after, the hills, the red harsh ground, and the grey, vast lake. Every time, I had woken up with a sense of drowning glued to my lungs, my skin. A few months later, details became more tangible and I began to feel like I was awake in my own dreams. Places and details would turn into new landscapes, spinning fast, vanishing before I could come to realize their true nature. Worried about these persistent visions, I asked John if I ever talked in my sleep or stood up and walked or did anything that could give me a hint as to what was actually happening to me.

'Are you sure?' I persisted as we sat inside a café in town on a heavy rainy day.

'Of course I'm sure.' He couldn't understand why I was scared. 'You are quite the opposite. Sometimes it feels like you're dead or something.'

'What do you mean, dead?' I asked, puzzled, my voice faltering.

'Calm down,' he said, reaching for my hand across the table, while I gripped my cup of coffee as if I could shatter it with just the power of my fear. 'Sometimes, and I'm saying sometimes, it feels like you've left your body or something. You just lie there, like you're not breathing.'

Like I left my body. Those words struck me like the thunder raging outside.

'I've tried to wake you up a couple of times, but you were just lying there like nobody's home. I've never thought this was serious because you usually are back, moving and stuff, a few seconds later. I'm sorry, I should have told you, but if it helps, I don't think this is something to be worried about,' he added with the typical small smile he had given me what felt like centuries ago.

'You know,' I tried to explain, 'it feels like something is coming my way. I know, I know,' I quickly added in response to his look. He was about to tell me his usual 'everything is fine'. 'I have this constant odd feeling of

17

imminent change, like I'm standing on the edge of something and I'm about to fall.'

'In your dream, you mean?' he asked.

'Initially yes. Now it feels like it's emerging into reality. I can feel it when I'm awake. I can feel it now...'

He looked at me with a mix of sadness and disappointment, like someone who had just lost the first prize in a big competition. He wanted to understand. He wanted to understand to control it. Or maybe that was me all the way, seeing in his eyes the cracks within my head. It wasn't long after that conversation, and not long before my thirtieth birthday, that things went into fast track mode. My dreams quickly came to life, filled with sounds and emotions, while reality became less tangible, confused, and places started to mix with impossible realities.

A group of people was laughing loudly. It was a celebration, a wedding, and a strong scent of magnolias floated all around. I could hear the calling of a name. Someone was late to his own most important day. There was no panic. There was no fear, and there was, before that sunny day. *How can you feel things that have been when you have never seen them happening? How do you know what you are feeling if you have never felt it before?* A long run of stairs was packed with people on both sides. There was happiness, there was loss, all at once. A tall man stood right at the top. Tension on his square shoulders, he adjusted his suit, moving his dark hair away from his neck. Three entities watched over him. *Am I meant to walk up those stairs? This sound, these feelings, I have to be part of it!* Certain this was my life all along, I was already moving my steps forward when my body froze.

18

I was stopped. One of the three celebrants had moved her eyes onto me. She was far away and suddenly behind me, in the split of a second. Her hand held me back, pulling my arm away, away from that happiness, that moment I wanted with all of myself.

'You are mistaken,' a voice to my right whispered. 'There are things that have been and are no longer, things that have never been, are waiting to be.'

I was mistaken? That moment belonged to me! As I turned to see and look, ready to ask what she wanted, there she was. An old lady was standing right before my eyes. I had never seen her, but I had met her before. She was there and she wasn't. I knew her, but she didn't look that way to me. She had the sweetest tone and the hardest look.

'There are things that have been and are no longer, things that have never been, waiting to be,' she repeated. And then she vanished, her place, her voice, and everything surrounding faded in the blink of an eye.

I was wide awake, staring at the ceiling, frozen in a broken vow I didn't get to make. I wanted to reach that top. I wanted to see and make the promise. I wanted to say yes. The old lady was gone from sight, but I could still hear her whispers, as if she had just moved somewhere over the wooden beams, inside the walls, hiding in my own home.

The days after that night, sleeping became more problematic. I wanted to know and I was afraid to know at the same time. I forced myself to stay awake at first. Then, to ensure I wouldn't dream again, I had music in my ears and read books before going to bed. Despite all my efforts, I found myself back again. In a moment of weakness, my

19

eyes closed, and my body found itself inside a small, old boat, floating on the vast, grey lake I had learned to recognize at once. There was no sound, no breeze, no life. Everything was flat, grey, as if mist had settled for days. Sitting quietly beside me was someone else.

'Hello?' My voice was flickering, low, as if it was traveling through the same water I was floating on. 'Who are you? Where are we?' Every word I said transformed into a useless bubbling sound.

I could see the other man sitting still, frozen and wrapped in too many layers of dark, worn-out wool. A greenish glow emanated from inside his garments, and his hands stuck through, each holding an oar, but to no use. We weren't moving. Then, the water started to rise, silently. It rose so fast I didn't have time to react. And then I was under. The top was now below, and the bottom was over my head. Flipped, submerged, there I was. I couldn't breathe.

'Let me out!'

The more I forced myself to keep my dreams under control by staying awake, the more I started to lose control during the day. Working became unbearable, and I began to lie about the reason I felt constantly tired. Trying to cheer me up and with my birthday approaching, John invited our friends to our house for a pre-festive celebration, thinking it would magically solve all the issues.

'You'll see, that's what you need right now.' He showed so much confidence that I nearly believed it.

'John, I don't think this is going to go away. I'm not going mad, I'm sure of it. Perhaps there's something that I have to figure out?' I asked, almost as if I were confessing it to myself.

'I personally believe you shouldn't give too much attention to these dreams. It will only make it worse. After all, they are just dreams,' he said, as if he could erase everything with the power of pure denial.

'I know, John. This is, after all, at the very core of my profession. I'm trying to think what I would see in someone who's experiencing the same. What I would say to them but…'

It wasn't important, and it wasn't real. Making it real would have made it important, or maybe it was the other way around. He had said that to me a few times. Too many times. Our friends came along as planned that night, two days before my birthday, and all of them came with the intention of saving me from going mad. They didn't know from what evil I needed to be rescued, but John apparently had dropped a 'to cheer him up' in the invite.

'So, what's going on? You're sad 'cause you're getting old and wrinkled or is there more?' Shannon asked, while helping me setting the table. Her boyfriend, Mark, already had his hands on the thing he loved the most, after Shannon. He was pouring some wine, when he smiled at me as if he wasn't taking any responsibility for that 'offensive' question.

'Shannon, let him be,' he told her across the kitchen.

'What?' she replied. 'It's not like this isn't going to happen to all of us?'

'Well, this has happened to you, how long now? Ten years?' jumped in Anita, trying to take my side. 'After all, he is the youngest of us all.' And she walked through the front door, out into the garden. 'Come out you, birthday boy! It's still warm outside, let's have a smoke,' she shouted, a few seconds later.

Even smoking wasn't giving me relief any more. There was no escape. My head would go straight to the madness I was going through. During dinner, we went in and out of the core of all my troubles, without quite jumping right at it. I was happy like that. They were my friends, but I wasn't sure I could share every tormented detail or expect they would react in a surprising new way, a way that would solve the issue.

'What do you mean "it feels real"? Like you are awake while dreaming?' Theresa was pretty late to every conversation, a bit lost in her own madness but always willing to help anyone.

'Not really. It's more like I can feel it. Like it's happening for real,' I tried to explain.

'You are the psychologist here,' Mark let out, smiling. 'Should you not know what this is?'

'You know? I read in an article...' And there Shannon started her mumbling about knowing everything about every single thing on Earth. '...and they said that it's possible,' and added a convincing face at the end. *What is possible?* I thought. I had lost her before I could tune in.

'I'm not sure what I'm about to say...' Anita said, coming from nowhere. She didn't usually make open statements to the public, not even in a small gathering of friends. I was listening, surprised. '...but I would say these dreams are coming to you for a reason. Don't get me wrong,' she continued before Shannon could take over, 'I'm not talking about ghosts or something like that! I'm talking about ourselves and our deepest thoughts.'

'Or it could really be a ghost!' Theresa's eyes enlarged. 'You know my Aunty Marge? She had one... I'd say even more than one, considering how mad she went in her later days!' And to her fingers spinning beside her head, we laughed, picturing the sad, funny look of Aunty Marge.

'What would someone look for...in a ghost, I mean?' Mark asked, leaving the table to get another bottle of wine and triggering an unhappy look on his girlfriend's face. It was almost like I could read her thoughts: *The more this conversation goes, the more he can drink, blamelessly.*

'Guys, let's not go all crazy,' John said, taking the bottle of wine away from Mark's hands. 'Next thing, we are going to talk to a priest or something. We are not kids believing in magic any more.' And at that last sentence, I felt somehow attacked.

'I think the obvious solution is most likely the right one. I think you are only trying to recall something, trying to resolve it.' And Anita had just put an end to the 'crazy talks'.

She honestly stated the obvious, there and then, but she was right. John redirected the attention to some cupcakes Anita had made for us, and I was happy to be dragged out of my misery for a little while. She had come that night without her boyfriend, but I didn't know how, I had forgotten to ask why. It was always all said or nothing said with her. I'd say I went for the latter, that night. When everyone was already gone and John was busy cleaning the kitchen, Anita and I went for our last cigarette of the night, sitting on a bench right outside the front door. The garden was already wet from the moist night and the smell of flowers was coming our way.

'Can you smell it?' I asked her.

'What? The grass?'

'Yes! Can you smell it?'

'Yeah. Of course I can!' she replied, laughing.

'You see? This is what I'm talking about. I can smell it in my dreams, I can smell it when I wake up. Not the grass, of course,' I quickly added, as she looked at me wonderingly. 'It feels real, Anita. Like now.'

'Are you sure you are dreaming?' she asked, looking up into the dark above the garden.

'Is there a chance I'm not?' I whispered, as if I was asking myself.

'Well, whatever this is, I think you need to allow it through. Something is trying to reach out. From within, from outside, I can't tell. But I feel you should give in.' And there she smiled at me, let the dead cigarette go, and stood up.

'I don't think it will be that hard. Whatever this is, it's growing. It's making contact more often. I don't know if it's just me or it's the house, those walls. It's like I'm watched.'

'No ghost talks, right? But I think I know what you are saying. I do feel a little bit strange when I'm here. Don't look at me like that! I'm not saying I'm daydreaming. It's more like a feedback, like a sound? Anyway, time to go. Breathe in. Let it flow. I have an idea for your birthday. We can talk about it tomorrow, when John is not around.' And after saying goodnight to me and him, she left.

After seeing Anita's car turning the corner, I walked to the far gates and closed them up. Summer had already started and I could feel in the air the sweet scent of flowers all around. Back at the house, I decided to stay outside just a little bit longer. It was as if I hoped that the clear, peaceful night would penetrate my flesh, inside my heart, cleanse it. I had moved only few steps away from the same spot where Anita and I were sitting a few moments earlier, when I started to feel the cold coming up from the ground. The scent of grass grew stronger. And there it came. I could see it with my eyes open.

Again, a group of people, loads of voices all around. No stairs this time, no feelings of loss or happiness either. *Just joy, perhaps?* A strange, upside-down tree branched its roots in the dark sky, surrounded by ceremonial stones, scattered across a rounded space. It was like I had been placed in a bubble with no perception of space and time. A man stood next to me, ready to begin. Suddenly the sky turned, the ground changed. Green valleys embraced his presence, as he stood at the edge of a forest, beside a tall, large tree. And above our heads, a voice whispered again.

'Things that have never been, are waiting to be. Please, remember. There is not much time left. Hurry!'

Chapter Two
The Birthday Plan

∞

That was the first time I was sure I had not been dreaming. I was standing right there, outside the house, when the entire world around me had disappeared. *This wasn't a dream*, I kept telling myself for a few minutes, after it had vanished. *Is something really trying to reach out?* On my way back inside, I had the urge to tell John what had just happened. *He's not going to deny it, this time.* I thought. *It was real... He must believe it! Believe in what? Something that nobody else has seen? Am I really expecting him to understand? No, he wouldn't.* The closer I got to those visions, the less I wanted to tell. So, there the night ended. A few smiles, some comments about our friends and up to bed we went, forgetting that, in the dark of my nights, I wasn't safe at all.

The following day Anita texted me to meet up and talk about my birthday. I was there reading her text thinking if it really was worth doing anything.

Anita

**Hoy. Let's meet up at the Treeshop at 1pm?
Time to plan.**

She didn't ask about my night. Did she have to? I knew she had thought about it. That's how Anita was. Strong like a castle but with tiny windows, to allow only small amounts of weakness or pain. Our conversation the night before was brief, direct but yet now closed. She knew, she understood and was now ready to move on to the birthday plan. I loved her very much and I knew she cared. So I pretended to be a bit like her and I went along.

Daniel

Sounds good. Can't wait to meet.

Anita

Bring a diary and a pen...

Daniel

O.O ok

That Saturday afternoon was a typical Irish summer afternoon. It had rained, and the sun had finally won against the odds, hot and shining. It gave us some hope that

27

we could still sit outside at the café. That place was Anita's favourite. It stood outside Castlecross, around twenty minutes driving, well into the countryside, but it had a massive field all around and, on a nice day, people could sit outside and enjoy the good weather. Although very popular, that day it was nearly empty. Driving in, I guessed people had decided to leave it for another time, due to the heavy storm just past. Anita was already there, trying to dry the table and the chairs on the patio before the waitress could get out and do it herself. I smiled while walking in, having seen something so typical of her. She was determined to sit in the open. I could imagine the conversation that had happened with the staff, before I even got in.

'Do you mind if we sit outside?'

'Well, it's pretty wet out there. We haven't had the chance to clean it up.'

'Oh, it's OK. I'm waiting for a friend anyway. I'll be outside then.'

A few seconds later, she was telling me about that exact same conversation. So predictable, but so funny. She was so ready to get that bit of sun that nobody could have stopped her.

Anita was standing up and I was standing up. The chairs were still playing the soft music of dripping drops, a last memory of the rain passed.

'So,' she said. 'Did you bring everything?'

'Oh, right. I forgot it in the car,' I said. By the time I had come back, the not-so-happy waitress had already started

28

drying everything as fast as she could, probably wishing we would get wet anyway.

'What do you need a pen for? What are we writing?' I asked, curious.

'Let's order something first? Then we can get this started,' she replied, with her nose already halfway through the menu.

No long after, she had already planned my birthday in every detail. John was going to work for the weekend and the bank holiday Monday too. Anita had the idea of taking the chance to go somewhere, 'for a bit of fun'. I knew she actually meant 'to get you out of that house, that bed and those dreams'. She would have never said it. She would have never said anything about John working on my birthday, and I was happy about it, because I'd given up the idea of having John not working on weekends a long time before.

Anita and I had been friends for many years. I always knew we shared a secret, an unspoken rule about telling each other everything and nothing at the same time. There was a sort of hidden etiquette about things we shouldn't have been discussing. If we really had to, we would do it briefly, once or twice, but that would be pretty much it. Although we talked a few times about things like family drama or arguments with our partners, I truly believed she never liked indulging in painful situations. Hence, once the topic was out, it would be addressed quickly and closed for good, straight after. At that point, when I thought we would never talk again about my situation, she opened up:

'I believe you need to write down what's happening,' she went straight to the point. 'And also the details of what you see and feel. If there is a reason, that's in those details. If that happened to me, I would write it down right away.'

'Oh, wow...' I replied. 'Is this why you asked me to bring a book and a pen?'

'Partially. I'm thinking also to write down our trip for your birthday.' And she sipped some coffee, like she had just said the most obvious thing on Earth.

'Our trip? Our trip where? When?' I asked, spilling some of my coffee.

'For your birthday!' she replied, like I was deaf. 'We have been saying to go to Connemara for ages now, the two of us. Now I feel it's time.'

I don't know why, my mind went instantly to Patrick. 'What about Patrick?' I asked, without even thinking.

'What about Patrick?' she asked back, as if she owned the right to ask that question.

'Don't you think he will want to come?'

'I wouldn't say so, but, anyway, this is our trip. It's going to be me and you.'

'Is everything OK with the two of you?' I knew I was forcing the conversation.

'Yeah...whatever OK could mean.'

The window was closed. There wasn't going to be any conversation around Patrick. No questions asked about why he wasn't there, at the pre-fake birthday party, nor why he wasn't allowed to come on our trip.

'I was thinking, we should go to those places in Connemara we planned to visit three years ago,' she continued. 'We were all booked in and everything, remember? Then you had to rush back to Italy...by the way' —she added—'how's your grandmother?'

'She is fine, I'd say. And yes, I do remember,' I replied, enthusiastic.

'Cool. What about we get on the road tomorrow morning? We should be able to spend the day there and some of the day after, before heading back?'

'Wait, I need to tell John first,' I replied. 'I nearly forgot about John, is that normal?'

'I told John already. He needs to know only if you said yes or no,' she said, like she had just organized a world revolution.

In less than one hour, we had the whole trip organized, places to go and see, where to get food, where to stop while on the road. It didn't strike me then, but during that hour I felt like a different man. I was so far from my recent dramas. It felt good. It felt right. I can't really tell if it was because Anita filled my mind with new ideas, or because that was going to be the exact moment that would change my life forever. But it felt like it was going to be right. We spent a few hours in that place, sitting on those squeaky chairs, looking at the open world in front of us. The sun was getting bigger and red but still not too close to the horizon, when we decided to head back. The plan was plain and simple.

'Pack your bags. Have a shower. Tell John you are going and then go to bed. We leave early tomorrow. I'll pick you up. You drive. Oh, have coffee ready!' she said, walking to her car. I was happy to do that. I really was.

'Anita,' I said briefly. 'Are you sure?'

'Oh yes. Don't ask me why, but I feel we have to do this.'

I stayed beside my car for a few minutes after Anita had left. It was like she had put in motion a deep dive in my thoughts and I was just standing still, trying to focus. My feet planted on a sloppy soil soaked with too much water, I was going back in time, when we were all set to go on our trip the first time. What would have happened if we had gone the first time? No flight to Italy meant not meeting John, our last three years would have been erased, not seeing my grandma. My grandma and her sudden sickness suddenly made space in my mind, strong and forceful, like she was in her youth.

The day I got the call from a neighbour of hers was a very bad day. I had just changed job, moved to one of these big corps that have all the best intentions and no soul, trying to put myself under the impression I could change the world…sitting on a chair…at an anonymous desk.

The call had surprised me at many levels. My mother was again nowhere to be found, probably wandering somewhere with other members of her cult. Honestly, I didn't expect to hear from her, but I couldn't stop thinking that the news should have come from her. It seemed like something in me was still holding to a supreme sense of justice, hoping she would have finally taken the place of a good daughter, a good mother. The lady living at number thirty-seven was my grandmother's long-time friend. They had moved into two old houses next to each other in a small village in the shadow of the big mountain, in the south of Italy, something like thirty years earlier. She was a lady in every sense. Even the way she had told me that my grandma had a mental setback was gentle and full of compassion. It reminded me the time I brought my first boyfriend home to meet the matriarch, and she was there, open arms and with a smile that would erase the entire hate in the world.

'Hi bimbo bellissimo (my beautiful child). It's Sara. Your nonna's friend.'

I was in the middle of my training for the new job I had just started, and I hadn't quite realized what that call was about, at first. All I knew was her and her sweet, sweet voice.

'Your nonna is not very well. She is physically OK,' she said quickly, before I could get worried. 'She had just a few, small episodes of mental disconnection.' I knew she was measuring her words.

'What do you mean?' I said, skipping the greetings.

'A few days ago she forgot where she was, just like that. We were talking about the heat, I thought she had a heatstroke. She came back right after and I didn't know what to say. Then it happened again yesterday, for a bit longer. Suddenly she was talking to someone who wasn't there…like a child with an invisible friend. I think her mind is playing tricks on her. She was mentioning her father…after all those years. It was really strange. Unfortunately this morning she went again and didn't come back.'

'Oh my God.' I let it out. 'Where is she now?'

'She is at the hospital. I'm just back home to get her a few things. She is OK, honey. She is OK,' she repeated, like she was trying to calm herself down more than reassuring me.

'Have the doctors said anything about it?' I asked.

'Well, you know, child, we are there more than here, at this stage. I think doctors are pretty happy to dismiss everything using the word *age*.'

'OK...' I was trapped in between my shock and her soft sarcasm.

'Now, listen to me,' she continued. 'She should be getting better fairly quick, I'd say. I'm just calling you to let you know, and if you could come over, I'm sure that would make things easier for her. It might speed things up, if you know what I mean. You know how much she loves you, right?'

Yes, I knew. I knew since I was little, when she used to tell me bedtime stories that brought me into many other worlds. I knew when things were not going well she would have always had a way out, there, ready for me. I knew when I used to tell her about dreams I had and she had an answer for it, each time. My dreams, her answers. Oh, how much I wanted to ask her once more. Especially after I had stood up in my garden, awake, frozen. Especially when I needed it the most.

But I knew she was gone. She had gone in one of her 'moments of disconnection' and had never come back. Shortly after, my mind confined the pain somewhere hidden in the dark and I was back again beside my car, my feet still firm on the wet ground.

34

I shook off my sense of regret and got in my car, rushing my way back at the house. I got home at sunset. John would be back only hours later, so I decided to pack my bags before telling him I was going to go on this unexpected trip with Anita. It didn't take long. I was getting more excited by the hour and, by the time John came back, all my things were lying in the hall, wrapped and ready.

'So, I see you are doing this?' he said, standing at the front door with his keys still in his hand.

'I am, yes. Do you mind?' I quickly asked, knowing that my bags there, between us, quietly listening to our conversation, already ignored any other opinion.

'Anita told me at dinner. She wasn't sure you wanted to go too. I told her you needed it very much,' he added, closing the door.

'I wish you could come,' I said, following him into the kitchen. That moment felt so familiar. That was what we had become. We were chasing each other after losing the beat. Our hearts used to play the same rhythm, once. 'I actually thought it feels weird that you're not coming and neither is Patrick,' I added, to prove I wasn't happy about it.

'Yeah, he didn't show up at dinner too,' he replied, taking his jacket and his shoes off. 'Something odd is happening here.'

'You mean between them?' I asked, lost in his blurry words. 'Or you mean here, here? Between us? Or just me?' I don't know why I went that far.

Is he making me feel I need to ask or I want to bring to light something that is secretly lurking in the shadow of our silence? I was again looking at him, lost in his thoughts, resistant to the idea of looking back at me. We were back at the airport. He talked but didn't engage. *Was it ever different? Have I, all this time, been connecting the two of us, all by myself?*

'With them, I mean.' He was finally looking at me. 'Has she said anything?'

'Nope. You know Anita,' I replied, without adding much more. I was getting closer, searching for a physical soft touch, but he looked tired. His body wasn't the same any more. Still like the day I met him, but a dark veil had covered his beauty. He was still there, somewhere, but out of reach. It was like if I was looking at him from the depths of the sea, his body deformed by the waters. He was still there, I was still there, but in between us, something had fallen.

'What time are you leaving?' he asked, moving away, distracted.

'She'll be here by eight o'clock. We'll be hitting the road shortly after,' I said.

'Are you back on Monday night?' he continued. His words were counted, expensive, hard to put together.

'Yes, I'll be only one night away from you,' I joked, trying to pull him closer, at least emotionally.

'You need a break, Daniel. I'm sure everything's going to be much better once you get a day to relax.' He was smiling. That was the first time he had reached out since that dinner with our friends. It wasn't much, but I heard hope and genuine interest for me, the insane man on a walk to dreamland with no return ticket.

36

I moved next to John and hugged him, like I had to prove my gratitude. I knew we had managed to get our first break from the cold war when he held his arms around me and his head moved slowly onto my shoulder. *Am I feeling his love for me? Am I feeling my love for him? Am I feeling relieved we have finally given in to each other, to show we have no enemies inside our own home?*

We briefly kissed, as we were both committed to seal the moment as a good moment, and then we moved apart. Somewhere, around us, in the space between our hearts, as we had moved away from one another, I felt someone else's presence. It was like something had come to bridge two lovers' gap and now it was letting us go. John and I spent the late evening talking about his big project at work. Something about a piece of art that wouldn't come together or wasn't ready for the big opening day. After a while, the TV took over. My eyes were moving from the noisy movie to the clock. My birthday was very close. *He must have checked the time as many times as I did*, I thought. We both used to celebrate the day on the spot, even just with a kiss. Two minutes before midnight, I decided to check on him, to show I knew he was vigilant to the arrival of the big moment. But there he was, asleep, tired, on the most uncomfortable chair someone could fall asleep on. I could have said something. I think I did.

'John? Are you awake?' But the answer was loud and clear. He wasn't.

I gazed at the clock once again, quickly imagining I would have time to wake him up, let him be the best boyfriend in the world, and get our moment going. But I didn't. It wasn't right. I felt selfish just thinking about it, so

I stood up and went back to check my bags lying on the floor.

If people usually blow on candles at midnight, I could light a cigarette instead, I told myself. So I grabbed my pack of smokes and went outside, closing the door behind me. The weather that day didn't have the best start for a summer day, but it was ending pretty well. It was unusually warm, a light breeze was moving my hair. The leaves of the magnolia trees were making that sound I loved so much.

I had just lit my cigarette when the door behind me clicked the sound of opening. I smiled without turning. I knew what was going to happen. John was about to hug me and kiss my neck, like he used to do. I closed my eyes, puffed my smoke away and I moved my right arm towards the door, to reach him. His hand grabbed my wrist, firmly but powerlessly. It didn't have weight at all and it was cold like the worst winter day. Everything around me started to lose shape, melting under too much fire, and a familiar voice said:

'Time has come. The years have gone by. There is no more to wait for...'

I knew that wasn't John. That voice belonged to something else, someone else. I turned my head around to see. I needed to see. I needed to know. *'If there is a reason, the reason is in these details.'* Those words were stuck in my head.

'Who are you?' I asked. 'Do I know you?'

There was no answer. A long white embroidered cloak hid a face that wasn't moving. I wanted to see! What else could I have looked at? My eyes went down to my wrist.

There, a long, grey hand held my arm with no harmful intention. I wasn't scared, it wasn't worrying. It was old, soft, nearly invisible. Under the strongest of my desires, my body finally moved and turned to embrace the truth. An old woman, with golden eyes like a tea too quickly made, was looking at me, pale, quiet, unchallenged. I could see her. I could feel her even if I knew she wasn't really there. I could smell her scent. Sweet, old, like a clean dress never worn. *Why is she not talking any longer?*

'Who are you? Please, make me understand...' I begged, whispering.

She attempted a smile and her head tilted down like she was willing to say yes, when she started to fade away. I knew she was about to go away. Another day with no answers was on my way. I would go insane. I was already going insane. Then I heard:

'Find him. Find the other one at the edge. Find him.' And then she was gone as she had come.

My cigarette was still in my hand, like time hadn't passed. The sound of crying leaves slowly came back and I opened my eyes to John, who stood there, at the door, in front of me, with a worried face, a birthday card and a chocolate muffin with a big thirty candle on top in his hands. That was the first time I moved further, beyond. The first time I entered my dreams with the power of consciousness. That was the first time John witnessed my mental instability. I was thrilled and I was petrified.

Chapter Three

The Trip

∞

John wouldn't say a word. I watched him standing there where, a minute before, his celebration for me had died. I looked at his hands has they moved down under the weight of misunderstanding. His mind was traveling as fast as light goes, and my mind was falling slowly, in the dark of my own heart. After so long together, that quickly became the most intimate moment we had ever had, as vulnerable as we stood, wearing nothing but fear.

'John...' I attempted, as I felt the power of my tears shaking my body. He dropped the card and the rest on the floor and pulled me into his arms, as strong as I could ever imagine. I was dropping way faster than my heart could beat for. He could not stop it. My body was his, but I was on a free fall.

'It's OK. I got you,' he said. 'I got you, I got you.' The more he said it, the faster I went. Alone, as alone I was born. 'Come inside,' he added after a few seconds, trying to pull me in.

I could not move. John went back into the kitchen fast, saying I needed something to drink, and there I was left, looking like that big candle on the floor, smashed, broken. He came back right away, smiling, with the strength of a thousand rescuers, and took my hand, pulling me into the house. That night was quiet. Whatever cosmic power was taking me, it decided I'd had enough for the day, giving me the peace I needed, not only for myself but for John and the two of us together. We spent the night in a reassuring hug, in a bed too big for two people who are afraid of tomorrow, his head under my chin, his arms against my chest. I was protecting him. I was protecting him from whatever had me in hand..

The morning after, I was up early. I knew Anita would be late as usual, but I wanted to get the time to roam around the house in silence, knowing that John was still in his deepest sleep. The muffin left there, crumbled on the floor, was the first thing I had seen coming downstairs. It didn't hurt me as it did the night before because John had healed me, partially, from my sickness. I quickly cleaned it up, dropped the candle and the muffin in the bin, and left the card on the island in the kitchen. I had my first coffee way before Anita arrived, and I was about to make a second one when she pulled up the drive. I gave another look at the card and some words came to mind as I ran to open the door before she could ring the bell. My first intention was to immediately share what had happened the night before but, after opening the front door, the entire scene of me going mad in front of John represented in my mind, making me feel I had to put some distance between us and my own house before I could feel free to open up. We had our coffee, put the bags in the car, and were ready to go. On my way out of the house, I went back into the kitchen and wrote something on the envelope of the birthday card:

I know you are doing your best and I love you for it. See you tomorrow night! —Daniel.

The first half of our drive went as fast as our talk. Anita and I discussed, excited, about a few places we wanted to see and things we wanted to do. It was only after a good hour that we realized we hadn't planned a pit stop in any specific place. Irish roads in the countryside are unique; we could have driven for a long time before finding a place where to get some petrol and something to eat. Here and there, we passed some deserted places with abandoned petrol stations, reporting a currency that doesn't even exist any more and a price that, today, would make anyone happy.

'Wow, it always surprises me to see things like this,' I said.

'You mean an old village with two deserted homes and a closed-down station?' she asked back, laughing. 'It's weird, I know. It feels like you are entering a different world.'

'Entering and exiting a different world,' I added. 'These places are one mile big, max. By the time you realize it, the village is already gone by.'

'I suppose people moved to the big cities at some stage and never came back,' she replied. 'We'd better check where we can stop before we run out of petrol.'

'We're halfway through. I'd say if we find something close, we could then drive straight with no other pit stops?' I asked.

'Yeah, let's do that.' And she started to check her phone, hoping for a decent connection to navigate the online map.

After a few seconds, she gave up. No petrol station, no village, no signal. Anita pulled out an old map I didn't even know she had in the car and guided me to the closest major road. There, we would find something for sure that was good enough. Proud of never being wrong, Anita was already celebrating our arrival at a big petrol station. Before I could even turn off the car, she had already jumped out, shouting she needed to use the bathroom. We spent a few minutes there, got the full tank in, and went to pay. Anita asked me if we should squeeze some breakfast time into our 'one and only pit stop, please we need to eat something,' so we questioned the woman at the till for any decent place to grab some food.

'Decent? Oh, lad. You joking me?' the woman replied, adding a very weird laugh. She had a funny accent, made more evident by the deep tone of her voice. 'There is John's Pub. That's the only place we have for about twenty miles?'

'John?' I said to Anita. 'I'd take it as a sign, after all, how bad can that be?'

The Irish pub was 'five minutes' walk' from the station. We parked the car and went on foot. We had some trouble finding it at first because it was part of a long series of tiny old cottage houses on the side of the road, and also because our heads were gone at our smartphones as soon as we got some signal.

'Looks like we have stepped into a civilized bubble. I got internet!' she said, her phone already on the map app.

'I wish we hadn't... I got ten messages from work already,' I complained.

'But it's the weekend!' Anita and I had talked before about the lack of well-being I had found in my new job. And again, she made that usual grimace of disagreement.

'Oh, look,' she continued, her phone right at my face. 'Mister *I never know what to do* has found already how to spend his day off.' Patrick had just posted on Instagram a 'fab day with the lads' picture.

'And that is bad because...' I said, not wanting to make a comment about it.

'It's not bad per se. But it seems like he knows what he wants to do only when I'm not around. Otherwise, it's all a "I don't know... We will see..."'

'Like he doesn't really want to do stuff with you?' I asked.

'Pretty much!' And Anita put the phone in her pocket. 'Wow, are we sure we want to do this?' she asked, looking at the outside walls of a large building falling apart.

'Well, maybe it's better inside?' I replied, pulling all my positive attitude into one short sentence.

Anita went in first. The door made a whingy sound as we walked in. The darkness in that place was pierced by sunlight coming through tiny windows, revealing a rail of dust too lazy to settle. A strong smell of wood filled our lungs as we moved across to the counter. An old man stood behind, polishing a beer glass.

'Hi there,' he said with a husky voice. 'Food or drinks?'

'Are we really staying here?' I whispered to Anita.

'It's not much different from any other Irish pub, is it?' she replied. 'I'm starving.'

'Food would be great...and two coffees?' I said to the old man, attempting a courteous smile, to which he replied:

'Take a seat.' And he lifted his hand, indicating the vast emptiness around.

We sat at a table, secretly agreeing to choose one close to the door in case the roof collapsed and we needed to run. A large woman turned up a minute later. Her blonde hair was tied up as if she had no time or will to get ready, and a big white apron with stains all over was staring at us, judging. No greetings, no smiles were given away that day. She came to the table, asked what we wanted, and walked away as fast as our hunger was growing. Anita and I looked at each other, laughing. With not many options on their menu, we chose whatever sounded trustworthy, trying to get on the road within the hour. As we were about to finish our breakfast, the old man came by, attempting a creepy smile.

'Not many strangers on this land...even fewer foreigners,' he laughed.

'Charming,' Anita said, making sure only I could hear it.

45

'We are just passing by,' I replied, 'on our way to Noah's Bridge.'

'Connemara?' he asked, putting more emphasis on his smile. 'There are better places than Noah's Bridge. There's not even a bridge there any more. You know that? Oh, I bet you know it, big fella.' And his face became creepier as he pointed a skinny finger at me. 'You have been there before,' he added.

'Oh, we wanted to go ages ago, but this is the first time we're visiting this side of the country,' I quickly replied. He was old and definitely losing his mind as much as I was.

'Oh, but you have,' he insisted. 'I would turn around and go somewhere better than those rotten lands if I were you. Here, the bill...if you are not having any more coffee. As I said, I suggest you go back your way and find a better place to...visit.'

Right after those words, Anita suggested to leave the place at once, after she had used the bathroom, and I agreed. Things didn't feel quite right. It wasn't just the old place pushing the weirdest ideas on us. It wasn't just the old man either. It was everything together. Sure I had everything with me, I waited for Anita by the door hoping she would come back in seconds. Standing there waiting, I suddenly realized no other customers had walked into that place since we had gotten in.

Glancing left and right, my eyes did another quick run around the pub. No wonder we were the only brave people having food there. Anita was on her way back, and I could see her face from where I stood on the other side of the room, her expression conveying so much that it was as if we were having an intricate conversation. *In there, she must have experienced the same level of service we had in here*, I thought. Without saying anything, we went to walk out, when the old man said:

'What the old tale says? There is no more to wait for...' And his hand was raised in a sad goodbye as I turned to look at him, surprised by hearing those familiar words.

'Did you hear what he said?' I asked Anita without hesitation once we had gone out into the real world.

'Yeah, he was damn right! Why would we have stayed any longer?' And she was already walking her way to the car.

'No, Anita. You don't understand. Those are the exact words that old lady told me last night!' I said, standing still by the door, trying to catch her attention.

'What old lady?' she asked, turning back.

My detailed story about the vision I had the night before started to unfold and, eventually, continued all the way to our final destination, which then sounded like a mistake, if we had listened to what that man said.

'Why didn't you tell me right away?' Anita looked upset.

'I was going to, and I did. What difference does it make if I told you now and not at the house?'

'You are right,' she replied, challenged. 'What did John say?'

'I got you...'

'I got you...' she bounced back, perplexed.

'And then he called the mental hospital and…the end!' I laughed. 'What else would you expect?'

'Did you recognize her? Was she familiar?' She quickly changed the topic, resuming her walk towards the car.

'She was…familiar, but I don't think I'd ever seen her before.' And I hopped in the car, ready to drive.

'OK, let's leave it like that, for now…' And with that sentence, our brief conversation about my mental illness had concluded. Or so it seemed, for a few minutes.

Right on time according to Anita's schedule, midday was upon us. We arrived in Noah's Bridge earlier than expected, or maybe it just felt that way because we never stopped talking. Anita had made the point that those dreams were coming from a distant past, something that happened to me years before. I kept rejecting the idea, mainly because I didn't remember anything that resembled the places and the people I had seen. I knew in my heart I wasn't really convinced of my own refusal, but I kept pushing back on her theory, in a desperate attempt to be more like John; this isn't happening for real. It never did. We went back a few times on commenting about the pub and how John would have hated it, especially considering his name was on it.

'To be honest, I don't even recall seeing the sign outside that creepy place,' Anita said. 'Are we sure that was the pub that woman at the petrol station told us about?'

'Well, she said it was the only one in twenty miles? I'd say that was pretty much all we could find around,' I replied, wondering if I had seen the sign myself.

48

'John's pub...you think that man was John? I don't see him as a John,' she stated, as if she knew what a John should look like. I knew how a John would look like. My John was always on my mind.

'Definitely, she wasn't John,' I said, laughing.

'Oh, she was definitely a Karen.' And to that, we laughed out loud.

'Right, it's the next exit to the left,' Anita said at one point. 'We should be nearly there.'

We left the main road, and a narrow one was all we could drive on, between fields full of bushes and trees. The green hills were dramatically broken down by large amounts of blue crystal water. Lakes popped up more and more everywhere we looked, mirroring the heavy clouds above us. Here and there, tiny islands appeared abandoned on their own, with lonely wild trees that had gone through too much wind. We were surely in Connemara. Anita was trapped in that captivating savage beauty and had stopped talking. We could clearly see some horses in the distant land running free, free from any fear, strong, furious.

'This is absolutely the most beautiful thing I've ever seen,' I said, interrupting the silence.

'I hope we are close; I'd love to stay here!' she replied. 'Let me get a look, we shouldn't be too far. Do you want to pull over? Get some fresh air?'

I was really up for it. After finding the right spot to leave the car, we parked it on a merciful break, at the side of that tiny road, and walked by the water. The hill came right down by the lake, with the road breaking through, like a flash of lightning. From above, an intricate mesh of trees

49

expanded all over, its magic coming right at us. We were happy to be there as if that was the first time we had ever seen a lake. Anita was already barefoot, touching the cold water, when I turned back to see if the car was still visible from that distance. 'Did we lock the car?' I asked.

'I think so,' she replied. 'But do you really think somebody else could pass by? I haven't seen a car in twenty miles.'

'That's actually true,' I said. 'Let me go and check. Don't you dare go swimming...'

'Are you mad? The water is freezing!' she shouted, while I was on my way back up the hill.

A few minutes later, I was already by the car, its appearance clearly indicating a desperate need for more time to rest. I took the chance to check the map once more, while I kept an eye on Anita to be sure she wasn't going to jump in the lake. The sun came and went in a fast loop and the wind had picked up, making my reading more difficult. I had just given up, when my attention moved to the trees far up. I wasn't sure what I was seeing. Large tall trees all the way to the left and right, and a breakthrough, towards the side where the road died off. There, someone stood.

'Hey, Anita! I'm getting a look over there!' I shouted. She turned and waved her hand at me, but I knew she hadn't heard a word I said.

On my way to know more, I rushed my steps, afraid it would rain soon. The sky was turning grey and the wind was getting stronger. As I walked, the trees grew bigger and more details added to peaceful scene. A wooden sign stood close to the breakthrough. Not able to read it, I sprinted faster, more convinced. Someone stood by the edge of the greenwood, a shape of a man waited just a few steps away from the sign that said: *Noah's Bridge.*

I couldn't believe it. *We've actually arrived? Should I ask him, just to be sure?* I walked past the sign, getting close to the first big trees. The land opened back a bit at the top, showing a small path down the other side; downhill, a crossing river flushed quietly between two sides, and on top of it, a stone bridge held the two worlds together. As if the man was waiting for someone or something to happen, he kept his right hand to the side of a tree, and all I could see was his wavy dark hair and his simple clothes.

'Hi there,' I said. 'I was wondering if you could tell me how far Elaine's Inn is from here?'

'It's just down the hill over the bridge. This place is not that big. You will find it,' he replied. His voice was soft and deep. He wasn't as young as I initially thought. Or at least his voice didn't make him sound like it. I walked a few more steps. I wanted to get closer.

'Great! Thank you.' I answered, as I stood beside him.

He turned around my way, just a little for me to see his face, looking young, perhaps younger than me. A few freckles marked his nose and cheeks up to his silvery green eyes. Those eyes could have easily been made of the same water Anita was walking in, down by the lake.

'Are you walking or driving?' he added, his face surprised, looking back the way I had come.

'Driving,' I replied. 'I left the car just over there.'

'Good! 'Cause I think it's going to rain.' And he smiled.

51

What did I just see? What did I just feel? I asked myself. It was the most peaceful smile I had ever seen.

'I'm Noah, by the way.' And his hand reached out to mine.

'Oh—' I stumbled over my own words. 'Is this place…is… Well, this is funny.' I had forgotten to raise my hand towards him.

'What is funny? My name? Well, I don't own the bridge and I don't own the village. I own nearly nothing, to be honest,' he added, smiling again. 'And you are…?'

'Daniel, sorry, yes…I'm Daniel. Nice to meet you.' But my hand remained still stuck down to my side. I had the feeling I was being stupid. I suddenly felt my sweat coming down my forehead. *Am I sweating?* Rain started pouring everywhere in just a few heartbeats. 'Oh crap! I need to run. Do you need a lift down?' I asked quickly.

'Don't worry…I like to walk under the rain,' he answered. 'I'll see you around.'

I stopped for a few seconds, just the time to look at him again and try to understand why it all felt so familiar. But my mind was picturing Anita already running back to the car, so I didn't hold myself any longer. She had just left the lake when I arrived at the car. Running, she screamed and laughed at the same time. The rain poured heavy, chilly and I didn't have the strength to wait for her outside, so I sat in the car holding the door open at her side.

'Oh my God!' she screamed. 'It came out of nowhere!'

'I know. I was just up the hill over there.' And we started laughing. 'I suppose we could always say we swam by the lake...'

'Well, I really wanted to,' she replied. 'We better go and find our way.'

'Actually, we are very close,' I said, very proud. 'This *is* Noah's Bridge.'

'How do you know?' she asked, trying to dry her hair with a bath towel extorted from her bag. Anita had managed to squeeze her entire world into a small suitcase, when I couldn't manage to put two pairs of jeans in mine.

"Cause...I just...met Noah,' I told her, pausing at every word.

'What do you mean?' And she stopped for a second. 'I thought there was no bridge, nevertheless a Noah?'

'Oh the bridge is there alright,' I said, turning on the car, smiling.

Anita didn't really believe I had met someone named Noah. The conversation ended there as we were already over the bridge, and to the right, a cottage with the sign *Elaine's* was just above our heads. It was still raining heavily, so I told Anita to wait in the car while I sorted our things out. The place looked nice and welcoming. At the front door, a middle-aged lady with a kind face looked through the glass. She gestured for me to bring our bags in, so I dropped everything I had just over the doorstep and went back to the car.

Leaving Anita with the duty of a fast check-in, I parked the car in one of the spots reserved at the back. By the time

I returned to the inn, Anita had everything organized, keys in hand and ready to go. The lady at the reception kept looking at us, probably trying to understand why we had taken two separate rooms, one next to the other.

'Right, let's go. I really need to change my clothes and dry my hair,' Anita said, walking down the long corridor on the left.

Everywhere was covered in a dark blue carpet. The walls were full of pictures, and white doors with golden handles nicely completed the charming look. As we walked to our rooms, some pictures held the present and past together, showing how Noah's Bridge must have looked like in remote eras. The village changed drastically from frame to frame. The only thing they shared was the same stone bridge by the river.

'Well, the bridge is there,' I said, while Anita opened the door of her room.

'Old man's tale,' she replied. 'Do we give ourselves thirty minutes before going out?'

'I think I could be ready in ten, if you want.'

'I need to dry my hair… Yours is long, but not as long as mine,' she replied, mocking me.

'OK. Thirty minutes will do.' I had to admit she was right.

I had no intention of waiting in the room for that long. I walked in, emptied the bag, changed into a dry white shirt and dark blue jeans, brushed my teeth, and went back out in the space of five minutes. The place was quiet, but a few people walked in and out of their rooms. At the front hall, the lady, whom I then found out was called Deborah, was still there, talking on the phone. She had just hung up when my attention went to a few *Things to See in Noah's Bridge* flyers on her desk, waiting to be picked up by a stranger like me. *How did that old man call me? Was it 'foreigner'?* I don't know why it came back to my mind there and then. *Perhaps it's because we are indeed tourists in a strange new place.* My mind was quickly captured by the phone ringing.

'Hi, Elaine's Inn, this is Debbie speaking. Oh, hi Marie. I got those things for you. Tell Noah to pick them up at seven?'

Noah? Did she say Noah? Is that the same guy I just met, up the hill? How many Noahs are there around? Is it like a thing to call all the boys of the village Noah? I wanted to ask. *If I really think about it, and I said it in the right way, it could sound like a tourist's question.* So I waited for Debbie to hang up.

'Debbie?' I started, right after she was done with her call.

'Yes, how can I help you? Is everything OK with your room? Oh, is the hairdryer missing from the room?' And she looked up at my hair as if she was about to go and get one for me.

'Oh no, no. I actually didn't even check. I was wondering…' and I repeated the words in my head to make sure they sounded right, '…I've heard you saying a name, Noah. I met a Noah just less than one hour ago.' She kept looking at me, trying to understand where I was going with it. 'I was just wondering,' I continued, 'is it a common name here, I mean, in Noah's Bridge?' In my head, I sounded OK.

55

'Well,' she said, 'this is a very old village. Pretty big, I have to say...for a village, I mean. Now it's all touristic...' Now it was me who looked at her, trying to understand where she was going with it. 'But I know only one Noah.' My eyes went wide open. One. One was good. 'There have been a few in the decades gone...you know, a tradition that came with the founders. Can't tell if Noah's family is related to them, but it wouldn't surprise me. It's said that a Noah built the bridge, and the tower to the east, and another Noah made the docks by the lake. There are also some other things the Noahs of our history have built, but they are far north, at the border with Mayo.'

'Nice. Thank you.' And I grabbed some flyers to make her believe I was done with my silly questions.

'So you met Noah? Where? Up the hill?' she asked.

'Actually yes.' I replied, surprised she had guessed so well. 'How do you know?'

'Noah loves his trees,' she replied. I think his mother Siobhan was raised in the country side. She kept bringing him there every time they had a chance. Oh, well, I'd do the same if I owned a house by a lake... What was I saying?' she added after pausing for a moment. 'Oh yes. the sign was knocked down by a storm last night. He went to put it back up this morning. The lady I was on the phone with told me just a few moments ago.' And she nodded her head like she was about to end the explanation. 'Now, please excuse me. I need to get back to my work. I hope you and your friend will enjoy your time here.'

And there she went, with a few sheets of paper, a pen, and the cordless in her hand, leaving me confused about all the things she had managed to say in a minute. Nevertheless, her Noah's Bridge history lesson was over.

Chapter Four

Noah

∞

I sat in the hall waiting for Anita to be ready. I felt hungry again. I felt like we had never eaten. Checking the clock, I realized it was way past lunchtime. My stomach complained once more. Anita showed up a few moments later, clothes changed, her dark straight hair dry, and the make-up was on.

'Oh. I see you're trying to make an impression here,' I said, making fun of her.

'Let's go. I'm starving!' she said, and without slowing down, she grabbed me by the arm and we walked out. The rain had stopped. The sun had found its way out, making the wet roads shine, as if glitters had filled the entire place around us. 'I can't believe I'm hungry again. We had breakfast something like two hours ago?'

'I was about to say the same thing,' I answered, looking at her like she had just read my mind.

'Oh, I'd love Japanese food right now.'

'Anita, this is not Dublin. I don't think we're going to find any weird restaurant here,' I replied.

'That's because you don't like it. OK let's see what I got in my notes.' And she pulled a small, chunky yellow notebook out of her purse. She had taken notes about all the things to see, to eat, to do. That was so Anita.

'Shall we just head down that way and see what we can find?' I said. 'To keep the adventure feeling going,' I added after she looked at me like I had just gone mad.

'Don't you feel we had enough adventures for today with that old, smelly place we went to?' she replied, giving me a look that declared victory hands-down.

Among all the places she had written down, there was a *Creative Workshop & Restaurant* that had a mix of art activities, food, a museum, and a stunning view of the major lake. Happy with the ratings, we decided to head to it. Noah's Bridge wasn't big—like Debbie had said earlier—but was well placed between two hills, enclosed by a river that would end its course on the enormous lake. At the centre of the lake, a small island floated, calm, rich in vegetation, and a few tiny buildings on its coast could be seen in the distance. On our side of that giant, blue host, the place we were heading tipped just on the edge, large and with a very old but clean look. To the right side, it spilled into the large green field filled with a few recreational areas.

The biggest one had big gazebos all over and a busy crowd walked around, looking at painters and their work, who were busy recreating the landscape in front of them. To the left side, the building looked gigantic, with a long, tall look, and the stores above the ground floor looked as if they had been badly positioned. Skewed, with white walls and dark brown, thick beams, it seemed like the entire place was a giant cake terribly made.

'We must be in the most peculiar place in the whole world!' Anita exclaimed. Enthusiastic about it, we walked down to the front porch. A young girl, with big eyes and bright red hair, wearing odd clothes, probably related to the art festival that had started there at the beginning of the week, came to greet us. She wore large dark green trousers, a white puffy top with no sleeves, and a horned hat with *Celtic Arts* printed on it.

'Welcome to the something, something...festival,' she said. She spoke so fast that I could only catch the first and last word. 'Food? Activities? Art gallery?' she asked, noticing our confused faces.

'Food!' we said at the same time, like nothing else mattered.

'Inside? Or would you prefer sitting outside to enjoy the view?' she added.

'Outside,' we said again simultaneously, eager to devour every tiny piece of that view.

We sat on a wooden patio, under one of the few gazebos close to the painters. Most of the people were there to watch, talk, and have a good time. Only a few had come to create the majestic pieces of art on their canvas. Some were big, others were so small they could have easily fit in two hands. They all shared the same beauty. Colours were harsh. Dramatic shades of red, yellow, and blue re-created the world around, failing still to meet the original, inspiring beauty. Further down, a group of men were putting together something for the night. A long dock held the weight of busy people walking up and down restlessly, oblivious to the heat the now-unchallenged sun was releasing.

'I wonder what's going on over there,' I said.

'Looks like they are preparing something for later on,' Anita replied. The menus on the table were left untouched. We were enchanted by the buzzy movements made by those busy bees.

'John would love this place. I'm not sure this is the type of art he makes...but it's still beautiful, isn't it?' I said.

Another young girl came by our table. She looked nothing like the previous one but she wore the same clothes and the same hat.

'What can I get you?' she asked with a happy voice.

'Oh,' Anita jumped in. 'We haven't even looked at the menu, I'm really sorry!'

'That's OK,' the waitress replied. 'Would you like to try our malt Irish whiskey before ordering anything else? It's our specialty!' Anita and I gave each other a quick agreeing look before I said:

'Yes, please! What are those guys preparing over there, if you don't mind me asking?' I added, before she could walk away.

61

'Yeah, that's for the Lugh's summer solstice event,' she replied. 'It's mainly a dancing fest. It happens on the last night of our festival week, on Crossing Island.'

'Is Crossing Island that tiny island on the lake?' I asked, unafraid of keeping her a bit longer. Anita's attention was split between our conversation and a juicy fish combo plate at the centre of page two.

'Yes. The boats leave from here every thirty minutes, starting from 7 p.m. You should go!' she added, with an overexcited tone I've heard only from a door-to-door salesman.

'Can I have also the fish combo?' Anita asked, as she was just back from a tasty trip.

I wasn't ready at all. I didn't have any idea of what was on the menu. Feeling the need for haste and on the principle that I hate fish, I imagined they had a burger of any kind on their list. And so I rightly guessed.

Seven p.m. Where did I hear that before? Oh, yes. Noah was meant to be somewhere or do something at 7 p.m.? I couldn't remember. Was he supposed to be at the inn at that time? Maybe I should have asked Anita not to leave the inn before seven-thirty and give me the opportunity to see him again. *But why do I want to do that?* I kept asking myself. *I haven't even asked Anita if she wants to go to this dance festival.* I replied to myself in my own head.

'I think we should go,' she said, interrupting my thoughts. *Is she reading my mind again?*

'Do you want to go?' I asked her, pretending the idea hadn't crossed my mind.

'I think we should. After all, what chances are there we could actually plan all this? I'd say we go. Oh, can't wait to try the fish!' And she had already changed topic. It was decided. We were going.

That was one of the few occasions when I wanted to say no, only because she knew exactly what I wanted. The afternoon went on pleasantly. We had food, walked around the gazebos, bought a few souvenirs, and spent a few good hours discussing what to bring to whom back home. During a debate around a hand-crafted notebook for sale in one of the tents, just around the time Anita was repeating, 'I think it's beautiful,' like she had said for pretty much everything we had seen earlier, I realized I was actually feeling great. I felt like I hadn't felt for quite some time. It wasn't just Anita, that place, or the book. It was everything together. It had snatched away my worries, my nightmares. I felt clean. I felt free.

Towards the end of our noisy walk around the place, skimming and searching for more peculiar things, we found ourselves in the museum section, where tons of pictures hung on the walls, and books piled up in every corner. An old lady with white, messy hair talked loudly in a corner packed with visitors. She wore shining glasses, heavily weighing on her pinched nose, and two puffy cheeks closed them up in a funny frame. Whatever she was saying, she had the audience's full attention.

'...and this is how it got its name! But the mysteries of Noah's Bridge are not over!' she said.

'Hold on,' I said. 'I want to hear this!' And we moved closer to the group.

'It is said,' the lady continued, moving beside a large, old picture, 'that these were the ones who built the village, originally. These five men and two women are considered the founders of Noah's Bridge, but the truth is...' and her voice had gone quieter, like a whisper, as if she was trying to resist the idea of sharing the biggest secret of them all, '...this place is much older than the date you see here, 1846! If you pay attention to this next frame here, you might notice something strange. This is not a picture, of course. It's a reproduction of a small portrait found reprinted in a book from 1954. The experts claim this to be a portrait, a painting of a man who lived here around the year 1940 called Noah Grágeal—but in some other findings, he is also named McCarthy—who lived in these lands in the eighteenth century. Do you notice anything?' the woman asked, smiling.

'It looks the same man to me,' Anita whispered to my ear. 'Look! The second man from the left, in the other picture and this one.'

'It really does. Must be related, I suppose...'

'No doubt, but how can they look so...identical?' Anita asked, accidentally raising her voice.

'Exactly, my dear!' the old woman exclaimed, addressing Anita's question. 'They could easily pass for twins! Some experts have dismissed the entire mystery by claiming *that two individuals may not be genetically identical, but family resemblances can be so striking that a photograph of one person can bear an uncanny resemblance to, let's say, his grandson, to the point where they can be mistaken for each other.* It's utterly ridiculous, if you ask me! Now, if we venture to

64

the other side, I shall entice you with even more captivating mysteries!'

Staying away from the moving pack, Anita and I got closer to the small portrait, trying to compare it with the large picture one more time. The group photo was taken from far away, blurring some of their physical features, but it was clear enough to spark our curiosity. For what we could see, despite the fact they had been living decades apart, both men looked identical. On top of that mystery, and without Anita knowing, I was puzzled by the same similarity with that young man I had met up the hill. He looked very much like those two old men.

'You know how much I love this, right?' Anita asked.

'You mean digging through history?' And my nose almost touched the glass covering the small portrait.

'Not only that. This uncovering old memories, putting them together to finally reveal things we knew nothing about.'

'This is more me speculating... You two! This way!' the woman shouted, moving her hands as if she wanted us to move along and join the group. 'What was I saying? Oh, yes. This piece is just a copy of a very old manuscript, the work of early Catholic missionaries. Among many things, it refers to pagan rites and traditions held by the people who called themselves Draoithe and lived here between the fourth century BCE and the fifth century CE. In this list of strange things they witnessed, they talk about a man, called guess who? Noah. Now' — and she lowered her voice again. We knew some more juicy gossip had found its way to us —

'the name doesn't say much. After all, it looks like a traditional name for this place, but still…is it not strange?'

'She is right.' Anita whispered. 'With so many invasions, change of traditions, religions. People names are often a reflection of those changes. That a name could stick for so long in the same place, a place that has witnessed so much…'

'And it's not just that!' the host's voice shouted, hinting at Anita who was obviously not paying attention. 'They describe him as brown hair, dots on his face, in other words freckles, stormy eyes and a very pale skin. Coincidentally, these are the same remarks of the other two we spoke about, just over there.' And after she had taken a brief pause, she said, 'I'll let you make your own conclusion.'

And so the guided tour was over. The group dispersed quickly, moving and roaming around, in search for other mysteries. Back at the inn, we decided we had enough time for a quick shower and to get some rest before leaving for the party. We'd had so much food, we both agreed dinner was not in our plans and, if we really wanted to, we would find something to get on the go. I convinced Anita to not get going before 7 p.m., knowing that she would be late anyway. That would give me the time to follow my weird instinct to try to *casually* meet Noah without instigating any suspicion.

I'd had my shower, shaved, and my hair looked OK. Trying to change style a few times, I eventually let it go, giving up on the idea that my hair would stay up. There wasn't much to choose from the clothes I had brought with me. We hadn't planned to go to any dance and definitely I didn't have any intention of meeting anyone special. Same jeans and a different shirt would do the trick. I hated it. I had always had the fixation of dressing great and being impeccable even on casual meets and greets. My eyes went to the clock on my phone. A few messages were left there, miserably begging for my attention. *Welcome to the UK*, said one. That was weird. *When did we actually cross the border?* I thought. John's was next.

John

Hey, hope you are feeling better already.
I miss u.

And then another one from him.

John

How's there? Raging I'm not there with you.
I hate my job ☺'

He missed me...and I missed him too. *So how did it happen that I didn't check my messages up until now?* I asked myself. *What a bad boyfriend.* The clock was ticking: 18.55. I was going to be an even worse boyfriend. I quickly texted back: *'Here is great. I'm feeling already much better. Miss u 2,'* put my phone in the back pocket of my jeans, gave another look at the mirror, complaining one more time about my hair, and left the room. I didn't know where to go and find Noah. I couldn't remember if Debbie had said anything else while I was eavesdropping. I took my chance by walking towards the hall. Nobody was there. Just a different lady at the reception.

'Can I do anything for you?' she said, noticing I was wandering undecided. The nameplate said Aoine. She wasn't Elaine either. *So far we have a Noah for the real Noah's Bridge and no Elaine for the inn,* I thought.

'No, I'm grand. Thank you.' She didn't know I knew about Noah coming over at seven. I had to take my chance. 'Do you know if Noah is here already?'

'I haven't seen him. Are you a friend of his? I believe he is going to be at the festival tonight…'' As if she meant *everyone is…*

I was a bit disappointed. All that Machiavellianism was done for nothing. Before I had the chance to get back to my room defeated, Anita showed up.

'Oh, hey. I see you're done already. I was going to kill some time waiting for you as I wasn't tired after all,' she said, all happy.

'Yeah…yes!' I was trying to think if I had to quickly lie or not. 'Very much the same for me…shall we go then?'

The sun was still pretty high in the sky, but the heat had faded away. I had a dark blue jumper with me and Anita had brought a black fancy coat. We knew our way too well. Being out earlier than we planned, we decided to walk around the village to take some selfies. I wasn't in the mood and my hair was all over the place, but Anita insisted I looked cool, and 'In any case,' she said, 'I'm fabulous enough for the both of us.'

A minute later, she added, 'I want to put few of those on Insta. So Patrick can learn the lesson.'

'What lesson? You're still thinking about his post?' I immediately asked, feeling like I was late to the gossip party.

'It's not just that. I'm over it. But you know,' she replied, posing at her phone, making weird faces, 'you need to pull a compliment out of that man if you want one. At the beginning was all nice words and stuff but now it's already a miracle if he acknowledges my existence.' I was confused. Why did I not know anything about it?

'You mean he doesn't tell you these "nice words" or he doesn't even think them?'

'He does think them when somebody else does first,' she said, 'or at least he says them, when he thinks he has to.'

'Did you guys talk about it?' I asked, taking a selfie myself just to pretend I wasn't starting an inquisition.

'Yeah, we did.' She put away her phone. 'And of course "I am too much when I make a big deal out of nothing!"' I knew she was quoting him there.

Patrick was a bit like that. They had been together for a while but Patrick had gotten worse at the whole effort of making things romantic. I wanted to keep the window open, so I continued:

'John is a bit like that, sometimes. It's like…I need to keep pulling him towards me otherwise he drifts away.'

'Is he?' she asked, like she wasn't sure about it.

'Well, this is how it feels,' I replied, ready to pull up my defence mechanism. I was trying to keep her window open, but inadvertently I made her look through mine.

'Remember when I told you John knew about my plan of bringing you on this trip?' I nodded yes trying to guess what she was about to say. 'He said the same thing about you…' And she looked at me briefly, before turning the corner and looking at a shop's items on display.

'He said that *I am* drifting away?' I asked, ignoring the weird jewels on a glass shelf. Her window might have closed, but mine was wide open.

'He didn't put it exactly in those terms but he feels you are getting too far to be reached and he doesn't know how to bring you back.'

I was shocked. John was…well…John. He was self-obsessed to the point of driving our lives around his things…and I loved it. I loved having him at the centre of my world and his world with him. *And he feels I am the one slipping away?* After all, we were living our life together as it started. He lost in his thoughts and me constantly after him. On the streets, I'd purposely let him walk ahead so I could see him from behind, as he could lead me through a world I didn't trust much. I loved seeing him making his space in the world with no fear. *Was he actually looking at me all this time, or was he complaining about not being the centre of my gravitational system any more?*

'Don't be mad,' she said, infiltrating between my thoughts. 'He wants you to be happy.'

'I'm not mad,' I promptly replied. 'It just seems strange that John does actually say what he thinks…'

'...or feels,' she added. 'That's exactly Patrick's problem.' And the game was back on her side of the pitch.

In other circumstances, I would have pushed the conversation further and brought home the match for once, now that she was going to play it. But I didn't. I felt guilty and I was mad. Actually, I really was. After a few minutes of awkward walking in silence, Anita asked me if I wanted to have a quick drink before heading to Crossing Island and I felt we needed a sudden turn around, so I said yes. We disappeared into a fancy bar full of lights and loud music and ordered two glasses of white wine. The atmosphere was festive alright. It seemed like the entire village was under some sort of drug that gives you the happy mood and I was jealously willing to get some, whatever that substance was. That's when it hit me. *I didn't have a smoke all day! How is it even possible?*

'Oh my God!' I shouted, trying to cover the noisy music. 'Can you believe I didn't have a cigarette since we left my house, this morning?'

'Noo, I don't want a cigarette. Maybe later!' she shouted back.

It was clear the music had covered every word I had said, so I took a cigarette out of my pack and showed it to her, pointing the way out, hinting I was going solo. We spent in that place a good hour, maybe more. Two glasses each later, the whole conversation about John and Patrick had gone forgotten. We were back in a great mood and the music was keeping it high and sturdy.

Around nine, we decided we were late enough to the party to make us look like snobby celebrities, so we left and walked towards the dock. The excitement grew rapidly and so was the alcoholic adrenaline. I didn't even perceived the feeling of travelling on a small boat with some other strangers and with the man who led the precarious machine. What I did feel was the music coming from far away, loud and distorted, mingling with the sound of the water moving away from the sliding boat. A brief thought of me sitting in there, on a dark lake, crossed my mind, giving me the chills. *Did I see the future? This future?* In a few laughs we arrived already to our destination and, some steps later, we knew already where to go first.

'It wasn't bad, was it?' I asked Anita, helping her to get up on the dock. 'We didn't even suffer the trip on the boat.'

'I suffer nothing that has holiday written on it!' she replied, laughing and almost tripping on the ground. 'More drinks? Shall we?'

The island looked like it was all one giant, bright Christmas tree. The sun had almost drawn at the very end of the lake and a massive gathering of trees hid the view to the other side. All around, a red-looking sand was enclosing the party in a holiday card and the music was calling us in. At the centre, some people performed a traditional Irish dance while many others stood up looking and clapping their hands. There was no age or race gap, they all looked like one moving body. To the right side, a few wooden carts sold drinks and finger food and, further down, some strange business unfolded under the protection of the rising night.

'Is that a fortune teller?' I asked Anita, pointing to one of the shopping carts.

'We should go later,' she said, trying to order two drinks. 'But not before I lose some of my sobriety... You know...Just in case she has bad news.'

If there were going to be bad news or not, we didn't know back then. After a few drinks and several random conversations with strangers coming and going, we decided bravery became us. So we walked back to the suspicious stand where a woman sat quietly, her body engulfed in an enormous amount of fake jewellery. Some of those looked like the ones we had seen in the shop, a few hours earlier. She held her arms firmly on a long, carved stick, her eyes, loaded with dark make-up, were closed. Her red lips were like a punch to our eyes, her weird look enhanced by the platinum hair and the black dress she wore.

'Hi.' Anita attempted a smile.

'Not you...*him!*' she said, sharp, her eyes still shut.

'OK,' Anita replied, looking at me with a face stuck in between surprise and annoyance.

'You are not ready to find your true self. He is. Seat!' And she finally opened her eyes.

'How does it work? Do I need to ask something?' I whispered in Anita's ear while she tried to keep her balance on a chair that was quickly sinking in the soft sand.

'There is no need. The questions are always the same. Will I find love? Will I become rich...? No. These questions are not good enough for you. I can see it. Although love is the reason why you are here...' And she pulled a small, brownish bag out of a pocket in her black dress. Inside, a few stones knocked against each other, making a strange sound.

'Well...we are doing this just for fun, we didn't know we were going to see a fortune teller here,' I said.

'I'm not a fortune teller, and nothing happens just for pure coincidence. I'm a Druí.' And she poured all the stones in a wooden plate. Carvings and writings of an unknown meaning covered the entire surface. Rolling, the stones randomly scattered across the plate. 'Your search for answers is going to lead you far away...very, very far. Physically and emotionally. There is also something very strange here...'

'Strange? Of course there is.' Anita mocked her, making her stiff.

'You see,' she continued, after giving Anita a bad look, 'these stones roll for me. They tell me the full story, every time! But look. Three of these seven stones have gone to the side, out of reading. It does not happen, ever!'

'Is that a bad sign?' I asked, trying to understand where she was going with it.

'It means I can't see half of yourself. This is...unusual. It's like a grey shadow is preventing me from seeing the other side, the side you have not come to meet. What I can tell you is that there is a long journey ahead. This stone here' — and she pointed out a crack in the wooden plate — 'it stopped on a departure. But it also means parting ways from something big. It also means splitting in two. This going somewhere won't be easy. Look at this second one,' she continued, her eyes almost shining from excitement. 'This is the stone of spirituality, divinity. It stopped here,

74

by the awakening symbol. Your journey will have an effect on your beliefs. And this last one, the rune of…"

'Of what?' I asked, noticing she had suddenly stopped talking, her eyes gazing away from us, lurking somewhere beside her shoulders. If someone had been there next to her, I could have sworn they were suggesting the words she was saying.

'The rune of…of fate. It went on its side. Not up, nor down. Right at the edge of this hole, here. Can you see this symbol?' And she pointed to a curved blade, painted at the bottom of the cavity. 'Whatever you do, be ready to take the right decision…or I'm afraid it's not going to end well…'

'OK, OK! That's it, let's go,' Anita said, standing up. 'This is putting me in a bad mood. This was supposed to be fun!'

'Why? Because it's not scientific? Because you can't research it yourself?' the lady replied, shocking the both of us. 'You are so entangled with your version of the truth that it makes you blind. But let me tell you this, before you go. There is another you there, somewhere, waiting to come out. Just cherish her and let her make you see!'

'What is a Druí exactly?' I asked, holding Anita onto her spot.

'A Druí is a carrier. A human being who's close enough to the other world to hear its whispers,' the lady said, collecting all the stones back into her bag.

'A carrier?' I asked again.

'A carrier of whispers…there are not many left…back in the days we Draoithe were many in numbers, waiting for the day to come, when our worlds, ours and the other, would finally merge. But it never did…and we grew old. Now, get this one to wake up, and watch your steps!' And she turned to the other side, dismissing us.

Anita had enough of that precise, sharp judgement and rude behaviour. Pulling my arm, she asked us to leave at once. I was attracted by that lady's words but I could not let that upset her. So I complied and, after thanking the mind reader, we moved back to a more pleasant atmosphere. One drink later, the whole episode had somehow dissipated from our minds and Anita and I were having fun looking at people dancing, drinking and talking with random strangers who were there just for the Summer Solstice Festival. A bit before midnight, someone on speaker announced it was time for everybody to dance. The music started to mix with more modern vibes, creating an irresistible desire to be part of that happy madness.

Anita had run to the dance floor—or whatever that could be called considering there was pretty much nothing but sand—and I followed right in. If we had been somewhere else, if we had been home, I would have resisted the urge to join her. I used to love to dance but I also used to feel out of place if I didn't have enough friends surrounding me. But there was no overthinking. It was pure happiness. We were there in the middle, dragged by the beat, moving along with so many others, losing and finding each other as many times as we could, without worries. We were safe and I had completely forgotten about my dreams, John, the fortune teller, my hair.

Then, between floating shapes and moving bodies, someone came by and got close. I knew his face and I knew his freckles. *Is he really here, dancing with us, or is the wine messing with my head, mixing reality with the pictures we saw at the museum?* He was there. I was sure. My eyes moved rapidly to find Anita. She was further down, away from me. I felt emotions I shouldn't have had. He was getting closer and I was getting excited. If he had come nearer, I would have let him. If he had touched me, I would have let him…and that was wrong. Trying to control that fear about my newly discovered emotions, I slipped behind a group of people dancing happily together and got close to Anita. I had no idea he was following me through.

'Should we head back?' I shouted.

'What? Why?' Anita replied. 'This is fun!'

'Listen…' I started saying, but there, another voice took over.

'Hey, stranger! Twice in a day, is this a sign?' His voice was as deep as my conflicting feelings. I turned around and instinctively grabbed Anita's hand.

'I assume you found Elaine's Inn,' he added, smiling. I could still see the light in his eyes in the dark of the hour. Something powerful was getting through.

'We did, thank you!' I replied, feeling I had an embarrassing face on.

'Come on,' he added. 'Let me offer you something to drink.' And his hand moved towards my shoulder.

In my head, the music slowed down and my heartbeat took its place. The more I held the grip, the more Anita felt the pressure on her hand. And then, the fear grew unleashed. He touched me. And we were gone.

Chapter Five

The Other Side

∞

What happened?' Anita said in shock, her head moving to the left and to the right. 'Where is everyone?'

I was standing still, next to her, in a never-ending shot between before and then. I could feel my body left behind on the dance floor. My eyes weren't moving. I was inside my head and inside his head. I could see myself looking at him and him looking back at me, in a nauseating loop. He was still there, with us, his hand over my shoulder, but I couldn't feel it any more. I could taste his mouth, his tongue, like it was mine. His voice in my head was my own voice, thinking over and over. My blue eyes had gone dark and bright again, warped in shades of colours and turned as bright as the sun goes, then settling in the colour of a stormy ocean. My sight was back. My consciousness was coming through.

'Is it you?' His voice was in my head. 'Is it you?'

'I don't know,' I thought. And he could hear me saying it.

'I've seen you coming, many times, as many times as I can remember.' And something inside me knew he was telling the truth. 'You are three years late. I've been waiting for you. I've been waiting for you all my life!'

An unnatural sense of guilt was raging up, fighting to come to light. And tears were flowing down, leaving my cheeks to float in the nothing where we were standing. And his tears came to keep me company straight after.

'Are we both crying, or is it just me?' I thought.

'Whatever you do, it's my doing. And whatever I do, it's your doing,' he replied. He could still hear my thoughts. He was in my head and I was in his.

'Where are we?' I asked. I could not see anything but him, and me through him.

'We are together...and together is the only place that matters.'

'What's the meaning of all this?' I asked again.

'We are meant...' And suddenly we were torn apart, shredded, our bodies took us back.

I had fallen on the dance floor and Anita behind me, pushed by a couple who danced carelessly. Noah stood where he was a few seconds earlier, his arm still up, his face in shock, and his tears still falling down.

'Bloody hell, I drank too much!' Anita said laughing, while trying to pull herself up. I was there, lying on the cold

80

sand, and I knew it wasn't the wine doing it. It had happened before, as much as every other dream I recently had.

'Are you OK?' I asked her, shaking the sand from my clothes.

'Yeah, I'm OK. I lost my balance or I got pushed, can't tell. Oh God, am I drunk already?' And she kept laughing. 'Why are you crying?' she added, once I stood up in front of her.

'Crying laughing?' I hoped she would buy it.

'Let me see if there is a bathroom somewhere here. I'm not going to pee behind a bush.' And she left slowly, with a funny walk. 'Did I come here without my shoes?' I could hear her shouting and laughing while looking on the ground.

Before I could see her gone from sight, I turned around looking for Noah. Whatever had happened, it had happened to him too. If he really had said those words, he had the answers to my many questions. He stood there still, where we had just left for our quick journey into the impossible.

'What happened?' I asked, hoping he would tell me the truth at once, no matter how brutal it would be.

'Are you OK?' he bounced back with another question.

'Answer me!' I shouted. Seeing his cheeks still wet sent me a clear and loud message: I was being rude.

'I can try to explain...' he replied, his voice soft. I could barely hear it. His hand was reaching out again, so I stepped back. 'Let's go somewhere we can talk, shall we?' he added, pointing somewhere far from the dance floor.

I wasn't sure about anything any more. I wasn't sure about what had just happened, what triggered it, if Anita had followed me through. Nothing was real and everything was cracking apart. But I said yes because I needed to know. I said yes because I was tired of pretending, of being worried. We left the crowd and the loud music behind. I gazed around looking for Anita but I couldn't see her. Over the shopping carts now closed and wrapped for the night, we moved close to the water, where a few big rocks were resting from the noise. He walked slowly, by my side, his face changing colour like the lights in the background, like his skin was made of glass. Same height, same messy hair, I believed for a second he was a copy of me, perhaps a better one.

'I know this must be confusing for you,' he started. 'It was for me, at the beginning. It still is, most of it, at least.' He looked right into my eyes waiting for me to say, *'Yes, it still is,'* but I had chosen to say nothing, to wait, at least for a bit longer. 'I had time to adjust, to understand. It will be the same for you once you let it come to you.'

I had no idea if he knew what I had gone through in the last few months, if he thought he knew but he didn't, if he was trying to help me or he had some sort of a hidden agenda. Again, I deflected his look and sealed my mouth.

'It all started a bit over three years ago. It was just dreams at the beginning...' And there he got my full attention. 'I didn't know what they meant and if it was normal having these strange thoughts in my head. Then it started to happen all the time.'

82

'Daydreams?' I asked, nearly too scared to attempt an empathetic connection.

'Yes,' he replied. He stopped walking and moved in front of me. The lights from behind me were crashing on his face, embracing his full beauty. 'I guess this has happened to you too, right?' he asked, moving so close to me that I could feel the heat leaving his body to reach mine.

'It has, since a few weeks now. It was nothing, at first. Now it happens constantly. I can't control it.' And the fear sneaked in through my lips.

His mouth attempted a comforting smile. 'I see…do you feel you are going insane?'

'How can I not? I see things that are not real. I feel them inside,' I replied, revealing some of my desperation.

'They are…real, I mean. At least to you and me.'

'You and me,' he said. *He is going insane like me, what a comfort! 'You and me,' like we are actually the same, two strangers. 'You and me,' like we are a story to be told at once.* I wasn't happy about it. I didn't feel I could talk about myself through the eyes of a man I didn't know. However, I wasn't alone any more. I didn't have to explain the madness I was going through to him. He knew. Someone finally knew. And to me, his beauty grew a little more. His eyes were locked to mine as if he was waiting for me to catch up, but I was miles behind. And he was waiting for me, anxiously waiting for me.

'Things that have never been, are waiting to be…'

'Oh my God,' I unwillingly said out loud. 'This is what she meant?' My face moved away from his as I gazed at the

83

far end of the lake. My eyes scanned the surface like it was the book of my life, and I was desperate to reach the final page.

'She?' he asked. 'Have you seen her?'

I quickly turned back to him, now convinced he had the answers I had been looking for. 'I have. Have you seen her too? I thought I'd imagined her. I thought she wasn't real.'

'She is. She was…' And I felt I hadn't quite understood what he meant. 'Look, this cannot come to you all at once. There is so much I need to tell you, and there is so much you need to tell me. I haven't got all the answers, but I went as far as I could on my own.'

Was he begging for help? I was so desperate to get rescued that I didn't realize he was lost too. I had to move faster.

'That thing that happened, just now. Was it real?' I asked.

'It was,' he answered.

'Where were we? Did it happen in our heads?' I continued.

'This is something we need to figure out together, I'm afraid. This is as far as I can go on my own.' He was visibly sorry. His face was looking for compassion; guilt was something we both shared. His body was craving for another touch, another risk to take to get to the land of the unknown. 'Shall we?' he asked, moving his hand next to mine.

'What will happen?' I was going to ask. But, somehow, I knew he didn't know.

His look was a force too strong to resist. He was pulling me into something. I wanted to follow him, to the end, if that it was.

A shy smile appeared in my face like I was telling him *'don't hurt me'*. And then, I took his hand. My entire body collapsed into fine dust. I could feel it slipping away, my soul travelling fast on its own, with him by my side. He was there with me and he was me. His mind was filling mine and I was seeing with his own eyes. Suspended into nothing, back we were, alone. There was no pain, my fear was left behind with the rest of the real world. Time had lost any relevance. We weren't moving, we weren't living or dying. We were just *being*.

I could feel his emotions mixing with mine. He loved, he had suffered, he had waited. I was embracing him as I was letting him in. And it was like we always were, never been apart, never started and never ended. We knew each other and we had been one, since the memory of our own self went. We had so many lives together, fought so many battles and lost the greatest of them all. We had gone broken, scattered to pieces, reduced to nothing. The emptiness around had left the space to memories coming now to life.

People were gathering from everywhere, celebrating. They had felt the desperation of a great loss but now rejoicing at a new beginning. Noah was there, standing on the top of long white steps, smiling. With him, three figures stood still, next to each other. At the very left, the first one wore a white cloak full of silvery marks. She held a long sceptre with a serpent carved on it all around. Opposite, in a dark old robe, someone held a golden clepsydra in his hands. The artifact had no up or down, and a green viscous liquid floated right in the middle. Between them, a glossy shadow, made of thousands of crystals, with bright eyes, stood still, open arms, wearing nothing but a silver tiara on his head. Noah knew I was never going to be far from him, from his heart. He knew I was close. Bells rang loud, the joy of the many around painted the sky of a bright blue. And there I was, a few steps away. Everything was exactly as I had seen before. Nobody would have stopped me, this time. Not an old lady, no fear, no regret. It was the day of my life. Mine to reach with my hand, so close…

A dark blade made of sadness and horror came to strike us down and I fell. Noah had just given his soft, kind, last look at me before the painful, evil dark hand of death landed down on our vows.

'Is this how we'll end? Noah?' We were both back, standing there, by the lake, hand in hand. I had touched his face before I had gained back possession of my body. With sadness of a lonely broken heart, my face close to his, eyes on eyes, our tears were one, and there, with my soul in pieces, I kissed him.

'Was that…us?' I asked, ignoring that I had just kissed a stranger, a man I had just met.

That wasn't my doing. I had no part in it. I was still free from any judgement. His answer felt like it had missed its right place. He was there with me but he had seen things differently. The place was the same, our feelings were equally matched, but he had seen his own view of our end, not mine. We were still two different beings, although our minds were bound together.

'I believe I saw myself dying...' he said in shock. His eyes dull, gazed at nowhere. 'I never got this far in my dreams. I've seen you before, there and in many other places. By the tree this morning; in your bed, I've seen the ceiling of a room. I've seen myself waiting for you, but what I just saw is beyond anything I have ever experienced.'

'Is this our future?' I asked, worried. What could I possibly do to bring him to this horrible fate?

'Does it feel like it is, to you?' he replied. Noah wasn't sure about it. He carried the look of a terrified bird with no direction, random, compulsive.

'What we do now?' It was like I could put no more than few words together. And again I was waiting for instructions, to be led by hand, like I was the lost child and he the protective parent.

'What's going on?' a familiar voice came right from my back, inquisitive.

Anita had just come back, shoes in hand, and a tribunal was already set to execute me directly from her eyes. We were still holding hands. No parole for me, ever. My mind searched fast in the empty bucket of hundreds of excuses. What could I've said to stop her from painting this new image of me, unfaithful, dishonest, mad man? And there the worst obvious words came out.

'I can explain.' My hand still glued to his. 'I got my answers, Anita. I think.'

'Oh,' she said. And that 'oh' carried the weight of what was about to come next. 'So now we cheat to find answers?

What is this? The new *Kiss a stranger Russian roulette*? Are you really insane?'

A bang after another. She had seen the kiss and now she was mad at me. I had disappointed her, or the idea of me had crushed down in her heart. I was Patrick. I had to answer for my not being perfect, for being like her boyfriend, for being unreliable and selfish. I was about to respond to the fight and begin the war, when her view of me pushed through my thoughts. I was going to give up my life, my love for John, my best friend's trust, for an insane fear. I had gone too far. *Is it not every criminal's best defence? 'Someone made me do it'? Where is my responsibility?*

My hand suddenly detached, like the magnetic force had just receded.

'Let's go' I said with all the determination I could find in me, without even looking back at Noah.

He was the sin and I had to let it go, there and then. Her rage was building up. It could have fuelled our way back to the other side of the lake. The strangers on the boat, sitting there with us, were unwillingly sustaining the partition wall between two nations at war. On our walk to the inn, the silence held sturdy and I didn't have the strength to risk a bigger argument. The slam of her room door made the final point. That wasn't over.

My room instead, was quiet. I wasn't used to coming back to an empty home, and, initially, I felt sorry for myself. However, not having John there was the best scenario I could hope for, I thought quite soon. Lying down on a bumpy bed, I could not sleep. How could I? So much had happened.

I had more new questions than answers. *How is it that we chose exactly this place to go on a trip? The same place we wanted to go three years earlier.* Again, my mind went down the road of ifs and maybes. A buzz brought me to reality. A message popped up on a locked screen.

John

Can't sleep. Are you still up?

He wanted to jump on a call, I was sure of it. My love for him moved my hands in a quick reply 'Yes,' but my dirty conscience held me back. I hadn't unlocked my phone. He didn't know I had read his message. It was better like that. I turned on my other side and left the awoken world, hoping I wouldn't have any dream for one night.

Chapter Six

The Secret

∞

The nice weather spell held enough for the Summer Solstice Festival to get to its end. Now that the world had moved over, the angry clouds and the so-familiar rain had come back to us. I woke up to its ticking sound against the window. It was still dark but the day had already started. Believing my old world had come back too with the awful weather, I stood up thinking the night before had never happened. John's text still comfortlessly lay in my phone, beside two more he had sent, sometime before morning. Scattered memories popped up while I was getting ready. The shower I took didn't quite do the trick of washing away the nightmare I had put myself in. With my bags packed and ready for the drive back home, I left my room starving and hoping Anita had waited for me.

Will she be still mad at me? I kept thinking. The reasons behind what I had done in Crossing Island had lost momentum. *How will I explain it to her?* I knocked at her door. No answer. I waited a few seconds, then I knocked again.

'How did you sleep?' she said in a flat tone, standing outside, behind me.

'Holy crap, you scared me!' *She must have left the room early and had breakfast without me.* 'Did you already have food?' I added.

'Not yet, no. I went to the reception and I asked at what time we are supposed to check out.' *She isn't rushing to get back? Is she OK with us staying here a bit longer as planned or is she trying to postpone as much as she can our long trip back…in a silent car,* I thought.

'How long do we have? Is there time for breakfast?' I asked her, ignoring that in my head, I was looking for a fight and a quick defeat. *Just let it out and be done with it!* I kept thinking.

'Sure. But somewhere out. A nice place.' she replied with that same flat tone. She sounded and looked as if in between wanting to punch me and wanting to stick to the plan: have fun and relax. I was clearly fighting against it. Outside was still raining. Whatever place we wanted to go, had to be close enough to walk. No way she was going to share the umbrella. I didn't deserve it.

She insisted on going to a place we had seen the day before, while looking at the shops, talking about John and Patrick. A quite long distance to walk under the rain but, that was her, I guessed, cashing the bill. So we went. Debbie

91

had let me borrow an umbrella so I wouldn't get wet, giving me the chance to circumvent Anita's revenge. We sat in a charming little bistro, between a bookstore and an antique shop, planning to go and check both, afterwards. The place was actually part of the same block and both shops were connected. People walked in and out, without really leaving the premises, and I was sure we had met a few of them the night before, on the dance floor. That was too much of an unwanted flashback. We were still in the middle of the crime scene and I, the biggest suspect, hadn't fled just yet.

'I think we met some of these people last night,' I let out, hoping that my remark could ignite a conversation and let it flow.

'Did we?' Again, her tone wasn't quite right but the wind was changing.

'Yeah. I clearly remember talking to that man over there,' I said, filling my mouth with a tasty scone.

'That mustn't be the only man you talked to, last night.' And I nearly choked. She had taken my hint in letting the topic out, but she wasn't making it an easy ride for me.

'There is a lot, and I mean *a lot*, I need to tell you…' I said.

'I'm sure you do,' she interrupted before I could show my unconditional sense of guilt. She continued sipping her tea, looking at some books standing on a shelf to the far left. She was angry at me but she played the game. She was still there, willing to stay in, hands on.

'Whatever happened…and I know this is going to sound stupid, no matter how I say it…it wasn't really me.'

She turned back, looking at me. 'I don't know what you remember, and I'm not sure you did actually see anything, but do you remember when we fell on the dance floor?' And she nodded.

'We left, Anita! We left for a little while'—I was afraid she wouldn't believe it—'and landed into nothing. It lasted only a few seconds because, I don't know, we fell? After being pushed by some random people. Do you recall it?'

'I remember being on the ground,' she said. This time she wasn't laughing like she had when that actually happened.

'You don't remember anything else? I was holding your hand. I'm pretty sure you came with me,' I said.

'Came with you where?'

'To…the other side, I guess?' She did not remember. I was devastated. That was my way out from our fight. If she did remember, she would have understood whatever had happened to me afterwards.

'I have no idea what are you talking about,' she replied 'I don't really know what's happening to you lately. I honestly believe something is odd here and you're not yourself. I know, I know,' she added, knowing I was about to debate her opening speech, 'this is confusing and you are worried.'

I was waiting for a 'but'. Nothing matters before the 'but'. Everyone knows that. I dropped my breakfast, my cappuccino was losing its frost on top and I was losing the hope she would actually let me explain.

'You are going through something bigger than you. Bigger than I can understand. I give you that. What I'm afraid of, is that you might be getting lost in this desperate searching for answers.'

Oh she was right! Anita had told it and I couldn't have said anything to deny it. All I could do was share what had happened. So I started to explain the events as they unfolded. She was listening carefully, wanting to understand, feel what I had felt, whatever these feelings were. I was ready to wrap everything up, be scolded for a little bit and move on, when she said:

'OK. OK. This is…OK. Wait a minute…' She was trying to sort things out. She had the same look she had when she had asked me if I had brought a book and a pen, a few days earlier. 'It's pretty clear and simple.' And I knew she was about to roll out a plan on bullet points, and she did it indeed.

'What you need to do is to ask this…Noah…' 'This Noah'—she was still keeping her distance from whoever made me sin. '…and ask him c l e a r l y what this is all about. You can't keep taking risks only because you think he has the answers. If he does, he has to hand them over.' And she had made her case. Anita had made things clear and crystal. I was now on probation, still under her grace, as long as I made things right.

We moved topic soon after. Now that Anita had made her point through, she could talk about the fun she had the night before. The decision to go on that trip was still a good one, despite my 'big mistake'. What was left to do in our trip plan, was the tour of the Connemara Whiskey Factory. The industry was well developed in the area, but the main

94

tourist attraction was an hour's drive away. 'If we went', she said, 'we wouldn't have time to take care of the other business'. We left the breakfast table and went to look at the shop beside. The impasse followed us.

'We can still go and forget about doing anything else,' I said, randomly scanning some of the books on sale, trying to gain some points.

'No. I have a better idea.' And she grabbed the book I was holding in my hand and placed it back where it belonged. 'Oh, look! *The Secret Wife*,' she added, picking another one just next to it, giving me a weird look.

'What is this other idea?' I asked, moving away from the book of shame.

'I actually found out there is a spa just at the back of the inn. I'm thinking of booking myself in for a good hour. That should give you enough time to talk to *you know who* and get it sorted.' And she floated away to the antique shop, at the other side.

She actually said, go and meet him…alone? Yes, that's a good idea, but how would I find him? I have no idea where he lives, where he works. I don't even have his phone number.

'How do I get to meet him? Do you also have an idea about that?' I asked her, trying to keep her pace, but she turned around and gave me again that weird look. It was too early for a good dose of sarcasm. At least on her side.

The only way I could find Noah was to get back to the inn and ask Debbie. The idea came just like that. Anita responded to my suggestion just saying:

95

'If it has to, it will happen. But remember, once done, is gone for good. You get this done and nobody gets hurt. John doesn't need to be hurt. It's going to be a secret we will bring to our graves. But promise, get your answers and leave!'

Having decided then she would have visited the spa for a good hour or maybe two, I told Anita we would meet back at the inn, before leaving. I would have enough time to find him and 'have a good talk', as she repeated while I was leaving the antique shop and she was brushing the dust off her hands after touching a century-old chair.

My visit to the inn was unfruitful. Debbie had no idea where Noah could be but she took the chance to ask, 'Are you friends or something?'

'We are…sort of…' I replied, handing back the umbrella I had borrowed.

A few more pushes and pokes didn't produce any result. She had no idea. My mind was running through all the places we had been, trying to find the one where I could meet him. *'Noah loves his trees.' Isn't that what Debbie told me just yesterday?*

Without hesitation, I ran through the streets, crossed the stone bridge as fast as I could. Ten minutes later I was up the hill with no breath, my heart madly pumping. The grass was soaked and I had almost slipped back a few feet on my way up. I could see the lake on the other side. The same lake we had stopped by, the day before, when Noah's Bridge was still just a nice place to go.

I wasn't wrong. Noah was there, same place, holding the same tree. It seemed like we had just gone back in time. I walked close to him. His clothes were wet, his hair under the weight of too much rain.

'This place, here. This is where I saw you coming to me the first time,' he said, before I could speak. 'I tried and tried to understand who you were, why did it feel like it was important for us to meet.' His voice sounded calm and deep. 'I was twenty-two when my dreams started. I saw you coming. I've seen you coming up the hill, over and over. I remember I couldn't see your face, at first. Eventually your blue eyes, your mouth, your skin, even your smile became clearer. I've seen your life, your things through your eyes like they were mine. It took me a while to understand I was actually experiencing pieces of your life through my dreams.'

I stood next to him, silent. I didn't have to ask any question, he was willingly confessing it to me. *How did he know that was real? How did he know he was seeing in the future?* I had never seen my dreams in that way. My visions had no meaning, had no time or space. For me, they had no clear purpose. But he knew I was coming.

'Did you expect me to appear a few years ago, didn't you?' I asked, remembering what he had told me, the night before.

'I did. But you didn't. I doubted it myself very much. I didn't know the exact day you would come, but I knew it was going to be soon. But you didn't...you never did,' he repeated. 'And so I stopped believing it, for a bit. It was like the idea of you had grown in my mind, bigger and bigger. I could feel it was going to happen very soon...and then nothing. It all went quiet for a good while.'

'Noah,' I said, looking in his eyes. 'Whatever this is, whatever has happened to you, I'm sorry. I'm sorry for the both of us.' And I also wanted to say: *'I'm sorry for holding your hand, kissing you.'* But this last part, somehow, got stuck in my throat.

'It's OK,' he replied, moving away from me. 'I'm done with this...whatever this is. I thought my days of madness were going to be over once we had met...that my confusion about my feelings...how I felt...*for a man! I'm so done with this!*' he shouted to the trees in front of us, as if he was challenging some invisible entity. I lost my words.

It didn't cross my mind. I loved men, loving another one, even only in my dreams, was no different. What if this had happened to someone else? Would it have been a woman? Would he have had dreams about a woman? Someone had made a mistake. Was it me, was it him, was it whoever was sending these messages who had made a mistake?

'Look, Noah...I'm really sorry,' I repeated. 'I had no idea. I have no idea about pretty much everything. I felt some sudden feelings for you, in my head...and I never thought it could be any different because this is who I am. I would have never imagined you could feel the same with being straight. Please accept my apology for kissing you.' But he still kept his face away from me.

I had no other words in mind. We were so close to grasping our answers. I felt I was about to reach them with my hand, and now, it was all slipping away. He had been waiting for me...but it wasn't *me* he had been waiting for. He had been waiting for answers, waiting to put an end to the nightmare we shared.

98

'It's OK,' he said again. 'There is no need to apologise. You believed some things, I believed some others. Do you want to walk back and talk more?' I think it's going to rain again soon and I also think you need to know all I know.'

And he turned around, calmer; he had changed again. We walked down to the bridge, went close to the inn and started to go around a few blocks, just to make sure we would be close enough, in case the rain came back. We stopped for a while at a bus stop and sat under the shelter. The village had changed dramatically from a day to another. It wasn't just the weather. The celebration had ended. Tourists had started to leave. Roads were nearly empty. Here and there, someone would walk by in the renewed silence. But he had more to say.

'I've been living in this village most of my life. My father was born here and so his parents before that. Yes, apparently Noah is a name that goes quite a lot in my family line. As a child I was pretty odd. At least that's what my mother used to say. I had this thing that I would talk to myself when alone, in my room. I had invisible friends. Who hadn't?' he asked, smiling. 'But my friends were not magical animals or superheroes. My friends were two old men and an old woman. Very weird, isn't?' And I smiled back at him. That wasn't the right time to define 'weird'.

'I don't know when it stopped. I suppose it happens when you leave your childhood. Anyway, I became a teenager, a young adult. Same thing that happens to everyone. I didn't have a real girlfriend, or a boyfriend...' he added. I didn't know if he wanted to be inclusive or leave that open for some reason. '...when I was in high school. College was a bit different. I wanted to be a nurse, so that took pretty much all my time and attention. I always had this feeling that I couldn't just take care of one person. I was meant to be caring for everyone.'

The charm in his tone, his voice, was still releasing a spell on me, a pheromone to my senses, a balm for my scars.

'When I was twenty-one, my mother got very sick. There wasn't much we could do. It went fast. Very fast. It hurt a lot, but I knew she had gone to the same place my dad went, years before. The day we buried her was the day my old, old friends came back to visit me. I still remember like it was yesterday. I was standing there, by her grave, with my dad's relatives and my parents' long-time friends. Members of our family were just gone. And there, over the gravestone, the three of them were looking at me. I left their side and I went over to...I don't know...see if they were real? Perhaps, even to thank them for being there for me. My hand went to the edge of the gravestone and theirs went to cover mine. I could hear them whispering, "The time is coming. Come back to us, remember..." I had chills on my spine.'

'Were they the same people we've both seen in our dreams?' I asked.

'Yes. They were. Oh, I didn't realize it till a few years later. But yes. They had never left me and, now that you are here, sitting next to me, I understand they are still here...somewhere.'

'What do they want? From you...from me?'

'I don't know. For years I thought I had to wait for you to finally know it. Everything ended with me meeting you.

It never went further than that.' And I could hear the disappointment in his voice.

I had done the same thing. Not that I knew I was going to meet him there, in that small village, but I was looking for answers myself, and only few hours earlier, I really thought he could give them to me.

'I haven't spent as much time as you wondering, but I truly believed the same thing. That the answer would come from someone, you perhaps. We were hoping in each other. I've seen you too, you know? In my dreams. I started to believe you were a sort of soulmate that I had to find…so the kiss…' and I took the chance to bring back my mistake into the conversation, '…was me thinking you were *the one.*'

'Oh, man! You are a romantic!' he laughed. I didn't expect such change in his mood, or mine, but I laughed too. That brief comment had lightened our hearts a little.

'I felt things for you too,' he added from nowhere. My chest thundered. 'Some times more than others. This hasn't been easy for me. But whatever these emotions are, they are indeed…strong. So strong that often I wanted to give them all up. It's a burden.'

'It is,' I added, my face showing the signs of it. 'It's impacting my life so much...'

During our long conversation the rain had come and gone. Anita had definitely finished her session at the spa. I wanted to stay a bit longer, maybe even more than a bit, but I couldn't. We couldn't leave things like that either. There was more to say, more to explain. I realized, despite the mistakes, the pain, the disappointment, we were not alone in that any more. I had to know more.

'I'm afraid I won't be able to stay here much longer. But, Noah, I don't want to let this go. I know already I would regret it, because this isn't over. Nor for me, nor for you. We lost already our chance, once. Please, can we stay close? At least for a little while? Just to make sure we can get to the bottom of this madness?' I said all at once, no pause, no breathing.

'I'd love to,' he said. 'And I hoped you'd say that.'

So we stood up, one in front of the other. The embarrassment was like a third giant man in between. We had found ourselves in a strange place between friendship, alliance and, perhaps, trust? A shy smile was exchanged and a laugh followed right after. And we moved close and finally hugged. Our cheeks were touching and his hands held me tight. He knew and I knew the risk we had taken by getting so close again. This time, we hadn't moved from our reality. We could still feel our bodies, our hearts beating. We both felt a warm, powerful embrace, not just between us, but all around us. Noah's old friends were keeping us together in a soft hug full of emotions. I closed my eyes to absorb it all and I whispered in his ear, 'Yes, Noah. They are still here.'

Chapter Seven

The Place That Wasn't There

∞

Noah's Bridge was behind us. We had gotten in the car just twenty minutes after my conversation with Noah. Anita waited for the moment we had left Connemara to ask what had happened, like that place had to be gone before we could be free to talk. Noah was still there when we had put our bags in the car and said farewell to Aoine and Debbie, and Anita wasn't happy about it. Her idea didn't exactly include having him there till the end. So she had left the two of us outside the inn and gone to the car, waiting.

'Please, call me whenever you want,' I said, after giving him my number. I knew this also wasn't part of Anita's plan, and she would have something to say about it, but what was happening between me and him, she would have never understood.

'Why do I feel like this is a mistake?' he asked.

'What? Calling me?'

'No...letting you go. I'm happy we finally met but it feels like...'

'...we are leaving things unfinished,' I said.

'Yes...' and he sadly smiled.

'This is not over, Noah. I need more and you need more. Unfortunately, we have many other things in our lives to take care of. But please...call me.'

Last thing I had seen before leaving, was his partial gesture, his last attempt to hold me longer. And my heart broke a little that day. This time around, Anita had taken the lead in driving the car. We had just gotten halfway through our journey back, when she finally stepped back into the whole Noah affair.

I told her everything that had happened, acknowledging my mistake, and explained the reasons behind it, *as there is no more there.* I omitted the exchange of phone numbers. I purposely missed out our intent to keep in touch. We went through the topic with a rational point of view, an emotional perspective and a more relaxed approach, to make sense of it.

The fact that Noah had been experiencing my same problems, was giving more space to the relaxed approach. After all, how could we justify that massive coincidence? We jumped then to the more practical, 'we need to focus on the real life and what's really important' approach. This perspective kicked the whole situation out of the car and out of question. If I cared about my happiness, my life with John, my mental stability, I had to keep my issues under control and remember what was real and what wasn't. Our last point of view was about my emotions. *Did I let this happen also because of my feelings?* There was something that I wasn't happy about, in my life?

I wasn't a fan of this last viewpoint because it hurt but, I had to admit, I hadn't even replied to John's messages since the night before. Where was John in all this? My mind went back to John's texts. He had written a few, but I had read only the first one. It was time to get a look at it.

John

Can't sleep. Are you still up?

John

I tried to call you anyway but you have no service.
Something weird has happened.
Call me tomorrow morning, babes.
Miss u.

What happened? What weird things can ever happen if I'm not around?, I thought. I was miles away from home and the nightmares had obviously followed me. *How could weirdness still manifest back home?* His next and last message read:

105

John

Couldn't sleep last night. I'm wrecked.
Someone knocked at the door twice
but nobody was there.

I'm sure cause Daisy went mad and the second
time I heard it clearly cause I was already up.
Going to the gallery in a bit.
Let me know when you are on your way home.
Miss u

'John said someone knocked at the door twice, last night,' I told Anita right after reading the text. I was puzzled.

'What do you mean, knocked? How can someone knock at the door if you guys keep the gates at the far side closed all the time?' she asked.

'I don't know. I'm just seeing this now…maybe I should call him. Hold on.' The service was pretty bad. No call was possible.

'The joy of being in the remote countryside,' she said, when I complained about the signal. 'I think we are pretty close to the pit stop we had on the way in. Shall we just go to the petrol station and try there? I'll get some coffee in the meantime.'

So Anita exited at the next crossroad and drove towards the station. We passed the old cottages where John's Pub was and we purposely looked outside, to see if the sign was actually there.

'See? There's no sign outside. I'm telling you that wasn't the pub that woman told us about,' Anita said, pointing at the building in ruins.

'I can't believe we did really have food in there,' I replied. 'Look, it's all in disrepair!'

At the petrol station, we filled the tank, used the bathroom and I went looking for a phone box. John answered.

'Hey... what happened? I was getting worried!' he said. A loud sound of people talking took over his side of the call.

'I'm sorry, John, I had no coverage at all,' I lied. *It is true for most of it*, I thought. 'I got your messages. What is this noise? Are you at the show?'

'Yes! I finally got the room for a week at the gallery, but there is a lot that needs to be done before I can put up my work and show it!'

'Oh, that's great! Come here, what happened last night?' I asked, jumping to the real reason I had called.

'I don't know. I had just fallen asleep after texting you, when I heard a knock from downstairs, at the front door. I thought I had left the gates open and someone had walked in. Daisy got crazy, barking. So I went and checked, but nothing. No one was there and the gates were locked. But then I heard it again. I turned on the lights outside. Nothing. I'm starting to believe we have a ghost!' And he laughed.

'Oh God!' I said. 'That's so strange. Look, I should be home in two hours, three max. I'll check the house and everything. Will you be home late?'

'No babes. I'll see you at seven. I have to go. Love you!' And he was gone.

This was exactly what I needed. Knowing that another crazy event was happening in our house, even without me in it.

'See? I told you! She said John's Pub is that way. We were supposed to turn at the corner, not go straight.' Anita had just come back as I was hanging up.

'So where did we go?' I asked, surprised.

'Oh, that's another funny thing in this entire trip to fantasy land!' she said, starting walking towards the car. 'The woman, the same woman we spoke with, two days ago, said there is nothing that way, and she laughed at my face. When I told her we had food there, she thought I was having a laugh.'

'What?' I could not believe it. 'What did she say exactly?'

'She said there is only John's Pub two minutes up that way.' And she kept walking, passing the parking lot, in the direction of the pub. 'See? That's the pub!' The place was sitting there, with a long dark green sign and golden letters all over.

It was nothing like the one we had been in. The building was in a fairly good shape. A few houses were connected to it and people were walking around.

'What the hell? How did we miss it?' We had passed by that turn and instead continued on the main road. 'Where are you going now?' Anita kept walking. She was going back to a place that apparently didn't exist.

Once we got there, the shock was the new front house manager. There was nothing. Windows were shut, doors were barely hanging on, their shape deformed by the time gone by. Not a single cottage in the block was inhabited. The two of us stood there, in silence, eyes wide open.

'You got to be kidding me,' I said, breaking the daze.

'This is so fucked up,' she said, looking around to see if we could had actually walked in.

'What are you doing?' I asked. She tried to pull the main door, hoping to get in. 'This place is in ruin. There's going to be nothing inside…'

'Is it? And how did we exactly manage to get breakfast, talk to that creepy man and use that disgusting bathroom?' And the door opened after she had put all her strength in the final pull.

The dust came out like a storm of crows finally released to freedom. Our mouths could taste it. The inside was even darker than it had been before. There was nothing to see, but Anita was determined to know. She was finally being me, the same me who was pushing forward, looking for the truth. After looking at our back, to make sure no one could see us breaking in, we slipped into the shadow and disappeared. Flashlights on our phones, we walked around into nothing.

There was no counter, no tables, windows were closed, patched with too much wood for the light to come in. The place was big but nearly empty. An old fireplace was falling apart on the far left. A broken chair next to it.

'I can't believe it,' Anita said. The pub we had been in was in a bad state, but it was nothing like that.

'I don't think we actually had breakfast at all,' I replied while moving around carefully.

'That explains why I was so hungry when we arrived at the inn,' Anita added. 'How is this even possible?'

'Do you think it's because of me?' I asked, getting close to her. Our faces were deformed by our bright lights and were creating scary shadows on the walls. 'Did I bring us here?'

'You mean...we were in one of your daydreams?' she asked back. 'But it was real! As real as the food I ate. I peed somewhere over there! Oh God...' she said like she was about to cry from disgust.

'Let's go, Anita. Let's leave this place.' And I dragged her out into the daylight.

For a brief moment the outside changed. As if we had walked through an invisible wormhole, the landscape had been swapped with a new one we knew nothing about. The road in front of us was gone, the old houses at our back had disappeared. A few steps away from us, a new, shining ground had formed. Like white marble had been poured all over, a bright expanse formed, a few large pillars rose to the sky, closing in arches, forming doors and windows. Through a large one, a stunning patio extended further out, its edge clashing against a blue sea. As if Anita had teleported herself from part to part, she walked around with confidence, pride, as if she belonged to that place.

Her hair up, golden bracelets wrapped her arms down to her hands. She turned around and said, *'If we don't hurry, they will find it! They will find the node. What are we going to do then?'*

But as it had come, the vision quickly disappeared. It was matter of seconds before I was brought back to reality. There, next to me, Anita was still looking at the outside of the derelicts, questioning her own sanity. As if I couldn't bring myself in adding more strange stories to her mind, I decided it was better not sharing what I had just seen.

'Are you alright? Daniel, don't worry. We will figure this out! Shall we go?' she asked.

'Yes! Let's go.' And in an instant I removed my latest vision from my mind.

We gave a few more looks to the outside while rushing our steps back to the car. Whatever that pub really was, we had fallen right into it and came out, somehow safe, twice. The food we'd had, the conversations, everything came back to us in a flashback. And yet, it had never happened. Back in the car, I drove because Anita was too agitated to focus on the road. We spent the next hour talking and talking trying to make sense of it. The three different perspectives about my experience were now reduced to one. No emotions, no rationality. Our only breakthrough had to be the more 'relaxed approach'. That couldn't have been possible to explain without an open mind on the supernatural.

'OK, let's say that happened because of you, right?' Anita decided to analyse it once more, before I left the car, outside my house. I could hear Daisy crying behind the front door. 'Let's say this whole trip was somehow intended to happen. We had to postpone it, Noah stopped dreaming about you for a while because of it. So far you had no dreams, right?' And I nodded. She was the queen of recaps in bullet points. 'Then the fate, or whatever this is, brings you back on track. We plan this trip. Then we can say it was all predetermined. Even me and you ending up in that dump hole.'

'Where is this going, Anita?' I asked, trying to fast-forward it. I wanted to hug my poor dog.

'I don't know...' And she sighed. 'This doesn't tell us who and why anyway. OK let's do this. I know, I'm taking over a bit' —*a bit?* I thought—'but let's do this. We give ourselves a break. Let's have a good night's sleep and let's see if tomorrow, or in the next few days, we come up with something? What you think?'

'I think you are trying to control this fear you now have too,' I wanted to say. But there was no point. I was tired. A lot had happened and I hadn't got any further in my research. I had only gotten more questions.

'Yeah, I think it's a good idea. You know, I feel better knowing that you've experienced some of my madness, in these two days. It makes me feel less...lonely.' I chose a soft approach.

'OK. OK. Remember, let's keep the whole Noah thing for ourselves, for now. There is no reason to make John worried or hurt.' The secret pact was still on. I was up for it. It would have made things easier anyway.

So Anita left the house and went home. The night came fast as I was unpacking my bags, feeding the dog, putting

112

on a wash and waiting for John to come home. When he arrived there was no cold distance. The two days away had turned things for the better. We hugged at the front door. Our hug was different. John wasn't Noah. I had no fear or thrill on touching him, but he felt like home. He made me feel safe, normal. I gave the impression I wasn't quite myself by holding to him so long and so firmly.

'Are you alright? Did you just miss me or something happened?' he asked, still with my arms around him.

I had no idea if he was worried because I hadn't answered his texts or because he could read me through like a book, two pages at a time. I went with just, 'I missed you. Very much,' and somehow that was the only thing I was sure of. That night we talked like we hadn't in a long time. He told me about the show, the trouble with getting everything organized at the gallery. Apparently the room he had reserved wasn't going to be free on time for his exposition, and they had to move it into a smaller one. His sequence of paintings, quite large, needed to be displayed one next to the other, requiring large walls.

He then went again to the strange happenings of the night before. Daisy wagged her tail, sitting on the floor, by the couch we lay on, giving her own version of the same story. With his head on my chest, John felt like the closest thing I had to a family. I played with his hair, and now and then we laughed. He asked me how the two days away had been and I managed to leave out the pub with his name on it, the festival, Noah. Then he asked me a difficult question.

'Do you feel better? I mean, you think you'll sleep OK tonight?'

'I'm sure I will, beside you,' I replied. I wanted to believe it, so I wasn't really lying, I told myself.

'I'm so tired,' he added. And his hand went right by my heart. Guilt was an enemy that I had learned to live with, in between win and defeat. I was going through probably the most difficult time of my life, and I couldn't share it with him. He was in it, and I had wronged him.

'John…' I started, '…there is something else I need to tell you… John?' He had fallen asleep before I could let out my full confession.

That night was a good night. We had gone to bed eventually, me with my secret and him with his worries about his job. I had to go to work the following day, so I hoped that my nightmares would leave me alone. And so they did. There were no dreams, no knocking on any door. Daisy spent a full night snoring on the couch.

Going back to work was a great way to put my thoughts aside, even for a few hours. I had to finish my last project and then I had to jump right into real work. A few years earlier, my best friend had referred me for the role, and knowing there was an unspoken rivalry between the two of us on who was better at pretty much everything, I wanted to make sure I was going to get a promotion soon.

Harry and I had been friends since shortly after I moved to Ireland. He had relocated from England one year after I did, and we got very close pretty soon after. When our friendship started, I was in my little 'rising star' moment. I had just come out, my college career in psychology was going great, I had already started my internship and I had just conquered my full independence as a grown man. For a twenty-one-year-old young man, I had worked very hard for it.

Harry, on the other hand, was a bull-like man in a body he didn't like, with no confidence in himself and with a giant snobby attitude that was secretly buried in his little self-esteem. With time, he had regained consciousness on what he could become, had made substantial changes in his life and his arrogance had started to spill over, here and there. We had a few small fights during the years together, but I had let it go because he was, in many ways, a very good friend. Although he had ancient opinions about pretty much everything—he often defined himself 'conservative'—he had accepted me as a gay man since day one. He had met my previous boyfriends, had gone out with me on crazy adventures, and he and John were close. On our lunch break, he asked me how my trip to Connemara had been.

'I feel like I've been out of the loop since forever. Two weeks back home and this place looks already unbearable.' This was his way of saying, *'I've been to England and now I'm back to this horrible country that I will never call home even if I've been living and working here for years.'*

'How was being back in Manchester?' I asked, pretending, as usual, that I hadn't noticed the obvious complaint.

'Oh man…great, great as expected! You know, good people, great fun. Went to see the match last week, you know? It was awesome.' *I know? Match?* I always wondered if he was happy with me being gay because he genuinely was, or only because he didn't care about what it meant? Me and football were complete strangers.

115

'Oh right… Was it good?' I had learned to play the game. But I hadn't learned the lesson. He started to talk about the players, who was good, who was bad, and something about someone not flagging a red card. At that stage, I wasn't really paying attention.

'I just finished that project on gender bias in the workplace,' I interrupted. 'Now this man needs to take things seriously!'

'Oh yeah…' he went. 'It's going to be OK. What can be hard in your job?' There he was. Harry at his worst. It was my work, so nothing too serious or difficult.

'Well, Harry,' I replied, 'I need to start working on this mental health program. This place is a mess! It's not going to be easy. The leadership here is quick to make big speeches about diversity, inclusion and equality, but when the time to act comes…all they can do is push out a silly virtual training or a pizza party. I really need this to work!'

'Right. But it's not like a real job, is it?'

'Excuse me?' I asked, looking visibly offended.

'Don't get me wrong. I mean, it's what you love, isn't it? It's going to be like…a game for you.' That was his way of fixing his rudeness.

'Anyway, Connemara was incredible.' I had to change topic. 'Great place to be in this time of the year. We met nice people and…less nice people. And also got in this strange place that was supposed to be a pub but it turned out being not…so good,' I added. I wanted to talk a bit about our weird experience but I knew Harry wasn't the right person to ask to keep an open mind. Instead, I told him about the good stuff and left out the odd events.

116

'Do we meet tonight? For dinner. Your place?' His way of saying *I missed you.*

'I'd like to but I need to check few things first,' I said. I had to check what the plan was with Anita. She had said we were going to give it a day to think about what had happened and then...then what? We never said it. I had to keep it open for further instructions.

'Right, let me know. I'm out of here at five.' And Harry left to go back to his work.

The day flew by. I got no texts or calls from Anita. I took the lead and I introduced the topic.

Daniel

**Last night was good.
No accident. You?**

Anita

Great! I've done some digging

Daniel

What

Anita

**Digging.
I've done some researches**

Daniel

About?

Anita

Daniel... wake up...

Daniel

Gotcha. What now?

Anita

'My place. At 7?

Daniel

Cool. See ya then.

Chapter Eight

Searching For The Past

∞

At seven I was already at her place. Anita owned a small, detached house in a nice, quiet estate in the suburbs of Castlecross, very close to the beach. She had moved there after her parents had left for Australia, deciding to take over the family home and make it hers. That was not long before Patrick came along. I remember she wasn't sure about the two of them living together. Anita had this obsession with planning everything in every single detail and, if she didn't feel sure or comfortable with doing something, she would postpone it until she finally was, or decided otherwise. I had the feeling she had started regretting it.

'Is John working late?' She asked while preparing some tea.

'He is. The show starts on Thursday night.'

'I see. I'm making some tea but we could order some pizza later?' She also wanted to have dinner together. *She must have done a lot of digging,* I thought. *And what about Patrick?*

'Is Patrick joining? He loves pizza.' I said, trying to understand.

'He is playing with his friends tonight. He won't be here before ten.' She poured the tea in our cups and went to grab some pages she had printed earlier.

'Here. I found something.' There were pages and pages of pictures, stories about Noah's Bridge, events that had happened in the past and much more. She had already ordered them in sequence based on what she thought was more important.

'You have really gone to the bottom of this, haven't you? Did you steal all these from that museum?' I said, smiling.

The first few pages were about Noah's Bridge. The village indeed existed for centuries. Data got thinner going far back in the past. There was a mention about the founders.

Noah's Bridge was, at first, a self-sustained small village. We have lost track on why the first settlers had chosen this place to set in, but there are records showing that the first family was called Carthach (now known as McCarthy—from ancient Celtic, tr. Loving). Some generations later we have a repeated mention of a Noah coming from the McCarthy family and the bridge also

120

appears more or less at the same time. Although texts are sporadic on this subject, it's generally agreed the name was carried on by descendants of the same family line.

Another piece read:

1880. McCarthy family members struck in deadly large fire. Young male only survivor, named Noah, 13, is now under care. Two more houses have now collapsed. Residents have been moved to the other side of the historical bridge.

And a picture of a young boy was beside the article. Again, the similarity was uncanny. Did the Noah I met come from that family? Then another one:

A good number of small villages are now deserted. After the Great War and the 1929 crisis—what many call now 'the great depression', hundreds of Irish have left for the 'new world'. Most impacted is the west coast. Connemara districts are seeing the highest emigration, with Noah's Bridge leading the race with only one inhabitant left, N. McCarthy, 26. Here Noah's Bridge's only resident.

The Herald—20.05.1933.

In a side photo, a man stood by some trees, an old bridge was visible at his back. This time, the resemblance was astonishing. Anita looked at me. She knew I had recognized that face.

'How this is even possible?' I asked, still staring at the picture.

'They are identical! I mean, the first picture there...I don't know. This young boy looks similar to Noah but I can't really tell. But this one...this one is the image of him,' she said, visibly puzzled. 'And there is more...'

The next page she had printed was a chronicle of recorded births and deaths. It went back to 1868 till 1995. Some parts which she had already circled stood out. *How did she manage to do all this searching in less than a day?* As a great writer and journalist, Anita had a talent for research and data. Her work was incredible. Incredible as the shocking truth she had dug out. The chronicle had a few McCarthys circled in red. Sarah, Conor, Philip, Sean...

'What am I looking at?' I asked.

'You see.' Anita moved my face towards hers. She was about to explain the reasons behind all that researching. 'I could not come to an explanation, as I'm sure you can't either, how a picture from years and years ago could show an exact, identical copy of a guy we just met. This and the rest we got from that lady in Noah's Bridge, remember? So I thought, and I know it might sounds crazy. I thought, what if...?'

'What if?'

'OK, look. These, on the left are the births. Dates and names recorded. Some of them are missing of course. Back in those days, registrations of this type weren't widely common. Here are the deaths records. These ones are a bit more reliable. Don't you see anything?' I was still trying to follow her thinking process.

'OK...OK. There is no Noah anywhere, right? This is what you mean? So this confirms the other article that he was the only survivor?' I asked.

'Daniel...there is no Noah *anywhere*. No baby born with that name and nobody dead with that name. Since 1868?' It was right in front of my eyes and I couldn't see it. She was right.

'OK. Wait a minute. Is it not possible he lied and his name isn't Noah?' I asked, trying to make sense of it.

'And so did Debbie at the inn? People know him as Noah.' We had stumbled into something. Was this something connected to my dreams? 'Now. Let's talk about you,' she said.

'What about me?'

'We have to believe you are connected to Noah. And if Noah has a very...blurry and *very long* past...what about yours? I mean, I know about your family and stuff, but I can't really dig into other countries' records that easily and, in fairness, it feels weird searching things about you without...you,' she admitted.

'What do you want to know?' I replied uncomfortably. 'You know about me moving to Ireland. You know about my family and I don't recall being immortal.' I added that last part with a good dose of sarcasm.

'OK. Let's leave aside this apparent immortality thing,' and she pushed back with a double dose. 'Do you know enough about your parents, your grandparents?'

'Well, I do. I think. And for the things I don't know, I have to say it's a bit late to go and ask my grandma. She can't even recognize me any more.' And Anita could feel the sadness in my words.

'OK. Don't worry. We can figure things out. Anyway, let's order pizza.'

Before we could even realize it, pizza had arrived and gone. We changed topic and went back right on it. There wasn't much I hadn't told her already that could find a match with Noah's history. We went through my first years living in an old house with my mother and my grandma, the absence of any maternal attachment, the distance my mother had always had, my dad not being in the picture.

Anita and I talked briefly about my father. I didn't know him and I had never seen him. All I knew was what my mother had told me. He was a bad man, up to no good most of the time, and she had left him when I was only one year old. Growing up, I had asked more questions of my grandma, who was always too gentle to say anything horrible about anyone. She had only said he had chosen a different life for himself and that I didn't really need him, because she was going to be there to protect me. And she had done that, somehow.

Patrick came back soon after we started talking about my great parents. Not wanting to tell him what that was all about, we dropped the conversation and moved to talk about work. Anita shared with me she had started to write a book on ancient Irish history and, funny enough, we were still on topic. Looking at Patrick, no one would say something wasn't right between them. He was in great form. He bombarded me with questions about the trip, John, and my work. While he was away to get a shower, Anita and I agreed to continue the conversation in the next

124

few days. In the meantime, I promised I would go on a memory hunt 'looking for signs'. What signs…I didn't know. I left her home just after saying goodbye to Patrick and I was ready to turn on the car and leave, when a text popped up in my phone. I imagined it was John, telling me he was coming home. But I was wrong.

Noah

I've been waiting to text you.
I thought I might just leave it a little longer
but I really wanted to talk.

I hadn't forget we had exchanged our numbers and I did want to text him myself, but I had some challenging feelings about it. *Should I write him back? What will I say? I have been thinking about you…but my friend even more because she has been investigating your past and now I don't know who you really are?* I thought.

'*I've been waiting…*' No. Better, '*Hi Noah, how are you?*' No, this wasn't good either.

Daniel

Hi Noah. I was just thinking about you.

Noah

How was the trip back home?

Daniel

Strange.. but we got home alright

Noah

Something happened?

Daniel

**Long story. What about you.
You wanted to talk. Something happened?**

Noah

Can I call you?

And there I stopped for few seconds. Was I making a mistake by telling him, *'Yes of course, we can talk'*? I couldn't bring up the whole story about the fire, the births and deaths over the phone.

Daniel

**I'm in my car. Driving back home.
I'll call you when I'm there.**

Noah

OK. Talk to you soon. x

John wasn't at the house when I arrived. I really couldn't imagine how I would explain taking that call closed in the bathroom. I let Daisy out for a run around the house, and followed her outside, phone in hand, thinking if I was really going to call him or not. The longer I waited the

126

higher was the chance John would get back home. *Stop being a chickenshit*, I told myself. And so I made the call.

'Hi!' he answered. So much enthusiasm in a tiny word.

'How are you?' I sounded purposely cold. For one, I felt I was plotting in the shadow, and second, after my conversation with Anita, I had my doubts he was trustworthy.

'I'm OK. Are you OK? What did you mean the trip back was strange?'

'Well...you know. Strange.' I didn't know if I should say: *You know, with Anita knowing about what happened between you and me.* Instead I went with, *Keep your mouth shut!*

'So she knows everything?'

'Yes. She knows. To be honest she knows even too much.' And I immediately regretted saying it, so I added a brief laugh to make it sound like a joke.

'That's not a bad idea. I never had the chance to tell anyone...until you. That made you even more special. You were the first and only one,' he said.

'Noah...' He talked with a soft, making me feel uncomfortable. This was going to be a practical conversation. A business talk. No romance.

'Sorry, I didn't mean it in a weird way.' He had taken the hint. 'Since you left, I haven't stopped thinking...about you and me...' No, he hadn't, obviously.

'Noah...look...'

'Daniel, please, hold on. Listen to me, one second,' he interrupted me. 'You know what I mean. I waited for you too long to have only a few moments together. It wasn't enough. I told you a lot but you haven't had the chance to do the same, and I feel this is what we need right now.'

He had told me a lot...well not enough, considering what I had learned after my little conversation with Anita. Or maybe he really was telling the truth? How can someone not die and not know it? There were only two possibilities: either he was lying to me or it was all true and he didn't know. Both ideas scared me.

'I know what you mean. I know this is important. It is for you as much it is for me. What you need to understand is that I'm not like you. These...emotions, these feelings mean something different for me and I can't go ahead if I don't start to see you in a different way.' There, I had said it.

'What if I am?' he asked.

'You are what?' I was confused.

'You said I'm not like you. What if I am?'

I was speechless. That wasn't fair. We had talked about it. We were both victims of the same sick game, but I was playing with my own weakness. He wasn't.

'Look, Noah. I want us to get to the bottom of this...whatever this is. But I don't want to make more mess than the one we can barely handle. I promise, I will help you to understand as much as you will help me and, I hope, to get this gone from our lives, but please. I need time to reflect.' I wasn't sure it was what I really wanted to say.

'Sorry. I didn't mean to... What do we do now? Will I just let you go and wait for when you are ready?'

'Yes, please. Can you do that?' I wasn't sure about that either.

'That's all I've been doing so far. Waiting for you.' He said, and my stomach twisted violently.

'I really want to know. I swear.' I replied immediately, trying to make it up to him.

'You call me or text me when you are ready?' he asked, nearly begging.

'I will.' And our phone conversation was over.

A few seconds later, John pulled over at the front door. His excitement was visible in his face, from the side window. Daisy jumped at the car door, eager for cuddles. Couldn't help myself from putting on a big smile.

'It's all done and ready. I can't believe it. It's actually looking great, babe!'

'The show at the gallery?' I asked.

'Yeah, silly, what else! I know it's late but do you fancy a quick drink? I really want to celebrate with my baby tonight.' He said it like he wouldn't have accepted a no for an answer.

And so we went. I had so much in my head, so I had to pull myself together and do what a good boyfriend should do. That was his moment and he deserved it. After giving Daisy her food, putting some fresh clothes on and closing the house, we were on the road to his favourite pub, The Garden. I was happy I had forced myself to go. We had a great few hours of talking, laughing and, for John only, drinking. I felt it was my duty to drive back and let him enjoy the celebration.

Some friends of his, including Theresa, joined us and the talk steered to the big opening, in two days. I always loved looking at John when he talked about his work. His eyes glowed, his smile was irresistible. The same spell he had put on me the day we met had strengthened its power. I just wanted to go home and be with him, in every way.

Having to go to work the morning after and with most of his friends gone, we eventually left to go back home. I was pretty tired and John was a bit drunk but I still wanted him very much, so I drove as fast as I could. We had just parked the car and were walking towards the front door, holding hands, my lips on his neck following him closely, when I stopped. I pulled him back the second he took out the house keys. Something was wrong.

'John...'

'What?' he said, a bit lost. The alcohol had taken over.

'John, the gates were closed...' I was getting very worried.

'Of course they were.' He wasn't focused on the matter.

'John... Look. The door is open...' I said, whispering, and he instantly washed off his dizziness and came back to reality, in a second. The front door was unlocked and slightly open. No lights on. No noise.

'Daisy!' he said loudly. Afraid someone could be inside, I pulled him again before he could rush in.

'Wait. What if someone is inside?' And we waited a few long never-ending seconds.

130

Not a sound came from the house. We listened carefully but all I could hear was my heart pumping in my ears. And then Daisy stormed out, jumping all over us. She was again happy to see John and to see me. She was OK. John looked at me for a moment, before moving forward and entering the house.

'Get your phone and be ready to call the Gardaí,' he said.

He slowly opened the door and moved towards the light switch. When the lights went on, in the hall, up the stairs and in the back corridor, I had the fear someone was going to be there, looking right at us. But nobody was home. John moved to the sitting room and I went to the kitchen. Nothing. There was no one. Everything was there as we had left it. Upstairs was untouched.

'You're sure you looked the door, right?' he asked.

'Of course I did. I'm one hundred per cent sure. And even if I didn't lock it, I definitely didn't leave the door open!' I said, a bit agitated.

'Calm down, babe. I know you didn't. Let's do another round of the house. You stay here at the bottom of the stairs. I'm going to check again upstairs, room by room, and again downstairs afterwards.'

The meticulous research didn't produce any result, gladly. We had no idea what had happened. For the following twenty minutes, we kept talking over and over, about us closing the door and us then finding it open. I had gone and checked some of the rooms again, and back again checking all the windows. I had to be sure. After the fear had worn off, we felt too tired to continue so we went to bed, happy that nothing bad had happened, but still vigilant, while my desire for him had gone somewhere far, without me noticing. Two hours or so after we fell asleep, Daisy came upstairs beside our bed and started pulling my side of the sheets with her paw. Halfway between nightmares and being awake, I felt her cold nose on my hand hanging down.

'Hey, what's up, baby? What are you doing upstairs?' I whispered to not wake John up.

Then somewhere, in the back of my head, I remembered what had happened that night and suddenly, Daisy being there, when she had never been on her own will, looked very strange.

My senses were on. I was staring into the deep dark, ears on. I could have easily been a dog myself. Then the first knock struck me.

I heard it clearly. There was no doubt. My left hand went to John.

'John...John, wake up!'

'What's wrong? Are you OK?' he asked, still asleep. Then he heard Daisy's heavy breathing. 'Why is Daisy up here?'

'She woke me up few seconds ago. John, I heard knocking...' And he immediately pulled himself up.

'What's going on in this house?' he asked, quite tired. John got out of bed, turned the bedside lamp on and moved close to the bedroom door, pointing his left ear outside.

'I'm sure, John.' And I got up as well, exchanging places with Daisy, who lay comfortably on our bed.

'I know, love. I am sure I heard it too, the other night. Stay quiet for a moment,' he whispered.

Then the second knock came. John stormed out of the bedroom and went downstairs turning on all the lights on his way down. Me, right behind him, I stood halfway down after John had stopped at the bottom of the stairs, petrified. The front door was wide open. I rushed downstairs, followed by Daisy, when my fear took a strange turn making me determined to see that through. John stood still at the front door. He turned the outside lights on, making the large field around the house bright to the far edge, where the darkness was still too powerful to overcome. After doing the round of our home, I went upstairs checking all the bedroom, the studio, the bathrooms. Still, there was nothing.

'There is no one...' I told John. He was scanning the outside world, like a predator too hungry to give up the hunt.

'I closed the door myself, Daniel,' he said.

'I know.' What else could I have said? That I had the horrible feeling this was all on me? That it was nothing but another crazy event connected to my dreams?

He locked the door again and walked into the sitting room. After a few seconds he came back with one of the heavy armchairs. I could see right through the plan he had in mind.

'The door is locked. Now the chair is in front of it. See this?' he said, pointing at the defensive strategy he had just put together. 'If this moves, even one inch, I'm calling the Gardaí! And if it doesn't, we'll get this door fixed.'

I didn't answer. His plan was far from perfect, but what else could have been done? Nobody had broken in. He knew it and I knew it. Rather than give in to the idea we were being haunted by one of aunty Marge's ghosts', John had decided to prove that the door was faulty. The door was perfectly fine. I was faulty, and there was no piece of furniture that would have fixed that.

Chapter Nine
Prophecy

∞

The morning after, John was happy to find out the armchair hadn't moved. It was still there exactly like he had placed it. Same position as he remembered. The clock ticked seven. I would usually be up long before him in the morning, but this time I found him in the kitchen, making coffee. Daisy ran happy outside; the weather looked good enough to let her free for a little while. The stronghold at the front door had been already removed and placed back in its spot.

'Please tell me you put it back this morning?' I asked, skipping the good morning and begging for some strong dose of caffeine.

'Morning. Yes, I put it back. It was there as I left it. Daisy is out.' And he handed over a boiling cup.

'Are you going to the gallery earlier today? You're not up this early, usually.'

'I might. I had some trouble going back to sleep anyway. I'll have the chance to get all ready and leave early. Will I pick up Chinese on my way home?'

'Oh God, yes. I love you!' And a kiss was strongly due.

'Right, I'll jump in the shower and I'm out of here...by the way, that cloak you brought from Connemara? It's pretty funky, babe. Why did you get it? Is it like a bathrobe or something?' And he went upstairs laughing.

I didn't follow. *What cloak? What is he talking about?* On the kitchen table, folded and in a silky cover, a half-open square soft bag was left there. I had no idea what it was. John had opened it and the wrap was left loose. I knew I had brought only a few funny fridge magnets from Connemara, but that was pretty much it. I remembered unpacking my bag and taking everything out. There was no bathrobe. I pulled it out and looked at it.

It was a long ivory cloak with no sleeves. It had a large hood reaching down the shoulders and gold engravings all around the edges. Symbols were printed all together, like words in sequence, but with no meaning to me.

Like a flash, it hit me. That strange present was left there by someone who had entered our house the night before. There wasn't any other explanation. But why would someone break in, take nothing and leave something like that instead? It had something to do with me?

I dropped it immediately, as if fire was catching in my hands, and moved away. I kept looking at it as if it were going to move or do something else crazy, but the cloak lay dead on the table, harmless. I wanted to tell John it wasn't mine, that it had appeared overnight, but what explanation would I give him? What if John wanted to tear it apart, once he saw it as the tangible proof that someone had broken in? And if it was left for me, as deep down I knew, could I let that happen?

So, I quickly wrapped it back, went into the spare bedroom and hid it from sight, at the bottom of the wardrobe, buried by tons of jumpers.

After letting Daisy back in, we both went to work. That was John's last day before the big show and while at work, I texted him a few times to make sure everything was going OK. I didn't mention anything about the Connemara souvenir and I hoped he wasn't going to ask.

At lunchtime, I met Harry who complained about me not letting him know about dinner. I wanted to say: *'If you stopped for few minutes thinking everybody's life gravitates around you, I might have told you what's going on.'* But I didn't.

The truth was that I had forgotten. I hadn't planned on staying at Anita's, but the conversation about Noah had taken over. Pizza was also too much of a good idea to renounce. So I put up the excuse that John wanted to go and celebrate his success but Harry wasn't much interested in that either.

That day went fast, and so did the day after.

I left work early on Thursday to be ready and on time for John's opening night. I hadn't seen his work yet. He never allowed me to see anything that wasn't ready, so I had to wait for the big event, like everyone else. Harry was going to be there and so were Mark, Shannon and Anita. I wasn't sure about Patrick, but I thought I was going to find out when I had picked her up, on my way to the gallery.

John had left in the afternoon, with his suit in a plastic cover so he could be there before anyone else, making sure that everything was ready. The reception was at 6.30 p.m. and John insisted I had the invite too or I would forget, so I kept looking at it, worried that I was going to be late. Wearing a sleek black suit and a black bowtie on a white shirt, and my hair pulled back, I was ready to go. The tight new shoes were already killing me.

At six I was already at Harry's. He waited for me at the front door. Nothing fancy in his clothes. A grey shirt, dark jeans and a pair of runners. Anita instead was stunning. She showed at the front door wearing a long black pretty cocktail dress, wide open at the back. Hair up, make-up impeccable. The first thing she said once she had gotten in the car was:

'Daniel, you look handsome.' And then turned to Harry: 'You on the other hand, what's that?' —but he wasn't even bothered by her comment.

'Anita, it's not a wedding…but you look beautiful! I'm just making sure the attention is all on you.' And he went on checking his phone.

'OK, calm down, you two.' And I smiled. 'The attention is all for John tonight, and his work.'

'What's new in that?' she snapped.

'And you are saying?' I replied, but I knew exactly what she was referring to.

'I'm kidding! Don't mind me. I'm just annoyed that Patrick won't be there,' she said, lowering her voice towards the end, like she wanted to tell me more, but didn't want Harry to be part of our secret circle.

'Yeah, where is Patrick? That man hasn't text me in like, forever.' That was Harry jumping in. The circle was opened to unwanted guests.

'He had something important to do with a relative of his.' And she said it like she didn't believe it or that 'the something' wasn't important.

'Right then, let's go. Let's make this night unforgettable.' I said, turning on the car. And so we went.

Dublin bustled, even for a Thursday night, and the gallery was no exception. Despite arriving on time, the place was already teeming with people. The exhibition had been arranged at the convention centre, nestled by the canal docks, where multiple events were taking place. The surroundings were abuzz with people hurrying about, filled with anticipation akin to the week before Christmas. The reception hall brimmed with clinking glasses of champagne, accompanied by a lively hum of voices and conversations. The atmosphere was simply delightful.

'Oh my God, look at this place,' Anita said, grabbing a glass of champagne. 'Are you getting one?' she added, knowing I might be the one driving back.

'Sure,' I said. 'John is keeping clean tonight. He will drive.'

'Bloody hell, so many hot girls here!' Harry added, with his usual savoir faire.

'See? Now you know why you were supposed to wear a suit!' she said.

'Sweetheart,' he replied, and I knew he was going to say something stupid, 'my charm is all I need.'

'Let's find John, please,' she said to me, while I enjoyed the squabble.

'Shall we?' I asked, taking her arm.

We went up the escalator, to the main exposition area. The show was at the far left. Once at the top, we found more people roaming around in a very happy mood. I saw John from afar. My heart took the same escalator we had, in a loop up and down. He was a God in a world of simple men. I don't know if it was the atmosphere, his stunning look, or me loving to see him in his conquering quest, but the closer we went, the more I loved him. His smile was there to greet me, at the entrance.

'You look incredible,' he told me. 'And you, oh my God, Anita. This dress is phenomenal!' And she blushed.

'Mister!' Harry shouted to John, from the back.

'Oh, you made it too. So happy to see you!'

John made no mention of Patrick. Probably, his mind was too busy to really think of who was missing, and Anita was visibly happy about the omission. The show was going very well. People kept making positive comments about the series of paintings John had produced and his face showed appreciation. Without further ado, we decided to enter the room and see it for ourselves. The space was pretty big. I couldn't imagine what the other one would have looked like, considering John was initially worried about the idea of moving to a smaller room. It could have easily fit 300 people, at least. Giant glass windows shined at the left, the chunky grey clouds gazed at the presentation too, and to the front and right, two massive walls sustained John's six large paintings.

'Oh my God, this is fantastic,' Anita said as soon as we moved in. John walked in front of us, leading to the presentation.

At first, I was captured by the room, the noise of people talking, the champagne glasses ringing at a touch. After a few moments, my eyes moved to John's work. There was something in it. Confused by my own first reaction, I went back looking at the first painting. It was pretty large, like the others. It could have easily contained all of us and three times more. The paint was dark. A shadow lurked behind a door adorned with trees, flowers, animals and many other elements of Earth carved into it. The dark figure had a hand at the door while kept the other one hidden behind, squeezing a heart. If John wanted to trigger a reaction, he was off to a good start.

I quickly looked to Anita, Harry and then the many other people around, looking for strong responses. But they were absolutely OK with all of it. So I went on and looked at the other pieces, thinking the answer might be there. The second painting showed a woman wearing a transparent gown. She held a small plant in one hand and in the other she contained the bright, explosive power of a star. This was definitely more appealing. An old man hunched and tired spun a wheel in the third painting. In the fourth painting another figure stood still. A tiara on his head, he was crowned with a multitude of tiny flames that

141

were melting and dropping as a golden liquid on a large planet. At the bottom, the fluid turned into what looked like spirits or ghosts, just before reaching the surface. The fifth painting had another woman. She held several sick men, women and children at her back. This one was again very hard to look at.

The final painting looked like two. The frame was all around the two parts but in the centre it had an opening. A man in each side, they both looked at each other like in a mirror, and their hands came together right in the middle. The man on the left had a shell in his left hand and the man on the right held a crowned heart. I got a look at all the paintings together. This was supposed to be one entire piece of art, so I tried to see the overall message. I couldn't understand. It was difficult to look at it. Whatever message it had, it was disturbing.

'So, I want to know. Your opinion is the most important, you know that, right?' John asked me. I was speechless. What could I have said?

'I…I…have no words.' I said the truth. I was shocked.

'Is it a good thing, right?' he asked, smiling and looking at me.

I couldn't keep my eyes off his work. I was trying to understand what he wanted people to feel. I quickly went to analyse it under a psychological point of view, an art perspective, something had to come to help me. Harry did. He moved closer to the two of us.

'You know me and art. I mean, it's massive and pretty great to look at it but…what am looking at, exactly?' And he smiled, embarrassed. I was glad he said it first. *What are we looking at?*

'No, you're fine,' John answered. 'Expressionism can be difficult to read. You see, the first paint represents birth, then you have growth, challenges, success, failure, and the last one is love which, for me, is the ultimate status a human being can strive to achieve.'

I listened carefully. It didn't make any sense. It wasn't expressionism, or not the art style I knew. There was no connection with what he said and what I saw. So I looked at them for a moment, confused.

'You didn't get it too?' John asked, a bit surprised.

'No, no. I was listening to your explanation and trying to connect with what you just said,' I replied. And my eyes went back to the paintings.

Something weird had happened.

The seven figures were gone. The two women and the five men had disappeared and been replaced with six incredible paintings. I lost my words again. *What did I see?* I looked at John and Harry once more and back again to the paintings. Still they hadn't changed back. I had imagined it. The real paintings were astonishing. John's work for sure.

'John, this is unreal. Really. I have no words.' And I meant it as both a compliment to him and a reproach to me.

'Thank you, babe,' he answered, like he had just started breathing again.

'I mean, this is so good. John you are unbelievable!' Anita had just come back from a close inspection of all six

143

paintings. She made comments about the size, the style, the idea, the symbolism.

An hour later the room was still full and we had moved close to the table with the drinks, as Harry was interested only in that and in the good-looking women coming and going. Busy, John entertained in conversation with old gentlemen and art teachers. I was still puzzled.

'Oh, don't tell me you are jealous of those old pensioners,' Anita said, after taking a glass of white wine for herself and for me.

'Sure!' I replied, laughing. 'I need to tell you something.' And I made a sign with my head to move away from Harry.

'What's wrong?' she asked, after we moved far enough.

'Something weird happened. When I gave the first look at those paintings, I didn't see what everybody else saw.'

'It happens with art, I suppose. No?'

'That's not what I mean. I saw something different. Different pictures, different things entirely...' I tried to make her understand.

'What did you see?' I was glad she was so open-minded with all my craziness.

'A creepy figure in the first, two women and some other men in the others...nothing like the real paintings.'

'Were you daydreaming again?' she asked, sounding nearly annoyed by it.

'What do you mean again? No. I was here with all of you. Everything else was normal,' I said.

'OK. Will you be able to remember...till tomorrow? We can discuss about this later.' And she looked around, as if we were surrounded by spies under cover.

'There is more.' I wanted to tell her about the cloak.

'What else did just happen?'

'Nothing else...something happened earlier. We can also talk about this later?'

'Sure. Now, pull yourself together, our best friend is here...' she replied. She referred to Shannon, who had just walked in, wearing a long, dark golden dress. Anita was not particularly happy to see her, and I could tell from her face and her voice.

Almost invisible, Mark walked beside his gal. His clothes were fancier than Harry's but it was clear he hadn't put any effort into it. Uninterested in the whole event, he parted from Shannon and moved to grab a drink at the far corner of the room. His lady instead moved towards us, conquering the space as if she walked on a red carpet. For every step she took, I could see Anita's nerves cracking a little.

'If this is not the event of the year!' she started, smiling at us. There was an unnatural mannerism in her moves, but she looked stunning. Harry's mouth was visibly drooling.

'Shannon, you made it,' I replied, hugging her. 'This dress is incredible!'

'Where is Mark?' Anita asked.

'Somewhere... Where is Patrick?' she replied, moving her hair to the side. I could have sworn I saw a sparkle at the corner of her eyes.

145

'I mean,' Harry said, in between moving forward and staying behind me, shy as a boy in his first day of school. 'If you ever need to get a better man, you have my number...'

'Harry, please,' Anita interjected, sharp. 'And fix your shirt, you look desperate.'

'This place is packed!' Shannon continued. 'I'll get a look at John's work quickly, then it's time for a few snaps. This is going to be huge on Insta!' And she moved away quickly, almost floating into the heavy space around us.

The wine and the many conversations lasted long enough to entertain us until the conclusion of the show. When everyone else had left, Anita, Harry and I stood at the entrance, waiting for John to be ready to go. He had a very pleasant night and wanted to prolong a bit longer. So we decided to get back to Castlecross and stop somewhere for a quick bite and, perhaps, another drink or two.

In the car, we talked again about the show, the people in there, the public acclaim. John was over the moon. Then, hitting me as cold ice down my spine, he started talking about what had happened at the house, a few nights before. Harry was amazed how I had managed to keep that from him and Anita was unusually quiet. I could hear her brain ticking.

'Did they take anything?' Harry asked. And I was about to say, *'No but they left something behind.'*

'We're not really sure if someone did actually break in. I think there are only two explanations,' John replied, while driving. I was waiting to hear it. 'Either the door needs to be fixed or we have a ghost.'

146

Anita didn't talk still.

'Do you want to stop home first, to go and check if everything is OK?' Harry asked.

'I wouldn't mind using the bathroom and seeing Daisy…' Anita said. *What is she trying to do?*

'We can, if you guys want,' John replied.

'Are you sure, babe? It's your big celebration night,' I asked.

'What if we stop somewhere, get some drinks and order food when we get home? In this way, you guys don't have to leave. We can call a taxi, right, Anita?' For the first time since I had known them, it looked as if Harry's mind was tuned in with Anita's.

'I like it. Are you OK with it?' John asked.

And of course I said yes. I wondered if the front door would still be closed by the time we got home. I knew Anita was up to something, and I knew Harry wanted to just stay comfortable, at our place. If John didn't mind, I was OK with it. So we stopped at one of those all-night-open off licences, got a few drinks and, on the way, ordered Chinese food, as John was disappointed we couldn't get it the night before. We were glad to find the gates and the front door closed shut as we had left it. On the other side, Daisy waited alone.

We had the kitchen table ready when the food finally arrived. The great mood, John's success and the nice experience were all guests at the dinner table.

Whatever Anita's plans were, I didn't find it out that night. Maybe it was the wine, maybe it was our happiness, but it all went forgotten.

Chapter Ten

Couples

∞

John's show was going to last till Sunday evening. Every day, he left early in the morning and came back late at night. Harry had organized a barbeque at Anita and Patrick's place without their full consent, but Patrick was happy about it, so when Harry invited himself over and asked me to join, Anita said yes. She asked some girls from the newspaper she worked with to come and join us, so when she recommended Harry to come wearing decent clothes, I laughed hard. I couldn't believe my ears when she told him:

'These are nice, well-educated girls. You can come as long as you leave your man cave look back in the Palaeolithic. 'Harry didn't take it personally. He just smiled and moved on. Patrick had invited a friend as well so, that

Saturday, we were a quite big group. Anita had introduced me and Harry to Claire and Liz and Patrick had done the same with his friend, Phil. The seven of us were sitting outside, in the back garden, enjoying the surprisingly good weather, and Harry was grilling some burgers, showing off his talent to the two new girls who didn't look very impressed by it.

'Patrick, did you tell Mark about the barbeque?' Harry asked, flipping some meat.

'Nope. He would bring Shannon with him and you know, Anita doesn't like her,' he replied with a flat tone.

'Since when?' Anita asked, looking annoyed.

'Well, it's not like you two are best friends,' I answered.

'I like Shannon,' she said, 'except when she is so difficult to be liked.'

'Come on, she is a good girl...big...you know...' Harry added, putting his hands on his chest as if referring to Shannon's breasts. In Claire's and Liz's eyes, he was losing more points at every minute.

'Not everything is about that, you know?' Anita said. 'Daniel, tell him.'

'Don't look at me! I like Shannon for anything but her body...'

'You know what I mean. I'm all about research, truth, data, history. She is so shallow, believes in everything she reads, anywhere, especially on social media.' And she looked up, in a sign of disapproval.

'Well, now that you're saying it...' Harry said, '...I might need to tell you that I've accidentally told her about the barbeque.' And a not so worried smile appeared on his face.

'You didn't!' Anita showed a completely opposite face.

'Accidentally? Oh Harry, come on,' I said, trying to take Anita's role before she could kill him. We still needed a cook.

Anita looked at Patrick, waiting for him to say something, but he wasn't going to step in that conversation, especially because he was too busy looking at the television, from the patio doors. Phil did the same thing. She moved from looking at him to looking at me, planning a mass murdering.

'Did she say she was going to come?' I asked Harry.

'She said she might be doing something with Mark. That's why I asked Patrick about him,' he replied. He was completely oblivious about the whole situation and especially why what he did was a bit too much.

I gave him the look of disapproval and he responded with the look of 'why is this such a big deal?' I gave up. With the excuse of getting some ice, I asked Anita to get inside. We didn't have the chance to talk about anything that had happened and, if I wanted to keep it secret, there was nothing better than making everyone believe we were going to talk about Shannon and Mark. Standing in front of the fridge, Anita and I started the conversation.

'I hate when he does that!' she said.

'Yeah. He doesn't understand anything that is not his.'

'I hope she won't show up. Now I really don't want her here,' And I imagined her pulling the ice as if she was picturing herself pulling Shannon's hair.

'If she does, we'll minimize the damage, don't worry.' I knew her aversion for Shannon didn't have its roots only in their different personalities. It had also a little of jealousy buried in it. Harry's remarks had just pinched that very secret chord.

'What about you? We didn't have the chance to talk since the opening.' She preceded me.

'Since that night, nothing new. Which is great. But I need to tell you a few things that happened before that,' I said.

'Well, spill it out!' she said sharp, making me feel as if she was picturing me as Shannon.

'Well, you know about the paintings,' I started, 'and you know about what happened at my place a few nights ago.'

'Is there more? How long since we haven't seen each other?' she said, putting the ice in a big jar.

Following her moves around the kitchen, I started doing something I always done in Anita's, thinking why that room looked so small. I wasn't sure if it was really tiny or the tons of books and sheets of papers scattered everywhere made the place feeling claustrophobic. The house was packed with old newspaper, magazines, books, notes. I could swear, I saw a notebook in the fridge, when I had taken the orange juice out.

'You know what John said about *nobody* breaking in the house?' I continued.

'Wasn't true?' she asked, ready to jump on the gossip.

'Technically it wasn't. But he doesn't know. Calm down, it's not like I saw someone and he didn't,' I quickly added, before she could stop me again. 'There was this weird stuff left in the kitchen and he thought I brought it over from our trip.'

'Wait, what? What stuff?'

'An ivory cloak. Pretty fancy to see but absolutely weird.'

'Was it just left there? And excuse me, John didn't say anything?'

'It was on the kitchen table the following morning, wrapped and everything. John had opened it already, way before I had woken up. He thinks it's a souvenir from Connemara.'

Anita gazed outside the window, as if she was checking the others chatting aloud, but she was actually thinking about what I had just said. Agreeing to have some fruit salad, I started cutting some apples.

'Where is this lovely present now?' she asked.

'I hid it…in the spare wardrobe.'

'Why?' She looked at me and I wasn't sure if she was just asking or giving out to me because I hadn't thrown it away.

''Cause it was clearly left there for a reason and I don't want John to stumble onto it again. Not before I can figure out why it was left to me,' I answered.

153

'You know this is crazy, right?' And she looked like there was something wrong with me. 'You found the front door open, twice, and also found something left there that doesn't belong to either you or John. And you hid it in the wardrobe?'

'I know,' I replied. 'But you know this has something to do with everything that has happened. I'm sure of it. We weren't robbed or anything. This is all part of the same thing.'

'You say it like it would make things better.' And this time I had no answer to that. She was right.

'It doesn't, but I have this feeling in my head that cloak is actually a good thing.'

'You know.' And she turned around with a sharp knife in her hand pointed at me as if she was going to kill me for saying something so stupid. 'This could actually be the very first time something tangible has come our way. So far it has been visions and stuff. This...this cloak is real!'

'Our way'. For a moment I had the feeling I wasn't alone any more. Not that the house wasn't packed with people coming and going, but mine and Anita's was a different kind of companionship. The fruit salad was ready but we kept talking about the cloak and how it fitted the overall picture. Claire came in the house while we tried to put all the pieces together, making some comments about Harry and how he was too full of himself. Then Liz came along, saying pretty much the same thing, to which Anita and I started to laugh out loud. After sending them both outside, carrying food and drinks, I found the courage to add the only news I had been withholding.

154

'I talked to Noah,' I said, while she was pulling some garlic bread out of the oven. She froze for a moment.

'When? How?' I had forgotten I had never mentioned to her about the two of us exchanging our phone numbers.

'Not too long ago. The night I came over for pizza. He texted me and I didn't want to talk to him, initially. You had just showed me all that stuff about him. But then I thought it would be a good idea...and so we talked on the phone.'

'OK...' she said, like she wanted to know more but didn't want to push too much.

I was about to tell her the whole conversation while we were collecting the rest of the stuff to bring outside when the bell rang. She quickly looked at me.

'Please tell me I just had one of your daydreams and *that*'—and she pointed at the front door—'didn't happen!'

'Leave it to me...and please, let me handle her,' I replied, knowing that Shannon would make one of her sarcastic comments such as 'Hi, thank you for *not* inviting me over!'

At the door, I had a pleasant surprise. It was John. He carried two bottles of red wine and a smile going from ear to ear.

'Babe? What are you doing here?' I said, visibly happy.

'The show won't start before six thirty and I left everything ready, so instead of spending four hours waiting, I thought to come back home for a little bit.'

'Awesome!' I was glad he had the chance to come over.

155

Having John around meant no more conversation with Anita about Noah or anything else related to, but I always loved having John around my friends. Strangely, it made me feel like he was closer to me, somehow. I also counted on the fact that Anita and I would sneak out for a smoke and a quick talk, at some stage. The group was glad to have John over too. Claire and Liz had the impression they had just met a celebrity. The afternoon went fast and full of talks and laughs.

That was, until the bell rang again. Anita had run out of luck. Shannon was at the door and Mark behind her. This time Patrick went to open it, so we never knew what her opening speech had been.

We had finished the meal already so the couple joined us for coffee, a cake and some drinks. The back garden started to resemble a world war map. John and I sat close in the middle. Patrick and Anita were at the left and Phil just next to them. Shannon and Mark sat by the kitchen window at the right and the new girls constantly moved in the opposite direction to Harry. If he moved, they moved the other way. It was hilarious. If that were a new board game, it would definitely be a couples game.

Observing them all, I had the feeling we would win hands down. John was considered the new idol and I was gladly to be the centre of his attention. He held my hand and told stories about our day-to-day life together. Mark and Shannon seemed happy together but we all knew Shannon consumed all the space in their relationship and Mark was...well...Mark. Present in their relationship as a nice, pretty accessory, Mark was the perfect chosen one. Beside his unchallenged beauty, he had no interesting

156

traits, his behaviour, like his words would fall flat in every circumstance. Wine being his best companion, he would turn to life only if a bottle of alcohol showed up in the room.

Anita and Patrick had been a strong couple in the past. I believed they still were, but I knew they were going through something lately. That day he was also interested in nothing but the football match on TV and Phil looked more like his partner, leaving Anita out. There, when I was about to declare victory, John told everyone about our last experience with the ghost. My mind went rapidly to the cloak, my conversation with Anita, my phone call with Noah, and I thought we were perhaps the worst couple in that board game. I had collected so many secrets already. I had kissed another man and I had been talking to that same man afterwards. Whatever great excuses I had, I was making our relationship sink. Around five John left the house to go home, get ready and drive back to the gallery. Harry proposed some card game and everyone was up for it. Anita and I skipped the first few rounds to walk John outside and have a smoke.

'Good luck, babe,' I said just before he left.

'It's hard, isn't it?' Anita asked, while John was driving away.

'Very much,' I replied, knowing she meant me keeping the secret from John.

'So, tell me about this call you had.' And she lit her cigarette.

'He said he might be feeling something for me.' I started with the strongest bomb.

'What? I thought he was straight?' she asked, almost falling from the tiny old chair she was sitting on. We both sat on two rusty old chairs, by the porch, and I couldn't understand why she found them so pretty.

'That's what he told me...and I think he is. He's just confused about the whole connection we had. He also said I'm special and other stuff like that.'

'Special at getting yourself in trouble...' she said, smiling.

'That was pretty much it. I did push back, though. I told him I need space to figure things out.' And she looked at me, surprised.

'What did he say?'

'That he had been waiting for me all his life, so waiting a bit more wouldn't make much difference.'

'Now, that's sad,' she said.

'It is.'

'Especially considering how long his life has been.' And we laughed, because we had suddenly remembered about the whole mystery around births and deaths. 'That's pity. I have to admit he is very good looking,' she added.

'I've been thinking about what you said. You know, my past,' I continued, ignoring her remark.

'What about it?'

'You know about my mother, and my father. It is pretty messy, isn't't? I think I should start thinking about it. Seriously.'

'Yes, do that. You know I'm by your side, right?' she said with all the affection she could show.

'I do. Let's go back inside and rescue those poor friends of yours from Harry!' And so back inside we went.

When we walked back, Shannon was already talking about some new challenges she had seen on social media, a new special diet, even more extreme than her last gospel around a different vegan alternative approach — where we were supposed to eat only raw bio-vegetables without washing them. Nobody was really listening to her. Mark had gone to sit with Patrick and Phil, Harry was checking his phone and Anita's friends were nodding their heads pretending a mute agreement, quietly promising themselves they were never going to come by the house ever again.

'Oh, Daniel!' Shannon changed topic as soon as I came out. 'I really wanted to stay longer at John's show but I've been busy with my new course on "achieve success through influencing" and this week was pretty intense.'

'Don't worry about it,' I replied, hoping that she wouldn't explain what that course was all about. 'We went home after the opening night and, anyway, John is too busy to also have the time to mind us.'

'Oh, that's so strange…' she said. 'I've read art is dead these days. I was shocked to see so many people who have no better interests.'

'Only the people who still have a brain,' Anita replied, sarcastic, before I could even realize what Shannon had just said was actually offensive.

'This is the social media era, Anita. Get out from the Renaissance. Anyone can do art just using an app,' she snapped.

I knew a big discussion was about to break. That was the usual when Shannon was around. I don't believe she had, deep down, bad intentions when she said things like that. Anita had said few times 'being stupid doesn't make things acceptable'. But I didn't think she was. Shannon had her opinions and she wasn't afraid to let them out, to the world.

'Right, first you have clearly no idea what art is.' At that 'first' I was about to run. 'Second, you come back from that crazy world of yours full of low-level gossip resold for great news and then, and only then, you tell me to get out from the Renaissance!' Anita said it out and loud. The tone wasn't even allowing to a passive-aggressive reply typical of Shannon. It was aggressive and final.

'My news stories are not gossip. And I don't know what you mean, to be honest. Don't be bitter only because you have, what, five followers?' She had used her big guns. For Shannon, life success was measured in followers.

'Speaking of Instagram,' Harry interrupted loudly, 'Claire and Liz, why don't you add me to yours?' And I laughed hard and Anita followed suit after seeing the girls' reaction, in fact breaking the escalation.

Harry was pursuing his selfish goal, but I knew there was a hint of pure altruism that only I could read. He had always despised confrontation or seeing people getting angry one another. That was his personality at its best. He only wanted to get along peacefully with his friends—and also, if possible, be the centre of the female population's attention.

We managed to defuse the evening, splitting into smaller groups, taking a break, making coffee. Finally, the boys joined the group as the match was over. Someone had done something they were not happy about, so they continued to complain about the game for thirty more minutes after it was finished.

Eventually one by one we all left. I told Harry I was going to give him a lift home so he wasn't happy about leaving Claire and Liz there without getting their phone numbers, but I promised him we were going to make it happen again, soon. I had to go back home and check on Daisy so I didn't want to stay too long and Anita was happy to continue our conversation—and also give out about Shannon—the next day. The couple game was over, and for that night there were no winners.

Chapter Eleven

Memories

∞

The next few days passed without major concerns. John's show was over, and the understandable tension he had brought home with it was now in the past. No other strange events happened in the house or to me. Although I took up the habit of checking the spare room wardrobe, making sure the strange gift was still there, nothing unusual happened to it or to me.

I thought for a while about what Anita had said on exploring my past looking for answers. If it was true that Noah's history was entangled with the situation, mine might have also been connected to it. Unfortunately, regressing wasn't easy for me. It never was. There was so much drama and pain in my life that something in me always refused to look back. The whole sexual orientation problem was surprisingly just a minor painful detail in the never-ending experience of an outsider like me. The day I came out to my family wasn't the greatest time of my life and, in fact, it wasn't the greatest family either.

My father was out of the picture and out of memory. There was no talking about him, there was no mention of who he was, why he wasn't there. I had learned that asking about it was only a way to attract trouble. My mother was the complete opposite. She was there and everywhere, over controlling, moved by the fear of her God and her beliefs. There was never love coming from her. She had never been a good mother to me or a good daughter to her mother but that was all I knew back then so, for that young silly boy, that was love. It wasn't the coming out that helped me to see things as they were. It wasn't the news, and their reaction to it, that made me open my eyes to the horrible reality I had lived on. It was gradual, subtle.

Flying back to those days wasn't going to be pleasant. I had closed that door the day I moved to Ireland and I never looked back, except when I had visited my grandma. She was the only keyhole, the only narrow passage to what it had been, despite the painful memories. I wasn't sure I could make it. *Anita has no idea how difficult this is. I can't make it. I prefer living in the darkness of the future than exploring the certainty of my old sorrow*, I kept thinking.

But time was going fast. I hadn't texted or called Noah and some weird things were still happening. Dreams stopped for a while but visions became more frequent. Short, almost imperceptible, they started to appear randomly like if they were part of my real life. The most peculiar thing was that, the more I had them, the more

163

strongly I felt as if an evil presence lurked within. At the beginning, although worried about the unknown, I didn't have the feeling it was coming from somewhere wicked. But things changed and changed fast.

A trip to my past was inevitable. The evil I knew was the evil my mother knew. The one she had taught me to stay away from and, for this reason, my instinct of rejecting her preaching had pushed me more into discovery mode. I refused to believe in what she believed, including her version of hell. She had joined a Christian cult when I was four years old. Back then, I had no idea of where this would bring us and I never fully realized the sickness within till I was sixteen. My grandma never accepted her choices and the choice of bringing me with her in such a twisted path. With the years, their fights became a regular until, one day, my mother moved out of her house, bringing me with her. She eventually met a priest of her church and decided to marry him. Being eleven, I had no say in the affair. That's when the greatest collection of my painful memories were stored.

The deep dive into my past became quickly unbearable. If I wanted to continue this research, it had to be in another way. What could I have done? I had no pictures of my teenagerhood saved anywhere; there wasn't much to imprint in a photo. I had no long-time friends back in Italy that I could call and start a walk in the memory lane. The day I came out and got kicked out from my mother's church, I lost all my friends. They knew and I knew, there weren't going to be more talks from that moment on. I was 'spiritually dead' and for them also literally, till the day I repented and came back confessing my sins.

That was never going to happen. I knew my sexuality was not something I could just turn off and ignore for the rest of my life. Being gay for me was like being hungry, happy, sad, alive. It was part of my mind and my body. But this was something they would never understand. Thinking about what it was and had been for a long time, I realized there was never going to be any other way. Love had found me somewhere, in one way or another. And then I let it in, let it heal my heart.

What the next step was going to be become clear to me. There wasn't going to be more lying down in bed looking at the ceiling or sitting on John's favourite armchair, forcing myself to reopen old scars. I had to touch with my bare hands the reality I had left behind. I had to get my answers directly, face to face. It was time to know where my father was, where I really came from. That was the only way. And what way would that be? To whom could I talk? My grandma was the only one who could have made full confession to me, open-heartedly. Unfortunately her mind was gone. Long gone.

Something inside me told me I had to give it a try, maybe as a start. I took my decision. I was going to go and get my answers.

I had to tell John first. How would I explain it to him, was the next big question. I had been withholding so much from him lately, that lies started to chain together with no way out. I had to tell another lie. Anita received a better treatment. As she took part in my secrets, I didn't have to pretend or find an excuse to go.

Around a week later I had my tickets ready. I was going to fly at the end of July and a week earlier I met her to talk about it. We went out to see a movie and grab something to eat. Right before the movie started, I dropped the hint saying I had to tell her something very important. It wasn't only about the flight but it had also something to do with a recent event I had kept to myself.

The day after I had booked my tickets to go back to Italy, I received a text from Noah. He tried to understand if I was still going to keep my promise of getting back to him. After a short reply from me, he decided that a phone call was needed.

'Daniel, I know you probably don't want to talk to me, you haven't texted me or anything for weeks, but I really need to talk to you.'

'I'm sorry, Noah.' No matter what, an apology was long due, I had put Noah aside for too long. 'I really shouldn't have kept you waiting for so long. I don't want to justify myself, but the main reason is that I've been trying to solve my side of the issue before we could do it together.'

'What do you mean?' he asked.

'I believe...' and I started knowing I was going to bring the whole past mystery into the conversation, '...the key to understand what's happening to us is in our past.'

'I see.' That was all I got. *Am I confusing him or does he know exactly where I'm going with this?*

'I have to be honest, I had done some research about you. Don't get offended, please. I didn't have any intention to spy on you. I needed to understand why you felt so important to me. And what I found has made me believe I need to do the same with my own history.'

'Are you concerned with what you found about me? 'Cause I am…if you are,' he added quickly.

'Not really. I was at first, but honestly…is there anything about us that makes sense at this stage?' Then I added, 'What do you mean with are you concerned?'

'I discovered the truth about my past only recently.'

'I see.' I don't know why I felt relieved by that. 'Well, as I was telling you, I started doing some digging about my life and I booked myself on a flight back to Italy. Yes, now that I think about it, I never told you that's where I was born. Well, that's what I believe.' And I added a brief laugh.

'You think there is something in there that might help you?'

'That might help us, I hope,' I corrected him.

'The fact you are still using the word *us* makes me feel so happy…'

'There is an *us*. I'm done with denying it.' That phrase came out just like that. The pain of my failed attempts remembering my past was speaking for me.

'Daniel?'

'Yes?'

'Can we meet again, before you go?'

'Noah…' I said.

'Please. If what you are about to do is important for you and me, I really want to see you before you go. You don't have to come back here. I'll come to you.'

What was I going to reply? I wanted it. I wanted to see him, to talk about the things I found, the pain I was going through, the risk I was taking by jumping back into a world of hate and fear. I knew I was making a mistake but all I selfishly wanted was to have someone beside me to whom I could open up completely and, if scared of the things we would find in doing so, I could simply leave behind. It wasn't easy to admit and it wasn't pleasant. Perhaps it was just an excuse I told myself to feel free to run to a man I knew nothing about. John popped up in my mind the same moment I said 'yes'.

'Are you serious?' he asked and I was tempted to change my mind. I had another chance to make things right.

'I think it's for the best if we do.' And I chose wrong, again.

'When are you going?'

'In around a week.' The worry he couldn't make it briefly crossed my mind.

'I'll be there in two days. Is that OK? If you tell me where you live, I can get a place close so we can meet.' At that stage I felt like I was doing something really wrong. What was I thinking?

'I live in Castlecross.' It slipped through my lips before my mind could even process it. Whatever I was feeling for Noah had a will of its own.

The two days went in a flash. I made no mention to John about the flights, nor about Noah's visit. Anita was my only safe place, the only person to whom I could express myself. Outside the cinema, Anita made clear she wasn't going home before she knew what I was hinting at. So we decided to grab some food in a place nearby, avoiding the crowd by sitting in a tiny corner, out of sight and out of hearing.

Neither of us was really hungry but we both wanted to spend some time in there so some food found its way in. I wanted to stay as long as possible but I didn't want to take the long route around.

'So, I'm going to see Noah after this.' I dropped it. Just like that. She stared at me and I could see in her face she gasped for air.

'Wait a minute,' She put aside her plate, moved her glass of red wine and all the stuff in between us to the side, so slowly that I felt her intention to make me suffer while waiting. 'You what? Is he here? Daniel, what did I miss?'

'You didn't miss anything. Well, anything about Noah. We spoke on the phone just two days ago. I told him something…' and this was the other news I felt she wasn't ready to hear yet,'…and he said he wanted to come and meet me.' That was the shortest way I could bring her up to speed.

'Right. We will come back to the whole Noah thing in a minute. What else is there?'

'I'm flying back home in a few days.'

'Good!' She was quickly done with it. I went on silent mode. She didn't add anything else and I didn't either. I nearly expected a third voice speaking from above, a narrator, to continue the conversation.

'It's because you want to know about your past, right?' she finally added, and I knew she knew me all along.

'Yes. I have found it difficult to go back with just my memories. I need to go and see what else is there that I don't know.'

169

'Your father…' she said. Again right on point.

'Yes. I have to. This is the major black hole I have. I can't tell if I know some things but I can't remember them or I don't know them at all. I want to try to talk to my grandma. She might have the answers I'm looking for,' I explained.

'I thought your grannie had lost most of her faculties?'

'Yeah. I'm afraid so, but I'm hopeful she could still be there, somewhere.'

'OK, let's go back to Noah.' She hadn't forgotten. 'Why is he coming to see you?'

'I told him we know. Well, I told him I know about him and his past. I also told him about my intention to go to Italy. That's when he asked if we could see each other before I left. I was going to say no, but the truth is that he is somehow connected to me.'

'This is what you think,' she said, bringing back the lost rational part of me. 'But even I have to admit…there are too many signs that this could be true. But my first warning still stands,' she quickly added. 'Be careful. Whatever this is, always think if it's worth sacrificing everything for it.'

We had this conversation before. She was right then and she was right still. I couldn't let my desire to know the truth become something else, another sinful desire that would hunt me forever.

'Where are you meeting this immortal man?' she asked sarcastic.

'Just around the corner. I told him we could meet at Jackie's.'

170

'A bar. A public space. Good! You are almost thinking like me,' she said. 'And I suppose this is why you chose this crappy place to have dinner...'

Anita never liked the Food House. Too much closer to a fast food than a more refined place with nice, fresh food. I tricked her to accept the low-quality alternative only because she was eager to know my news and the place was unusually quiet. Few minutes later we had already left. She got in her car and left, but only after repeating, 'Be careful!'

So I turned around the block and went to meet Noah at the bar. My mind wasn't really tuned to the upcoming event. It was like Anita had taken over and my body was in her full control. I was going to meet him in about few seconds but I was as calm as a puddle.

During the good season, the weather allowed bars and pubs to have tables and chairs outside. Jackie's was just on the main square and the unusually dry furniture were all there, in order, row after row. There wasn't anything out of place about that picture, except for a man I had learned to recognize in a heartbeat. His dark hair, the freckles on his cheeks were something that enchanted me before. But the grey storm in his eyes, that clear water staring into nothing, the thin green line all around: he was irresistible. I was only few steps away, when he turned his head up and saw me. A big smile suddenly stretched his freckles in a warm sign of happiness. That was the moment I regained consciousness of my own mind and my heart went from zero to speed light in few seconds. He stood up to greet me as I was close enough to say 'hi'.

'Hi Daniel, I'm so happy we're meeting again.' His smile filled the space around us.

'I'm happy to see you too.' I was. But I shouldn't have been.

'Thank you for letting me come and see you. How are you? Oh, wait, shall we sit and have something to drink?' he asked, moving the other chair to make space for me.

'Yes, I'd love that.' *Thank God he didn't ask for food. I couldn't possibly get anything else*, I thought. I sat right in front of him, this time in my side of the world, in between things I knew and that felt normal. He looked like the only surreal element left. His beauty was not made for all that.

'Tell me about your plans. You are going to Italy?' he asked.

'I am. It's a long story, but I promise I'll leave out the things that are not necessary. I won't annoy you with silly details.' And I smiled.

'I honestly want to know everything about you, everything you feel comfortable to share' he added, after seeing my face showing a sign of embarrassment. It wasn't because he seemed to be so much into me—and that alone had been confusing me since our last phone call—but because I really didn't want to share my other life, the life I had managed to bury for good.

'I will. But first, tell me'—I had to slow him down—'how was the trip here? Where are you staying?'

'All good. This town wasn't so hard to find. I'm staying just a few blocks away. I booked myself in for two nights. I'll be gone before you leave for Italy.' I don't know why, in my mind, there wasn't going to be an after that night. The sound of 'two nights' got my attention. How many times was I going to just ignore Noah existed and that he wanted to spend time with me?

'Nice!' I replied, hoping he hadn't seen my first reaction. 'That means we could meet again tomorrow,' I added, to sound more convincing. *What is wrong with me?* The more I fought myself the more I fell right into the trap. *'Be careful!'*

'Do you work tomorrow?' he asked.

'Nope. I'm free till the weekend. I planned to get my stuff ready, you know? Do the last few bits before leaving.'

We got our drinks and started to talk about all the things I hoped we would talk of. I told him about Anita's research, and my intent to do the same with my past. I was going to give him the opportunity to answer all the questions I had about his history, his birth, his family, but I felt I owed an explanation right away.

'Everything you found it's true,' he admitted. 'I did some research about my family way before my visions started. It was more about a young man trying to find his roots, answers to a different kind of question. I never got much. This until the day my life changed. That's when I decided to dig deep, really deep.'

'It must have been very difficult.' I let out.

'It still is. I have no answers to so many things, sometimes I would like just to give it all up and, I don't know, start a new life somewhere else.'

'Why didn't you?' I asked, honestly curious. That was a topic I knew even too well.

'Because of you,' he replied. I didn't know what to say to that. 'When you came to me, the first time, you appeared

173

in my dreams, I didn't know what it meant. You know, I told you about it. But day after day it became clearer I had to stick to what I had. Although they had no sense at the beginning, with time things started to become clearer. You came to me as feelings first. Then your voice in my head, your face. And then, after a while, it was like I had switched from outside to inside someone else's mind. I saw places I didn't know of. I saw your home, your bedroom, your dreams. I heard your thoughts in my head as you were looking at the ceiling of your room, after the many nightmares. I could feel you completely. I knew something was coming. Something was meant to happen to me. So I waited, I waited because of you.'

'You said you have no answers to many things.' I wanted to push away that 'because of you'. 'Does this mean you don't know why there is nothing about you, pretty much anywhere?'

'Correct. I have found no reasonable explanations. With time, I started to think I would understand better once I had met you and, don't panic, but I don't believe I'm too far from the truth.'

'So you are looking for answers. This is why you are here.'

'Not just that. I don't think so. I believe you can help me with that, but this is not the reason why I'm here,' he replied. His eyes did not leave mine. His face was locked to mine like a planet to its star and I didn't put up any resistance to that gravitational attraction.

'So why are you here?' I asked, my heart beginning to race faster.

'The same reason you are. I can't stop thinking about you.'

There. He said it. I knew he was going to say that because I would have said it too. The thought was electrifying and petrifying all at once. *Are we experiencing love? Attraction? Or we are both victims of our sick visions? 'Be careful'* popped up in my head again. I had to tell him about John, there and then. He preceded me.

'Your eyes. I kind of noticed the first time, but I never quite realized it.'

'What about them?' I asked. And my thought about John grew small again.

'They looked blue at first. But now they seem more like they are changing colour? More grey than blue. No, actually very silvery.'

'What are you talking about?' I asked. My eyes had always been blue as far as my memory went. I had to go and check, so I pulled my phone out and checked through the camera app.

A shocking truth revealed itself to me as I stared at my twin. He had really grey shiny eyes. I did look again. I closed and opened the app back once more. My clone was still there, the same look, the same crystal colour in his eyes. That was madness. Noah didn't lie. My eyes now looked like his. I put my phone away in the attempt of hiding it. But there, Noah still stared at me. Same look, same colour mirroring mine.

'I'd say you didn't know?' he asked, smiling. He enjoyed my not-so-secret panic.

'This is the first time something like this has happened to me,' I replied.

'Do you think tomorrow we can find some time to talk more about us?' he asked. I was still behind in the conversation, stuck with the camera app preview in my head. 'I mean, us in this situation.'

It felt as if he moved back and forward. One moment he tested the waters, checking if I had the same feelings for him, then withdrew to the more general meaning of us sharing the same difficult experience. *Is it not one of the best ways to get close to somebody?* I thought. *Sharing dramatic events is one of the strongest bonds in life...* He had done that before, the first time we met, and on the phone and now there at Jackie's.

'I think there is a lot we need to say to each other, indeed.'

'How do we want to do this? Shall we meet for a walk? Do you want to come to my room? Or me coming to your place?' he asked. That was exactly what Anita would have considered a red flag. Me and him, alone in a room. I had to find another solution.

'I have the perfect place. We need help, Noah. I don't know how many people know about your situation, but I have somebody I care very much who knows. You met her.'

'Anita?'

'Yes. I'll pick you up tomorrow and we can go to her place. We can talk about anything, don't worry. She might even help us! She has a very...how can I say it? Practical perspective on pretty much anything.' I wanted to avoid any intimacy. That was the only way I could achieve that.

'I trust you. Sounds good to me,' he said, after spending a few moments thinking.

I wasn't sure if he was disappointed by me taking the distance or he was really evaluating the idea of having a third person listening to our conversation. My brilliant plan had a flaw. Anita had no clue about it and I wasn't even sure she was free the day after. I remembered her saying something about work but I couldn't recall if she had said she was going to work from home or she had a lot of work to do at home. Home was the only thing I could think of. It had to work. So I quickly sent her a message.

Daniel

Help. he wants to meet again tomorrow for a talk. Has proposed his place or mine. I told him I'll bring him to yours. Need a safe space and a true friend.

Anita

I'm wfh tomorrow.

Daniel

Is that a yes?

Anita

What else? You dumb. Txt me when you are on your way. Patrick works all day

That went well and fast. I felt relieved by her message but I knew I was asking too much from her. In the other

177

hand, I was sure she was happy to be the watcher over my shoulder, preventing me from doing anything silly. Two drinks each later, Noah and I stood by the front door of his B and B. We delayed the goodbye long enough to make it awkward so I said:

'Are you OK for me to pick you up at eleven? I'll get up early, do everything I have to do and I'll be here.'

'Sounds good to me. Is there any place here you suggest I could go for breakfast?' he asked.

'Sure. Right around the corner.'

'Can you stay a bit longer?' he asked, his face turning sad.

'I really have to get going,' I quickly replied. 'I look forward to seeing you tomorrow.'

With his sad look still focused on me, he moved forward, towards me. I expected a hug but I was afraid more would come my way. For a brief moment I thought I could let the darkness of the night be the secret keeper of my mistakes. The whole place was shut down, ready for the long sleep, and I had no way out but just to move away. So I did. I stepped back just enough to be out of reach, causing Noah to stop immediately.

'A hug?' he whispered with a broken voice. I had hurt him with the power of a simple step. So I moved close and pulled him to my chest, my arms around his shoulders, as strong as it needed to be for my sorrow to reach him.

'Can you feel it?' he asked. His body still bound to mine.

The ground started to quiver below our feet, sending a strange soft vibration right up to our bodies. My ears

178

turned rapidly dull as if we had just fallen under deep waters. All I could feel was our heartbeats and Noah's body in my arms. Then it became nothing. There was no sound, no light. Everything was wrapped in a dark bubble and we were the only thing trapped in it.

'What's happening?' I asked him, looking right at his face. My voice came out and bounced back to me over and over.

'What's happening?' he asked me back, immediately after. It was like an echo, bouncing back and forth between us two.

And then we were alone no more. A dark figure of a man emerged from the black surface right behind Noah. I had seen him before, but where? *Whatever is happening, this is one of our visions,* I thought. *There is no need to be afraid.* The new presence wore a full vest covering his form, but his face and hands were still visible. His eyes reflected the soft green light coming from an artefact, a clepsydra he held in his hands. Before I could free Noah from our hug and tell him to turn around, the man spoke.

'He is close. Whatever you do, you have to move fast. I can feel it in the cracks of my wheel. He has felt your presence. I can't keep you away from time too long.' And his artefact pulsed slowly with an intense bright light.

'Who are you?' I asked. Noah voiced the same exact question as if we were both speaking together.

'I'm the only Time you have left. You need to remember…' And his figure quickly flickered and started to fade.

'We are trying! Help us!' we both begged.

179

'You are the only one who can come and rescue me. Help...*me*.' And he vanished into the dark.

The front door was back and so were the soft streetlights around us. We were back in our reality. Or had we never left? That vision was different. We didn't left our bodies or moved away. We didn't watch that scene from behind. We were in our present and that present talked to us. Whoever that was, it was real and had just come into our lives.

'The old friend has come back,' Noah said, his head still over my shoulder.

'Do you know him?' I asked, releasing my arms.

'He is one of the three I told you about. Did you hear what he said?'

'I did. Whoever he is, he won't help us, looks more like we need to help...him?' I replied, disappointed.

'Only one,' Noah whispered, looking at me. 'Seems like only one of us can help the other.'

'But we don't know how...'

'Please stay with me tonight, I can't let you go after this.' He was begging again. Same sad look on his face.

I knew what he felt, because I felt it too. I didn't want to leave him alone but I knew I would be making a mistake staying.

'I know how you feel, Noah. But I can't stay. I really can't. I want to, but I can't. Please, go inside, put everything that has happened on hold until tomorrow. I know I'm asking you a lot. I'm asking a lot of myself too, but please...wait until tomorrow!' It seemed like all I could ask

180

Noah was to wait. Every time he asked something from me, I told him to wait.

'OK,' he replied. His hands moved to touch my face, holding it like he was searching for something in my eyes. 'You heard what he said. Let's not waste more time. We need to do this.'

And he turned around, opened the front door and gave me a last look as if it were the only one left to give, as if he were going to let go. The door shut closed on our feelings, our worries, our deepest desires. We were parting ways and moving closer to each other at the same time. We were bonding as fast as I was resisting it.

Chapter Twelve
Friends Of Friends

∞

The morning after, I put most of my stuff in the suitcase and left it on the bed, in the spare bedroom. Now that the luggage stood there, visible, I had to tell John what it was for. The best excuse I came up with was that my grandma had a setback and I was rushing back home to see her before it was too late. Little did I know I was being the prophet of her dark future, without me realizing it. John knew a lot about my past. We had the chance to talk about it, here and there, but I had never shared the worst parts of it, as if I were sparing him — or maybe sparing myself — from feeling the pain leeched to my memories.

'When did that happen?' he asked, visibly sad. I regretted saying that lie quickly after seeing how upset he was. But I had to go ahead with it.

'It just happened. I had just the time to think about what to do. You know, I don't like going back there but I have to.'

'Let me see what I can do. I'll go with you!' he said, dropping his morning coffee to run and check his schedule. I stupidly didn't think about that possible reaction. Why was it strange, thinking that John would react that way? John cared about me and he always knew how close I was to my grandma.

'No John,' I said, grabbing his arm before he could leave. 'It's not necessary, really. I'll go, do what I have to and be back right away. Also, what about Daisy?'

'We can ask Harry to mind her. Or Anita?' he replied.

'It's OK, John, I'm honest. I'll feel better knowing you are here taking care of our lives.' I didn't know how to push back. My sense of guilt blocked my deceiving creativity in lying effectively. Thankfully, John made things easier.

'Alright. If you feel this is the best way, I'll stay. But please, keep me up to date while you're there.'

'I will. Of course I will!'

I saved myself another day from explaining to him what was really going on. How far would I go? One hour later, John went to the big city to discuss a piece of modern art the council had requested from him after seeing his paintings at the show. I was still at the house, looking at my suitcase lying on the bed, in an open-heart surgery mode, undecided. My face turned to the wardrobe. The keeper of the strange gift stared at me, silent. I imagined myself taking the cloak and putting it in the luggage, twice. Somehow it felt like the right thing to do. *What if I need it?* I thought. *Why would I need it, though?* I quickly asked myself. *This is stupid… Why am I doing this?* My head was cracking up. My phone rang. A message from Anita quickly brought me to reality.

Anita

When are you coming?

Daniel

**I'm picking him up at 11.
I'll be there at 11.15.**

Anita

**Cool. Patrick is gone to work.
I'll make some coffee'**

Daniel

**Same. John's just gone…
After seeing the suitcase**

Anita

What did you tell him?

Daniel

'That grandma is sick.

Anita

**You chicken shit.
See you in a bit.**

Few minutes later I put some fresh clothes on, pointlessly brushed my hair and, after feeding Daisy, I left the house. I was still early for the appointment with Noah, so I texted him to see if he was up to meet already. He was having breakfast a block away from his B and B so I told him I would join him before going to Anita's. On my way to town I kept repeating to myself that the day would be just fine. Noah and I were going to talk about the situation and Anita was going to be the moderator I so much needed.

I found Noah sitting inside a small coffee shop sipping some cappuccino. His smile was framed by fresh foam when he saw me. As simple as that, I found it funny, lighting the serious mood I had artificially put on. The place was pretty busy but he sat at a two-seater table, so I joined him, and ordered a cappuccino for myself too. Before I could sit, he stood up and hugged me.

'Oh, wow. OK,' I said, smiling. 'How did the night go?'

'Not bad,' he replied. 'I did what you said. I put everything on hold and went to sleep. What about you?'

'Same. I woke up pretty early, prepared my suitcase…oh, and I gave the news of me leaving soon.'

'Gave it to whom?' he asked, taking the hint.

'John,' I replied with a tone that opened up to a bigger revelation. He looked like he wanted to know more, reasonably. 'John…is my boyfriend.' And a long frozen silence joined us for breakfast.

'I see,' he finally said. I felt there was more but he didn't add anything else.

185

'I know this is something I should have told you earlier,' I said. 'It might sound like a stereotype but...it's complicated.'

'Yes it does...sound like a stereotype, I mean,' he added. He was resentful and he was right to be so.

'I'm sorry. I felt like it was never the right time to tell you, and with everything we're going through, I've been struggling with my feelings. Honestly, I don't know what to do or what to say to make it right.'

'You mean between you and him...or you and me?' The greatest question of them all. I didn't have the answer. It was me and John but also me and Noah and everything in between. I didn't answer.

'Look, I know this is greater than just having a boyfriend. It doesn't make me feel good but, to be honest, neither does me being so into another guy.'

'Tell me more about this. You said it before and I've been thinking about it,' I asked, hoping this would also move the topic away from me omitting John from the story.

'There's not much to say. I had feelings for one or two girls growing up. I never thought I was going to be any different from any other guy I knew. For me, the real difference and real issue, was my life in general. I had no space for anything else, or interest if that mattered. Then you came along. The visions of you, of us meeting, with time became a desire, and the desire became then obsession. For a while, at least. I thought about it. I thought if that made me gay. I wasn't attracted by other guys. I wasn't attracted by a *real* guy. Just this man in my dreams.'

'So your feelings for me are not for me as a guy,' I said.

186

'I don't really know,' he replied. His face was desperately looking for answers, comfort and certainties. 'When I met you, up the hill… Oh God you made me the gayest man in the world…' And his smile showed some embarrassment from saying it out loud. 'I felt like all I wanted was you. But it's not physical or at least not only that. It's this wanting more of you. Like an obsession.' And he smiled and looked the other way as if he had just told an uncomfortable secret. 'Regardless. I've been thinking about it, since you left Noah's Bridge. I feel I can rationalize it when you are not close to me.'

'What happens when I am? Close to you, I mean?'

'I think you know. I never managed to hide it, have I?' he replied, turning his face away one more time.

His cappuccino was nearly gone but Noah held on to the last few drops as if he was trying to make it last forever. I was charmed by his face, his gestures, his movements. It wasn't because I felt something for Noah but because I felt his feelings like they were my own. I didn't want him to feel bad, rejected, wrong. I wanted to just say: *'You are entitled to be and feel whatever you want to.'*

'I think I know how you feel, Noah,' I said, trying to catch his attention, moving closer. 'It has happened, it is still happening to me too but in a different way. In my case it's not about liking a man but liking *another* man. It doesn't make sense. I have a boyfriend and I'm happy with him but I can rationalize it only when you're not this close. When you are, everything gets blurry. When you look at me, I can't even recall my own name.'

187

'If we feel the way we feel, shouldn't we let it unfold?' he asked, finally looking back at me.

'What if we feel the way we feel because something else is happening to us? Would you be happy to then find out it was all a mistake?' I replied, showing the greatest of my worries. He got me right away. Noah shared the same fear.

'You're absolutely right. You see, it's easier for me going along with it, 'cause I have very little to lose.'

'A loss is a loss. I don't want you to regret anything,' I quickly replied. I didn't want to cause all that waiting, but it wasn't supposed to be just me being careful. He shared the risks and responsibilities.

To my last sentence, Noah pulled back. I didn't understand if I had disappointed him or he was just having a reality check and accepting the status of things. Few moments later, we left the shop and got in my car on the way to Anita's. The drive went unusually quietly. His mind was probably going back and forth to what I had said a few minutes earlier. I wanted to make it right, so after parking the car at Anita's, I said:

'Noah, before we go in.' And I grabbed his hand to stop him from getting out the car. 'Let me clarify what I meant earlier on, at the shop. I don't want to push back on our attempt to find the truth. I don't know what's going to happen from now till then, but I promise, I'm not holding you back. I'm not holding back anything that has to happen. If that includes us, being more than we are now, I'll let it happen, but only if it's the right thing to do. Do you understand what I mean?'

'I do. I know what you are saying. I'm sorry if I got upset. It's just because I've been waiting for so long that now I'm eager...too eager, I know.' And he smiled. His hand held mine back for few seconds and then we left.

Anita was at the door before I could ring the bell. I think she had secretly looked through the side window even if she pretended she hadn't, greeting us with a clearly fake:

'Oh! Good morning boys!' But she sounded so fake to me that I gave her a quick weird look. And she replied with another one, like saying, '*Don't! You are in trouble already!*' to which I responded with a genuine smile.

'I believe you remember Noah?' I asked, pushing him a little closer to the front door. It felt like he was afraid of her. *Like everyone else*, I thought, laughing in my mind.

'Of course I dooo!' And that *do* lasted long enough for her to look at me like saying she wasn't happy about being part of my betrayal. *Or was that my sense of guilt? That do lasted long enough though...*

Soon after, we all sat in the messy kitchen. The patio doors were wide open even if the weather wasn't the best for a midsummer morning. A light breeze was coming through and some of the papers left abandoned here and there kept spreading their wings ready to fly. Anita made some coffee even though we had said a few times there was no need. She was leading the meeting, in her place, with her rules.

Noah gazed around, trapped by the charm of tons of books piled all over the room, newspaper magazines forming messy bushes, and a strange smell of old dust too precious to settle floated in the air. He must have felt like

189

me the first time I stepped in there. The years had gone by but the place remained the same. Anita had collected more books and notes since the day we had met but, strangely enough, the house seemed able to digest it, showing the same amount of little space through the time.

The first time I walked in Anita's house, was shortly after we started to work together, long before she took the job at the newspaper agency and I got into the corporations world. We were both in our final year of our master's and ended up working together on the same project. Anita was putting together her final essay on social demographics and I was working on my last exams on social media impact on mental well-being. As we were in the same course, we ended up talking to each other more and more often and, eventually, decided to combine our efforts and team up for a better result. She was brilliant with research and data. I was good with humanistic topics.

Shortly after we started spending time together, Anita's heart began beating for more than just history and numbers. I still vividly recall my reaction the first time I stepped into that madhouse. Everywhere appeared clean but old, brimming with books. It felt like I had stepped into a library. I was sure it had to be the work of more people than just Anita's. Her home was her parents' home. They had moved to Australia just a few years prior, to join the rest of the family, but Anita had stayed behind to finish college so I assumed they had turned that place into a history museum. I was only partially correct. I soon found out Anita's parents were academics. Her mother was an English teacher in high school and her father was a history researcher, book critic and book writer. They might have started that chaotic collection, but it was Anita who had mastered it. It was then, in between history and dust, that our friendship emerged from the messy lives we were living. It was the two of us initially, then Harry came along. There was no John, but soon there was going to be a Patrick.

The first time Patrick walked into the house he wasn't impressed. He wasn't much bothered by it either. For some reason, Patrick wasn't able to perceive anything that was secretly special, hidden. A treasure could have been easily waving at him but he wouldn't have seen it. In some ways he was Anita's opposite. If she loved digging, uncovering, he was happy with status quo, being carried over into things. There was a fire burning in Anita's heart. A desire of movement towards discovering. Patrick was immutable, uninterested in most of the things, most of the times. They met at her place, a night we were celebrating the end of our academic journey. We had decided to invite only a few friends over for dinner and drinks but allowed them to bring whoever they wanted. It was a friends of friends kind of party, with only one limit: space.

'I know we said to bring over whoever they wanted, but this is madness!' Anita had said to me and Shannon.

'I didn't bring anyone. I know there's not much space here,' Shannon had replied, looking around. Back then we weren't experts on Shannon's snobby sarcasm. 'But Mark insisted to bring over his friend Patrick.'

'There are not too many people yet. We can manage, can't we?' I had said.

'Harry's not here yet. Do you want to bet he's bringing the whole town with him?' Anita had replied, knowing how little concern Harry would have had.

Eventually Harry had not brought anyone, 'or anything', like Anita had kept repeating for a week, and the number of people wasn't bad once some of us had spilled outside in the backyard. That night Anita and Patrick had met and talked. Somehow the spark had made it through and turned their hearts on fire, maybe helped by those old books we were surrounded by. The weeks had become months, and months turned to years. Anita and Patrick continued their lives together with very little adjustment. They were exactly the same together as they were as single individuals. He kept his space, she kept her many interests. Eventually Patrick moved in, finding home in between tons of books, but they never really fully merged into becoming a real couple. Instead, they started writing their own version of love.

I wasn't sure if that was the best way to be in a true relationship or not. I was completely taken by John, my air was his to breathe, his shadow was mine to be with. But in all those years, Anita was quite the opposite. She was strongly independent, almost detached from her own feelings from Patrick. In the many conversations we had, I knew Anita loved him dearly. *Somehow, many forms of love must exist*, I kept thinking. Absorbed in the memory of that long-gone past, I could still hear their voices, one on top of all the others.

Returned from my unexpected flashback, I was brought back to reality by Anita mentioning my name while 'interrogating' Noah with multiple questions. She could have easily been a cop and he an already condemned criminal. I waited a few seconds to understand where we were at with the incrimination. She asked about Noah's past, his place, his date of birth, everything that had been previously discussed between me and her and me and him. Nothing new was there. He said again the same things with no resistance or hesitation. For every answer, Anita looked at me as she was linking whatever had happened to Noah to whatever had happened to me. There was a *'See? Same thing,'* unspoken sentence showing on her face every couple of minutes.

'You see,' she continued after joining us at the kitchen table, bringing our coffees, 'in one hand we have all these tiny, tiny details, things that as they are, don't make any sense. Events, dates, things that happened to both of you…and me,' she added, turning her eyes up to the ceiling, 'and in the other hand, we have…nothing! Not a hint, a trail to follow. Every time we look for an answer, we get a new question instead,' she concluded, clearly puzzled and a bit annoyed. I wasn't sure if she was mostly upset by the impact that craziness was having on me, or by the fact she could not solve the mystery related to it.

Some magazines around the sunroom had picked up on her restlessness, flapping their pages with an added sense of warning. The sky had turned grey, getting dark rapidly.

'There is also the timing issue,' Noah added right after.

'What do you mean?' I asked.

'It started with me, right? Then faded away and started with you, like it moved from me to you. Now it's

193

happening to the both of us and it's getting faster. It's happening more and more often. Like...'

'...like something is reaching us quickly.' I finished his sentence.

'Is it about one of you, the first gets served kind of thing? Or is about *both of you* and the first that solves it?' Anita asked, triggering a sudden silence.

Rain started to come down and the temperature around the house dropped suddenly. We all could feel the quick change but the conversation led our minds, oblivious to anything else.

'I think is about me and Noah, together,' I replied. Somehow, that *together* meant a lot to him. His smile to my words showed just more than agreement. 'These events brought us together and something has definitely happened, almost every time we touched, more than once.'

'Maybe this could work...on demand, I mean?' she asked quickly.

'Like we try to make it happen?' Noah added.

'Sure. It did work before, right?' Anita was already tasting the joy of the sudden solution.

'It doesn't work like that.' I stepped in, breaking the growing excitement. 'I mean, it didn't happen *every time.*' And I could hear already Anita asking: *'How many times did you touch?'*

'It's true. We hugged last night, before going to bed, and something happened, but then just earlier we held hands and nothing happened,' Noah said, trying to support my

194

statement. I could hear Anita asking, '*What does that mean? Hugging before going to bed, holding hands?*'

'Something did happen last night,' I immediately replied, before Anita could say anything. 'Before leaving Noah at his B and B, we hugged and someone appeared to us. It's true, nothing happened *to us*. We were there, by the front door, and never moved, but someone did show up."

'Hugging?' she asked. It was like she hadn't heard anything else but that. I knew where she was going.

'It is the only thing you heard?' I asked.

'I mean, you were hugging when that happened. There was a physical connection, like before.'

'There was a connection when we held hands in the car, here, just outside...and nothing happened,' Noah added, sceptical.

'Maybe it needs more!' Anita replied as she stood. Quickly leaving the table, she went searching for a book in the sitting room. 'It's not only physical, but it also has to have an emotional...' And we couldn't hear any more as she moved to the far side of the house.

Some of the open windows started to move back and forth. The weather was rapidly changing for the worse. There was a storm coming. The room had lost most of its brightness like the angry clouds had found their way through the walls. On her way back, Anita switched on the lights with none of us noticing we had gotten swallowed by the dark.

'Remember *Psychology & Memory: A Biologic Approach?*' and she showed us a massive book we both had to study in

195

college. A painful memory popped up from the front cover. 'Remember that part about the nature of memories? I did my exam on memory recall vs collective memory.'

'And I did mine on emotional memory...are you saying...?'

'Yes. What if these are *memories*? What if they need an emotional trigger to come up? After all, haven't you both had them during some sort of emotional distress?' *'Emotional distress...'* Why did it sound so bad?

'Hello?' Noah waved at us.

'Sorry Noah,' I said. 'You see, memories are not all the same. The way we recall them, the way we create them. It's believed that memories can be generated by different parts of our brain. These parts generate them in different ways and with different intensity. Emotional memories, like the one you remember by *feeling something*, are different from memories of a sentence, a number, etc.'

'Normal memories can be forgotten. Emotional memories can come back triggered by a repeating event. This is why some historic events seem to be in everybody's memory more than other stuff. Myths, legends, they all are connected to extremely emotional events. The truth around them is long gone, but our beliefs still remain,' Anita added right after.

'But if emotional memories can come back, why don't we remember?' Noah asked after a bit of silent thinking.

'Because the emotion comes back, not the memory of the event itself. You can feel sad, happy, mad, like you felt back then, without remembering why. Sometime, if the feeling

196

is strong enough, you can also remember what caused it,' I replied.

'If this is true it would explain the blind spots in our visions…but how can we explain the way they manifest? It seems they can spill out in the real world, involving the people we're with,' Noah asked.

'True!' Anita replied after taking a small break. 'But we know that. We know there is an element of craziness we need to accept.'

'Craziness?' I asked, pulling the book from her hands.

'Call it mystery, magic… I'm just saying we can't rationalize that part just yet. We better take it as it is, for the time being,' she replied, closing the book before I could do anything with it. 'Shall we?' And she moved her hands across the table like she wanted us to start an exorcism of some sort.

'What are you doing?' Noah asked, visibly puzzled.

'Don't mind her. She wants us to conjure some old people that can tell us the truth,' I replied, laughing at Anita. Her hands hung there, looking for ours. Her fingers were moving rapidly as if she said, *'Stop the crap. Give me your hands and be done with it.'*

After quickly looking at each other, Noah and I eventually gave up and took Anita's hands. As we expected, and to Anita's disappointment, nothing happened. If what we discussed was true, there wasn't any emotional element in that gesture. Or there was, but of a different kind. Noah burst out laughing a few moments later, followed by me and eventually Anita too.

'OK, OK…no panic. Mistakes are normal…after all we are exploring a very unknown territory here,' she said, trying to contain the laugh and sound professional.

We stood up in silence for a few more seconds, holding hands. The effort to contain our laughter diminished as our attention shifted to the sound of the heavy rain pouring through the open windows. We knew then that the weather had changed.

'This is not working,' Anita said, releasing us from her ritual. 'I better go and close the windows before we get flooded.' And Noah and I gave each other a quick smile.

'Let's try again,' he said. 'The two of us.' And he moved to Anita's place to come closer and took my hand.

'This is not working,' Anita repeated, quickly coming back to the table. I wasn't sure if she wanted something to happen or she was making sure nothing would happen between just the two of us.

'Let's try one more time, this time think something about me and you,' Noah said, our hands still together.

What could I focus my mind on? The first time we met? The kiss? Everything was a loud judgement against my sins. My emotions were ones of guilt, sadness, confusion, at first. Then the memory of the laughs we just had took over. It was nice to be with him. He was a good man. I was happy I had met him. A sudden crack brought me to reality. Heavy thunders started to strike on top of our heads. We were still there, by the table, and Anita stood still at Noah's back.

'This is not working,' she said again.

Anita's tolerance for Noah must have grown since the day we met him, I thought, after seeing her putting a hand on his shoulder.

'This is not working. I'm not ready,' she added. It was like she was on repeat. She didn't move. She stood there still, in the dark of the room, her body lit only by the flash of thunders. *When did the lights go off?* I thought. Her hand was on Noah's shoulder but I could feel it like it was on mine.

'Come home. You need to know. Time has come. Come home,' she said with a voice that I knew but didn't belong to Anita.

'Grandma?' I asked, with a broken voice, nearly a whisper.

And there she was, in a small corner in between too much history and paper, this old lady I knew, sitting in a deformed armchair, looking at her own grey, wrinkly hands. She stared at them like she was taken by surprise, brought back to a younger life without warning. I knew her. I loved her, very much.

'Grandma?' I asked, trying to stand up and get closer. Anita's hand held me still, preventing me from moving.

She turned her face up to me. Her eyes sparkled in disbelief as if she had come back from a long journey and she was now home. A tiny smile had appeared on her face.

'Daniel…is that you?' And tears went flowing onto her tired cheeks. 'I need to talk to you. What time is it? Can you tell her I need more time?' And she stared back at her hands, her body. 'This is not right. I don't understand...I'm afraid I lost it...'

'Grandma, it's OK. What did you lose?' I didn't know what to say. I was in shock. Had I left and gone back to Italy without realizing it? *Am I seeing the future? What am I seeing?*

'Come home, this is not going to work without it,' she said, and her voice mixed with Anita's in a wobbling sound. Then a sudden bang! The wind had smashed the patio doors open, breaking the vision in thousands of pieces, too many to be saved, too many like the books we were surrounded by.

With her hand still on Noah's shoulder, Anita said, 'This is not working, we better find another way!'

And I was there, staring at the nothing where my grandma was, just a few moments earlier. *Did they see her? Were they with me or was she just in my head?* It had worked. It had worked, indeed.

Chapter Thirteen
My Name Is Rita-Louise

∞

For a few moments none of us said a word. Noah and I were still sitting by the kitchen table and Anita had just gone to close the patio doors. A strong wind started to whistle all around the house; alone, the only one who had something to say was whistling loud while we stood there, listening carefully. At first, I had the impulse of keeping that vision for myself. For some strange reason that was something I didn't want to share, something that belonged to me. She was family. *My family.* There was no magic, it wasn't supernatural. It was just me, thinking about going back home, missing my grandma and maybe pitying her condition. But at Noah's question, I spilled it out.

'Are you OK?'

'It was only me, then?' I said, my face holding to that very same spot where she stood. I could still feel her.

'I'm not sure. What happened?' Noah asked. Anita was quickly catching up with the events as she moved closer to the table.

'I saw my grandma…just a few moments ago…she was sitting there.' And both of them turned their faces to a pile of books abandoned in a lonely corner. A tired, fading plant stood just beside an old cabinet, stuck in a never-ending attempt to reach the sunlight.

'You saw her…you mean like…' Anita attempted to ask if I just had one of my daydreams. Somehow, she sounded afraid to say it.

'Yes. No! I don't know…I think she was.' I had no time to think.

'Daniel?' Noah moved closer, his eyes searching for mine. 'Are you OK? I didn't see anything. Whatever you saw, it wasn't here. You must have seen her in your own mind.'

'What are you saying?' I knew that vision was different. Was that enough for him to say I had just imagined it? *Is he annoyed because I went to dreamland alone this time?* I thought. *Was that me misunderstanding?*

'We were holding hands, trying to make it happen, and it did happen, for you…but not for me. I think you went solo, this time,' he explained. Why was I so ready to jump on defence? I was somehow angry, worried.

'Tell us more,' Anita added, and she pulled a chair and sat close to me, waiting.

From that moment, the day went on without any other stranger events. We spent hours talking about my grandmother, my upcoming trip to Italy, Noah's attempts to find the truth, all things we hoped could give us a full picture, but it felt just like minutes.

The storm had passed and the afternoon sun had started to dry up the surroundings. When the place was dry enough for us to go outside, we decided to take some fresh air and walk towards the beach nearby. Planted at the edge of the northern coastline, Anita's home was one of the closest to the sea. On most days we could feel the breeze coming from the ocean and smell the salt in the air. The grey Irish sand was unlimited, scattered across the full horizon, we had the world at our feet. The low tide had expanded the land we could navigate with our eyes, small rocks were left exposed, glittering; we were just few tiny dots in a shiny desert. The entire place was quiet. Someone had brought their dog for a short walk and then had disappeared from sight in a blink, like a mirage. The usual crowds had stayed home, probably pushed back by the recent storm. Seagulls celebrated the freedom in random circles through the sky; now and then, we could hear them calling from afar.

Without noticing it, I started walking faster and left Noah and Anita behind. My feet dreamt of a new magic, as if they could help me in rising above the ground, a quick fly to snatch the unattainable truth. I was in a hurry. The newly discovered friends were enjoying a busy conversation and I heard them laughing every so often. Their voices reassured me of something else I didn't quite understand. Back then I had no idea how much these two people would eventually mean the world to me.

That beautiful place wasn't going to be the only one we would discover together, it wasn't going to be the only one we would impress in our memory. Our journey towards the truth would soon open up to things beyond our imagination. And yet, we had no idea of the magic we would soon yield.

I was trapped by the vastity of that empty space. There was us and then nothing for miles. Perhaps, someone else in the far end would think the same. *There must be someone else. If I only were a bird... I could fly and see. See things in a different way. I could see it all,* I thought. A few minutes later I walked back to Noah and Anita.

'I think I know what I need to do next,' I started. 'It is true that all these events make no sense as we have experienced it. And I think it's because we are seeing it from the wrong angle. We have experienced pieces of something we can't see entirely because we are in it, in the moment.'

'I'm not entirely in it...but I can't see it either. What do you mean?' Anita asked. We stopped walking. Our hands went hidden in our pockets, safe from the rising cold.

'I don't mean seeing it as an outsider, but more like seeing it from the beginning till the end. Like it was one thing entirely.'

'That's more or less what we have been trying to do, right? Put all the pieces together?' Noah added.

'True. But not completely. There's a massive piece of knowledge missing. We know what we don't know about

204

you, right? It doesn't help the fact that we don't know it, true, but bear with me. I think I need to get to the beginning of *my* story. We need to know what is missing there,' I replied.

'Sure. This is why you are going back to Italy in few days. What are you exactly thinking about?' Anita asked. We had spoken about it few times already. *'The secret is in the past,'* was her motto. What was new in me going now? she meant.

'Now I know what to look for. I know what questions I need to ask and to whom,' I said, turning my back and taking the way back home as if I could actually start the inquisition immediately.

The sun had moved across the sky and had started to die behind the hungry hills. I had to head home. I had been out all day and I wanted to go back home and hug Daisy for a little bit. My eyes quickly moved to Noah. I knew our time together was about to end and I didn't know if I wanted to drag it longer or get it over with. He was at the centre of the greatest challenge of my life, up till then. In a few weeks I had gone from feeling something for him to feeling guilty because of it. From thinking he was someone I wanted, to thinking he just held answers I needed.

And now my mind was turning again. Noah wasn't the thing I wanted. Noah was someone who shared a journey with me...for a little bit. Now this was my journey only. The answers were in my past, not in his. *Am I selfishly leaving him behind?* After walking back to Anita's place and saying goodbye, Noah and I got in the car and drove to his B and B. Anita had promised Noah she would continue some digging and decided they would be in contact from that moment on. If I was determined to stop a love story at its very beginning, a friendship was getting started instead.

Noah and I stayed in the car for a little while. Our minds busy thinking, creating, doubting. He had come to Castlecross to be with me, looking for answers that didn't obviously come. I had let it happen with no resistance, hoping for answers that didn't obviously come. And once again Anita had gotten caught up with all that confusion. Were we mistakenly rushing into long-term solutions or was this never meant to work?

'Was it worth it?' he asked, breaking up the silence.

'What?' The hint was clear but I didn't want to get it.

'Me coming here. We didn't move that much ahead.'

'True,' I admitted.

'But I loved every second we spent together.'

'Really?' Again, the hint was clear but I didn't want to pick it up.

'Yes. I mean you, me, Anita…I had a great day!' He was still playing the game of coming close, withdrawing and moving closer again. I had moved forward. I was on a mission. *No feelings allowed!* So I thought.

'I'll leave shortly. I hope I can get some answers. You know? Move forward a little bit?' I said, changing the topic.

'Will it be difficult? Are you worried?'

'No.' I wasn't really. 'I'm more…troubled. Going back to a place I don't like, surrounded by people who were not good to me, it's not pleasant. I'm doing it because I honestly

206

think there is no other way, but believe me, I've been fighting against it.' And I had indeed.

My head had put up all the resistance strategies it knew. Up till the very moment I said goodbye to John, at the security check at the airport, I was about to change my mind and be done with it. The night I had left Noah to get back to John I felt as bad as if I had cheated on him. I had done nothing, Noah and I had not closed our last night with a kiss, a hug. No sweet promises were exchanged. I think Noah knew how serious and difficult my near future was going to be and he had said goodbye with a pure and simple: 'Please, be strong. I'm with you.' But I felt bad. I felt bad because I was leaving someone I loved, a life I had built with sacrifice, to run away with my fantasies, my daydreams. *Was it worth it?'* Noah's question was resounding in my head like a bad joke. Anita had said something similar not long before. *Am I stupid enough to ignore not one, but two different warnings?*

Although I had said nothing about the real reasons I was going back to Italy, John had picked up some strange vibes. He repeatedly said he was going to come with me, if I let him. I could have told him to come. I could have told him the truth; on the plane, perhaps, where he couldn't run away. I had the chance to tell him what I was going through up until the night before I left, the night Noah had asked: 'Was it worth it?'

John prepared a nice dinner for the two of us. On my way in, I found my luggage on the floor, packed and ready. A light blue enveloped letter just on top tried to catch my attention. I knew John was going to write something sweet. He was always up for meaningful gestures; in between my

207

runs trying to go after him, John had taken the lead. Like in a game, every time I slowed down, every time I stopped making him the only thing that mattered in my life, he had run back to save the flame from burning out. Now he had done it again. I was going to go on my own for a little while and John had to make sure it didn't mean anything bad for the two of us.

'I thought we could go all crazy, romantic...before you go?' he said, introducing the dressed kitchen table with shaking hands. He was a magician, and I had enough magic for a day.

'Oh my God. What did you do?' I asked, exaggerating my reaction.

'Well, considering you are leaving tomorrow, I got your luggage ready over there, a nice dinner to be served and...I'll give you the chance once again to ask me to go with you!' And a smile came along.

'Thank you, babe.' Beyond the reasons, over the madness, John was still my safe place.

Yes, I wanted more attention and less gravitational pull. He was taking the space, the air, and I had been happy with it, but not any more. Not when I needed to breathe. But John was still John. His eyes carried the weight of the years together or, maybe, I looked at him with that weight, but it was love. Imperfect, difficult, but it was love. That night ended on the same note it started. John made sure I knew he loved me, like there was a chance I wasn't coming back home. Once again, we fell asleep on the couch, holding hands. Those same hands were in someone else's just few hours prior and now they were in his. Two different men, two different reasons.

Hundreds of miles later, I landed in what, a lifetime before, used to be my home. Someone I knew very well and I loved very much waited for me at the airport. Eléna didn't look like me at all. She was my sister and I was her brother but we didn't share a drop of blood. We shared life, pain, happiness and most of all, a terrible family. Every chance to get back together was the right one. The moment I planned my trip back to Italy, Eléna was on top of the list — if not the only one — of the people to inform. And she never disappointed me. There she was, with a smile so big it could embrace the entire terminal. She was ready to jump on a long-awaited hug.

'How long has it been? Two thousand years?' she said, holding back tears from flowing, hugging me as strong as she could.

'Oh don't get all soft on me now,' I replied, smiling.

It was extremely hot. Midsummer extreme heat was something I had forgotten. The air boiled, I could feel my skin getting burnt by the minute. After what it felt like days of walking, we got into the car, the air conditioning waiting to greet us.

'Do we go right away or you want to stop by my house and leave your stuff there?' Eléna asked.

'I'd say we go now for a quick check and then we go to yours? In this way I can check with Mrs Sara what's the situation. Have you been there lately?'

'Oh God, last time I was up there...must have been Christmas.. You know that even if she and I are not related

I always liked her very much. But I guess I didn't want to get the chance to meet *you know who*...' And she added an annoyed face along with it.

'Yeah. Speaking of *you know who*...' I started.

'Don't worry. I'll go and check first,' she interrupted me.

'No, I didn't mean that.' But that was actually good thinking. 'She hasn't been around, has she?'

'Look, I have no idea nor interest in finding it out.' And that was pretty much confirming the status quo. We both hated Victoria and we both didn't want to talk about it.

In between speedy cars, scooters, tons of beeps and mad drivers, we left the hot city, up to the very edge of a hill at the volcano's feet. From the far distance, in between the dark green of the immense landscape, the solitary mountain sat on its throne, conquering the world around. A white hat on its peak, a flat cloud floated left and right, putting the crown on the unchallenged queen. My grandma had always lived there. Although I knew she had been there for the last three decades, I didn't recall her talking about any other place she had been before. It was like she was born there only then, like she had just appeared from nowhere. We left the strong heat behind. The mountain had always stolen a few grades from the hottest summers and for me it was exactly what I begged for. After so many years in Ireland, I had lost the gecko skin and its DNA, while my sister didn't even notice the difference.

'Oh nice. A fresh breeze, finally!'

'You call that fresh? Close the window, the air con is on!' she replied, like the outside air was poisoned and I was compromising the safety of that bunker on wheels.

The car was pretty old, squeaking at every turn. There were no tech features of any kind but the air con was spot on. If we had died by losing a wheel or we had suddenly exploded, we would have done it with our fresh faces on.

'Are you ever going to change your car?' I asked, laughing.

'What's wrong with it? She is beautiful. Loyal like no others.' she replied without taking offence. For Eléna her car was just like life. It was what it was and she would make the best of it.

'Don't get me wrong, it's a strong car' —and I suddenly stopped breathing when she overtook an old lady's car, increasing the speed and making the car produce a very suspicious sound—'but cars are so cheap now, you can get one with all the comforts.'

'Comforts make people weak,' she said, sounding like she was born a century earlier. 'Also, imagine buying a new car and getting it destroyed shortly after?'

'Is there a risk?' I asked, worried. I had forgotten the crazy Italian way of driving. There was no rule or maybe there was one: first gets served first.

A half hour later we had already pulled over. Our destination was on the left. That place hadn't changed a bit. Everything looked frozen in time, not a single detail had changed since last time I was there, actually…since my memory goes. The heavy cement monsters were fewer compared to the city, everywhere trees popped up, on both

211

side of the streets, creating lines of pure nature. Grandma's house was an old two-storey square building with iron balconies all around and a flat head. Some of its skin had fallen off from the sharp corners, revealing the age and the true nature of history. Some of the inhabitants sat in a park just a few metres away, enjoying the only air con they knew: the relief of big pines shadowed down, mercifully.

A sweet old lady next door carefully looked at us getting out the car. Her senses had picked up the great surprise. Instantly recognizing me, she hurried herself up to the front gate to meet us. I had the feeling age ceases to show at a certain point. Must have been at least ten years since Mrs Sara had shown any change. She looked the same three years earlier. For a moment, I had the impression they were all frozen in time, like that place, the big mountain, everything.

'Oh my bimbo... Sweet child, what a surprise!' she exclaimed, moving her arms forward. *She must have been cleaning or in the middle of doing something in the house before coming out*, I thought. She carried the smell of soap mixed with some sort of salsa and it moved softly around us, like a second, bigger hug.

'Sara, it's so nice to see you... You look incredible, still young and fresh!' I said with a big smile on my face.

'Eléna, why didn't you tell me he was coming? Oh, never mind. I'm happy to see you too! Come here!' and the hug embraced us both.

'How is she?' I asked immediately after. I wanted to get down to business immediately, good manners had gone forgotten.

212

'Oh my child,' she replied, pulling my chin with her soft, skinny fingers and a look full of compassion and loss. 'She is, you know…but she is OK today. She is good!'

'Is she by herself right now?' I asked. I had to be sure we weren't going to have any unpleasant encounter.

'Your mother is not here.' She knew exactly what I meant. Although she wasn't family, she was the closest thing to a sister to my grandma, so she had been part of our lives since the beginning of time. 'Carla, the girl that minds her, is here, of course.'

Carla was Sara's friend's daughter who lived a few houses away and had started minding Grandma a few years prior. That girl wasn't the most outspoken human being I had ever met, actually was quite the opposite. Pretty skinny, she had the strength of a full-grown man and a sharp face that reminded me of a mouse, including big brown eyes and prominent teeth.

When she opened the front door I gulped a bit, like every time. If everything else was stuck in time, unchanged, the inside of the house had deteriorated fast. Even with Carla's efforts to keep it clean, walls had lost shape, the big floor tiles were cracked in several parts and the entry corridor felt more like a time tunnel than just a simple room. From the far entrance, we spotted the massive doors leading to the huge back field, wide open, like Grandma loved it. I could already see the many orange trees with the eyes of my imagination, even before they appeared in front of us. With just the power of my memory, I could anticipate their colours, their scent. There, between us and them, someone sat quietly. We moved closer, following Carla to the far end of the house.

213

'Signora, you have guests,' Carla said, in a very strong accent. Somehow, she looked even more shabby that I remembered.

La *Signora* sat on a large chair. Her legs rested on a high level with the help of a wooden box, an improvised step, probably stolen from a fruit stand at the near market. She had changed. She had lost a lot of weight in the last few months and the skin had given up to the time passing. Her silver hair, long as always, was pulled up in a rushed way and a few strands flowed down carelessly, holding still to a pretty but tired look. She stared at the field in front of her without a real meaning, like she was just waiting for something to happen and, in the meantime, letting the time and life pass by. Carla brought her back to reality after saying again she had guests.

'Signora, Daniel is here. With la Signorina Eléna.' And that remark was her way to remind us that I was family. Eléna not really. None of the others picked that up.

After a moment of embarrassment quickly replaced by a smile, my grandma finally turned around, looking at us, acknowledging our presence. With the remains of an old, but yet solid lady manner, she welcomed us.

'Hi, I'm Rita-Louise. What can I do for you?'

Chapter Fourteen

Son Of No One

∞

The shock of seeing *Nonna* unable to recognize me was something I had learned to silence. Yet it still hurt. My sister's hand was already over my shoulder, a gesture of comfort, in case I needed. But I was ready to take it. I knew this would happen. It had happened so many times that it had become a sort of routine. The first signs of dementia were subtle, small. I don't think anybody noticed anything in particular.

In time, I would learn that the first stage of that horrible disease had started even before I had left the country. What the doctors said a few years earlier, if I remember correctly, was that it had started when Grandma was close to her seventies. Back then I used to think her forgetfulness was mainly a consequence of the life she had lived. Single mother—and single grandma—she had worked all her life as a nurse, with no signs of fatigue, she had been on the front line for too many years. Eventually, when she retired at sixty-seven, her body and her mind began to pay the price. This is what I thought. It was a payback, pure and simple.

Things got worse rapidly while I was away and, eventually, it led to me coming back home, helping her to navigate in a world of everlasting fog, experiencing the pain of seeing her memories going for good. Somewhere in my head I kept thinking someone in the universe held every living being's fate, measuring its length, plotting its end down to every tiny detail. If that was Grandma's price to pay, that master of punishment must be evil.

'She looks good, isn't she?' Sara said with a smile that felt a bit out of place. All considering, she looked in great form.

'Thank you. I feel my hair isn't looking great, though,' she replied, trying to fix it as well as she could.

'Why? Signora Rita, are you invited to a ball and you didn't tell me?' Carla said laughing, going back inside to attend her many duties. Even with her strong accent, she still lifted up the spirit.

'Please sit down,' Rita-Louise said to me and Eléna. She pointed to two chairs left to the corner, by the rear wall of the house. It was like she wasn't acknowledging Sara's presence because she knew her. '*She's Sara. If she wants a chair she will get one.*' That gave me some sort of relief. Although I was a complete stranger to her, she could still hold to some of her memories.

Eléna and I pulled the chairs from the sunny spot and moved them closer to Grandma, who was enjoying the fresh shade the balcony above was projecting down. The sun had heated the plastic of the chairs and had made them soft. I had the feeling we were going to break them just by putting them down, never mind sitting on them. Midday heat was beyond us and sitting outside, in the shade, felt like a smooth way to get back to the roasting weather I was so familiar with.

With the years, Grandma had started to confine herself to more cooler places, away from too much heat, but her dark skin was unquestionably marked for life by the sun she used to be so in love with. *'The sun burns away any problem,'* she used to say. Why was I so different now? My eyes stared at her, looking for the things I knew we shared but there I was, suffering the hot world I was born into, my skin pale, my eyes not dark like hers. *Have we always been so different?* The thought came up fast. *Or am I putting some distance from her and from the pain I feel?*

'See those trees? You can't really see it now but those are orange trees,' Grandma started. 'Further down there are a few lemon trees as well. My father planted them when he moved here, after the big war, after he retired from the navy. I'm not sure why, but I think he needed to hold himself to the ground, you know, after being for so many years out in the sea.' And her hands mimicked the emotions attached to her words.

'How long was Great-Grandpa in the navy for?' I asked, without even thinking.

'Twenty years and more. Great-Grandpa!' And she laughed at that word. 'He would have hated that word. Thank God none of us ever gave him that chance.'

'Grandma, he was alive up until I was four. I remember him.'

'Oh, were your parents from Valverde?' she quickly asked. I was sure she was trying to remember if she had ever met my parents. In a way, that was funny.

'No, Grandma. We moved here when he got really sick, remember? You, Mum, me.'

'Don't be silly! I never met you in my life!' And that wasn't funny any more.

How could she remember the most random details, things that happened when she was young, people she had just met two days before, but had forgotten big chunks of life, including me with it? It was disturbing.

'Signora Rita, how long have you and Sara known each other?' Eléna jumped right in the conversation.

'Oh, years and years. Isn't true, Sara?' she said, looking at her lifetime friend taking a chair and sitting beside us.

'Years!' she repeated, but with more emphasis. 'Oh, the things we have seen... You can't even imagine! Do you know this shit hole of a place—oops! Excuse my language,' she quickly said, '—thought at some stage that we *were special friends?*' And she whispered that last word and laughed hard right after. Eléna and I were puzzled.

'You were what?' Eléna asked.

'You know...*lovers!* I wasn't married, she wasn't married. People started to talk. Your mum was already a teenager, they must have thought she was adopted.' And she kept laughing. After realizing what she really meant, Eléna and I burst into a big loud laugh.

'Yeah, he was adopted. But we never told a soul,' my grandma started, suddenly breaking up the fun. It was like she had picked up on a pitch and she was now singing solo, an entire new song nobody knew. 'I had a very big responsibility, you have no idea. But it had to be done. The most beautiful little boy anyone had ever seen! The brightest blue eyes he had...' And she moved her arms as if she was still holding a baby in her arms.

I tried to understand what part of her long life she was describing to us when Sara gently moved her hand to my leg. It was like she was telling me to not get upset with what I had just heard.

'I made some iced tea. Anyone? Drink it. It's very hot today!' Carla just showed up out of nowhere, shutting off everybody's thoughts.

'Thank you, Carla. Are you staying for the night?' Sara asked me.

'Oh no. I just wanted to check what the situation looked like and see if I could come back tomorrow and stay longer,' I replied.

'You're visiting your parents tomorrow?' Grandma said. 'Good. I knew since the moment I saw you, you were a good young boy.'

We spent the next hour jumping randomly from a topic to another based on where Grandma's mind decided to lead us to. It was a nice time to be together despite the circumstances and I did truly believe she was happy to have us there, whoever we were. After making some arrangements with Sara and Carla on my next-day visit, Eléna and I eventually left and headed back to the noisy city. The evening was upon us; the sun had moved behind the volcano painting a red, violent mesh of colours while clouds popped up, small and bright, from the hot mountain. Like a fast train we sped down the hill, air con off and all four windows wide open. The air was still warm, like a distant fire still burning underneath the ashes. Happy we went, hungry and looking forward to something to bite.

After arriving at the house and changing our outfits, the two of us started some funny, spirited conversations about where to go for dinner. As always, it wasn't a clash of preferences but a desperate attempt to have everything we could think of without being able to give up on a specific food. Eléna and I were like that. A conversation never started and never ended. We were on a continuous talk, about everything—food was a recurring node to any topic, all the time. It was natural then, that we had already left the house, started to walk down the city centre, and we had still not decided where to go. We went back to her main issue in between our random talks. Eventually—and predictably—we let our noses and our eyes decide on the spot.

'What's the situation with your man?' I asked while sat down in a funky restaurant specialized in all kind of burgers.

'There isn't a situation,' she replied. 'There is just, I don't know...disappointment, at this stage...'

'Why is that?'

220

'Because it's what now? Six years? Six years that we have been working together, being inseparable, he needs me for *everything* and still...he doesn't know what he wants,' she replied, picking up the menu with the same frustration she had in her voice.

'Have you told him you have enough?'

'Of course. I left him a few times. You know that. Every time, I get him closer to me, for a little while, but then we go back where we started.'

'Maybe even in a worse position than you were when you started...'cause you are getting more tired and disappointed, every time?' I asked.

'Pretty much. Maybe I should just do what you did. Be brave, leave everything and start over,' she said, tasting the fresh beer the waiter had just brought us.

'Oh no, thank you.' I said to the waiter. 'I'm not into beer at all. Can I have some white wine?'

'White wine, with a burger?' Eléna asked and her hand intercepted the glass of beer standing in front of me before it was taken back. 'I'll drink his, don't worry,' she said to the waiter.

'So, tell me...why are you here? And don't tell me you missed me. I know you hate this place too much for that to be enough...what's happening? Did you and John break up?'

'Oh God no,' I started.

'The two of you are getting married and you are having second thoughts so you run away!' she interrupted me.

'Noo. Stop talking madness!' I said, laughing. 'Nobody is leaving anybody and no one is marrying anyone.'

We sat by a small table outside, right on the street. There were tons and tons of tables scattered everywhere, belonging to different restaurants, but together they seemed to be a floating sea of tea lamps and boats wreckage. There were not too many people around yet. That spot was the centre of the city night life, but we were too hungry to wait for a busier happy hour. By the time we got our burgers at the table, the crowd had grown bigger and louder. The music had picked up. I heard the radio from the restaurant speaker saying something about the heat and the volcano having an unusual increased activity but parts of songs coming from different directions overtook my attention, covering my ears. Busy flies had started to pinch frenetically and my legs soon became itchy.

'I forgot what it means being in a hot country and surrounded by flies...' I said, scratching away.

'You forgot the basics. Here, put some of this spray on. It'll help.'

'Will it, or is it one of those crappy fake things you buy cheap and then complain about it afterwards?' I replied, smiling.

'It wasn't cheap and you are free to let them eat you alive.' And Eléna sipped some beer from what had been, for a second, my glass. Hers was long gone.

'Oh, hey stranger! Eléna told me you were coming but I didn't know it was today.' From the street, a voice shouted right at us. It was Andrea, *the one who doesn't get it, the undecided*.

'I did tell you Daniel was coming today, that's why I took a day off, remember?' she replied, her words barely passing through her teeth.

'Sure, sure,' he said, as if he hadn't really listened. I guessed that was why he 'didn't know it was today', as well? 'If you had told me you were here, I would have booked that fantastic place on the coast. Here is...you know..." And he made an unimpressed expression.

'Here is just fine.' I stepped in. I never liked the way he had to decide for everyone what was good and what wasn't. I did understand that his job, the power that came with it, might have given him the idea he possessed a stronger judgement on the most ludicrous details, but that had a direct consequence on my sister's life. Her decisions were his decisions. Her comments, ideas were his. 'To be honest, I was so hungry that any place would have done the trick. Don't worry.'

'What are you guys doing tomorrow?' He seemed to have the unpleasant intention to stay there as long as was needed for my burger to get cold.

Before I could speak, Eléna said: 'There is a lot of catching up we have to do.' And I was listening carefully. Whatever she was saying I was hearing it for the first time. 'Then shopping, food...and more shopping of course.' And she added a smile at the end, long enough to be seen as a payback.

I said nothing. My plans were quite different. I was going to spend most of the day back in Valverde, with my grandma. I was playing a bigger game there, a game my sister wasn't aware of. We never spoke about the details of how we were going to do what we were supposed to do, except the fact that she was going to give me a lift and pick me up afterwards. The rest was up in the air. *Maybe Andrea would like to express his opinion about the agenda*, I thought, smiling. For a brief moment, it felt like the two of them had the urge to get into a big fight, so I zoned out quickly, took out my phone and pretended to make a call. Talking to John was actually a good idea. I dialled the number. Their voices went lower, they nearly read each other's lips, or that was what I was trying to do waiting for John to pick up his phone.

'Hey babe! How's it going? Are you with your sis?' he answered.

'All good here. Yes, I'm having dinner with Eléna in this very moment, I thought to give you a quick call.' And the two of them suddenly got louder. Someone said something about giving space, and something else about lies...and truth...

'Is it hot? Oh, I wish this was a trip of pleasure. I would have come with you, no excuses! How is Grandma?'

'Grandma is fine,' I said, without thinking. 'I mean, as fine as she can be...all considering,' I added, trying to keep up with my own lie. *Lies... truth...wasn't that what they were fighting about?* I thought.

'I'm really sorry, babe...it must be horrible... Is there any chance she can make it alright?' he asked. How bad did I describe it? I couldn't remember.

'I think she will. I mean, things are not improving in some areas'—I walked on slipping ice—'but she is still

224

strong. We talked today. Just a little bit. Then her mind went who knows where.'

'That's sad... I'm really sorry, hun. Listen, I'm about to get home. Daisy must be starving by now. I'll text you when I'm free then you call me if you can?'

'Sure. Hug Daisy for me. I love you!' And I hung up after making sure the fight at the other side of the table was over. They weren't talking any more. Whatever the fight was about, it had come and gone in seconds.

'I'm on my way home. Have a great day tomorrow,' Andrea said. It was formal, borderline cold, but that was him all along. In the back of my head, something told me he was going to offer to pay for our dinner, and I instantly begged the Gods to not find myself in that situation. Fortunately he left without such a gesture.

As the night continued, Eléna shared they were seriously at the cusp of a bad breakup. Too many misunderstandings, things not said, fights not really resolved, had built a version of themselves they didn't recognize any more. She had my full understanding. In my own way, I was moving towards the same outcome. Of course me and John were different. There was less sharpness in our differences but John was indeed the one who had driven our relationship for long.

I was the busy bee attracted to his smell, his big gestures, his power of conquering the world he stepped in. He was the one that told our stories to our friends, to my friends. He owned us and I loved it. I wanted it to be in that way...up until a few months before. Now the charm had started to fade. I was waking up to new needs. I had a mind

225

of my own, an unknown purpose to discover that wasn't his. John had no idea of the road I was taking. I was driving myself again, like I had done for all my life. My life before him. My life before I had given away the reins to love, to him.

Back home, we got comfortable in our shorts pyjamas while the conversation flowed non-stop. We had picked up some ice cream to have when, in full relaxed mood, we were going to watch some trash TV but neither of us was going to slow down the talk. My sister's home was unbelievably small. Even a pet would have struggled. There was only one large bedroom, split in two by a wide wardrobe. A bed to one side, a couch with telly and stuff to the other. The kitchen was a small but functional corridor and the sitting room was just a table with two chairs. Although small, that apartment was perfect. Everything had its right place, there wasn't much to move anywhere.

'I still don't get how a girl tall like you can actually fit so right in this apartment,' I shouted through the bathroom door.

'There is no need to talk that loud. I'm just here a few steps away,' she replied. 'Will I prepare the ice cream?'

'Sure... Sis?' I had to ask. 'What are all these multitude of small, tiny ointment tubes? They're everywhere, coming out from every drawer.'

'Those are samples I get every time I go to the pharmacy,' she said laughing. 'Try them out! They really work...just make sure they are for the face first.' And she laughed louder.

'Why don't you buy just a full one like normal people?'

'Are you mad? You know how expensive these things are?' she replied while I secretly tried one that said *aloe and lime*. My eyes felt the shock right away and I started to cry as I walked out the bathroom. My sister could not stop laughing as I desperately tried to get the mask off my face as fast as I could.

Soon it was 2 a.m., we had gone to bed but we still talked through the wardrobe. It was like we had so much to say and so little time, we had to tell it all at once. We went back to the beginning of time, when her father met my mother and eventually got together. It was funny, but also unbelievable how we initially hated each other. Then, slowly we had started to bond together, driven by the same rebel way to see life. We were troublemakers to the Christians' world, sinners and impenitents who now laughed at our past struggles.

Eventually, I got so tired that the couch stopped feeling uncomfortable and I fell asleep, in between words travelling on the way between us, left hanging in the air. Our last conversation about the future and the unknown slipped into my dreams, transformed into scenes with little logic. Grandma had come back from the land of the lost ones. She was young again, full of energy, and she talked about the future, my future.

Another man stood next to her, both gazing at the sea, with the big mountain at their back, and the unusually silent city in the distance; they stood on a wooden jetty. To the far left, two big ships pushed their metal hulls into the dark water, like long sharp blades cutting through the surface. The night had just fallen.

'You know, it has to be done,' the man said. He looked much older than Grandma. 'I've made a promise, and when I'm gone, that promise will be your promise.'

'But how are we going to explain it? I'm forty-two years old. I can't have a child at my age.'

'True. But Victoria is seventeen, soon eighteen...' he replied. That was strange. Even in my dream I could feel it, that was too familiar. Their faces, their names. They were my family.

'Don't be ridiculous. She is too young to have a child! Can you imagine what the people will say?' she strongly rejected the idea.

'It's the eighties, Rita. If it was OK with me, nearly twenty years ago, for you to have a child with no man by your side, I'm sure it's going to be OK for Victoria to have a child on her own.' The old man insisted in pushing his decision on Grandma, as if he had the authority to do so. If what he said were true, he would be my great-grandfather. How was that possible?

'What's going to happen then?' she asked, defeated.

'The boy is in the ship, in my cabin. We'll bring him home with us tonight, when everyone is gone. Get Victoria out of the car and bring her here. She will have the main responsibility in raising this child. You and she will both come to live at my place, where no one knows you.' And he left, with no further words, his face, hard and unsensitive, showed no doubts.

Grandma was left there, her eyes watching the start of a nightmare that was never going to end. Called to respond to a distress signal, she had silently accepted the unwanted burden.

Chapter Fifteen

A Secret In A Shell

∞

The morning after, I was up way before Eléna. Since that dream, my mind started to go on its own, through places, ideas, conjectures I didn't quite like. What was the meaning of all that? Was I just making that up or had I really *seen* something that had happened in the past? After my sister was ready, we went out to get our breakfast nearby. At ten in the morning, the sun was already punching our sleepy faces with so much energy I started to feel faint. On one hand, I was glad to spend the day at Grandma's because I knew the temperature there would be more pleasant. Eléna didn't show any trouble with the heat, and I was melting away like a snowman in the desert.

We both sat outside a bar, under the shade of a giant white awning. Eléna laughed at the heat by drinking a short hot espresso. I chewed the ice in my drink.

'Sis?' I started. 'If I'm correct, Andrea spends a lot of time with the officials in the navy, down the harbour?'

'Yeah. He has his own boat, licence and everything,' she replied, unimpressed. 'Why?'

'No why…I just…I might need to get down there, for a quick look. I need to check something,' I said, hoping she wasn't going to ask again why.

'I can ask him, if you want. But let me warn you, if we get there with him he will ask us to go on a boat trip.'

'Would it be so bad?' I asked, happy she didn't question further.

'No, no. It's summertime. It's nice out in the sea. It's just…when you are with him, you know when you leave, you don't know when you come back,' she said. I couldn't say if she was happy about Andrea's passion or not. I didn't push for clarification.

'OK. Let's see how today goes…we might ask him tonight or tomorrow,' I proposed.

So we finished our breakfast and got in the car. Twenty minutes later we were already in Valverde. Not many cars around for a Saturday morning, but we guessed many people must have been away for the holidays, trying to escape the suffocating wrath of the summer. Eléna and I agreed she would drop me at Grandma's and I would spend a few hours there while she walked around shopping. We would sync again at lunchtime and take it from there. I loved the plan because it would give me the chance of being alone with Grandma but my sister would still be a snap away, in case I needed her. Carla was at the door a few seconds after I knocked; her face hadn't changed overnight and had neither my reaction in seeing her. She spoke to me with a flat tone, sounding already tired.

'Come in,' she said. 'Let me warn you, today is not a good day. She's being a nightmare since last night.'

'What's wrong with her?' I asked, closing the door behind me. The corridor felt darker than usual, and pleasantly colder.

'The same crazy dance. That's what's wrong with her. She couldn't sleep last night, stood up shouting my name, three times in the space of few hours. I don't know what happened. It has been a while since last time she acted like that. Even her voice sounded different!'

'How is she now? Has she calmed down?' I asked, looking around to see where Grandma was.

'A bit. I told her you were coming, she gets always in a good mood when she gets visitors...want coffee?' she asked, moving away from me, heading to the kitchen. She had no interest in engaging in any other conversation.

'Please...that'd be nice. Is she in her bedroom?'

'Yes. By the bay window.' And Carla moved out of sight.

Stepping in Grandma's bedroom had always had a strange feeling. I knew the room inch by inch, I had spent so much time in it. Her bed was my bed when I was sick. Her TV by the corner was the centre of my lonely weekends. Her giant wardrobe was like a secret passage to my dreams when I used to carve some space in it and read my favourite books in there, over and over. Then, one day, Victoria and Grandma had a horrible fight, and my mother left for good, bringing me with her, and so the magic, the fun and my dreams were over. That's when that room became so important to me, and as I walked in, I could still feel it was.

Grandma sat by the bay window like Carla had said. She wore a very light pinkish shirt, her hair looked exactly as it had the day before, and a soft white throw covered her legs. Her face was turned away, towards the window, but I had the feeling she was asleep. I moved closer quietly so as to not disturb her. I squeezed in between her chair and the side of her bed and sat there, looking around; the walls were quiet but Grandma's stuff spoke words of older times. There were pictures scattered everywhere with all sorts of frames, many more that I remembered.

I could easily recognize the ones with me, Mother, Grandma. I was quite sure I had seen a younger, pretty Sara in a few of those and a late Great-Grandfather in some others. *I wish she could look at these pictures and remember her life as it has been,* I thought. *Hopefully she did have a good life.* A small, old photo on the bedside locker got my attention. Although tiny, the picture was packed with people. I was sure I had seen it before, but something looked odd, as if I was noticing it for the first time. There was Grandma, Victoria, a man—most likely Great-Grandad—holding a baby, and two other men and an old lady to their right. These last three looked a bit different, greyer, like the

233

picture had faded away with the years...but only on one side.

'This was taken the day after we got our little boy,' Grandma said, taking me by surprise. It was like someone else was speaking for her. Grandma moved like a pawn, in between sadness and pain. Her gestures were slow, fragmented, as broken as her memories.

'Hey 'Ma. I didn't mean to wake you up,' I replied, taking her right hand. Hers felt colder than mine, her skin like a fragile veil, heating up on my touch. ''Ma, are you cold? You hand is freezing!'

'We didn't know what to do, you know? Back then you don't just appear with a year-old boy out of nowhere,' she continued, ignoring what I had just said. 'But nevertheless, it was the best gift we could have had...my Daniel.'

'Grandma, what are you saying?' I asked. *What did she mean? Is she remembering correctly? If that boy was me, how did I just appear, out of nowhere?*

'Victoria never understood that,' she continued, like I didn't just speak. It was like she had to tell her story at once, before it slipped away from her mind. 'She knew the boy was special, but for her, he was more a special-needs little child, something to be ashamed of, something that needs constant, tiring help. But of course she knew very little. Exactly like a special-needs child, Daniel was a precious stone, something to protect, to love for what it was, not for what it wasn't. Instead, Victoria decided to turn herself to that horrible, horrible religion of hers!' And her face turned dark, full of anger. That was a vivid memory, no doubt, for her like it was for me, marked for life by my mother's wrong choices.

'I never understood why she chose that life,' I said without even thinking. Grandma listened, this time.

'Because she was afraid…she was afraid of who she was, who she is. She was afraid of all the things happening around her. And, like everybody else, when we are afraid we run for protection, security. We believe what our mind wants to believe to feel safe. And she believed that her knocking door after door, preaching her gospel, would save her from her destiny, her son's destiny.'

'So she chose that life because of m—because of Daniel?' I had almost forgotten to play by Grandma's rules.

'She chose that life because of her fear, nothing more.'

I was stunned by the way her mind could be so sharp on that topic. Grandma hated most of Victoria's decisions but that was the battle she had never learned to let go. I knew she had felt my same pain when we left her home and I became the victim of a terrifying mother, too quick to silence me with violence than listening. I believe she regretted letting us go, letting me go.

Even in her new memoryless world, Grandma was still right. Victoria had chosen a fundamentalist religion because she felt unsafe, unprotected. The more rules her God had, the better. The biblical gates would have kept the evil away from her soul, if she had managed to stay pure and saintly. *What about me? Was she so abusive because I wasn't pure? After all, me being gay was only the cherry on top of the cake*, I thought.

"Ma...was Victoria so bad to...Daniel, because she knew something about him or also because he was...difficult?' I asked, and my heart trembled a bit.

'Let me tell you this'—and she turned around in her chair, her body fully oriented towards mine—'I know it's going to sound bad, coming from me as I'm her mother, but...Victoria was bad and that's that. She had to fight battles with her own demons even before Daniel came along. She still is, I'm telling you, she still is! That girl never quite moved on from the fact that her father left her. Never understood I had been left too. No, it was only her drama to have. She was almost happy to need rescuing. That's what drove people's attention to her. And the more she turned bad, the more she needed to be rescued. Eventually she met that man...what was his name...oh my mind is playing tricks on me!' she said, making me laugh. 'Oh, never mind! He showed her a *path of salvation*. He legitimated her status of victim. What rescuer greater than God could she find?'

Her words unmercifully opened old scars. Everything she said had a direct impact in my life, my childhood, the man I was. But I didn't care much, this time. This time I was there to ask those questions, I was ready to take it, to take even more than I could imagine. Then Carla showed up. She brought my coffee and tightly held some large papers under her arm. Her walk seemed stranger than usual; she dragged her feet as if she had been pushed in against her will.

'Here, Daniel. That's your coffee. And here loads of magazines for Mama Rita. I know you like to read them.'

And she put the papers on the bed, next to me, finally free to get back to her funny walk.

'Why did she call you Daniel?' Grandma asked, her expression showing the many troubles of her mind as she tried to understand. For a moment, I pondered what answer to give. Then, I decided to use her own technique by changing the topic.

'Grandma, who are these people to the right?' Ignoring her question, I took the small picture frame from the table and brought it closer to her face. 'Get a proper look. I can see you. I can see my mother...is this Great-Grandpa?'

'Yes, that's him,' she replied after struggling in readjusting to the topic shift.

'And who are these other people?' I added.

'What other people? It's the four of us, that's all. Let me see, again?' The picture had faded from one side only, the side that mattered. I moved closer and with my finger I pointed out the two men.

'See here? It looks like there are three people?' I said.

'I can't see much, Danny. My eyes are tired.' And she turned her face back to the window.

I was thrilled, nearly in tears.

She had just called me Danny. Something, somewhere in her mind had made the click. Who those people were didn't matter any more. None of those pictures were worth their past as much as a single word mattered in our present. Unfortunately, Grandma closed her eyes and her mind left the room before I could ask anything else, before I could hold on to that *Danny* a little longer. So I sat there, at the edge of her bed for a few more minutes, maybe to check if she was really asleep or maybe just to indulge in the brief happiness I had just tasted.

Eventually I went to see Carla, to check what she was up to and give her back the empty cup of coffee. She was unloading the washing machine in the utility room and I could hear her badly singing broken lyrics from a song the radio was playing in the background. It was one of those moments when you don't want interrupt somebody, so I decided to head outside, where the day before we had spent some time, at the orange trees, enjoying a thankful cigarette.

'That's bad for your health!' Carla showed up from behind, scaring the hell out of me. Same face, troubled expression and a big basket full of wet clothes.

'Oh Carla,' I said, after putting myself back together. 'Grandma fell asleep. I think she's tired.'

'Yeah, of course she doesn't sleep at night, then. You better go and try keep her awake, if you can.' And she started to fold some clothes over a few rubber wires, carelessly.

'Does she often fall asleep and wake up just like that, randomly?' I asked. Grandma's changeable behaviour was unsettling.

'Yes...most of the time. But there is nothing to be worried about.' Her face disappeared behind big, long sheets flipping over the wires strongly shaken by her harsh movements.

In the next hour, I went back and forth from 'Ma's bedroom a few times. I woke her up two or three times, had a few small random conversations and gone back to Carla who was, at every turn, in a different room of the house doing something different. My time there was spent thinking on how many things someone like Carla could find to do every day, in a home with only two people, thinking how old that house was and how much renovation it needed. John would have loved to get into a project like that. Then, I realized Grandma wasn't the only one in that house with information.

'Carla, when was Victoria here last?' I asked her, while she dried up some plates.

'Let me see,' she started with her usual flat tone. 'She left three weeks ago, after being here for a few days.'

'And how long was she gone before that?' I added.

'Oh God, I can't remember. Maybe another three or four weeks. She comes often but only for a bit. She is busy with her other family.'

'Other family?' I asked, surprised. It wasn't really possible.

'Yaaah, her family...the one with the Bible and their books. She calls them brothers here...sisters there...like they are family. For real!' she added, with some judgement in her voice. 'If you asked me, that's not right. A grown-up woman like her, with a son and a mother in need, that goes around with other strangers calling them brothers.' And her head nodded in a visible sign of dissatisfaction.

'I know...I know. Nothing new in there,' I said, trying to not wind her up. 'Have other people been here, in the last few months? People that you don't know or people who have no reason to be here?' I asked, trying to change topic.

'No, not really. The doctor is here from time to time. Sometimes your mother brings a girl with her, but that's only for a few minutes while they are doing their Bible stuff, knocking at people's doors. Why are you asking?' And she put down the last plate before she could dry it.

'No reason,' I quickly replied. 'Just making sure you and Grandma haven't been disturbed by strangers...you know, people that have no business here,' I added after noticing Carla started to look worried. I only wanted to make sure Victoria's *brothers and sisters* were not coming and going from Grandma's house at their pleasure.

'No, no. Nobody,' she replied. 'Well, a couple of weeks ago something strange actually happened. Someone I've never seen before was at the front door. I thought he might have had the wrong address or something, but when I opened the door he specifically asked for your grandma.'

'Did he mention her name?' I asked, sitting down by the kitchen table. Carla had just moved the plates back to their place in a cabinet and poured me some fresh coffee in a clean cup.

'Yes. Not at first. At first he said something weird, like he was sorry for being late. Then he asked about her.' And she pointed to the other room with her skinny finger.

'Did you get to see him well? Do you remember what he looked like?' I asked.

'Oh sure. Old-looking, white beard, the darkest eyes I have ever seen he had! I could have sworn it was Christmas Eve! He came back, a few times. Never walked in! No...no.

240

I wouldn't have let him in. A stranger... Imagine the trouble I would be in by now!' She sounded funny to me. She was more worried about her reputation than about the event itself.

'OK...now you need to tell me the full story. Get a cup of coffee for yourself too.' I said, intending to find out everything about that man. I'd been in that strange new world full of mysteries only a few months, but I had learned to recognize when something was not...ordinary.

'Right. He came first on a Sunday. Your mother was here but she was at her church for the Sunday mass. When the bell rang, I thought that was her. *She must have forgotten the key,* I thought, but she didn't. That wasn't her!'

She was telling the story like a pro. The suspense in her voice came through as if she was about to share the greatest gossip of all time. Her eyes zipped right and left and narrowed as she got to the juicy parts. 'I opened the door and this old man with a grey-and-white beard and a long jacket was looking at me. I think this was after Christmas...yes it was! It was last February. But there he was. A late Santa Claus in front of me.' And she smiled. 'Now, you know what happened. But when he asked me about Mrs. Rita, I said: *No sir, I can't help you. I'm not allowed to let anyone in without permission. Good day.* And I closed the door.'

'Did he ring again?' I asked.

'No. Of course I went to Mrs. Rita's bedroom and looked through the bay window. He was still there, at the door, staring into nothing. This for a good few minutes. That's strange, isn't it? Thank God I didn't let him in!' She asked

241

and replied to her own questions before I could even speak. She was hilarious even when telling creepy stories.

'So that was that. Then two days later he came back. Your mother was already gone so I wasn't very happy to see him there 'cause I had nobody to call, if I needed. This time, I checked from the window and when I saw him at the door I didn't open. I just sat there and waited until he was gone. Again, he stayed there for a few minutes, doing nothing. Then he left. He wasn't alright in the head, I'm telling you!'

She stood back up and left the table to go and get the cooker started. Lunchtime had arrived and I hadn't achieved what I wanted to. I only had more questions. That had become a habit and I didn't like it. Every time I tried, I had no answers and more questions. I texted Eléna to check where she was at.

Daniel

Bought much?

Eléna

Not really.
Buying time at a coffee shop at the mall.
Are you ready to go?

Daniel

I wish. 'Ma is in dreamland

Eléna

As...

Daniel

'Asleep. I'm talking to Carla.

Eléna

What a holiday :D

Daniel

Can you give me some more time,
like 1 hour?

Eléna

Sure. Text me when you are ready.

I didn't want to go back home with nothing but doubts. I had no one else to rely on for those matters. Eléna had stepped into my life way after I had left Grandma's home and she had no idea how messed up my childhood had been. Of course she and I had talked about the major issues, especially the ones that were still happening when we got together—after my mother had married her father—but I had willingly left behind some things I didn't want to talk about ever again. Somehow our relationship was like the one I had with John. I loved her very much, and in a way that meant protecting her from knowing, from feeling what I felt. The only relationship I had where I could open up again about my past struggles was with the same woman who could not remember me. I had to try again. Grandma was my only chance but, first, I had to finish my conversation with Carla.

'Carla, is there something else you are not telling me, for some reason?' I asked, putting the empty cup in the spotless sink.

243

'What? Noo. I never lied in my life! To anyone!' she said, trying to sound convincing.

'Not saying and lying are two different things. I'm not saying you are lying. I believe you. I'm just wondering if there is more that might *help me to help you* if something happens in the future…you know what I'm saying?' And I hoped she would get the hint…somehow.

'OK. I didn't say it 'cause I'm sure it's nothing. I don't want to sound like I'm not able to do my job…so please promise you won't tell a word about what I'm about to say.' And she switched off the fire; the green sauce in the pot went dead and a weak smoke carried a yummy smell around the kitchen. I knew then I was starving.

'I promise. Now, spill it out!'

Carla's expression changed quickly, the suspense mode was on again and I could clearly see it. She dragged me outside the house, through the big doors to the back field, and slowly closed them up.

'Your grandma went nuts…' she started, whispering.

'What do you mean?' I said, my face showing the obvious confusion. We all knew already she wasn't quite there.

'Noo, you don't understand. That man came back the following Sunday. Again, I went and checked through the bay window. This time Mrs. Rita was in the room, sitting where she is sitting now. Oh you had to see her! She started to move back and forth, like that—and she swung her body right and left—I didn't know what to do. Then she started to say something like…*waiting, waiting to be, waiting to be*…over and over.

Those words were unpleasantly familiar but I was too interested in knowing the rest to stop her and think about what Carla had just said.

'Was she having like an attack?' I asked.

'I don't know. That had never happened before. She started to get very upset and started to cry. Then she said: *Daniel, bring me the shell, bring me the shell.* Like for a whole minute or more! You had to see me there...with my hands on your grandma and my face back and forth to her and to the window.'

'I can only imagine,' I replied. I was trapped by that story. As strange as it was, it fitted right into my usual madness.

'And wait! In the middle of this, when Mrs. Rita was getting very, very upset, that man turned his face to the window and looked right at us. I nearly pissed myself! He couldn't have seen us, with the curtains and everything. I'm telling you, it was like he could hear your grandma!' And she paused there, looking for any reaction on my side. I was completely still. There, I had another massive question with no answer. That wasn't going well.

'You think I'm mad, don't you?' she said.

'No, no. I told you, I believe you,' I quickly replied.

'Good. 'Cause, I'm telling you, something odd is happening in this house,' she added. 'You know, sometimes...I feel like there is someone in this house, other than la Signora...watching me, listening to what she says... You know, sometimes she leaves her room without a warning, without asking for help. Once or twice she took

245

me off guard and went to the attic. The attic! Imagine if she fell! It would be a disaster!'

'What she went there for?' I asked, worried.

'No idea… It's like if she is possessed! Both times I found her there, searching in old boxes. There is one in particular she is obsessed with… But anyway! This is it,' she added, wrapping up. 'The old man stayed there a few seconds and then turned his back and left. After that day…I never seen him again.' And she went mute, looking at me, waiting.

Whatever that man wanted, there was a connection with Grandma, and Grandma had mentioned my name. *Yes, Carla must have thought that wasn't important,* I said to myself, *but it is something.* The timing also felt suspicious. It had happened before my daydreams started. 'What is the connection?' I whispered.

'Connection to what?' she asked.

'Oh…to Grandma's illness,' I replied, trying to come up with a rational answer. 'Look, I appreciate you telling me this. I need to find a way to talk to 'Ma, now. Let me see if I can wake her up, in every sense.' And I left Carla outside and went back to 'Ma's room before she could say that my attempts were just a waste of time.

'Don't get her upset!' Carla said, before I could walk into Grandma's room.

'Carla?' I said.

'Yeah?'

'You said you feel like you have been watched?'

'I do… But please don't say it to anybody. I can do the job alright!' And she ran close to me, ready to beg. Somehow I realized only then Carla wasn't just close to Grandma. She also needed the money.

'I won't.' And I touched her shoulders with my hand. Her worried face looked uglier than usual. 'You are doing a great job!'

Grandma was still there where I had left her. Her arms were down and her hands, joined on her lap, held on to the picture I had questioned early on. I moved closer to see if she was still awake when she turned her head to me and smiled. Inside me something moved. I had the warm, sweet feeling she was back with me, the real 'Ma I loved so much. With a simple smile, just by the way she looked at me, I knew she had finally recognised me.

'Daniel, my love…you are so big.' And my legs lost their strength, leaving me weak. Happiness pulled me down, so I quickly sat at the very edge of her bed, my eyes wet, my hands rushing to reach hers.

"Ma?' I could barely speak. 'How do you feel?'

'I'm feeling…good,' she said with a magical peaceful smile. 'I'm so happy to see you. Where have you been?'

I could have said so many things. I could have said I had always been there, that she was the one who was gone. I could have said about the time that had passed, the things that had happened, but I could only cry.

'I'm happy to see you too. I've been out of the country…for work, you know?'

'Good boy. You are building a life of your own, don't cry. You can't be with your nonna forever.' And her left hand moved softly on my head. 'You always had big hair...' And she smiled again.

"Ma?' I wanted to live that moment forever, but I knew she could go anytime, so I hurried, 'There is something important I need to ask you.'

'I know, my child. I know,' she replied, looking at the picture she held. She was back and she had done it fast.

'Yes, it's about these people, I think, but there is more. Some things have happened to me, lately. I've discovered truths and events I wasn't aware of and I'm not even sure if I was meant to, but I need to fix this and you are the only one I trust, the only one who might know,' I said all at once.

'You can't fix it, my love.' And her smile left her dark face. 'You can only let it happen.'

'What do you mean? Please tell me what's happening to me?' I asked desperately, as if I were running against time. She had the answers and I didn't know how long I could keep her confined in her sanity.

'Hold on. Carla, can you please go to the attic? There is something I need you to take.'

I hadn't seen Carla entering the room. She stood silent by the door, in shock. She had heard Grandma talking and she knew she had come back, against the odds. Now she was asked to go to the same place where she had found her suspiciously searching for something, twice. She responded to *Mrs. Rita* with a 'Sure...sure,' and left the room at once. Grandma had asked her to bring back a *small chest with a shell carved on the top,* something she needed me to see?

'Whatever I'm going to tell you, it's not something I'm completely sure about. It's something that came from your great-grandfather, and the story I know, it's the story he told me,' she started, with a serious tone in her voice.

My body was petrified by realizing the moment had come. I was about to know, at a step from the truth I was, and in between me and it, there was only a mysterious shell.

Chapter Sixteen
The Praetorian

∞

I was forty-two years old when it all started. I know this might hurt you, my child. Whatever I'm going to say to you, it won't change this simple fact: I love you with every inch of my soul and I always will...' And she paused, as if she waited for me to be ready for the blow. 'You were already born, I don't know when, but you were already there when it all started, when you came to us. My father had sent a few letters couple of weeks before he came back, saying he was on a mission bigger than he we could imagine and to be ready for when he would be back. As you know, your great-grandfather was in the navy all his life. He had been in every corner of the world and nobody really knows—or knew back then—the things he had seen and lived through. Three days before he docked, a half-page letter arrived. It was his. He wrote he was coming home with a gift, 'A gift from God.''

I was listening to 'Ma exactly like I used to when I was a little boy, ready to go to sleep, with her sitting on my bed, by my side. Her voice had changed with the years, but the effect on me stayed the same.

'At that time, your mother was a late teenager. She didn't really care about her granddad and his adventures so, when I forced her into meeting him the night he came back, she wasn't happy. Now, you know how difficult for your mother life was...growing up without a father, with only me taking care of the family. When you arrived, she wasn't happy. She wasn't happy at all. Now that I think about it...it wasn't only that. She was like a cold stone. Like she could not feel anything at all. The night my father came back, he came back with a child. The sweetest boy anyone had ever seen! His eyes were crystal blue, like the ocean, and his head was full of hair. Your skin was pale and soft, you were the most beautiful thing I had ever seen...'

And there she said it. Somewhere in me, I knew this was the kind of truth I was afraid to get. I had collected so many hints about my unclear past, the love my mother had never felt for me. I wasn't hers. I wasn't meant to be loved like a son. I was no one's son. That was exactly what I was. I suddenly forgot the reason why I was even there, asking those questions. An old one had come back. An old *why* had come through, why my life had been so difficult, painful? There was no mystery or magic. I wasn't theirs, and that was as simple as it hurt.

Carla came back before I could ask anything of Grandma. She brought in a small black box with a pinkish shell carved on top. The wooden chest looked pretty old, ruined in a few parts, and yet, it was still intact. A lock held it shut. After handing it over to 'Ma, she stood there, beside the two of us, in shock and still puzzled by the events.

'Thank you, Carla,' she said. 'You can go now, and please make sure nobody interrupts us, will you?' And the poor woman left the room with a pure face of disbelief. I was sure that in her mind, the memory of that weird man had suddenly lost the top spot of all the crazy things she had witnessed.

'Is this box connected to me?' I asked. I had thousands of questions, but that one was the only one that came out.

'It is,' she said. 'That night, my father didn't bring just you with him, but also this box and a story. His story and your story. He said the child he had rescued was a gift from God. My dad was chosen to look after him, to be the supreme protection, a Praetorian.'

'A what?' I asked, without hesitation.

'A Praetorian. It means protector, bodyguard. My father called himself in that way…and later he called me with that name. He said the responsibility was going to pass from one generation to the other. So I became your protector when he passed away.'

'Protecting me from what? Was there someone after me?' I asked.

'I'm afraid I won't have all the answers, my child. There are many, many details buried in foggy statements, things that my dad said that made no sense at all. But I'll tell you

252

all I know, even if it's not much. Because I was too old to have a child,' she continued, 'your great-grandfather decided that you were going to be, for everyone else, Victoria's child. It made sense, for him, that she had you, being almost eighteen years old she fitted better in the story. I resisted, believe me, I did! I knew your mother. It doesn't give me any pleasure to say it now and it didn't give me any pleasure then, but I always said Victoria wasn't fit to be anyone's mother. Not at that age, and I can say now, not ever! There was something missing in that girl, she wasn't just too young to be a mother. She wasn't right. It was like she had come to this world without a heart. Of course, your great-grandfather didn't listen. His biggest worry was to keep you in the family and having Victoria as your mother was the only way we could let it happen. So she became legally your mother.' And then Grandma stopped for a moment.

Her face turned sad, her eyes wandered in the air as if she was trying to decide what would come next. I had the fear she had lost momentum and I was about to lose her again.

"Ma? What's wrong? I'm OK, please continue,' I had to know everything she knew. I couldn't pause it just to allow my sadness to come through, it was a risk too high to take.

'Nothing, my love. I was just thinking about the day you both left. You can't remember. You were four, I think. We had a very bad argument over some decisions of hers. She had taken up the habit of meeting with some people from that religion of hers. She had started to talk about the end of the world, a God that would save only her and her brothers and sisters...and I knew she was only trying to escape reality. She knew the mystery around you. She had seen the things you could do as a child and she believed their God was the only hope for salvation. One day she would become the Praetorian and I couldn't let it happen! But you were legally hers. I couldn't stop her.'

'What things did I do, as a child?' I had stopped at that remark and I couldn't followed the rest.

'Oh, well...sometimes just things any child would do...you know? Talking to imaginary friends, laughing at things that we couldn't see. Nothing very unusual. But then there were episodes when you would disappear. Like vanished! One moment you were playing with your toys on my bed, the next one you were gone. It was terrifying! Some others you would cry for no reason, like you had just been hurt. We both knew these things were part of the mystery around you, but I never felt like you were in danger, or I was in danger. Unfortunately your mother did.'

'I don't understand. Why was I crying?'

'There was no apparent reason. But if you asked me, I could swear it was your heart. It still is. You are so entangled with feelings, emotions. You always have. It's like if you were fully made of a pure heart. I can't tell how many times you would touch my face and smile or cry as I would have if I had let my feelings come out. You could read me with a touch. But your mother...the few times you did the same to her...oh, it caused the most wrathful reactions!'

'What is in the box?' I suddenly changed topic. Any talk about my mother would hurt. I really didn't want to know more.

'Funny enough, there isn't much. There is a shell, a real shell. There is also a letter my father sent before coming home and another small piece of paper with something written on it.' And Grandma showed me a tiny key she had secured to her necklace and hidden under her shirt. She had worn that key since forever and now she could finally put it to use.

The tension mounted within me. She had just told me what the box contained, but I was sure some sort of spell would emerge the moment she opened it. I stood in silence while Grandma unlocked the chest. The carved shell on top flipped, and the lid clicked open. Inside, there were three items like 'Ma said. An unexpected chill crept up my neck through my spine, like I had frozen for a moment, as if a short breeze had left Grandma to come to me. A passage of knowledge, a passage of truth, transformed in a real, tangible sense of transfer.

My hands held hers for a brief moment. We both held on to that chest like children looking for candies. Then my eyes moved from its contents to Grandma. I was going to say I was expecting some sort of magic to happen but I couldn't. She looked at me but her face had gone beyond, staring at nothing, and the terror of losing her again took over.

''Ma?' I said. ''Ma, are you OK? Are you still with me?' But she didn't respond. Then eventually her eyes focused again.

'Daniel? The three people I wanted to talk to you about...' And she rushed her words, scrambling like she had not much time left and didn't know in which order to proceed. 'They came in with your father...I mean my father. They were there and they weren't. It was like memories in the shape of people. They had come from a long-gone past and they gave us you. They are the ones you are supposed to call family. They didn't speak a word but they were there! The only one who seemed to be more real than the others, it was the woman. This old woman is the one who kept you alive here and she is the one who passed that duty on to us. We were meant to keep you safe until the age... But there is another one. She said there is another one...another child with a crowned heart. But they are only one! Do you understand?' And she rushed her words even more, her breathing went fast, her hands twisting in between mine.

"Ma, it's OK. Calm down. I'm here. I'm not going anywhere. You are not going anywhere,' I said, holding her firmly. The chest fell onto my lap and the contents were about to spill out. Grandma continued:

'She said: *There are things that have been and are no longer, things that have never been, are waiting to be...* It's over, Daniel. Victoria never made it. There is no Praetorian after me, so next it's finding the other one. Do you understand?' And she smiled at me again, a different smile than before. A sad but full of love smile that I would remember for a long time.

'Daniel? You are so big!' she said again before her mind would go into pieces, scattered into nothing.

My arms moved around Grandma and I found myself hugging her tight, trying to calm her down and—I believe—trying to hold her there, with me. Eventually she stopped breathing heavily and her hands slipped down onto her lap. As I moved away from her a bit, I knew she had left me again. Her eyes had turned off, her smile was just a painful memory, and she had gone quiet. I spent there what it felt like hours, just looking at her, fading away again. I could not hold her, but I was grateful we had another moment together. Grateful we had those few minutes, not just because she had told me the things I needed to hear, but also because that moment was like many others we had in my childhood, when she used to make me feel special, safe, loved.

Shaken and with tears in my eyes, I attempted a text to my sister to let her know I was ready to go. It had been years since the last time Grandma had been back with us and I was sure she wasn't coming back anytime soon, probably ever again.

Later, I would be sorry to learn that she wouldn't return at all, that it was all meant to happen, that it was all set in motion...by me, by destiny...by magic. She could have easily been a pawn, moved at the right time, for the right reason...to win a game we were all playing. After spending some time looking at her, thinking about what she had told me, I decided to leave. Just when I stood up, she woke up again and looked around the room. With a worried expression in her face, she shouted:

'Carla? Carla? Here! Come quick!' And then she looked right at me. 'Who are you? Do I know you?' And she started to panic.

I had just moved back towards the door when Carla rushed in. As she entered the room, she ignored me completely. She quickly run to Grandma and tried to calm her down.

'It's OK, Rita. This man is an old family friend who happened to be around and wanted to come and see you. You were asleep, tired, so he decided just to come and say hi and leave, isn't that right, Daniel?' And she looked at me, her eyes praying for me to stick to that odd version of the truth.

'Ye... Yes, sure! I just wanted to see how you were keeping. You won't remember me, my parents lived down the road. I knew your dad!' I added, trying to sound convincing. 'He was in the navy, wasn't he?' And I hoped that question would make her believe we knew each other.

'Yes, he was...' she said, slowly. 'I'm afraid I'm not well enough to talk much today. I'm sorry...Mr...'

'Yes, yes... Please let's leave Mrs. Rita having some rest, shall we?' Carla interrupted me before I could talk, rescuing me from coming up with a random family name. After all, even if I didn't really belong to her family — like she had finally confessed to me — we still did share the same name.

We walked out of the room at once. I was still holding the open chest in my hands, thinking what had just happened, but Carla hadn't noticed it. Her only attention was on quickly defusing the situation. Before she could look better and see it, I went and put the box in the bag I had with me. It was a criminal's gesture. I had never taken anything from that house for myself, ever. Now I had secrets, I became a thief, I had extorted the truth from a fragile old mind. Whatever road I was on, it had *Turn Back* signs all over.

Eléna arrived ten minutes later. She came in, understood what the situation was like and got back in the car, ready to go. Before leaving, I went back to Grandma's room to say goodbye. I knew she wasn't feeling well and what had happened was too much for her to take, but I wanted to see her face once more. So I opened the door and let myself in. She was awake and still in the same spot I had left her. Noticing she had seen me, I said:

'Gran... Mrs. Rita-Louise. I'm going home. I wanted to say goodbye and wish you the very best.' And I moved closer, looking forward to hugging her one last time.

'Thank you for visiting,' she said, smiling. 'I told you yesterday, I knew you were a good boy...' And she raised her arms, welcoming my hug.

Grandma had gone back to the day before. She could remember I was there, what she had said, but nothing about our latest conversation. In a way, I felt like that was the right closure. She wasn't hurt, suffering any more. That smile was the only thing I wanted to see as I left.

Few moments later, Eléna and I were already driving back to the city. She asked how the day had been, but I just vaguely replied that Grandma had zoned in and out all morning. I made some comments about Carla and how well she was taking care of Grandma, just to make it sound like I had something to say, and I hoped Eléna wouldn't ask for more.

Back at her home, I hopped in the shower, changed, and suddenly we started a random conversation around

259

children, while we were getting ready to go out for the evening. Eléna had finished first and she sat on the couch while looking at me fixing my hair. She made some comments about my fixation on being *absolutely perfect before going out* in between our remarks on building a family, having kids of our own. We were both against the idea of having children. It didn't matter that she wasn't in a strong, stable relationship. It didn't matter I was in a gay relationship. We agreed *we didn't have the experience, the background...or the support system* — a family — for that matter.

'Does it ever feel wrong?' I asked.

'What? Not wanting kids?' she asked back.

'Yeah, but also not having anyone to look after or someone who will be there to keep the memory of us.' And my mind went back to Grandma.

'A bit, yes. But if I think about our family...I don't know. If our parents were bad, imagine how bad would I be considering that I even miss the desire to be a mother... I'd probably we worse.'

'Don't be silly. That's not possible. And, anyway, I don't think they desired it either,' I quickly replied. I could still hear 'Ma telling me about Victoria, how she didn't want me, how she didn't want to be a mother. 'I bet Victoria never did.'

'My father chose your mother despite everything. He always did. So I don't think he did either, to be honest.' And Eléna stood up, ready to go out.

'Anyway,' I said, spraying some aftershave all over my head. 'Are we good to go? Shall we?'

'We shall!' And we both fled the house, leaving behind the sad thoughts about becoming parents.

On our walk to the city centre, I called John to check if everything was OK back home. I missed him more than it showed and his name had popped out constantly in my talks with Eléna. Eventually I picked up my smartphone and made a videocall. I was excited to see him. John didn't answer right away. The moment he saw me video calling, he had gone to get Daisy outside so she could be in the camera too.

Eléna was happy to see him. Last time they had seen each other was two years earlier, when she had come home visiting. She'd had one of her historic fights with Andrea and had decided to quit her job, leave him and take a break. I was happy to be there for her, but the truth was I knew it wouldn't last long. A week later, she was already on her flight home, getting back to her love, forgiving and forgetting.

'Babe, how's going? You out?' John asked, pulling Daisy on his lap. Her cute, fluffy face had popped up for a brief moment.

'Yes, we're heading downtown for dinner...'

In the space of a few seconds, I was completely ejected from the conversation. Eléna took my phone and started to talk loudly in the middle of a busy street. Despite the fact that John spoke a very broken Italian and Eléna didn't really know a word in English, the two of them talked non-stop, moving their hands to facilitate understanding and when that became too difficult, they asked me to perform a real-time translation.

261

Once the major topics, house, dogs, work, love, had been discussed, I finally managed to take over the phone call. John complained about preparing a dinner for one. That was his way of telling me he missed me. We managed to talk about pretty much everything before he had to go and have his dinner. I was glad Eléna could not understand much of what we said. In that way I managed to tell John some parts of my conversation with Grandma. I obviously omitted any reference to the box, to my origins, but I felt he could take the rest with no risk. In that way, he was where I wanted him to be, close to me, by my side, in that confusion and pain I was feeling and I couldn't share with my sister.

For a brief moment, I pondered the way I was compartmentalizing every relationship. Anita, John, and Eléna—they all held a fragment of me, but not the entirety. Each could access a distinct piece, their own portion. My life was transforming into a jigsaw puzzle, with different individuals grasping different parts of the whole. I was, indeed, the living proof of the very mystery I was navigating, the mystery I could not solve still.

If there was something I had learned, it was that in the right place, with the right mood, I could almost summon my daydreams. *I have done it before, could I do it again?* I wanted to know more about the night I was brought under Grandma's protection; I wanted to see the details about the moment my great-grandfather had brought me to her, by the harbour, covered by the secret mist of the sea. So I asked Eléna again if we could meet Andrea the day after, and see the boats and yachts swinging peacefully under the sun.

'Oh yes. I forgot to tell you!' she jumped to reply. 'I have already asked and Andrea said we can all go tomorrow.'

'That's awesome!'

'Yeah, but remember what I told you? We will end up spending most of the day there, and you have only one day left before heading back home. Are you sure you want to do that?' she asked while we sat in a tiny, cute pizzeria. The smell of fresh pizza bread was enchanting, the music in the background was typical of the region. Everything made me feel like I was right in the middle of a postcard.

'Of course I'm sure. If you are happy to spend the day by the sea, I'm happy with it. After all, with this bloody heat…what else could we do?' I knew the trade was a bit unfair. Spending the whole day trapped in a boat, with the two of them…just to be able to see that harbour. *But it has to be done,* I thought.

'OK. Let's do it. Did you bring your swimmers?' She asked as she was already texting Andrea to confirm..

We spent another beautiful, relaxing night together. As usual, we never stopped talking. It didn't really matter how long we had been apart or how long we had been back together. Our talks were everlasting, no matter what. Topic after topic, pizzas left the spot to a shared dessert and the dessert to tons of cocktails. We moved from one place to the next a few times and by midnight we were already close to home. Just outside Eléna's apartment, by a big square, we sat on a bench beside a drinks kiosk.

The air had cooled down just a bit and a weak breeze turned our last drink even more refreshing. One by one, all the standing, noisy customers had finished their drinks and left. When the kiosk was about to close, we decided to head back home. There and then I was pretty sure the alcohol we had in our system wasn't much. After all, we walked straight, talking fine and our conversations made sense. Yet, the morning after, I had no recollection of anything that was said. I only remembered the happiness, the laughs and the pleasant breeze.

Chapter Seventeen
By The Sea I Came

∞

My final day in Italy arrived. As we planned, Eléna and I were going to meet Andrea at the harbour and get on a boat for the day and enjoy the scent of the sea. Although I wasn't completely happy on wasting the entire day trapped in the middle of nowhere, it was summertime and I was sure I would enjoy a day of swimming. After all, life in Ireland wasn't really that kind of life. I had to get the most of it while I could. The two of us had a quick breakfast in the house, made some panini for our lunch on the boat, got our bags organized and left around eleven.

'I got a text from Andrea last night, but I saw it only this morning,' Eléna said, while we walked down to the bus stop. 'He said two more people will join us. Oh, don't worry, it's a nice couple. He is sixty and she is fifty-something.'

'Andrea's colleagues?' I asked. I was actually happy to have more people around than just the two of them.

'Yes. The boat we are using today is actually theirs. I think when Andrea asked them if he could borrow it, they might have said they were going to join. He couldn't really say no, you know?' she said, waving at the bus to make it stop.

'Make sense. Well, at least with more people we won't risk being short on talk topics,' I said, smiling.

Eléna's home stood at the very top edge of the city centre, at the opposite side to the sea. Being the city placed right in the volcano's valley, the area look like a giant slide, with high hills at the top on one side, and the sea at the bottom on the other side. Moving from one point to another felt like slipping away, crashing down like a river to its delta or, if going the other way around, like climbing Everest's peak. To speed our way down, we decided to use the old, unbearable public transportation. Between the downhill run, the bus being in a very bad shape and the pure crazy driving style of every car around, I felt dizzy.

The heat in that vehicle of death was possibly ten times worse. I could feel the burning engine roaring fire in the inside but the people around me seemed to have no issues at all, like living an ordinary day in an ordinary city. Stripped of any excessive clothes, I wore only a pair of shorts and a white T-shirt. With my flip flops almost fusing with the floor, I could see my near future: a part of the roasting machinery. What felt like twenty years later, we arrived.

'Oh God thank you!' I exclaimed on our way out.

'You don't suffer from bus sickness, do you? You never did before,' Eléna asked, walking into a coffee shop just a few steps away from the bus stop.

'It's not the bus, it's the heat! Why do they not put air con in those buses?' I said, complaining.

'For a five-minute ride?' she said, paying at the till for two small bottles of water.

She handed me one of the two, and without hesitation I snapped it from her hands as if that was the antidote to a mortal poison. Few blocks later we arrived and stopped at two massive doors by a giant baroque building. A plate on the left side said: *Associazione Nautica Militare* (Military Navy Club). The structure enormous; its shadow enveloped the entire parking lot and some of the other buildings right in front of it. For a moment I hoped we could stay there all day. The cooler, darker atmosphere was nice to taste. Then, a tall man in uniform opened the doors. With a dark skin, dark green eyes and a square face, he was a pure representation of a southerner.

'Hey Eléna. You're not on your holiday yet?' Apparently they knew each other. I chose to disappear in the background and avoid any explanation as to why I was sweating the hell out of me.

'Well, Andrea hasn't closed the office yet…so I guess I have to keep going…' she replied, smiling. And we walked in.

'He is here, in the Comandante's office. Will I call him?' he asked, after we walked into the main big hall. The room was gigantic, with the ceiling so high I could barely see its corners.

'No, leave him. Just tell him we are here. I'll show my brother around. Oh, by the way, he is Daniel.' And she finally introduced me to Marco.

The big hall had another set of doors opposite to the main entrance. Wide open, they showed a glittering blue picture, its beauty coming right through. Over the doors, a long set of stairs descended directly to the sea, its end leading right into the big harbour. It was a magnificent place to be.

As I knew, Andrea was having one of his usual long conversations with some people in an office to the far right of the building, and Eléna and I waited for him just outside. After a few minutes, I thought to put time to a good use and go and explore the harbour on my own, while my sister waited for him.

With the simple excuse of wanting to give a quick look at the port by myself, as Andrea would want to go on the boat straight away, I left her there and went down the stairs.

The beauty of the landscape astonished me. Dozens of small and large boats floated on a big blue silky floor. Seagulls roamed around the tips of the sails, looking for a spot to stand on while singing loudly.

Some yachts looked impressively big while others barely held afloat, old and with a colour consumed by the scorching sun. The harbour looked like a giant's arms, trying to embrace the vastity of that beauty and everything with it.

To the far right, the land rose abruptly and steeply, and a portion of the imposing mountain came into view popping out the side of the building, with a cloudy hat bending on its side. The closer I got to the bottom of the steps, the bigger everything became, multiplying in numbers and sizes. At the end of the stairs, the port split in two, left and right.

To the left, it split again into loads of small docks. The way to the right led to a big round courtyard, where some large cabins stood quietly amidst a loud chattering of people coming and going. I couldn't picture where exactly the event in my dream had taken place but I knew I was in the right spot. My great-grandfather had been there many times and definitely he was there the night I had arrived.

Before deciding where to start from, I stopped for a few moments thinking on how I could trigger the vision I wanted to have. I had the tiny box with me, but I wasn't sure it would be enough. I needed more. If I were going to make it, a quiet place seemed the right place to be, while wandering in another world, another time.

So I chose left and walked down the docks looking for a lonely spot to sit. Whatever I was going to summon, I had the feeling it wouldn't quite like the bright of the day, the sounds and noises in the background. I couldn't find that moment to be mentally moving. I walked down several docks and eventually, towards the end, I found a spot behind the shade of a huge yacht.

With my feet hanging in the air, few inches away from the surface, I looked at the image of myself warping and deforming in the water. I knew I didn't have much time before Eléna and Andrea would start looking for me. My mind briefly went to Anita, Noah. *What would they say to help me make it happen?*

Suddenly I realized I had with me everything I needed to try right away. As my hands delved into the bag I carried, the small chest swiftly emerged into the open. It looked smaller than before, still old and consumed by time. The pink shell stared at me from the top of its cover and I imagined what hands had held it before mine, before Grandma's. *Who had it made? Who wrote that message lying silent inside?* I thought. I had the key ready in my hand, ready to reveal a secret only two people knew, me and 'Ma.

The soft click preceded a cracking sound made by the opening lid and the lock flipped upside down. My eyes gazed at the three items inside. I secretly hoped something else would magically happen this time. A real, big seashell rested in a corner and two pieces of paper lay just under its weight. One was much older than the other, part of its left side was badly damaged and some of the words written on it had faded away. As if I was performing a risky surgery, I gently moved the seashell away and I pulled the two pieces up, slowly taking them out. The fragility of those archaeological finds overshadowed my initial intent and, alone in my personal bubble, I kicked the world out, fully focused on my discovery.

The aged piece of paper bore a lengthy sentence, its vital secrets now faded, with sections obscured by time's passage, and both its beginning and end lost to the ages. It seemed as though this fragment was merely a remnant of a larger piece, its essence now irretrievably vanished.

There are things that have been and are no longer
Things that have never been are waiting to be

Those words were familiar. I had heard them before, in one of my daydreams. I could still recall the thrill and shock I felt the first time that sentence was said to me. Now it had come back in writing, proving that everything had always been connected, my childhood, Grandma, my madness. How much more was I yet to discover?

The other piece of paper was in a much better condition, although the sheet had gone yellow and the ink was turning grey. The handwriting was small, sharp. That was Great-Grandfather's letter.

Dear Rita,

Time has come for me to be back home. I should be docking at the harbour around midnight on the 29th, ten days from now. I won't be alone. God has rewarded me with a precious gift, a little boy I need to take with me. I won't be saying how important this is by letter. Make sure you and Victoria are going to be ready that night. There is much I have to tell you and much needs to be done. Please, it's vital you keep this to yourself. Victoria will need to hear this from me and me only. Looking forward to see you both.

Francesco

Well looks like Great-Grandad didn't say much, I thought. There wasn't anything new in that small letter. It didn't matter how many times I read it, the content would remain the same, unmeaningful compared to the magnitude of the secret he was carrying. I read it again, over and over, trying to pull more than that letter could actually give, but with very little result.

The seashell was the last piece to examine, so I put away the papers and took it in my hand. It was pretty big, in shades of ivory and brown, with lines marking the surface and a golden dot in the middle. The inside was whiter but empty. There was no secret in that item either. Whatever the mystery was and wherever it hid, the chest wasn't the key.

I sat in that spot for a few more minutes thinking why that object was so important, why I was supposed to have it. I knew about the first message and I heard Great-Grandad's words directly from 'Ma. The only piece left, the unknown element I didn't have yet, was the shell. I gave a closer look at that silent, inert artefact one more time and then I capitulated to the brutal truth. There wasn't any magic in there, in that place, in that box.

Determined to not waste the rest of the day, I went back and joined Eléna who had moved from one office's door to another. Apparently Andrea had managed to finish one conversation only to start another one. Her face was calm, she was smiling here and there to the people who were walking by. I couldn't understand how she could cope with that, with him spending hours in building relations with the sole intent of being venerated, moving her around like she was his to manoeuvre. I wanted to say something. I wanted to transfer my frustration about being stuck for the day to Andrea, blaming him for not having achieved any result. But I quickly realized that wasn't my call to make. I was disappointed with myself, by not being able to evoke my visions. Andrea was the same he had always been and it was me who had asked him to bring us there. I couldn't be mad because I was paying the consequences of it. Sitting by the chairs in a corner, beside my sister, I accepted the waiting.

Fifteen minutes later, the other couple arrived. At first sight they looked they had come out of a cartoon. He was as short as his wife, his dark hair had fallen off from the top of his head and his belly was compensating for the very skinny woman he had on his side. She was few inches away from being a bare skeleton, with dark skin and smashing pointy sunglasses. Her very bright curly red hair stunned my eyes, and her voice was so high-pitched that Daisy would run away. After looking at me with a funny smile, Eléna stood up and introduced me to the weird couple.

Although they were strange and at times very peculiar, by the end of that day I had grown to like them. The stories they told, the jokes they made…they were not that bad, after all.

So the day finally started when Andrea had done charming the world and we got onto the boat and left the harbour. The day was incredible. I had forgotten how much I needed the sun, the heat over my body, like I needed to remove any inch of rain, humidity and darkness from my bloodstream. We spent the day sailing, swimming, chatting, and laughing about pretty much anything our minds focused on.

The breeze of the speeding boat was like a balm to the scorching sun. Here and there we stopped at some beautiful spots to swim, refresh our bodies, drink some champagne. If that was my country once, I had surely forgotten why I had left. Later in the afternoon we left the boat to dock by a tiny village I had never seen before. The entire place had a yellowish-pink shade all over. It had the colour of a warm vast desert interrupted only by the splashes of green and blue of the many small, terraced houses scattered around like a cluster of mushrooms. Most of that place was closed down for the midday break. At night, it would magically come to life and hundreds of people would sit at the restaurants, bars or walk around with the local music playing in the background. Unfortunately we couldn't stay much longer. We had sailed south for three hours and the way back would take as much so, eventually, we went back to the boat and turned back home.

We arrived back at the harbour when the sun had already died behind the mountain. Small red lights resembling spilling lava at the top of the volcano were already visible from the sea. My skin had started to give back some of the heat like it was made from the very same fire. I was roasting, feeling happy but tired. We parted ways from the odd, funny couple right at the dock where we left the boat. As Andrea and Eléna went to give back some of the tools we had borrowed for the day, they asked me to wait at the top of the stairs. Wanting to see the other side of the harbour, I happily agreed.

The place looked nothing like it had few hours earlier. There was nobody around and the cabins were closed shut.

274

The big courtyard had long ropes piled up in round buckets, filled with the heavily spreading smell of the sea. Everything happened so quickly I can't really remember how I did it, but I clearly recall thinking what a perfect moment it was to induce a daydream. It didn't last long, but it was powerful.

In the blink of the eye, in between my steps, some people appeared out of nowhere, fading in slowly as they moved and talked. An old man with a grey beard talked to a group of people, moving his hands and whispering. It looked like he had something important to say. I moved close enough to see his face. It was Great-Grandad. He spoke to 'Ma, Victoria and three other people. That moment was so similar to the picture I had seen in Grandma's bedroom, I had the feeling it might have been taken then and there, that day. I moved like a ghost in between memories. I needed to see everyone's face, printing them in my memories. I wanted to be able to recall any detail of that event if I needed to. Victoria was so young I could barely recognize her. Her hair was long to her hips, straight and dark like I had never seen before. She was the only one not talking, for a while. That was an adult conversation and she didn't have the right to say much.

'I swore an oath, Rita. I can't take it back!' the old man said firmly.

'I don't even understand what this is all about. What did you bind yourself to? Is this like a gambling situation? Did you lose a bet and now you've been asked to do something crazy?' Grandma asked. What she had told me was true. She had fought that decision from the very first moment. I always thought she became suspicious and protective with

275

time, because of our family situation, but I could see she was already like that, before me.

'It had to be done. I had to go and rescue that child,' he said. The other three people, two men and a woman, stood there in silence, like they had nothing to say.

'You don't go and find a child just like that! Tell me the truth!' She forced him to come out in the light with no other options.

'Six months ago, on my expedition to Scotland, we had to make a rescue in the Atlantic Ocean, by the Irish west coast. A large boat had gone lost in the open and the strong winds had reduced it to bits. When we arrived, there wasn't much. Just a man with serious wounds, unconscious, lying as if he were dead. We docked in Galway and brought him to the hospital. I stayed there for two days, waiting for our cargo to go and come back from Scotland. I had told the captain I wanted to stay and make sure he would make it through the night and he allowed me to do so. Three days later he died in his sleep without ever regaining consciousness. The day I was supposed to embark again on my way to the ship, I met a very strange woman who told me my work there wasn't finished. Without a warning, I found myself in another place, a home, a very old Irish cottage in the middle of nowhere. Keeping me company, there she was, standing, looking at me and holding a small baby boy, sleeping in her arms.'

The story Francesco was telling, was fascinating, frightening but so familiar. Whatever he had experienced felt like the visions I'd had. I could have easily been him and lived the things he lived. The other three people in the group didn't speak at all. The only ones engaging in

276

conversation were him and Grandma. Victoria moved away a little bit and stopped listening to that story. For a while, I had the feeling my family wasn't acknowledging the presence of these 'strangers'. They were part of an invisible background against which the rest moved slowly. I tried to get closer while Great-Grandad continued:

'While I tried to figure out how I moved from one place to another, and after realizing what I was seeing was actually real, the woman spoke to me. She said the life I had spared from the sea, was a destiny fulfilled. That man who died was the child's carer, his protector. Now that he was gone, the only one allowed to do so, the one who would become the new Praetorian...was me.'

Every detail Great-Grandad added was a strike to my heart. My origins, my history, the answers to my questions moved further back. I had grasped the truth, the beginning of my journey for a tiny moment, to then seeing it slipping away again. It was right at the point when he called himself 'the protector' that something odd happened. Although the other three figures hadn't moved at all, their faces locked into the background of that vision, one of them suddenly turned his attention on me.

The tallest of the trio moved his gaze right on my spot, as if he could actually see me. A fast chill moved across my body, from my feet to my head. That wasn't possible. I was seeing through history, I was watching a scene that had been recorded in the space of time, unchanged; I could only recall it, resummon it from its ashes, but I could not change anything of it. Yet he looked right at me, trying to call my attention. A green sparkle briefly glow within his grey shadow. *What am I looking at? Is this a memory or something else?*

'So, I hope we are clear. That's the end of this conversation and we will never, *ever* speak of it again!' Great-Grandad had just concluded.

What did I miss? It was like I had skipped a big chunk of that conversation. They had already sealed its end, agreeing on what the future would look like, as they moved from their spot, leaving the premises. I had been distracted by somebody who wasn't even part of that conversation. *What was the meaning of all of that? Was it intentional?* The family made their way home, the challenge had been accepted, and the ownership of a long, traumatic debt had been moved from a name to another.

The other two men and the old woman faded away without moving, their path leading them somewhere else, sometime else perhaps. In the final glance of a closing curtain, a green shiny drop poured on the ground, in that same spot they had just left behind, lonely, mute.

My vision was over. I was left alone, in the dark of the coming night, and the emptiness looked at me whispering of a thousand questions. Eléna waved from the far end, at the bottom of the long stairs, telling me to hurry up. So I did, conscious I had somehow achieved what I wanted, with a last puzzling question in my head. *Where did I come from?*

Chapter Eighteen

The Way Home

∞

My last night with Eléna and Andrea went pleasantly well. Tired from the long trip and the many hours under the sun, the three of us decided to go to a place close to home and get something refreshing to drink on our walk back. Although I always had mixed feelings towards Andrea, that day and that night he was surprisingly laid back, humble. It wasn't all about him, his achievements, his double meaning questions, where I had to think twice in case he thought I was pretty much nothing compared to him.

He was open to a new perspective; his questions about my things, my life, were asked with genuine interest. For a while, I thought it was because he wanted to get back into Eléna's good graces, but she had already taken down her walls of resistance—as I knew she would—so I decided to do the same and give him a chance.

The following day was met with tears and sadness. Eléna started to cry since the moment we left the house to go to the airport. Eventually, after I took my bag out of the car, she asked me to get a quick coffee at the bar, on the ground floor. I knew she was dragging it out, and so was I when I said yes.

'It's your fault,' she started. 'You don't come home for only three days. Who does that? It's unfair...'

'It's actually four with today,' I said, joking.

'You know what I mean. We had time to do nothing!' she continued.

'I know, I know. But think that I wasn't supposed to be here anyway. Whatever time we got to spend together, it was a gift.'

'Speaking of which. Why did you come home then? You never told me.'

'I know it sounds odd, but I thought...with Grandma's condition...I had this weird feeling.'

'As if she could be gone anytime?' And I nodded yes without saying anything else. I had to keep it as vague as I could. 'When are you coming back?'

'When are *you* coming to visit?' I said, right back at her.

'You know what the situation is like. With Andrea and everything,' she replied turning her face from me.

'He doesn't own you, you know that, right? You do have your own mind and will.' I finally said it, at the end of that trip, hoping that she wouldn't have the time to reply something silly or that we wouldn't get into a fight over my cheeky comment.

'I know, I know.' She chose the easy way out, admitting it and moving on. In that specific topic, she had outsmarted me. 'Well this visit was too short. I'm expecting to see my brother again, soon!'

My brother...these words meant the world to me. She wasn't family by blood but indeed she was family to me. She was my second chance after the first horrible disaster. *Now she's what? The third?*, I thought. *If my family wasn't the one I knew, if I came from somewhere else, what would our relationship be? A destiny's second backup plan?*

'What's wrong?' she asked, noticing I had lost myself in a narrow lane of thoughts.

'Nothing. I was just thinking that...I agree with you.' I replied, trying to pull myself together.

We eventually parted ways at the boarding check. Before I could go in, she gave me the strongest hug she was capable of. It was like I was leaving for the war and she feared she wouldn't see me again. And to that feeling, a form of premonition infiltrated my heart, making it sink.

Soon enough, I had travelled for miles and landed back home. John had texted me saying he was going to pick me up at the airport, so right at the exit, I started to look around trying to spot him, in between tons of people hugging and greeting. An initial, disturbing surprise greeted me, or at least trying to. At the far end of the arrival pod, I saw someone who clearly resembled Noah. My head started to spin. *Why is he here? We never agreed to meet again once I was back in the country. Does he not understand I have to juggle a difficult situation with John already?*

I continued to move forward, looking at the same spot and, at each step, the chance I could actually be wrong grew smaller and smaller. Then, when we were only a few feet away, and Noah started to smile at me, the only man I truly waited for suddenly hugged me. John had come in from the right side, straight at me from my back, and his hug squeezed my body like my sister had done a few hours before. For a few seconds my eyes remained locked to Noah's. My mind was already moving towards John but my body lagged behind. Finally I turned to him, smiled and gave him a kiss.

'Oh, it feels like you have been away since forever!' he said.

'Well, tell that to Sis. She said exactly the opposite.' And I kissed him again, like the first kiss wasn't quite right, pure...still affected by Noah's presence.

'Let's go, you can tell me everything in the car...oh, let's hurry up. I left Daisy in there and she is dying to see you!' And John took my bag and started to walk back, with his hand glued to mine.

I was rescued from the danger behind me, but a final look was due. Noah stood there where I saw him last, his smile was gone, his eyes had gone dark and I felt the vivid hazard I had just risked, right in my bones.

Daisy's welcome was of a completely new level. She started to go mad even before John opened the passenger door. After that, was jump after jump, her tail going like she could even fly with it, and she never left my side until we got home, gates closed, door shut. I was home, I was never going to escape again. Bags on the floor, my shoes left behind, I had left that house being Daniel and come back being no one. The space around me was exactly as I had left it. I had changed but the world hadn't. *Who knows if some other events have happened, while I was away,* I kept thinking while I moved around, making physical contact with what I knew it was mine, my world.

'Everything alright, here in the house?' I finally asked.

'What do you mean?' John replied. *Obviously why would his mind go right to the freaky stuff,* I thought.

'You know, any suspicious movement, the front door being possessed, the usual.' I tried to sound funny.

'Nothing. It was as boring as you could imagine. Me and Daisy alone. Oh, speaking of which... Keep the spare bedroom door shut. Daisy has picked up the habit of nesting in the wardrobe.'

'What? Since when?' I asked. It didn't come to mind at first. The cloak was hidden in there.

'Right after you left. I think she was sad, looking for you or something. Some of your clothes might still have your scent, you know? I had to take her out of that wardrobe three times!'

'That's odd,' I replied, but I'd just realized the hidden gift was lying in there. 'Did you check if she damaged anything?'

'It looked alright to me. I'll get a look at it tonight,' John replied.

'It's fine. I'll do it. I have to unpack my stuff anyway.' And I kissed him to close the topic and move on.

John had to leave the house in the afternoon for an art job he was commissioned for from an old man living in the small village next to ours. As agreed, we would have a romantic dinner later, but nothing too complicated, a takeaway as we liked. So I brought my bags upstairs, got in the shower, changed and got ready to leave the house again for a quick trip to meet Anita. As I was about to walk down the stairs, my eyes went to the spare bedroom. The door was shut as John had left it. His story bounced back and forth in my head. Without hesitation, I decided to take a look in the wardrobe and make sure the cloak was still there. After all, I had witnessed so many weird things that anything seemed possible. With my surprise, it was. Dead, flat at the bottom of my stuff, Daisy's shape still imprinted on a blue jumper at the top of the pile. Nothing was touched. Everything was there as I had left it.

I walked out the room making sure the door was closed behind me, gave a quick rub to that beautiful creature who had obviously missed me, and went out the house. Anita had a full busy day in work but she had texted me saying she would happily go on a lunch break with me if I was up to it. I knew she wanted to know what had happened in every detail. I hadn't said much in the past few days and she was dying to ask all the questions.

We met in a very small bistro just opposite the newspaper office. The time was perfect, no other customers were in, except for a young girl, probably a student, sitting at the back. We took the seats at the window, ordered

284

coffees and a couple of sandwiches. When we were sure no one was close enough to listen, we jumped right in.

'Right, tell me everything. I have hundreds of questions,' she said, all in one breath.

'Wait. Questions for later.' I replied immediately, noticing she was just about to fire away. 'I have to tell you something that happened this morning, after I landed.

'OK. And then we go backwards! I like when a story is told backwards...' she said, smiling.

'No, no. This thing is different...ish...' I replied, sipping some coffee before letting it out. 'Noah was at the airport this morning.'

Time froze at once. She didn't move, her eyes fixed on me. I waited for her reaction, sitting still. Then she started to trip over her own words.

'Wha...wait... What? No, you mean...what the hell is he thinking?' she scrambled.

'I don't know. He was right there!'

'Are you sure it was him?' she asked, pausing.

'Of course you had to ask... I'm sure it was him! I saw him with my own eyes. He was standing there, few feet away,' I replied, knowing she would have questioned my sight if necessary, to remove the possibility that I'd imagined it.

'I can't believe it... I told him John would go to the airport and pick you up...like a normal person would expect, right?' she said.

'What do you mean? Did you talk to him?' I felt as if I had skipped a few episodes of that new relationship.

'We...texted. While you were away...a few texts, nothing crazy, before you go start making a drama out of it,' she said, moving her hands forward.

'What did you text about?' I felt entitled to know.

'Nothing weird. He said he hoped everything was OK with you...that he wanted to call you, text you. I told him to give you some space. Then he asked me if I was going to pick you up...and I said John was. That's all!' And she started her sandwich like there wasn't much else to add.

'OK. Sorry for being pushy. Seeing him there...it freaked me out.'

'You bet!' she chewed out. 'Now, tell me everything.'

The twenty minutes we had felt too short for us to be able to squeeze everything in. I left some parts out, things I could tell her later on, but the essentials were all there, with a few minutes spare to get her thoughts, her reactions. Anita listened carefully, making a few comments here and there or, sometimes, just talking to herself as if thinking out loud.

'Alright, listen,' she said, standing. Our time was up, she was meant to get back to work, so she hurried up her final words. 'I have to go, but there is more, isn't there?'

'A bit, yes,' I replied, putting on my jacket.

'OK. You go and have a nice time with John. We can meet again tomorrow. And please, enjoy it! God knows at least one of us deserves some love...'

'What's that supposed to mean?' I asked, following her outside. 'Is everything OK between you and Patrick?'

'Oh, Patrick... Don't let me get started...' And we crossed the road and reached the front door of the newspaper building.

For a brief moment I felt like the world had moved on, without me. I had been away only a few days but, since I was back, people were acting funny. Noah showing up at the airport, Anita being elusive. I quickly dismissed my thoughts. I was being 'dramatic', like she had just said.

'Anita, hold on,' I said, pulling her arm. 'Is everything OK? I mean, did I miss something important while I was away?'

'Yes, yes, everything is OK, I mean. You didn't miss much. I really have to go, but I'd like to get together tomorrow? I'll tell you more then.'

'OK. I'm back to work tomorrow. We meet at six?'

'Works!' And she walked in with a brief smile on her face.

Something had happened indeed. I knew it was about Patrick but I also knew I could never force Anita's opening window. That wasn't the right time to open up and probably wouldn't be tomorrow either. It was funny to think we were in Noah's Bridge only a few weeks earlier and we had managed to talk about ourselves so smoothly...so defencelessly.

Will she be like that again? I thought while I got back in my car.

The night came fast; by the time John came home, I had already washed all the clothes I had with me in Italy, changed Daisy's bed and cleaned the house. Although John had kept it in an impeccable status, I had the urge of cleaning everything, bottom to top. Whatever I was doing to the house, I was doing it to my brain. The washing, the dusting...it was all me trying to make a sense of my thoughts, my doubts.

Just a few minutes before John showed up and right after I had finished emptying the dishwasher, I went to smoke a cigarette, trying to cool down the last bit of stubborn turmoil. With my phone in hand, I texted Anita about meeting her the next day and while I waited for her answer, Noah's face popped up in my mind. He was there. I was pretty sure of it. I could easily recall the visual memory of that morning, right in front of me. I wasn't wrong. He was there for a reason. I wanted to know that reason.

'Please tell me it wasn't...' delete, delete. *I shouldn't start so aggressive*, I thought.

Daniel

Were you at the airport, this morning?

A few minutes later, still no answer came. John's car appeared at the gates as I was about to walk back in. Daisy started to push in between my legs to go out and greet him, so I picked her up and waited there, sharing her same joy on seeing him.

288

That night was a great night. John and I ordered our favourite takeaway, talked about pretty much everything we thought of and watched a movie we both loved. We snuggled together on the couch sharing some popcorn, his head on my side, right on my heart, where he belonged, my arm on his shoulder; I could feel him breathing at my same pace. The life we had was summed up just right there and in the immediate thereafter, when our bodies turned up the fire inside, transformed in passion in the space of a few movements.

Our hands were everywhere that mattered, frenetically increasing the speed, succumbing to the pure pursuit of desire. We ended up upstairs, on our spacious bed, as we had done many times before, proving we still had the emotional and physical spark pulsing inside. His warm body and the scent of his skin was leading me where my lips yearned to go-fast, slow and fast again. His hair brushed against my chest and my stomach, sending me into a frenzy as if I were hurtling at the speed of light toward the centre of the universe. I was his and he was mine as nothing else had happened between us. We had drifted apart and come back together, drawn by the fiery desire of our flesh, our eyes and our hearts.

Falling asleep with that certainty in my head was the best way to close a very long day, a day closing its shutter for the night, with me knowing I was back home, where I belonged.

The morning after, I was up pretty early. I left John in bed, his body conquering the entire surface, arms wide open. I gave him a quick glance before heading out for the day and everything felt safe, sweet. I carried my phone all

289

morning, on my way to work at the coffee shop, in the office, but for some reason I wasn't paying attention to it. During lunchtime, Harry and I talked about my trip to Italy. To make my story a little more visual, I decided to show him a few pictures I had taken on the boat. Just as I took my phone out of my pocket, a message popped up on the screensaver. It was Noah.

Noah

When can we talk?'

Daniel

Were you?
At the airport, yesterday morning?

I replied to his text almost automatically. I didn't want to talk. I wanted to know why he was there and I wanted him to answer honestly. The situation wasn't starting off well, so I pulled up the stronger version of me—the me that doesn't tolerate diversions—silencing that part of me that gives only one second chance. I had known Noah long enough to realize he was able to elicit the most conflicting emotions in me.

For some reasons I was attracted to him, almost unable to resist his gravitational pull, but I also felt hurt, nearly physically in pain when I was near him. The divide in my mind had grown wider since I had seen him there, waiting for me, without a warning, ready to destroy my life. Yes, I wanted to know why he was there, and that was the only thing I would listen to.

I quickly went back to Harry who had already moved on to a different topic. In the space of the few seconds I spent replying to Noah's text, he had started to talk about a girl he had met. *No, wait…he didn't meet her…oh, I get it now, he wants to meet her but he hasn't, so he is fabricating the most improbable future right in front of me…* I thought, while Harry did his usual thing of making up stories that had no foundation. Harry had always done that. In his stories, he was the hero destined to be, the man every woman—who he was interested in—desperately needed. Half selfish and half naïve, his approach was in part funny and in part grotesque. *Why does he need to hide himself behind these fantasies? There is much more beauty in him if he only would allow it through.* Having used already the *uncompromising version of me* with Noah, I let Harry free to fly with his fantasies, enjoying the absurd ride. This time Noah's reply came fast.

Noah

It's complicated. Can we talk?
It might be easier to explain…

Daniel

It's actually not…complicated
Were you?

Noah

Yes I was. I needed to talk to you.
It was important, it still is.'

Daniel

What are you trying to do?
John was there. Are you trying to make me
break up with him?

No answer came after that. In the quick back and forth, I had completely zoned out. I could still hear Harry's voice in the background but I had no idea what he was saying. All I could feel was fear and anger directed at Noah...and at myself. I had brought this on myself and I struggled to keep things apart, reality from fantasies. I was Harry but worse. I had believed in my fantasies and I had tainted my reality. How could I have prevented it from persisting? How could I have stopped Noah?

Most of the day flew by. Busy trying to get back to the work I had left behind, I didn't noticed it was time to leave until well past the time I normally did. Back in my car, I went home, fed Daisy, got some stuff I wanted to show Anita and quickly got on my way to her place. At the turn of the estate, a few feet away from the promenade, a surprise waited for me. Noah's figure cut the sea in the background in two, hands in his pocket, face with no expression; he could have been easily a statue, an ornament for the people to see on their walks. With no attempt to get closer, he just stood there, waiting for me to get out, like it was my turn to please him, to obey.

292

Chapter Nineteen

A Stronger Will

∞

We spent a minute or so just staring at each other. I got out of my car, my backpack on my right shoulder and my phone in my hand. He didn't moved an inch and I was firmly planted on my spot. My strong will there to protect me, I wasn't going to let go. His beauty was as strong as my disappointment. Both were still there with all their power to condition my mind, to break me in two, to defeat me.

His clothes were simple, weak against the scenery behind him; Noah was surrounded by an infinite blue that pushed forward its pure demand for attention. Yet, he still won over the landscape. He was irresistible to the point it was irritating, nearly annoying. The early rain was about to come back. The road, the sand and the entire place was still wet. That summer evening was warm but ready to turn its course. Before it was too late, I started.

'You couldn't just wait...could you?' I asked from a safe distance.

He didn't pick up the hint. I was ready for a fight and he wouldn't attack. *Maybe that's what he is. A coward who would make his move from behind, when I'm most vulnerable? When my defences are low?*

'Why are you here? Why are you so pushy?' I continued.

'What did you do?' he finally replied with a serious look on this face.

'You know well what I did. I was gone for only few days and you couldn't wait to come forward and make me risk what I care about the most?' My voice got louder.

'What did you do?' he repeated. I was confused. *What part of my last few sentences did he not understand?'*

'You know what I did. And you know you should have waited for me to call you. But you couldn't do that, right? You simply can't just wait.' And that was the entire problem, right there, in the open.

I had been asking Noah to wait since the day we met. I felt guilty for pushing him back several times, but I was also sure that was the safest approach, the only way we would get our answers without compromising our lives. Noah was constantly in a rush. Being at a completely different stage of discovering, he was miles ahead and he was ready to act. Ready to act at my expense, at any cost.

'What did you do, Daniel?' he asked again. What else was there? Was he asking about something other than my trip to Italy? Finally surrendering to my obduracy, he left his spot to come closer.

'What do you mean?' I asked, lowering my voice. It was like he had just defused the tension by taking the first step.

'You look different.' And his eyes zipped around as if my entire body had suddenly changed.

'I'm...I'm the same. What are you talking about?' His proximity turned my stomach like a wave; he was like the moon changing my tides and I could feel it.

'There is an aura around you...like...a copy of you just behind your body...but bigger...' And his hands moved in my direction, as if he was about to touch my shoulders.

'Please don't!' I said, promptly raising my hands. 'I'm the same. It's me. There is no aura, please stop this magic nonsense.'

'No you're not. Something has changed,' he said, slowly moving back.

I looked at him, trying to make sense of everything. It wasn't only the scary moment at the airport that pushed me away. It was the whole connection between Noah and the unknown, Noah and the danger I felt so strongly taking over my mind. He was again tearing down my certainties by questioning who I was. Feeling the pressure of taking myself out of that situation, I turned around, towards Anita's home. I was there to meet her, nothing else and no one else. As a second surprise in the space of a few minutes, there she was, walking out of her house, moving closer. She had seen us from the window but I wasn't quite sure how much she had actually seen. *Did she hear me shouting at Noah?*

295

'What's going on?' she asked directly. Her folded arms sent a pretty clear message. She had picked up the vibe and, judging from the look she had given Noah, she was standing by my side, no doubts.

'Hi, Anita. I'm here because that's the only place I know. Two days after I went back home, something happened. I knew I had to come back and meet Daniel as soon as possible. I had only two options: come here—as this is the only place I know I could find you—or meet you at the airport yesterday morning.'

Noah's face was the finishing touch of a convincing excuse. *He knew only Anita's place because I brought him there. He didn't know where I live, where I work. What else could he have done? Text me...*

'Why did you not text me?' I asked.

'Because you would have told me to wait...like you always do,' he replied, sounding annoyed and hurt.

'Noah, there is a reason why I tell you to wait. It's not like I enjoy pushing you back.'

'And there is a reason why we can't wait. I don't enjoy pushing you either!' he replied, nearly mocking me.

'Boys...let's just chill, alright?' Anita interrupted. 'You both have your reasons. Let's clarify what's going on and decide who does what and when next time...sounds fair?'

After a brief moment of hesitation, Noah and I raised the white flag. We were entering into a temporary truce stage under Anita's supervision. Eventually, the three of us moved to Anita's place. As the weather still held, we sat in the back garden drinking some weird tea Anita had in her collection. Despite the fact we had all agreed on talking to clarify, silence was the most welcomed guest. We sat quietly, sipping away, the tablecloth with its pattern of white and blue flowers moving gently with the warm roaming breeze.

'Is Patrick working?' I asked. I felt that was the only safe question I could ask.

'Patrick has moved out. He went back to his parents,' she coldly replied, like that was yesterday's news.

'What? When?' I quickly realized she had given me the hint the day before…that was her way of letting me in.

'Few days ago. Nothing important to discuss right now…we have better business to discuss here…' And she adjusted her seat, raised up her shoulders and moved forward like she was waiting for me to tell her what this important business was.

There was no talking about Patrick and it wasn't because Noah was there. It was because she was hurt and she wasn't ready to revisit her pain with me. I was looking at her, trying to unlock whatever door she had put up in front of me, but she wasn't giving up. Her small smile was asking me to *'move on, not now please…'* The only thing left to do was to take over the conversation and let her be free to decide.

'Noah,' I said. 'Why don't you start? What is this important reason why you couldn't just wait?' I might have called a truce but I wasn't hiding my feelings.

'I know what you are thinking. I'm just pushing you to the limits for my own selfish desire. Well, you're wrong,' he replied. His expression changed, his will was getting stronger. 'I had a vision…of you. You held a shell in your hands.'

That very moment he captured my full attention. He knew about the shell…what else had he seen? Could he access a secret passage to my life, to my emotions?

'Four other people were in the room with us,' he continued. 'An old lady sitting in a chair and three others that I couldn't really see. I know I'm just assuming here, but I'm pretty sure those three people were the ones I met before. Then, one of them looked at me, like he could see me…he could feel my presence…and so he spoke to me. He said: *"There is another one.. with a crowned heart. Two become one. Next it's the one. Time is running thin, to a time when there won't be time at all."* I knew that was different, Daniel. We're somewhere we've never been before. We have to let it happen.'

Noah's entire story was a shock after shock through my heart. He wasn't only seeing through me, my life. He was also listening to what I was listening to. *Those words.. Those were the words my grandma had said before going back to the emptiness of her lost memories…* I couldn't believe it and I couldn't fight it back. Noah had complete access to whatever I was holding on to. If he were there to destroy my life, I wouldn't have been able to stop him. He was there to conquer and I was there to be taken.

'How would you do that?' I heard Anita's question, but her words sounded as if she had talked wrapped in a bubble. My thoughts were overtaking the ongoing conversation.

'We have to go to the other side. Like we have done before,' Noah replied.

'And still, how do we do that?' Anita asked again. She stood up, moved close to me and put a hand on my shoulder in an attempt to bring me back. After I smiled, she went and topped up my tea.

'I don't know. We try whatever we can?' Noah replied.

'What else is there we haven't tried?' Anita asked, sceptical, leaving an uncomfortable silence afterwards.

'There is something new…' I started. 'Grandma had this with her and she gave it to me when I went to visit.' And I pulled out the small chest from my backpack.

'What is this?' Noah asked.

'This is something connected to me, to my past. There are three things inside, one wasn't there originally, I think. It's a letter written by my great-grandfather. The other two…well I don't know.'

My revelation had brought new energy into a tired, restless group of people searching for the truth. Both Noah and Anita moved closer to get a vivid look at everything I was showing them. Thoughts and ideas were shared, conjectures were made. The entire new story about my past fuelled more speculations. The three of us put aside the horrible atmosphere we had begun with and started to resemble the trio we had been only a week before, by the beach. The sky above us had turned darker from the upcoming evening, pushed further by the bad weather approaching. The wind had picked up a bit and the tablecloth had started to flap, spilling around some of the falling raindrops.

'We should move inside, boys,' Anita said, standing up.

Noah and I left our chairs behind and moved like a double shadow attached to Anita's body. He quickly collected all the teacups that needed to be rescued and I carried my precious gift with me.

As we were about to walk in, a sudden and intense shock struck me, paralysing my entire body. The sound of the falling box was accompanied by the crash of the old porcelains touching the hard floor by the patio doors. Noah went on his knees, crushed, frozen. Anita had just turned around in time to see me falling down too. In an attempt to come and check what had just happened to us, she came closer, her hands reaching towards both of us, undecided who needed it the most.

With my face looking right at the wet grass, I gazed at the box lying defenceless, the lid wide open and the shell upside down. Then it happened. The ground wobbled for a brief moment, turning its colours, shape and form. The bright green grass left its space to a dark brown pattern and the place around us changed in the blink of the eye. Still holding her position, Anita kept her hands on both of us, her gaze fixed over our shoulders. As everything we knew melted away before our eyes, we stood frozen, held prisoner of our own shock, astonished by what was becoming all around us.

'What is this?' Anita said with a broken voice.

'Isn't this happening only in my head?' I asked in reply.

'Where are we?' The spell on Noah's body had vanished and he was finally free to move.

Every single piece of reality had changed. We weren't in Anita's back garden any more. We were not in a blurry vision either. Around us, a real place took shape, with final details being added right as we got back on our feet.

Chapter Twenty
Runae

∞

The three of us stood on a rounded piece of land, small enough for us to see its full circle, but large like an atoll surrounded by water. We were the only inhabitants of that silent world. There was no one else and nothing else. The quiet horizon stretched as far as our sight, with no sounds of life, no sounds of anything; our voices were lost into nothing. At our back, at the edge of that small island, a couple of large, red rocks were stared at us, muted. A long, dead tree spread its contorted branches in the air, bringing the worrying omen of a dangerous vision.

The giant sea had no beginning and no end, its surface flat, unnaturally still. With no motion or waves its colour looked grey like the sky it was reflecting. In the far beyond, a cloudy fog floated in between above and below like no third dimension actually existed, and within, tiny sparks flickered all around.

'I don't think we are still in Castlecross,' Anita whispered.

'Do you think we did actually move? Or is this just a vision?' Noah added, moving backwards towards me, his shoulder close to mine.

'Does it make any difference? I wouldn't be able to tell anyway,' I replied, as I reached for Anita's hand. Something told me we had to stay close together.

Our voices sounded sharp and deep. There was no echo, no space to absorb it. They would just remain there, beside us, like a fourth guest who doesn't know where to go. We took a few steps, just as much as we felt it was safe, but we moved like a pack, glued one to another, our faces looking in three different directions. There was nothing to look at, no hint to where we were, no form or shape to catch our eyes. Then, something in the fog changed. The electric sparks started to increase in size and number. From the very left, it advanced fast, as if it had a direction, a will…and it was getting closer.

'What's that?' Anita asked.

'Looks like a storm?' I replied.

'I hope not. There's nowhere to get cover here.' She was right. There wasn't anywhere to go.

Before we could think of anything to do, the fog and its storm reached ashore, shaking the sea's surface, splitting it in two, as if doors suddenly opened into something, in large narrow waves. We lined up, ready to welcome our fear; none of us felt safe, none of us could escape. The same water, dead up until then, was came to life, surging from below, forming a liquid, transparent shape.

Arms and legs appeared first, then shoulders, hands and, at last, a head. The crystal body started to pull colours from the ground, as if it was filling itself with the soil of that same land we stood on. As we watched, petrified, the final details appeared. Long, dark hair folded into intricate forms, wrapped by stems and leaves; red lips and blue eyes turned the water into a human being, and the sand covered parts of the shiny skin.

'Teny phara fle fö ish,' it said.

We could not believe our eyes and ears. *What did it just say?*

'Humans perhaps?' And she said again, 'There is two too many.'

That thing had just formed from pure water and it talked our language. *There is two too many? This doesn't sound good at all,* I thought.

'Anyway, welcome to Runae. I have been waiting for you since the end of Time, since the mirrors spoke of your arrival.' And the creature nodded its head to greet us. The sudden fear lost its grip on our hearts. It was welcoming us. The immediate danger was gone.

'What is this place?' I asked. It had just called it Runae, but that name meant nothing to us. We still had no idea on where we had been teleported to.

'This is the conjunction node. The ground you stand on is the only way in and out of Runae,' the creature replied. Its body had become completely human, its skin was no different than ours. Whatever magic witnessed, it was stunning.

'Who are you?' Noah asked.

'I'm Aura, the gatekeeper. Unfortunately this place is not safe. Nowhere really is. We can't stay here too long. I need to get you to the other side.' As she spoke, she moved closer, her feet still in the water, but her outstretched arms extended a dangerous invitation.

'Daniel...' Anita whispered. 'We know nothing about this...gatekeeper...this place. I think we should go home.'

'You can't,' Aura replied. 'You need Time, without, you won't succeed. Now, please, take my hands. We need to go!'

With not much of a surprise to me, Noah had already moved forward. He was determined to know, determined to get in contact with the truth, whatever that was. On the other hand, Anita started to walk backwards. She was the wisest in our group and I could see my same fear growing in her eyes. I couldn't go further without her and I couldn't go back home without him. Once again, I had a choice to make and, being worried sick, I could only hold on to the middle ground.

'Noah, hold on! I'm not sure we should do this,' I said, grabbing his arm before he could get out of reach.

'This is just a dream, Daniel. What are your worried about? I'm done waiting... I need to know, with or without you!' His expression didn't allow for any argument. I could not persuade him to wait any longer.

Right as I was about to let him go, my hand ready to detached from his, the words I'd heard so many times and had become so familiar, repeated in my head: *'Things are waiting to be'. Am I letting go my future as well? Am I losing Noah, the truth about my past, all at once? Am I cowardly leaving a fight that I am meant to lead? I have been in the wrong side of history too long. I have been living a lie, protected by Grandma, waiting for this moment to happen.*

So I gave a final look at Anita who stood behind me, her face telling me to run away. I could feel tears flowing down my cheeks as my hand strengthened its grip, as I realized I had to follow him. And then, we both did it. Our fingertips touched the soft, immaterial hand of that creature who, in the weakness of our souls, had laid the road to the pitfall of our hearts.

Noah lifted ahead while I briefly resisted the attraction, my eyes holding to Anita's whose fear spoke loudly. In the flickering of our last moment, our bodies imploded into nothing. In the snap of a short breath, I felt Anita's arms around mine, holding me tight.

The sky dove into the depth of our minds, the sea reached the highest peaks of our fears as we plunged down, like tiny bullets cutting through the water. Everywhere around was blue and black and all the shades in between. Reborn as dolphins, we crossed the sea without breathing, without slowing down, the three of us clinging to the trail Aura left behind, virtually attached to it, led by its charted course. There was nothing to see. The dark of the far seabed and the speed of our crossing made

306

impossible to distinguish anything else but ourselves swishing fast, one beside the other until, a few minutes later, the journey finally ended and we were back out in the open.

We got out to a previously invisible other side, beyond the fog now lurking at our back. We had crossed an invisible wall by diving through the dark of the waters and were soaking wet, at the edge of a new land we were destined to cross. Aura stopped just at the edge of the shore, her body needing the same water we had just learned to explore. She waited for us to put ourselves together, then eventually said:

'That's as far as I can lead you, I'm afraid. As gatekeeper I have to stay close to the node.'

'You mean you can't leave? Ever?' I asked. I had the feeling she was somehow physically attached to that world, like her life depended on it.

'I'm afraid you are right,' she replied. 'But not just because I'm the gatekeeper, but because I am an Aqualymph. Our kind is bound to the same water we were born into. I can come to the surface, from time to time, but just for a little while.'

'Does that mean we are on our own now?' Noah asked, moving closer to Aura. He believed that creature would lead him to the beyond he was craving, but he had to come to terms that wasn't the end of the journey, that was just a pit stop.

'I'd say you are,' she said. 'I wish I could come with you but, if I leave, I will break the ties with my own nature, my soul. I'd survive, my body would survive, but I'd be corrupting my spirit to the point I'd transform into something terrible. I could try and lead you further up, through the Gochi river, but I must stay here. Someone else might follow you. Someone who should not be crossing these lands.'

I listened to her voice, looking her face, her body. Everything felt real, it felt like it was happening outside my pure imagination. I dripped real water; my fingers were wrinkled and I could feel the humidity and the heat coming from the ground. Anita and Noah were in my same world; we were all experiencing that incredible reality.

Aura continued: 'And this brings me to something important I have to tell you. There is not much time, I'm not the only one who knows someone has just passed the gates. The Crimson Queen is holding this world in her grip. My fellow Aqualymphs have left this place long time ago, turned into pure madness and evil by lies and deceptions, and they have now become her servants. Please be careful who you get in contact with and whom you put your trust in.'

'How do we get back home?' Anita interrupted. She had reasonably only one goal in mind. She wanted to go back, right away. It wasn't only the weirdness of what we were experiencing but also the fact she hadn't planned it. She wasn't ready, we weren't ready. Would we ever be?

'You need to get to Time first. I really must go now.' And Aura scanned the area behind herself, her eyes closed into thin lines, gazing towards a coming danger.

'What do we do now?' I asked to the group.

'You cross that land behind you. At the seven hills, get to the stone road, through the silent forest. Don't stop till you reach the Chomps' Village. If you are in luck, the old Key master will tell you everything you need to know. Feralaih Tu!' And Aura turned around, her body losing its shape rapidly, turning back into water.

The far-off sea surface started to shake, white splashes riding fast towards us. Aura's last word was 'Run!' and then the water she was made of turned into a giant crystal wall, ready to stand in between us and whatever was coming our way.

We had no time to think. After a few seconds, we sprinted to the top of the shore, away from the sea, the image of a crashing wave echoing in our minds. Something had breached Aura's defence, scattering it into thousands of droplets that shimmered against the enormous red sun beating down on our heads. We had to run, and we had to run fast.

Panting heavily, we reached the far top of a small hill. The distant sea had turned into a tiny blue line lost on the horizon; we believed we had run far enough to feel safe. Taking a moment to rest, Anita knelt on the soft ground, her hands on her chest, struggling to compose herself. After making sure nothing was behind us, I collapsed onto the wild grass, gasping for air as fast as I could.

I stared at the strange sky, knowing it wasn't our familiar blue ceiling or our sun. The sky was a vibrant purple, fading into green at the horizon. The enormous star overhead appeared three times larger, its reddish hue pulsing strongly as if it were alive. Noah struggled to move forward, his willpower overriding his body's limitations.

309

Though he couldn't breathe, he continued to walk, steadily closing the distance to his target and putting some distance between us.

'Please...tell me this isn't happening...tell me we are going to wake up in few moments, in my house,' Anita said, panting heavily.

'I don't know, Anita...this is...something else. I never felt this way before. I truly think we are not home any more.' And I gazed at her, gesturing for her to look up, to see for herself how different everything was.

'He doesn't seem concerned?' she asked, watching Noah walking in the far distance. He staggered as if he were about to collapse on the ground.

'Noah is pushing...I'm pulling...and I think this is getting risky.'

'What do you mean?' she asked, getting close and helping me to get back up.

'He wants to move forward, I want to wait. I'm afraid we have to choose, or we'll be stuck in the middle. And this middle doesn't look any good,' I said, pointing at the space around us.

'What lies ahead doesn't look any better,' she said and we started walking again, trying to catch up with Noah who had stopped by a tree, at the very beginning of a greenwood.

We descended the other side of the hill quickly. The sea was no longer visible, erroneously encouraging us to think the threat was gone as too. At the bottom, a large forest stretched to the left, with hundreds of trees clustered together, forming a dense mass of shadows on the ground. As we got closer, the strong scent of vegetation filled our noses. Noah stood still at the entrance of that enchanted world, taking a brief rest before resuming his journey.

'Shall we rest here for a few minutes?' Anita asked immediately. A clear disagreement appeared on Noah's face. Still, worn out from the long run, he refrained from replying, visibly challenged.

'We need to stick together,' I added, before he could voice his objections. 'Let's follow Aura's advice. Running without knowing where we're going or what we're running from could land us in big trouble. Let's take a rest, stay vigilant for any danger, and then continue. What do you think?' And Noah nodded in agreement, lowering himself to the ground, his shoulders resting against the tree, his eyes shut.

'I can't believe it...' Anita let out, a few minutes after we had settled by the same tree. It looked as if we were holding it up, like three table legs.

'This is definitely the most vivid vision I've ever had. Remember the one on our way to Noah's Bridge? The pub? This feels way more real, doesn't it?' I asked, my eyes still fixed on the path behind us.

'Oh God, yes... More real and somehow more pleasant! And now it just reminded me I need to pee... And this time I'm not going to risk it...God... What is this place?'

'This is where we were supposed to be,' Noah said. For a moment, I thought he had fallen asleep.

'Were we?' Anita turned around, looking at Noah. 'I'm pretty sure that thing... She... Was it a she? Anyway, she said we were two too many.'

'You think this was meant to happen only to one of us?' I asked.

'It looks like he' — and Anita pointed a judging finger at Noah —'is the only one who wants it... So, yeah, I'd say so!' She wasn't happy with Noah's assertive behaviour, and she had finally said it, loud and clear.

'I want it because I'm the only one who understands it. And so should you!' Noah replied, looking at me, back in full strength. 'She has nothing to do with this... and you know it.'

'I'm right here!' Anita was ready to pick that fight right up.

'Please, stop it! Both of you. Stop it! You're too pushy, risking our safety to get what you want, whatever that is... And you know Anita can't fully understand what we're going through, but she's trying, so please, stop pushing!' I let it out, all at once."

Maybe my brain wasn't able to process that place, those series of events, but one thing I could handle and was determined to control: them. My words had left an empty space filled with disagreement and unspoken thoughts, but they had worked.

We took the time to understand and process what was happening, waiting for our clothes to dry, our bodies to rest. Then, in the quiet of that peaceful moment, a faraway but clear sound began to emanate from inside the forest. It was like a repeated thump, as if something was being dropped on the ground, crashing down over and over.

With our shoulders tense, ears pointed in every direction, we discerned more than just the sound. A deep but childish voice repeated unclear words, as if someone were singing along to the rhythm we had heard before, as if accompanying the drums echoing through the forest. The sound drew closer for a brief moment, and we stood up, only to lose it slowly as whoever was performing seemed to move away from us.

'Should we go take a look?' I asked.

'Well...it was a nice song...whoever is singing it can't be...bad, right?' Anita asked, raising her hands in an obvious question.

'It's getting quieter...it's moving away. If we go, we need to go now before we lose it.' Noah left the security of the tree, entering the darkness of the forest, where the red sun could only reach so far, struggling to light the ground, the wooden walls, the countless inhabitants of that unknown place.

And so we followed, our steps hurried, our faces kissed by a rapid sequence of light and darkness. Unbeknownst to us, we were embarking on the journey of our lives.

Chapter Twenty-One
The Sleepyheads

∞

As we entered the deepness of the greenwood, the melody became stronger and clearer. Someone sang happily from somewhere above our heads, as if their voice came directly from the invisible sky. Eventually, we reached what felt like the centre of that sound and, confused on where to head next, we stopped. It came from everywhere around us, yet, we could see no one. Then the song stopped.

'Human sfrangeeer… Where do you come from?' the voice said.

The three of us looked everywhere, our eyes scanning the surroundings, looking for a face, a body, someone. A few feet away from Anita, a pile of strange orange vegetables gathered quietly. From right above, the voice continued:

'We don'f see human since looong fime...you don'f speak fhe human fongue?'

'Where are you? Show yourself!' I shouted in the air.

'You fell me firsf whaf you doing here...' Whoever they were, they had a very strange way of speaking. Their words sounded incorrect in parts and their tone was the one of a little boy.

'We are heading to the Chomps' Village...' Noah said. For a moment, I had forgotten that was exactly what Aura had told us to do.

'Why?' he asked. The voice clearly came from above us.

'We are looking for the Key master,' Noah continued.

'My dad!' he exclaimed and a distinct sound of a popping bubble accompanied his voice

Something appeared at the top of a nearby tree; on a lower branch, nestled among the foliage, a small round pink face peered down at us. His nose was large and circular, his eyes positioned on the top sides of his head, pushed up by prominent cheeks. He wore a dark green, hairy top, giving the impression of grass growing all over his skin. Two chunky arms emerged from it, holding three large orange pear-like fruits. His bottom half resembled that of a dog, with large brown paws dangling from the branch, swinging in rhythm with his last song. We gazed up at this incredible, comical being, brimming with more questions than we could articulate. Anita spoke first.

'Is it not dangerous up there? I'm afraid you could fall!' It was amusing that this was her foremost concern, but then again, it was typical of her.

'Yeah, how did you get up there?' Noah added. The tree he perched on was towering, its lowest branches far beyond our reach, let alone that of the diminutive creature with short arms and legs. I wondered if he could jump very high.

'Whaf do you mean, how? I'm a Chomp!' he proudly declared, standing up on a very skinny and fragile branch.

With his arms fully extended to the space around him, he let the fruits drop to the ground, narrowly missing Noah by inches. Just when we thought the ancient tree might buckle under the creature's weight, we realized he wasn't standing on it at all. His paws hovered a foot clear of the branch, his body swaying from side to side. He descended slowly to the ground, revealing his diminutive stature. His head barely reached Anita's hips, and his curly brown hair added only a few virtual inches to his height.

Attached to his body, a pair of vibrating wings frenetically moved from his shoulders, covered in hairs and adorned with brown feathers. How such small wings could enable the stout creature to fly was a mystery. He seemed to be made of pure air, light and ethereal, moving like the free wind in the skies.

'I am Frusk!' he said once he had fully landed, pointing to himself with his right thumb.

'Hi Frusk, I'm Anita,' she replied, looking at me and Noah with a cracked smile on her face. She was happy and in shock at the same time, like the rest of us.

'No! I'm FRUSK!' the small creature replied. Anita had said it wrong.

'Yeees, and I'm Anita… These are Daniel and Noah,' she added.

We had some language issues right from the start, but in the end, none of us had actually stopped for a moment to consider that he spoke our tongue. Anita adopted a childish tone, spelling out her words slowly as if she were talking to a baby. It felt as though we could have easily been anthropologists in contact with a newly discovered civilization, and Anita was interpreting the linguist like a pro, using grand gestures with her hands.

'Well…Frusk… Can we speak to your parents?' Anita moved forward, bending down to get closer to the Chomp's face.

'I'm Frusk!' he insisted, folding his arms in obvious disappointment. Anita turned to us, hands in the air, wondering what wasn't clear.

'I think it might be Trusk?' I whispered so as not to offend him. 'He seems to use "F" instead of "T"?'

'Right…' she said, sounding unconvinced. 'Let's see… Trusk?' And she looked directly at him.

'Correcf!' he shouted, a smile on his face, his wings flapping rapidly, lifting him a few inches from the ground. Anita looked at me in disbelief.

'A lucky guess, perhaps?' I said with a guilty smile.

'How can we find the Key master?' Noah asked.

'No… he means…' Anita jumped in, trying to clarify Noah's question. 'Would you mind telling us where we can

317

find the Key master?' And she pronounced every word deliberately slow. Noah rolled his eyes in frustration, to which I responded with a sheepish grin.

'Fhe Key masfer is my dad. He's in fhe village. You need fo falk fo him; I'll bring you. We need fo move quickly. Rain is coming!' Trusk replied, pointing to the sky.

I doubted it would make much difference; despite the heat, we were still pretty much soaked. So we followed Trusk into the depths of the woods. A multitude of tiny stones paved a narrow road crossing the land from one part to another. In some areas, its layout had been completely destroyed, making it invisible for a good length. If we didn't have that little guide, we would have probably gotten lost in the forest. Trusk walked at a brisk pace, carrying so many of those orange fruits on his shoulders that he made it look like they didn't have any weight at all. He began to explain why.

'Us Chomps come here for good fruifs! We can move big fhings wifh our small hands. No problem for Chomps fo carry all of you fogefher! fhe foresf is nof safe for fhe ofher side, so we only go close fo fhe village. You're lucky I was looking for big fruifs foday!'

'Why is it not safe?' I asked, walking close to him.

'Chomps are hiding! Nobody can know where we are.'

'Hiding from whom?' I asked, my eyes landing on strange marks carved into the bark of some old trees.

'And what about us? Would it be unsafe for us too?' Anita added.

318

'Can you disappear?' he asked, stopping his walk and looking up at us, his hands mimicking the effect of an exploding bubble. Two fruits fell to the ground.

'Um… Not really, no,' I replied, smiling, feeling like I might be disappointing him a little.

'Oh, very unsafe for you fhen!' he said, his expression serious as he resumed his walk. 'Bad fhings around here. Fhe foresf helps fo hide us, buf we always keep wafching. Dad will explain everyfhing you don'f know! Come on, hurry!' And he began to walk faster, aided by the downward slope in front of us.

'Who do you hide from, exactly?' I asked, falling into step behind him.

'Fhese lands are full of perils… Eyes wafching all fhe fime, looking fo find us and our Flare…'

'Trusk,' I continued, 'do you always speak this language, or only with us?' I could still hear in my head the first few, strange words Aura had said as she welcomed us.

'No, never. Fhis is fhe human fongue. Humans used if long ago, before everyfhing ended. I do remember how to say words, buf nof well enough!'

'It sounds perfect to me,' Noah chimed in, smiling at us.

'Before what ended?' Anita whispered in my ear, seemingly attuned to anything tinged with danger.

At a brisk pace, we approached the end of the woods, emerging on the opposite side from where we entered. The trees had become scarce, but the dim light remained as the red sun had disappeared behind giant dark clouds. Just

319

outside the forest, Trusk suddenly stopped and looked at the sky.

'We have only a liffle fime! We need fo fly!' And he dropped all his fruits on the ground. 'Hold my hands; I will fake you home!' His arms stretched toward us.

We understood Trusk's urgency, but none of us were entirely sure whether to comply with his request. However, having experienced the incredible sensation of diving in the depths of the sea, we exchanged quick glances and all moved towards the Chomp, grabbing his hands as we took off. The feeling of losing contact with the ground, the rush of air through my hair and skin, my weight becoming nothing, was unlike anything I'd ever felt. Visions and teleporting were one thing, but now, after experiencing diving in the sea and flying through the air, we had lived through the most electrifying events of our lives in just a few hours.

'This is amazing!' Anita shouted, her words easing my mind. Knowing she was experiencing something incredible, after being petrified and worried sick about our situation, felt like the best gift I could give her.

The warm air grew heavy rapidly, and electrostatics built up as I felt my hair fizzing in my ears. Though we were floating just a few feet above the ground in open space, the light dimmed around us. The dark clouds obscured the purple sky, the sun completely vanished from sight, and flashes multiplied amidst the flurry of clouds. The feeling of wet air grew palpable.

'I'm sorry...' Trusk's voice trailed off as we began losing speed.

320

The ground grew closer, enlarging every detail. The three of us, still holding to the Chomp's arms, could feel the wet rising and, eventually, it started to rain. The sky had opened its rage on us, unmercifully, punishing us for taking the easy way out. Almost before we were aware, we'd reached the surface, crashing fast on the hard soil. Scattered like broken pieces, we split apart across the large field.

Noah dropped first, his eyes warning his feet to get ready. He had managed to get down easily but I crashed further down, close to the bottom of the hill. Anita had fallen in between, Trusk's arm still in her hands; he was peacefully sleeping, snoring away. The rain came down as fast as the thunders shook the space around, making us slip several times. Back on my feet and with pain all over my body, I headed back to make sure they were all OK, when I saw Anita getting back up, shouting and laughing.

'You won't believe this... He's asleep!'

'What do you mean, asleep?' I asked, out of breath, holding a hand to my side. I had the horrible feeling I had broken something.

'Look!' she said, moving away to show the little creature lying on his side, arms and legs relaxed, loudly snoring.

'Are you guys OK?' Noah had just arrived, his face covered in mud.

'I'm OK, all considered...it's lashing, I had just dried up!' Anita cried, looking at her clothes now covered in dirt.

321

'I'm not sure…' I answered. It was like something had slipped under my ribs, crushing them. 'Oh, crap! I lost my box!'

The wooden chest I had with me, hidden in the right pocket of my jacket, had fallen somewhere around. The panic of losing what it had possibly brought us there took over my mind, completely obscuring the fear I had felt just a few seconds earlier, with the fall. Somehow, I had the certainty the pain I felt had to be caused by the box being crushed between me and the ground, so I headed back where I had landed.

To my pure joy, the chest was there, knocked on its side, the lid open but upside down. I was confident the contents were still inside. Anita and Noah followed me down and arrived just as I realized one item was missing. One of the two letters was gone. Great-Grandfather's was still there but the other one, the important one, the one with the words I had inked in my mind…was gone.

'It's gone… It's gone…' I repeated. I was desperate. If I had to choose what to lose from the items in that box, what would I have picked? For sure not that letter.

'What's gone?' Anita asked, getting on her knees, beside me.

'One of the two letters. It's gone. The one with the words,' I said and I knew she would understand right away.

Under the heavy rain, my hands skimmed over the ground blindly, searching for a miracle, desperate to reclaim what had been taken from me. Noah and Anita, soaked but determined, joined in the hunt for the lost paper. They understood the significance of the box and its contents, knowing it might have brought us to our current predicament. If there was a way back, it likely involved the same medium. After several minutes of fruitless searching, we reluctantly conceded defeat. The letter seemed to have vanished without a trace, leaving us standing alone in the vast, stormy landscape.

'Daniel, we have to go! We can't stay exposed like this,' Noah urged, his gaze fixed on me, defeated.

'Yes, I know,' I murmured, feeling utterly lost. The letter could have been carried away by the wind, lost to us forever.

'The important thing, I believe, is that you know what it said. You know the words. That's what matters,' Noah reassured me. Though it didn't ease my sense of loss, I knew he was right. I took his hand and rose to my feet, ready to move forward.

'What do we do with him?' Anita interjected, gesturing toward Trusk, who remained asleep on the wet ground. 'We can't leave him there...'

'No, we can't,' Noah agreed, bounding up the hill.

A short while later, we descended from the hillside, this time on foot and without any special powers. Noah carried the sleeping Chomp on his shoulders, visibly fatigued by his weight. Anita led the way toward the river, where the water surged with the force of the storm. My mind remained fixed on the spot where the box had fallen open. I had lost something crucial, and the weight of that loss hung heavy on me.

As we approached the bottom of the hills, the rain subsided, leaving only the gentle sound of water droplets falling from leaf to leaf, rock to rock, creating an incredible, magical atmosphere. Civilization came into view as we rounded the edge of the hill. A wooden bridge spanned the river, and a few signs stood planted in the ground, broken and battered. Abandoned homes dotted the landscape, silent witnesses to some unknown past.

Seeking respite from the elements, we settled in the shade of the hills. After laying the Chomp on a soft hep of grass, Noah ventured closer to the river, intent on deciphering the worn signs. Despite our shelter, the lingering humidity made it difficult to dry our soaked clothes and hair.

'It feels like I'm back in Italy,' I said, panting.

'It's not just the heat...it's this weird, gluey, sticky air. It feels like I'm stuck to my clothes. Look at my hair!' she replied.

'The hair isn't my worry any more... We are going somewhere we have no clue about, running from something we have no idea about, hoping to find help from somebody we don't know,' I thought.

'Well, the signs are unreadable,' Noah said, returning.

'Nothing left?' Anita asked.

'Some parts are still there, but I can't tell what they say. It's like...a different language,' he replied, sitting down.

'Did you try replacing the T with the F?' I asked, making the two of them laugh loudly. That was our first laugh since we had moved beyond...a laugh we had been waiting for since forever..

While Noah and Anita discussed what to do next, recalling Aura's words and speculating about when Trusk would wake up, my attention was drawn to the buildings in the distance. There was something peculiar about them. If the place had been abandoned, why did it appear as though smoke was rising from one of the roofs? Was it the sign of a fireplace, or was something burning?

'Where? I don't see anything... Why would someone light a fire in this heat?' Anita replied to my observation and standing up.

'Should we go take a look?' Noah suggested.

'Okay, but let's stick together,' Anita insisted, pre-empting any suggestion that she would babysit the Chomp.

So we quickly rose to our feet, with Noah hoisting Trusk onto his shoulders, and once again, we moved forward. A few steps after passing the bridge, we encountered a strange sensation, as if we were suddenly wrapped in plastic. Our ears felt muffled, as though submerged in bubble gum. The sticky sensation Anita had mentioned earlier intensified, and an invisible barrier pushed us back. After a brief struggle, Noah managed to push through, while Anita and I grappled with the resistance a little longer. Eventually, the pressure subsided, the repellent lost its effect, and we felt free to move once again.

'Did you feel that? What was it?' Anita asked, inspecting her hands and feet before glancing behind her.

'It was like passing through a bubble,' I replied.

'Guys?' Noah interrupted.

Before us and all around, the previously empty landscape transformed suddenly. It became bustling, with numerous small houses lining both sides of the river. Smoke indeed rose from two or three homes, and a lively little town materialized before our eyes.

The buildings had high roofs but unusually short doors and windows, almost squatting close to the ground; it was as though they had melted under the intense sun. Scattered here and there on the ground, a countless number Trusks lay fast asleep, as if they had suddenly dozed off without warning. Some appeared to have collapsed to the ground, much like we had earlier. Lying atop broken pieces of wood or on windowsills with half of their bodies still inside their homes, they seemed unaware of what had happened. A chorus of loud snores replaced the sound of raindrops, as a new enchantment unfolded before our astonished gaze.

'I can't believe my eyes...' Anita exclaimed, her mouth agape.

'It's like dozens and dozens of him, everywhere,' Noah remarked, surveying the scene.

'This must be the weirdest and funniest thing I've ever seen in my entire life,' I said, gazing at the scattered group of sleeping Chomps. 'They are all the same... I think we got lucky. It seems this is right where we were supposed to be. Which one is Trusk's dad?

'Are we sure they're okay? I mean... is this normal?' Anita asked.

326

The scene before our eyes surpassed imagination. No vision had ever taken me this far. Neither dream nor nightmare had ever conjured such an impossible sight. Everywhere we looked, multitudes of strange creatures lay dormant before us. And yet, they spoke loudly of an incredible, new truth.

Chapter Twenty-Two

Revelia

∞

We were walked around slowly, making as little noise as possible, trying to not wake them up. In between wheelbarrows full of vegetables, chests of wooden sticks, stands with tools of all kinds, those strange creatures lay around like they did not expect to fall asleep so abruptly. Some of them had items still in their hands, like some work was right in progress when they had fallen asleep. Noah walked further up the road and, stepping into a house porch, left Trusk on a chair, beside the front door. Then he walked in, uninvited.

'Do we all agree this is the place Aura told us to get to?' I asked, refraining from entering the house.

'I'd say so...look around you. These are all...him!' And she pointed at Trusk, who was gibbering something in his sleep.

'OK, so we wait here? Will they wake up, eventually? If they will we can talk to this Key master and go home,' I said, sitting on the porch steps. I was planning ahead. I knew she would like that.

'How long are they going to sleep for, would you say?' Anita asked.

'Not for long. It won't rain for another while,' an unknown voice answered.

Taken by surprise, both of us stood up, looking around. *This isn't Trusk's weird voice; none of the Chomps have woken up yet. Who is talking?* A thin figure moved from behind the house we had stopped by, turning the corner. It walked slowly, keeping its distance. I wasn't sure if it was afraid of us or if we should be afraid of it. As it moved around, our bodies turned in sync, keeping our eyes on it; like the Earth with its moon, we danced in a circle.

'Don't bother asking...' it said suddenly. 'My name is Revelia.'

'Do you live here?' I asked, after a few seconds of silence. Somehow, that being had already answered the first question I had in my mind, before I could even ask it.

'No. I'm a Leonty, not a Chomp...a female of my kind,' she said, her left hand hovered over some of the items left behind by the sleepyheads, without touching them, her expression showing a degree of judgement.

'How did you get here?' Anita asked, remembering what Trusk had said earlier on.

No one knew they existed. How did she know where they lived? The Leonty showed no interest in answering our simple question. She didn't engaged; her attention was only for the Chomps. As if she were on her own quest, interested only in what she was after, she walked around, distant from us. Her skin was light green, nearly grey in colour; marks inked all over her arms, neck, and part of her face came together in beautiful shapes and forms. Her hair looked hard, rigid like wooden sticks, she had long red ribbons tied to it. Her body was covered by a deep dark green layer with golden marks, she looked naked, her form was free from any clothing but, except for arms and face, her skin was still hidden.

'I come here, now and then,' she said, finally moving closer. 'The question is how did *you* get here?' And details on her face became clearer as she walked closer. Her lips were grey, the black signs on her skin enhanced the beauty of her eyes, crystal clear as if their colour had vanished.

'What happened to them?' I asked, unwilling to answer her question.

'It's the rain. It's the Chomps' weakness. In the exact moment the first drop reaches the ground, they fall asleep.'

'Just like that? Is it not dangerous?' Anita asked.

'Just like that,' Revelia slowly repeated. It was like she intended to lurk behind the curtains of our minds, her eyes fixed on us but seeming to gaze right through us. 'With the ages, Chomps have learned to predict when the rain will come. They can feel it in the air, in their skin. So they stop

330

whatever they are doing and seek shelter from the storm in their own homes. This scene here...what you are seeing, it's extremely...unusual.'

She looked puzzled. She wasn't friendly, and the tone of her voice was deep, severe. Like a wild cat, her moves were soft, but her face was hard, as if fighting was what she knew best. The Leonty clearly had no idea why the Chomps were caught by surprise, and I could have sworn she had hinted that we were the cause of it. After all, two strange events had just happened, right there, in the same place: them and us.

'I'm Daniel, this is Anita,' I started. 'We are here to talk to the Key master.' Anita looked at me with a reproachful look. She wanted to keep that information to ourselves.

'The Key master is not here,' she replied, looking around to double-check. 'He is probably in his home, further ahead.'

'Do you know him? Can you show us where he is?' I asked. Somehow, I felt she was willing to share that detail. Anita, on the other hand, looked at me as if I were gambling with our lives.

'There is no need,' she replied. 'I've seen you walking in, talking to him. I'm confident you won't need my help. They are waking up.' Her eyes briefly flickered, a red flash passing right through.

What did she mean by 'we have already talked to him'? I thought. Before I could ask any more questions, the Chomps started to wake up. Some of them got up quickly, their faces confused. Others had already seen us and started to talk among themselves, whispering. They all panicked, moving away from us as if we were a plague spreading fast. They could have been scared of us, scared of Revelia, or scared of what had just happened to them; in the space of a few minutes, a giant invisible hole had appeared between us and them.

'Who are you?' a Chomp shouted.

'How did you pass the wall?' another one asked.

'Tu vïv phat in hara sring?' a third Chomp added, looking at Revelia.

'I did not bring them in here,' she replied. 'They were already inside your dome. Treekan's son brought them into your home…'

They knew each other, and they knew each other well, but they were not up for a friendly encounter. There was something odd, a pulsating fear emanating from their words. Their bodies were rigid, their hands defensively positioned. Anita and I found ourselves caught between two opposing sides, on the verge of a war. Then, suddenly, a scream shattered the frozen atmosphere. Noah came right out of the house, tripping on the last few steps by the porch. He was being chased by an upset Chomp who wan after him with a tool in hand, screaming: 'Shprengar, Shprengar!'

Trusk woke up right when Noah slipped down the steps, a few feet from him. Getting up quickly, he stopped the infuriated Chomp.

'No! Fhese are nof sfrangers! Fhey are friends!' he shouted, arms open in Noah's defence. 'He is Noah. Daniel and Anifa,' he added, pointing his short, chubby hand at

332

us. Anita couldn't help but smile at the strange sound of her new name."

'Where did they come from?' someone in the crowd asked. 'These are not...what are these? I've never seen strange creatures like these. Not even before the Great Dawn. They look like...Humans?'

Anita and I looked at the Chomps in disbelief.

'Seriously?' she asked me, whispering. 'We are the strange creatures?'

'What is the Great Dawn?' I asked the crowd.

'See?' one replied. 'They are not from here!'

The group got louder. Many of them were getting impatient, and loud suggestions of actions arose among the gathering. We had upset what looked to be, at first, a peaceful kind. Now they were ready to charge.

'We have come from the gate over the sea!' Noah shouted, taking his chance to explain, to show them we were not enemies. The crowd went suddenly silent. 'The gatekeeper helped us to cross the waters and told us to look for the Key master. Trusk brought us here for this reason.'

The little beings looked at each other in shock. After a few seconds of mute dialogue, their voices started to chatter loud once again.

'Where do you come from?' someone asked.

'Earth?' Anita replied, with a question mark at the end. 'What? Don't tell me we are still on Earth? Whatever this is...is not it,' she said to me.

'What is Earth?' Questions mounted. 'How did you pass the wall of our dome? Why is the Leonty with you?'

'Quiet!' a deep voice shouted, covering the buzz.

A Chomp stood on an old, small chariot. His hands on reins, he rode an unusual carriage with big wheels, a small seat, and a strange animal at the front, pulling it. His face was Trusk's face but older, his eyes were accompanied by two big chunks of grey eyebrows at the top, and his nose looked large and flat. Positioned on his chariot, despite the funny look, he had the demeanour of a leader. All the other Chomps had gone silent, eyes directed to their master, all waiting for instructions.

'Why have you come here, unannounced?' he asked. For a moment, we thought he had asked that question to us.

'I didn't have the chance to tell you in advance,' Revelia replied.

'You know you are welcome here, but you are still a Leonty. The blood in your veins is of an evil magic. I trust you remember our deal?' he said.

'I do. And I trust you remember what I'm capable of. You can guess why I'm here.' And she looked right at us. Whatever she referred to, it didn't sound good at all.

'Trusk,' the old Chomp said, 'Bring your friends to the Flare. I'll meet you there. The Leonty will follow me.' And he turned his chariot around; the strange animal started to pull it up the hill.

The Leonty carried a disappointed face. She was going to comply with the Chomp's request, but she wasn't happy about it. Confused, we left the crowd behind, in the cluttered chats that were building up again, following Trusk in his puzzling, funny walk. Halfway through, he resumed his singing. *Is he oblivious to the whole atmosphere or are we worrying too much?*, I thought.

'Waree pha forash égó farher tu, farher tu...'

'I feel like we stepped into the middle of something. I wish we knew what this something is,' Anita said, walking right behind Trusk.

'Did you feel the tension between the old Chomp and the Leonty? What was that all about?' Noah added.

'And the tension between them and us?' Anita replied.

'It doesn't matter. The gatekeeper said we had to find the Key master to go back home, right? We found him. Let's hope we are a step closer,' I added.

I didn't know if that was what I really wanted or what I should have wanted. My mind played trick after trick. I had never been in a vision for so long, and no vision had ever been so real. I was guilty of having brought Anita into that crazy world, and I was worried I could not bring us back.

'Don't you have the feeling we are moving forward more than going back?' Noah asked.

He was still there, pushing to move ahead. He wasn't thinking about me or Anita. He wanted to grasp his truth at our expense. My heart beat to another rhythm, another music, and I had lost somehow my inexplicable attraction to him. Few minutes later, we arrived at what looked like the centre of the village. Houses were massed together, some on top of each other, their sides almost squeezed in a suffocating hug surrounded a circular courtyard, creating the illusion of a big, old country village. A bright light came from its centre, and we were heading right towards it.

'Here, fhis is Flare. Fhe big house in fronf is fhe old fulcrum.' And Trusk pointed to a large building with dark stones and wooden doors.

It had a large piece missing at the top right, like a bomb had destroyed its head and two large, long logs held the left side as if they were preventing it from collapsing. The buildings surrounding the yard enclosed the space in an unnatural dark. The daylight struggled to pass through the alleys, and its centre was lit only by a flame shining right from the ground. Trusk walked past the Flare like it was unnoticeable, something he had seen millions of times, but the three of us stopped by to observe that magic in the making. In between the paving stones, a circular hole brought to the surface a warm sort of energy. It was bright, flickering at times, and like a flame, it projected shadows all around the buildings' walls.

'The Sháten Déil is the very reason why we still exist,' a voice said. The old Chomp had walked out of the giant building to greet us. On his left side, the Leonty still followed.

They walked side by side, like an odd, mismatched couple; Revelia was twice as tall and twice as beautiful. The Chomp had a heavy walk, stripped of any harmony; in contrast with the soft walk of the Leonty beside him, he walked fast, in a hurry.

'Tell me. How did you get here? How did you pass the wall?' he asked, echoing the earlier crowd we had left behind.

'We got rescued by the gatekeeper first, and Trusk afterwards,' I answered.

'A gatekeeper? How?' he said, as if he was asking himself.

'It's true. I've seen it. A gatekeeper helped them cross the Soulless Sea,' the Leonty replied.

'How does she know? Why is she talking like she can see everything, like she is simply watching a movie?' Noah quickly looked at me and Anita, the exact same question in his mind.

'I found fhem af fhe edge of fhe foresf, Fafher. Like she said.' And Trusk pointed his finger to Revelia. 'And fhey said fhey were looking for you. Like she said.'

'Can someone explain to us what's going on?' I asked, interrupting.

'Fafher, I don'f fhink fhey know anyfhing...' Trusk continued.

'Very well,' the old Chomp stated after looking at us for a few seconds. 'I'm Treekan, Trusk's father, and protector of the Flare. I'm the oldest Chomp alive and the Key master. This was our home since way before the Great Dawn, when the end of our kind was near...' He continued to talk, walking around and moving his arms like he could paint their history with the power of his bare hands. 'The Flare, the magic contained in this place, was our only chance of survival. It protected us from the evil that spread in every land of this world by wrapping everything nearby around in an invisible dome. Inside this safe place, we are shielded from any danger. Only Chomps can come in and

337

out of its walls. There are few...risky exceptions, of course.' And his eyes went to Revelia.

Treekan stopped talking, as if his side of the story had come to an end and now, it was time for somebody else to take over.

'Runae wasn't always the way it is now,' Revelia continued. 'Our world had wonderful creatures scattered all over its surface, living peacefully. Despite our differences, our unique abilities, we had lived in peace and harmony. Until the day the evil rose from the Cloudy Mountain. Pain and death suddenly became...ordinary. But it was nothing compared to what we faced after the Great Dawn. As it's written in the Ancient Mirrors, a race managed unexpectedly to gain great power over the others. Over all the beings living in this world, one had emerged as victor. From being almost extinct to be the one ruling them all. In between blood and fear, the Crimson Queen conquered every corner of these lands, leaving a trail of death behind.'

'Everywhere, except this very place!' Treekan interrupted. 'The very centre of our power and our protection was hidden from her. She knew we existed, but she could find us no longer. And most importantly, she could not find the Flare.'

Noah was completely captured by their story. His eyes were fixed on the Flare, his mind flying with the wings of his pure imagination. On the other side, my hope could not take off. I held onto the ground, my will focused on getting back home right away. I scanned their words looking for details that would have made that possible, but it was fruitless.

338

'Why are we here?' I asked, sneaking my question in between their talks. 'Why did we get in here? Why now?'

'Because you have the key, and you obviously used it,' Treekan replied.

'The box?' Anita asked, looking right at me.

'I've had that box for a few days. It didn't do anything before,' I answered. 'Since the moment Grandma gave it to me, I've been holding it in my hands, I've opened it, checked the contents inside... Nothing strange ever happened.'

'We were together, this time,' Noah added, finally diverting his look from the warm flame.

'What you have, the key that brought you here, it's something we have been looking for since the war,' Treekan said. 'Come with me, I'll show you how Runae came to be and how long we have been waiting for you.'

And the old Chomp turned back towards the broken building, with Trusk following closely behind. They were inviting us in. Revelia hadn't moved an inch. Her mind was troubled by our presence, and her face reflected her stubborn hesitation.

After exchanging a brief, challenging look between her and us, we walked away from the flame, leaving the light behind, our shadows fading rapidly..

Chapter Twenty-Three
The Crimson Queen

∞

Like little ducks in a row, we followed Treekan right to the crooked building with in our minds the desire to know everything he could share. Two large wooden doors, three or four times bigger than needed for us to pass through, waited for us. Crossing their watch, I couldn't help but wonder if Chomps were once taller than they were now. Large columns and balconies filled the entire space inside. Here and there, parts were gone, matching the empty spots in the far-off high roof. The sunlight was coming right through the big hole above our heads, fighting a war of shadows against many candle flames flickering from high stands.

The giant space we walked into resembled a large, single area, with features giving the impression of a space caught between the interior of a palace and a church. At the far end, a curved wall closed the way further from part to part. Large mirrors hung side by side; some had gone dark, consumed by time. A few were cracked in parts, and some were missing entirely, leaving a silent shadow in memory of their long absence. What was left of old drapes and ornate furniture gave us the idea that it had been a beautiful building, once.

'This place is incredible!' Anita exclaimed, her voice echoing in the emptiness around us. 'Whatever this is, it must have so much history within...'

'You are right. What's the way they call you?' Treekan asked. Anita was puzzled by the old Chomp's manners. Nevertheless, she answered the question.

'Well...Anita... This place indeed contains history, much more than its walls themselves. See these mirrors? These are the Ancient Mirrors. They contain everything there is to know about us, them' —and he pointed at Revelia—'and Runae. Forgive me...I should have said, they did. Most of these reliquiae are dead, gone, broken with many parts of the building and our hearts.'

'Do you mean...you can see the past...in there?' Anita asked, moving closer to a cracked mirror, her face looking back at her, distorted.

'Not really. You can't see every past. You can only see your past.'

'What's the point of seeing my past? Should I not know my past already?' she said. Anita was seduced by the idea she could get access to that great amount of knowledge.

341

'For once, our own past is not always so easy to recall.' And to that sentence, my soul shrank a little. 'And when I say your past, I mean your kind's...'

'Do they go one way only? Can they show us our future?' Noah stepped into the conversation. Once again, he was moving further.

'No,' Revelia replied. 'But I can.'

'So you can see the future in these mirrors? Not just the past?' Anita said, moving closer to another one. Her reflection was blocked out by a grey dark shade all over the dead glass.

'Not really. The Ancient Mirrors have not that power. I do. I can't see yacs ahead, I can't see every detail, even if I want to. But, sometimes, I'm able to see a few rhocs further, before the random mix of decisions could make it impossible.'

Trusk had gone to sit in a corner, on an old bench, quiet. His legs were swinging again, like he had done before, on top of that tree where we had met. Our faces were coming in and out of sight, against the shadows of our bodies and those tired walls. We were exploring a world of possibilities, waiting for the magic to be revealed. Treekan moved to the far left, close to one of the few mirrors left standing. His hand reached the ornate frame; he stared at it as if he was venerating the magic within. Eventually, he resumed:

'This story has not a real beginning. These mirrors were made by magic and blood; they were created the very same moment the Great Dawn began. For some reason, they can't go too far before then; they don't tell how we came to

342

be, how we came to exist. But we do know how it ended, how we ended. There are stories, traditions that shed some light on what we were before the war, before the mirrors. Where they don't reach, some of my oldest memories, although weak now at my old age, come to help too. Runae was a world full of life, once. Chomps were not the only kind running free across the lands. Leonty were there, so myriads of Aqualymphs, Humans, Valahans and the Garughals. Then, slowly, an evil force started to spread from the far mountains to the northwest. It brought fear, panic and judgement. Long wars came right after. Our God and protector had found a way for us to temporarily shield ourselves from the wicked magic by giving us a new power, the Flares.'

'But it wasn't enough...' Revelia added, her face looking as if saddened by troubled thoughts.

'In an instant, so my old memory tells me, we were woken up to a sudden new war, a war like no other, like if our star had fallen on us. In a flap of our wings, we found ourselves close to extinction. In the dark of that terrifying time, my father and I went to meet the leaders of the other kinds for counsel. The world as we knew was dying. Although Erion, our star, was gone from sight, hidden by a heavy, black haze, our sky was red and bright, lands were torn by a poisoning darkness and flashes were running all around us. Everyone who attended that meeting was petrified, scared of the unknown. The Humans had proposed the idea to use the magic given to us by our God to protect our world and our lives. If we had put together our powers, we could have spared the time necessary to find out what was happening. Decisions had to be taken quickly. Despite an initial disagreement, especially after what had happened between the Humans and the Leonty, the council eventually agreed. We were going to summon our greatest protection.'

Treekan stopped for a few moments. His face had turned sad. Something unpleasant was waiting to be revealed. My mind and my eyes moved to Revelia, a Leonty. *'Her kind wasn't willing to help? How long can these creatures live? Was it possible she was there too?*

The Key master eventually moved towards the middle, skipping some of the mirrors now in pieces, and stopped in front of the one Anita stood close by. He briefly smiled at her, then continued:

'We came here. Ten of the most powerful beings, two of each kind, the ones who had learned to practice the strongest of all magics. All except the Leonty. After all, there were too few left to be of any help and the hate between them and the Humans was too great to be overcome. Anyway, far away from here, at the five temples, in an incredible coincidence, the Leonty called Una came in contact with the source of all that terrible evil, the one who unleashed its rage on all of us. It seduced her in a maleficent pact, an agreement that would have spared her from being erased from memory. In exchange, she would enslave and keep under her magic someone that could not be destroyed, someone the evil had raged in battle with, in the far skies above Runae. As the evil wasn't able to win against our God, destruction was turned into a cage instead. An eternal prison under Una's supervision.'

Our ears were all for Treekan but our eyes gazed right at Revelia. Although we knew she wasn't Una and despite the fact we weren't sure she was evil too, we had no trust in her. We were the Chomps back at the village, looking at her with suspicion, worried. She didn't show any emotion to that story. It was as if her kind wasn't put on stand for judgement. She was quiet, her eyes engaging only with Treekan's. Whatever their deal was, she was still welcome in there.

'The ten were forced to move the plan ahead without the help of the mind benders, the Leonty. They gave their energies, their true selves, into the hope of salvation. Their lives were given to their Flares in a spell of supreme protection. In that same moment, just before everything was over, these mirrors appeared, bringing with them a new power, and here they still stand, despite the odds.

'Some of them are in ruins, in pieces. When did that happen?' I asked. I was completely taken by that story, by the events that had unfolded. It wasn't my history; I had nothing to do with it, but I still wondered how I was connected to it.

'Like this place, these magic tools withstood the rage of the war that happened afterward, when Una, intoxicated by the power given to her, spilled the blood of many, many innocent lives, declaring herself Queen of Runae, Queen of our red blood now penetrating our lands.'

'The Crimson Queen…' Noah whispered.

Treekan nodded in agreement. We knew that name was an omen of fear and sorrow. We finally understood why. Revelia turned her face away, looking at the far big doors, her face showing shame, guilt. Whatever her connection was with Una, she didn't want to be part of that injustice.

'These Flares...the ones you just described...is that one we have just seen, one of them?' I asked.

'It's the only one left,' Revelia replied, finally looking back at us. 'All the other stones are gone, gone like the one who generated them. One by one, my sister managed to absorb their power...after killing all the ones standing to protect them.'

'Although she has her hands on your Flare, she doesn't own its full power,' Treekan added, looking at Revelia. 'She is keeping you and your sisters alive, so its magic is shared amongst you.'

'Her sister.' Those words had given meaning to her sense of guilt. She might not have done it herself, but someone very close to her had. Anita moved away from the mirror she stood by and moved closer to me. Her eyes spoke of worries I also had. We had walked into a strange, destroyed world; we were in between factions at war, and a possibly dangerous enemy stood only a few feet away from us.

'How is your Flare still here?' Noah asked, ignoring that Anita and I had taken distance from the rising peril.

'Because our Flare is ours. It has our inner power. It makes us invisible to the external world. We don't know how we got to have this power, just as we don't know how we came to be in the first place. But it saved us. At the peak of the war between the Humans and the Leonty, there were no so many Chomps left. Eventually, we managed to master our Flare; we disappeared completely and started to increase our numbers again. She knows we are still here, alive. But she can't reach us,' Treekan replied.

346

Was his confidence misplaced? Wasn't a Leonty, the Crimson Queen's very own sister, there, with them? Our feet were already pointing at the big doors. My face and Anita's were locked in agreement. We had to get out. We had to get back home.

'You don't need to fear me,' Revelia said, looking at the both of us. Once again, she could reach inside our heads. 'No, I can't read your minds, but I can see your immediate future, the decision you are about to take.' And her eyes flashed red again. This time, in the dark of that old place, we saw it clearly.

'What does it mean?' Noah asked, looking at us.

'It means we want to go back home,' I quickly replied. 'I'm really sorry to hear what happened to you, to all of you, but this is not our world and this can't be the reason why we're here.'

'We just want to go home,' Anita added.

'I'm afraid this is not possible,' Treekan replied. He moved away from the magical artefacts and walked across the room, on his way out. 'You came here because you have the key to your world. You need our key to leave this place.'

'Where can we find this other key?' I asked. I felt like we had just become prisoners.

'There is only one being that can get in and out of our world, the real Key master. And he is unreachable, at least for any of us.'

'I thought…Aura told us you were the Key master?' I asked.

'I've been called that because I'm the only one who knows…the only one who knows about the real one.'

Treekan was about to walk out of that place. We held still, petrified by the idea of not being able to see our world again, our loved ones, my John. When he noticed we had been left behind, he turned again and continued:

'Before the Crimson Queen, before the Flares, before the madness, Runae was under the protection of an incredibly powerful being. We all were. Life on our planet might not have always been aware of his presence, but he walked amongst us now and then. We knew him, and we met him when we needed him the most. We call him Time. Time, like the power he possessed. Time, like the hocs, rhocs, and yacs that are not passing by any more. He was our protector until that day came. The day he was enslaved. The day his power was taken from him and given to Una, who now holds her grip on a day that never ends. He owned the key that allowed him to come and go.'

'Are you saying time doesn't pass here? Were you all here when all this happened?' Anita asked in disbelief. If she was right, so Noah's apparent immortality could be explained?

'Exactly, little human. It has been for a long time. Of course, we can still die if our bodies get damaged, but if they don't, we grow old in an infinite future, until the day we just… vanish. We don't know how it really works. We had generations and generations after Time stopped Erion in the middle of the sky. We had little ones of our own. But they all get frozen past a certain age. My son, Trusk, has been like this since twenty yacs. I was younger than he was when it all began. I got to grow with the pain and sorrow

348

walking in these lands for so long,' Treekan said, his face showing he had long given up the idea of a normal life.

'So, he doesn't have the key any more? She has it,' I said as if I were talking to myself.

'She does,' Revelia replied.

Suddenly the conversation came to an end. They had lost any hope of changing their fate, there was no question on how to fix that. We were now stepping into their lost dreams, sharing the emptiness of a way through that was never going to come.

'Why would Aura tell us to come here for help? If there's nothing we can do, if we came here for no reason, why did she say to come to you?' Noah said to Treekan, walking out through the doors.

That question was everyone's question now. Somehow, that detail had slipped our minds, and Treekan was now standing still, looking at Revelia, searching for answers he wasn't sure about. He questioned the fact we had actually met her. Revelia was his focal point of certainty. What did she say? *I've seen it.'* She was, once again, confirming it.

'It is true, Treekan. The gatekeeper helped them to cross the dead sea. They came here because they were told to.'

'Even if it happened...' From his voice, he was fighting against the idea. 'What are we supposed to do? Tell them to go and fight your sister? Tell them to free Time? Maybe you would suggest we give them the power of our Flare so they can sneak in, unseen?'

'I can't see what you have not decided yet!' she replied, matching his stubbornness.

349

'I can't do that! There is nothing to decide.'

'This is what we have been waiting for!' And Revelia rushed her feet out of the building, following the one we believed was the Key master, on his way out. We were silent, unwanted guests. There was no help coming.

'Isn't that convenient? You telling me to help them, who knows at what cost? We are the only kind left standing. I won't help these three strangers to only send my race to certain death!' Treekan's rage mounted. He was acting rightfully as a leader. Leader of a small but important group of beings who had survived against the odds. We could not ask for anything that could come at a high price.

'Key master,' I said, walking faster to reach him. The Flare was already at our back; the village opened up to the large valley at the bottom where we had left so many Chomps questioning who we were. 'We don't want to cause any trouble to you or your people. And definitely, we don't want to compromise your safety. We have been trying to understand a lot of strange events we've witnessed, and this search has brought us here. Like you said, we have the key to leaving our world but nothing else. Do you know, at least, how was it possible? Do you know why we were able to cross the gates?'

He stopped again. My words had reached him, deeply. His face changed and the anger slowly left the space to a weak look of empathy. He understood our trouble.

'Time is the Key master,' he repeated. 'Our protector had the key. He could leave this place whenever he wanted. We are bound to our lands. He wasn't. If you are not bound to yours, if you were able to leave your world, that makes you the protector of yours.'

'There is really nothing to protect, in our world,' Anita said. She talked to Treekan but also to me. 'Yes, our world is...well...complicated, but our kind is not in danger. We have never experienced the history you have. To be honest, I wasn't even supposed to be here. Daniel is the one. Daniel and Noah.'

'If you crossed the unreachable pass, then you are one of them,' he replied sharply. Then, after a long sigh, he continued. 'I don't know how you managed to get here, and I don't know why. I do believe you are not a danger to us. I'm happy to have you all staying in my home as long as you need to figure this through. If I can, I'll be happy to help you with whatever solution you will find. Now, Trusk, please bring these little Humans home. Make sure they have everything they need.'

'Where are you going, Fafher?' Trusk finally spoke again.

'I'm going to face a great gamble, I'll go to the dead sea. I need to find this gatekeeper. If what they say it's true, I might faint seeing her after all this time.'

Treekan left us there. The five of us were a mismatched group of people who had no idea of what would come next. Revelia still waited, in the depths of her visions, for a turning point that was late to arrive.

'I can't stay longer. My sister will start to suspect. I'll be back whenever I can.' And she made her way out of that place, without looking back, leaving us in shock at hearing she was still under the Crimson Queen's watch.

Without showing any worry about what Revelia had just said, Trusk started to walk down to the edge of the village, to the same spot we had found all those sleepyheads lying down. It was like he wasn't afraid of her, like he knew she had no bad intentions, even if she was still a Leonty, closely monitored by her evil sister. Noah was followed Trusk closer, hurrying to get back, while Anita and I walked slowly. We needed a moment for ourselves.

'Do you think we're still in my backyard? Like we are…I don't know…asleep and dreaming about all this?' she asked.

'I can't honestly tell. In a way, I really hope so. We might just wake up, someone might wake us up…' *Someone…who?*

'Bad thing Patrick is gone, isn't it? We could have hoped.'

'Speaking of which' — I took the hint — 'I know it's weird to talk about this while we are…here, but are you going to tell me what happened between the two of you?'

'Oh Daniel, I don't know. I can't really think straight right now. He said some things, I said some things. Then he had his stuff packed and he was gone.'

'Might he come back?' I asked. We were very close to Trusk's home. He had summoned someone at the door. A chunky Chomp had come out of the house to greet him.

'Do you hope so, so he can wake us up? I wouldn't hold my breath waiting.' And she turned the topic quickly. 'Do you think it's safe for us…and for them, to stay here?'

'Where else can we go?' I knew we would go back to the Patrick affair, just not then. 'If we are not at your place any more...if we are really gone, then John will be waiting for me. We were supposed to have dinner together. What time would be now?'

'Who knows. Did you notice, now that the sky is clear, their sun hasn't moved? It's still there in between the high hills. I think it's true. Time doesn't tick here.'

And so we reached the house. Noah waited for Trusk to explain everything to the other Chomp, who we thought was his mother. We couldn't tell the age of those beings, nor their sex. They were all alike, unlike anything we knew. The only thing that felt similar to the way we knew life was their sense of family, the way they were together. So we walked in, greeted by a very welcoming Chomp who was busy preparing some sort of food on top of a strange cooker. The side of what looked like a kitchen had three boxes made of stones, one on top of the other. Inside, three pots shook, their fat bottoms burning on the raging fire and a foggy steam shouted from their heads. The smell filled the house, while Trusk explained why he hadn't managed to bring those strange fruits he had left in the forest to come and rescue us.

The house was incredibly small for the three of us. Everything was reduced to a miniature. Simple in style, it had large wooden beams crossing from part to part. A small staircase popped up from the far back, rising to a second floor. The doors and all the windows were pretty low, nearly at our feet, and all over the floor, the wooden panels squeaked under the weight of our walk.

Keeping our bodies slightly bent, we looked around, trying to not annoy the welcoming family. Everything we saw was fascinating, from the rustic shelves in the tiny kitchen to the strange plants in the corners. One side of the sitting room was fully open to the outside. Like a porch in between the inside and the outside, the world out there could be seen. Few Chomps in the distance carried on with their work, tirelessly, under the heat of that large sun peeking from behind the hills.

Trusk shared with his mother, Reela, all the things that had happened that day, to him, to us. She didn't look at us as if we were a dangerous species had come to put them at risk and, instead, as she listened to her son, she became more and more understanding. After a few brief conversations with the two of them, the three of us sat outside, by the unusual porch, waiting for the mysterious dinner to be ready. Reela was finishing up a few things by the cooker, and Trusk had gone outside to borrow a few larger chairs for us.

'I have to say, despite everything, this place is incredible,' Anita let out.

'We couldn't be further away from our reality, could we? Everything is... so strange...' I added.

'I've been thinking,' she started. She sat on a step close to the road, her mind lost in the horizon, the red star shining on her dark hair. 'If you've never been able to come here, and you were meant to, somehow... what has changed?'

'We have that chest we didn't have before?' Noah replied from far back, inside the house. He barely sat on a tiny chair, struggling to keep himself from falling.

'I tried to use it before,' I said. 'Bear in mind I had no idea how, and I still don't know how we made it happen, but I really tried to evoke some sort of vision while I was in Italy.'

'It's because we were together!' Noah repeated himself.

'It's possible, but we have to come to the conclusion we are not having a vision this time. We have left, for real,' I continued.

'If we did leave, whatever made it possible, made it possible for all of us, not just you or Noah.' I could see Anita's brain spinning, trying to unlock the impasse, find the missing piece.

'Let's say the box is…I don't know…a teleporting device. Whoever uses it can travel through space?' Noah asked. He moved close to me and Anita, sitting on a more secure ground.

'Treekan said the key allowed only Time to come and go,' I replied.

'Not exactly. He said only Time could, because he had the key,' Anita pointed out.

'So he could bring anyone with him, if he wanted to? Is this what you're thinking?' Anita recalled it right, but I was still doubting that was the right path to follow.

'We know you two are somehow connected. We know the box didn't work before, when you were alone. I think the only possible explanation is that the box is the key and

355

you both have to use it, together. Oh, and of course, it might happen that you bring anybody in close proximity with you.' And the brain of that entire operation looked satisfied, like she had grasped the only possible solution.

The three of us went silent, listening to our own minds, thinking about what that meant. At our back we could hear Reela preparing the small table, moving some piece of furniture to the side, allowing us to sit and have food.

A few minutes later, Anita resumed: 'Whatever happened to these people, it must have been horrible. Imagine being the only kind left alive and not being able to leave your home…constantly under a giant threat.'

'And being afraid of trying to fix it. If there is something worse than a problem, it's the risk you need to take to solve it,' I added.

'You are very sweet and kind.' Reela had just joined our conversation. 'We have been living in this way for long time. Fear has let us go…just that bit to let us live in peace. Don't worry about it. We will be fine. And so will you, after you eat your food. Let's go. It's ready!' And after smiling at us, she moved back in.

Without knowing, we had built our first bridge between us and them. We had the help of Trusk, but it was Reela who made us feel really welcome. So back in the house we went, helping Trusk to move the last few bits and place the odd chairs he had managed to find around the table. He had not found a piece of furniture that could fit our size, so instead, he had brought in a few large empty wooden boxes. Once flipped upside down, they became good enough chairs to sit on.

Knowing that the Key master, unfortunately, wasn't going to come back soon, without further hesitation Reela brought the delicious food to the table. We had no idea what we were going to eat, but it didn't matter. We were starving.

Chapter Twenty-Four

A Risk Worth Dying For

∞

Grey shadows moved fast across the cold stones, lurking, waiting for instructions that had not yet been given. Long it had been since they were sent on a deadly mission, and now things were changing for the better. Abandoning the sacred waters and their true, pure form, they had chosen a life of death, charmed by so much power, they could not oppose it. The water they belonged to, the same water they were made of, had left its spot to a malicious nature, like their soul had left their vessel in ethereal steam. They were now hers to shape, hers to bind to her will; in exchange for survival, they had chosen a life of slavery and horror.

In a crowd of irrelevant henchmen, a different being kept her distance, far way up, unreachable, like her power was. She stood by a narrow window carved into the old stone, looking outside, silent. The raging star turning her skin purple, her eyes red as a statement to her massacres, she was the only radiant thing in a dark, gelid room. Her shadow, projected against the wall, large and dark like her soul, was pierced by sharp, thin rays coming from the other windows in the round room.

The tower of despair and wrath was at her will, powerless like any other creature that walked that world. Her hands, as if choking an old piece of paper, twisted in anger. After so long, that was the first time she had to face a threat, the first time since she had proclaimed herself Queen. A deformed, grey creature had come closer, the one who had just delivered that message she was now devouring between her fingers. Someone had come to Runae, someone carrying a message that had gotten lost and now it had found its way to her.

'You are saying you don't know who they are and where they have gone?' Her voice was deep, threatening, slow.

'We lost them at the dead sea, my queen. The gatekeeper prevented us from getting to them,' the being replied, his voice like a whisper, like a snake ready to eat its prey.

'You mean one of your stupid, useless kind,' she replied. Her face was still fixed to the outside world, like she could reach the far land and see the truth for herself. 'Even without the Anún Déil, she still troubles my rhocs!'

'We are not Aqualymphs any more, my queen. Since the day we met that stranger who walked through that very same gate. We were woken up to a new reality, to the truth of what the real power is…you! We serve you only, and for

359

you we have become spectres.' And his shape turned a bit, as if he bowed to Her Majesty, in respect and fear.

'Not before you joined the Humans in your quest to destroy my kind!' She recalled times long gone, an unpleasant reminder they were now in an eternal debt with their queen. 'When did you follow their trail, have you found anything else besides this?' And she showed the paper back to its original bearer.

'No, my queen. That was it. We believe they headed to the old Chomps' village. You know we can't fight their power, we could not see them passing the silent forest of Garaglon.'

'These meaningless creatures... Once again they step between me and my destiny!' And her eyes turned to fire. *'There are things that are waiting to be...* Yes, there is death waiting to be. And they shall have exactly what they are looking for. Call my sisters! Tell them I want to see them *now!'* And she left her spot to go back to the depths of her lonely home, her servant gone back behind the shadow of her evil will, vanishing from sight.

Hundreds of steps below, over the ruins of an ancient stronghold, the spectres moved restlessly, like fog pushed by the wind. Stone walls protected their space, like a kingdom at war, sentinels were made to stand forever at their spot, waiting for danger that should never come. Over the fortress, harsh reddish and green lands rose steeply into a high hill. On top of it, five temples sat like a crown on its head, white their making, tall their pillars.

Close to her destination, Revelia was walking fast, hurrying to meet her sisters by their home.

'Where have you been?' A Leonty, similar to her in every way, had just reached her by the first temple.

'What is this tone, Demetra?' Revelia replied.

'We have been summoned. Your sisters are waiting for you by the temple of Grace.'

'Summoned for what?' Revelia could read already through the first few pages of time, but she wanted to hear it directly.

'Rumour has it someone has crossed the gateway. Our queen demands our presence.' Demetra's voice was harsh, her magic spying through her sister's intention.

'Why do you even bother trying? You know I can block your power. "Where I have been" is none of your business. It might be even the case that I'm already aware of what has happened.' And she moved past her sister, dismissing her quickly. 'And her name is Una. Stop calling her queen. Your sister could kill you tomorrow, if she wanted to.'

A small group of Leonty was ready to walk down the hill, hurrying to get to Her Majesty's presence. They were only few, a small number compared to the Chomps who had survived against that very kind. Without adding any more words, Revelia joined the group and walked with them to meet their master. In the secret of her own thoughts, Revelia knew she would soon find herself in the queen's hands and her terrifying magic. Knowing the great power Una withheld she felt as if she walked right to her death. Her sister could not come to know she had met those strangers in the enemy land. Whatever mission they had come to accomplish, Revelia knew it was hanging on to her ability to overcome the queen's power.

As she silently walked towards the harsh desert accompanied by her sisters, she gazed back at the highest hill, where the largest of all their temples stood. A glimpse of an imperceptible future darted in her mind. A long sequence of events flashed before her eyes as she tried to understand it. With the many actions yet to unfold, her vision escaped her comprehension.

∞

Countless miles away, the five of us enjoyed a delicious meal, a mix of roots and other vegetables that didn't look so attractive but smelled and tasted fantastic.

'Are we having lunch or dinner?' Anita asked, smiling.

'Does it matter?' Noah replied. 'It's incredible!'

'Yes. It's very good,' Anita said to Reela, still talking slowly, as if they would struggle to understand our language.

'Anita, they clearly speak our tongue, stop this weird talk,' I told her, laughing.

Reela was visibly proud of us appreciating her cooking and, in between bites, she started to ask a few questions about us.

'So what do you do, in your world?'

'I'm a journalist and a researcher,' Anita replied, without adding any explanation, while chewing a chunky root.

'And is it hard? Is it dangerous?' Reela asked.

'Oh no, sorry. It's mainly research. I check for information, specifically about the past. I study history.'

'Oh, Like my Treekan! That's incredible! And what about you?' She turned her attention to Noah.

'I'm a nurse. I take care of people who are sick or people that need physical help.' Noah was being more detailed.

'I'm a psychologist,' I added, noticing Reela had looked at me, ready to know about me too. 'I take care of people's minds. You know, people who are worried, or struggle with their thoughts and feelings.'

'This is fascinating…' she said. 'You can't imagine what it means for us to meet other beings. We live here and only here. We don't know what's out there…but it's safe here, so we don't leave our village, ever.'

'Mofher, we know whaf's outside fhe Flare profecfion. You make me go every fime for rafions and branches…'

'This is because you have the gift. One of the few left!' she pushed back.

'What gift?' I asked, intruding in their back and forth.

'Trusk owns the very power of our Flare. He can disappear from sight, if he needs to. Only Treekan, Freesk, and Gallor can do that!'

'Fhis is whaf Freesk says. I never seen him do if…' Trusk replied, challenging her.

'Son, that's because he is too old…his mind doesn't work well any more.'

'I thought you weren't getting old? Time doesn't pass here,' Anita asked.

'You are correct, but our bodies still move ahead, slowly but surely, and Freesk is as old as my Treekan. Anyway, tell me more about you. Can you disappear too?' And to that, Trusk laughed, remembering the conversation we had not long before, in the woods.

She was fascinated by us, our lives, what we did and eventually how we got there. The conversation soon turned to more pressing matters. Us stepping into their world was something of extraordinary proportions, and she was very vocal about it. After finishing our meal, our talks continued for a little bit longer, and Reela and I ended up in a solo conversation while we cleaned some of the utensils we had used. Some of the dishes we put away were pretty heavy, like they had been carved from stones. We hadn't had the help of any spoon or fork; instead, we were given a few large square, flat tools. I was still smiling, thinking of Anita's face when I had spilled some of the juicy soup all over the table.

'I'm sorry Treekan had to go meet the gatekeeper, and to a great risk,' I said. In the background, I could hear Trusk engaging in an exciting conversation with Noah and Anita.

'Oh, don't worry about it. My fearcel can look after himself. He is very resourceful...when he wants,' Reela replied. 'Oh, tell him to help me out with the farm and he could die. But when it's about our people, our safety...he is a force of nature.' And she left the dripping wet dishes on the windowsill by the kitchen. Apparently, they would be left there to dry with the warm breeze coming through.

'Reela?' I asked, looking at the light coming from outside.

'Yes, dear...'

'How do you know when to do what? I mean, if time doesn't pass, how do you know when to work, eat, sleep?' Anita's question about lunch and dinner still crossed my mind.

'Is it different? In your world?' she replied. The Chomp was as curious as much as I was.

'It is. We have days and nights. Days when our star is in the sky and nights when it's not. It happens constantly. We do everything when it's daytime and we rest when it's nighttime.' I tired to explain it as best as I could without getting too complicated.

'Oh... That's fascinating. We have some old tales that speak of something like that. I wasn't born before the Great Dawn, like most of us. But Treekan knows. He knows the past. He talks about strange things like the one you said...sometimes.'

'So you don't sleep? Other than when it rains?'

'Oh, we do. When we are tired of too much work, or for Treekan, after our meals.' And she smiled. I had no idea how long they had been together, but listening to how she talked about him, they must be very close.

'How did you call him? Fearc...?'

'Fearcel. It means mine. For people that are meant to be together.'

They might have been different, on a strange planet, but they did share our concept of soulmates, our sense of togetherness. That felt deeply comforting. We were different on the outside, but their feelings were familiar.

'I feel we might rest for a little while,' she said.

'You do that too, after your meals?' I asked, smiling.

'Not really, not me. But the rain is coming, maybe in a little bit.'

And she moved outside, where Trusk, Anita, and Noah sat, chatting. She called his name, and he stood up and complied with an order we couldn't hear. A few moments later, he came back and started to move two large panels from the side of the house and placed them right in the

366

open side of the sitting room, closing himself, Noah, and Anita out.

'Fhe rain is coming. Liffle bif and we go,' he announced to Noah and Anita who looked at him, puzzled.

When Trusk came back inside, the two followed him in the house. Reela had repeated the announcement as if time was ticking faster, and we felt as if we were running late to catch a plane. Something was going to happen.

'It will go on for a while. Please feel free to stay here while we are gone. Please, for any reason, do not cross the wall. You are safe as long as you stay within the reach of our Flare.'

And the two went upstairs; with their funny walk they climbed the little staircase, preparing for something they were used to and that we had started to understand only recently.

Noah and I moved just outside the front door and sat by the entrance, while Anita roamed around, captured by all the strange things that welcoming family had. It was in that moment that a familiar urge of having a coffee and a cigarette came back to me, making me feel, for a moment, like I was just home. We sat quietly for a few minutes, by that strange house at the edge of the village. Everyone had disappeared from sight, preparing for their expected little rainy nap. This time around, there was no tool left behind, no business left unattended.

Noah stared at the space around us with a sense of achievement, like he had finished his greatest work and was now sitting by it, contemplating. Right when I thought he couldn't be more pleased about his discovery, tasting the pleasure of knowing there really was something he was destined to reach, he resumed his tireless hunt mode.

'There must be more,' he started. 'This can't be all there is to know. Whatever this place is, whatever I was meant to be part of, I don't think this is just it, you know what I mean?'

'To be honest, I'm beyond amazed about all this. I don't think my mind would be able to take even more. But I do understand that's not the same for you?' I was still fighting his restlessness. If we were both part of something, we were sitting at its opposite ends.

'I am amazed... Don't get me wrong. I would have never, even remotely, imagined a place like this would exist. These people, their world, their history. But I can't stop thinking how is this going to mean anything to us? If we are dreaming—and at this stage, we all know this is not really true—why are we dreaming of it? And if we are really here, how is it that nobody knew? We can't possibly be the first ones discovering it, right?' He had a point.

'Guys, have you seen any sort of...bathroom?' Anita asked from inside the house.

'Yes, you are right,' I continued, ignoring Anita. 'I never had a vision about this place. The things I have dreamt of have nothing to do with this place, as far as I can tell. I have been trying to discover my past, where did I come from, a bit like you. I do believe we are not from here. But still, this is an enormous event! I don't think it's so strange that I want to put our reasons, our goals aside for a little bit and try to figure this out'—and I pointed to the world in front of us—'first.'

368

'With figuring this out first, you mean leaving…going back home,' he replied, almost taunting me.

'If it's necessary, yes,' I responded sharply. I had felt his pain, I had shared his fears, but I wasn't going to be criticized because I wanted to put our safety first.

'What if we are here to save these people? To save this…being…what is his name, Time?'

'Assuming this is real, how are we supposed to do that? It looks like these people are way beyond our reach. They have magic, Noah. Not smoke and cheats. Magic!'

'You know?' Anita jumped right in, sitting a few steps away from us, on a tiny chair. 'I think this is real.'

We both stopped talking and looked at her trying to fit into a too-small, fragile chair hoping it wouldn't break. After struggling for a few seconds, she finally found a comfortable spot, on the floor, the shade of the large porch covering her from the motionless star. Large hungry clouds moved in the sky at a fast speed.

'Think about it,' she continued. 'We were hungry and have been fed. We have been running and been tired. We needed a bathroom and…well, let's leave it there, let's move on.' And once again, in the middle of our worries, we found ourselves laughing hard.

'It has never lasted that long either,' Noah added, referring to our daydreams.

'Also, these people have history, facts, events. How could we have ever made this up?' she continued.

'Okay. It's real then. It has to be. What does this tell us?' My last hope that we could actually wake up in Anita's

369

backyard, being able to scroll this from our shoulders and go home, to John, to Daisy, died painfully, leaving a trail of gloom.

'That we have to do better than this. So far, all we have been doing is running and walking. We need a ride home, and to do so, we need to come up with a plan.' There she was, Anita at her pure best.

For quite some time, I thought I had lost her. She had been unusually quiet, strangely passive to the events. The more laid back she was, the more I was pushing to go back home. I felt responsible for making her part of my madness, part of my worries, and I wanted it to be over, quickly. Her last words, her true personality emerging back to the surface, had made me feel stronger again. Finally, with the first drops of rain, my blind will to shut down that oneiric journey had returned.

'Now, did I say also we felt tired and fell asleep? No? 'Cause I really feel like I need to rest a bit. I feel like I'm turning into a Chomp...maybe this is all about...we all were meant to...' And, with the sound of the pouring rain, she quickly fell asleep, her last words stuck in between her lips.

It felt like a usual hot summer afternoon back in Italy, where everybody disappears from sight, gone to take a refreshing nap in the shade of their bedrooms. There was nobody left. Anita snoozed off pretty fast, and Noah and I sat still on our same spot, silent. Our brains travelled solo for a little bit as we had taken the hard decision to part ways, at least mentally. I gave him a look here and there, trying to read his mind like I had done before, in our shared vision.

His dark hair had finally dried off, his grey-clear eyes gazed at the horizon as if he could actually see the far-off, invisible wall we had crossed earlier. My mind went through time, to the first time we had met, in our world, our reality. Eventually, the same spell Anita had gone under, got to me as well, and with my head resting on a wooden pole of the roasting porch, I fell asleep.

Whatever happened afterwards was a secret from both me and Anita. We were suddenly woken up by the arrival of a familiar face. We had no idea for how long we had been sleeping; the star was still in the same spot, but it was like we had been gone for days. Treekan had just arrived. The rain must have stopped long enough for him to reach the village. Other Chomps moved about but Trusk and Reela were not around. We quickly stood up, waiting for important news.

'How did it go? I'm really sorry you had to go and risk your life for us. We all are,' I said immediately.

'There is no need to apologize,' Treekan replied. 'Where is your friend? I need to speak to you. All of you.'

My head turned to Anita and then Noah, to the exact spot where I had left him, but he wasn't there any longer. Anita raised her hands in response to my look, and I quickly thought he must have been somewhere nearby.

'Noah must be in the house. Did something happen?' I asked.

'I managed to speak with Aura, the gatekeeper. Oh, you have no idea about the surprise I had in seeing her again... Anyhow, there are things that are more ancient than me. Things that go beyond my memories. I have to get to know what it was way before the Great Dawn, things I have forgotten with the many yacs passed. Whatever reason brought you here has to be connected to it. Let's find your friend and head back to the Flare. We need to check the Ancient Mirrors once more.'

Without further ado, Anita and I re-entered the house to tell Noah we had news. The two hosts who had gently welcomed us were nowhere to be found. The house was empty. No Noah, no Reela, no Trusk.

'They must have gone for a walk together?' Anita guessed.

'Yeah, you could be right. How long have we been asleep?' I replied.

Before we could go and extend our search outside the house, Reela appeared from the top of the hill. She was in a hurry.

'Your friend...' she said, panting. 'Your friend is gone!'

'What do you mean?' I replied, responding to her panic. I had no idea what had happened, but my mind had already gone to the worst.

'Your friend... Noah? We woke up and found you here, asleep, just the two of you. He wasn't in the house any more. Trusk went downhill, looking for him at the wall. He should be back shortly. I've checked everywhere, at the Flare. I asked around. Nobody has seen him!' looked at Treekan, visibly upset, like she had lost her own child while she was responsible for our safety.

'He must be somewhere around, let's not panic, Reela,' Treekan replied, his hands up, trying to calm her down.

But I knew, somehow, that wasn't true any more. I had learned to know Noah's rush to get into things, his restless attitude towards knowing, understanding. Waiting in a sleepy, motionless village must have been too much for him.

'I think he's gone,' I let out, looking at Anita. She stared at me, looking for details, reasons. There was no other reason than that. Noah was being Noah. He had moved ahead.

'Here is Trusk,' Reela yelped.

'Nothing, Mom. He is not here. I checked over the wall too, for a little. He wasn't there.' His face showed his sense of failure.

'Why would he do something so stupid?' Anita whispered to me.

'Because he believes he has to take the risk. He wants to know and wants to know now,' I answered, defeated. In my mind, I had accepted it and let him go.

'If everything they've told us is true, he's risking his own life? Is it a risk worth dying for?' Anita's question fell there, in between the five of us, unanswered. We were all afraid to say it, but I knew. For him, it was.

Chapter Twenty-Five
The Great Dawn

∞

Our heads were fixed on the invisible spot where Anita's question had landed unheeded, while Reela's eyes pointed at Treekan who had gone silent, like the rest of us. Then he finally spoke:

'Let's not despair. He could still be around. There are urgent matters that need to be addressed. We need to go. Trusk!' He shifted his attention to his son. 'Go to Guroho and Saae's house. Tell them to go and look for Noah. Take others if needed, but do not, and I repeat, do not, cross the wall again! There are spectres around. I could feel them close as I was shifted.' And Reela's eyes got bigger.

'*Shifted?*' I asked.

'*Spectres?*' Anita asked at the same time.

'Yes, horrible, malevolent creatures. I saw them gathering in hordes in the outskirts. They could not see me passing through, fortunately, but they could still feel my presence.'

Treekan had his son's same ability to disappear. Chomps had proven to be very resourceful. It was no surprise they were still alive.

'We need to go, now,' Treekan said to Anita and me.

After the scary stories we had heard, the magic we had discovered, the fear of being in a strange new place, we found ourselves obeying his order with no questions. We left aside the important fact we had lost Noah and we placed our trust in Treekan, dangerously. A few moments later we were all speeding up back to the Flare, our target getting to the Ancient Mirrors as soon as possible. Although we had spent the first few minutes listening only to our heavy breathing, eventually we started to ask Treekan a few questions.

'Sir, if Noah left the village…if these…spectres have found him…'

'If that's the case, they are probably bringing him to their queen by now,' he replied, before I could finish.

'Does that mean…they...will…harm him?' Rushing to ask, words struggled to come out. Anita looked at me in shock. Whatever reality we were experiencing, harming, killing perhaps, was too much. The whole new experience wasn't welcomed any more.

'Most likely,' he replied, as if that was the obvious conclusion. 'She will extract every piece of information first, then he won't be needed any more.'

'Oh God!' Anita's breathing got shorter and shorter till she stopped walking. 'This can't be real. Daniel, we have to wake up!'

'Anita, we are not dreaming. This is not my doing.' And I wished it was. I could have ended it in the blink of an eye.

'Humans, you don't understand,' Treekan stopped and came close to Anita, his hand on her shoulder. His face finally showed us some empathy. 'We need to move fast. If your friend is really out there, his only chance to survive is in our hands!'

We picked up the pace again, even faster than we had yet. We'd been running since the moment we had landed in Runae, but this time we were not running away. We were running looking for something. We eventually passed the Flare and headed to the crooked building. The flame in the ground was worryingly flickering, at times losing strength, as if it was fighting to stay alive against an evil, gelid force. Treekan pushed the big doors wide open, carelessly, and we hurried inside after him. At the finish line, the mirrors hung in silence, some of them waiting to be questioned. Treekan showed no interest in any of the ones that were still intact; instead, he put his hands at the centre of the wall, just below the frame of a cracked mirror, and pushed the frame away.

A portion of the wall detached from the rest and twisted around itself, placing the cracked mirror at the back, and a new, shining one took its place. There was a new, secret mirror in front of us. Its frame ivory, with golden ornaments all around, its glass had no reflection, no replica of the three of us staring at it. A pure silver liquid slightly moved on the surface, waiting.

'This is the first of the first ones,' Treekan said, his hands slowly hovering over the surface. The silvery fluid was moving, following his gestures, like something inside was waiting to come forward. 'The first of the Ancient Mirrors to appear, the first me and my father explored. It retains every piece of memory since the Great Dawn.'

'How long has passed since then?' Anita asked, moving closer.

'Time is long gone,' the Chomp replied. A shadow had covered his eyes. 'Not just his personification who lies in chains, in the evil queen's grip. Time as a measure of past, present and future was gone the day she enslaved him. But these Mirrors continue to count the hocs, the rhocs and the yacs.'

'Yacs?' Anita was trying to speed up her learning process. History, and the ability to read it through, was her strength. She needed more.

'Yes, before Erion stopped moving, we counted its coming and going. Rhocs are for one coming and going. Yacs is three hundred times that.'

'Days and years,' Anita whispered, looking at me.

'The first Mirror counts twelve thousand yacs,' he continued. 'We don't know, and probably will never know, how long Runae existed before that. I know only what happened a little before and after the Great Dawn and everything that happened after that. It's baffling how we live in a rhoc that has no time and we have very little time to go through it, now. I wish I could share everything I've learned from searching through history, but we are here to look for something more specific. We need to go to the very

377

beginning, when Time was taken from us. I need to remember what I saw back then, when I was young, the memories that I completely lost.'

Anita and I were silent. There was so much to know and yet, we were in a rush. Noah's life could depend on how fast we found what we needed, what Treekan was looking for. Silence was our only possible contribution to speed things up. Treekan moved right in front of the First Mirror, his hands on the ivory frame, his eyes closed. His lips were ready to cast the spell.

'A yac for yac. My yacs for your yacs, to buy your oldest secrets, the beginning of your true self... Show it!'

And the surface started to pulse, faster and faster. A strong light surged from its deepest memories and it spilled outside the frame, moving around us, embracing the three of us in a wobbling, ethereal sphere. Our world changed again, we were being teleported once more somewhere else, this time not through space, not through worlds, but right across time. Nothing else moved, the existence beyond the mirror's light had remained untouched, unchanged, but we could see it shifting, rewinding events, moments, people. It was as if we could look at history in the making, backwards. Till it finally stopped.

'Where are we?' Anita asked.

'Or when,' I added.

'We are right before the Great Dawn, shortly after the Gods' war,' Treekan replied, while the space around us settled into a new shape. 'It's said that the Gods who created Runae and everything within engaged in a war against the evil. Our God and protector of Runae was Time. He fought hard and resisted a power that could not be defeated. Because he could not also be overcome or completely destroyed, the evil trapped him in the deepest of the lands, below the five temples, in the hands of the Leonty. There, he was given in slavery to them, to be watched, restrained forever. Time's pure essence penetrated our world and our life, turning everything into a frozen memory, for all time. Around that time, the Ancient Mirrors came to be, one by one, starting with the one we are looking in, right now. The Great Dawn was about to be.'

With our ears enchanted by the Chomp's voice, we travelled through time, matter forming right before our very eyes, like we were part of it. My mind briefly went to that night by the harbour, in Italy, when the vision of Grandma's past had formed just around me. Was I experiencing the same, unknown power then? A familiar place materialized around us. A large, quiet ocean embraced a tiny piece of land. On it, someone in the shape of a man had just appeared, crossing the node. Defying the power of the Gods and the magic of the ancient portal, he walked the same steps Anita, Noah and I had walked not long before. Like a copy of our own history, a gatekeeper was on her way to greet him.

'I'm Aura,' she said, immediately after taking shape. Some other beings, identical copies of the one we had met, formed behind her. 'The God of this world has put me as a gatekeeper. We were not expecting anyone. This gateway is open only to the Gods. Who are you?'

379

'My name is Lëogan,' the man said. In between the messy, white beard, he attempted a wicked smile. 'I'm here 'cause my world is in danger. I come to ask for help.'

'What world are you speaking of?' The Aqualymph stared at her guest suspiciously. Something wasn't right.

'Earth. We are under attack! We need your help, your power, your magic to face the enemy!'

'If what he says is true, we need to bring him to the council!' another Aqualymph suggested.

'Yes, please. I need to talk to them!'

In the snap of two fingers, the vision collapsed, twisting lights and shadows, forming a new landscape. Temples appeared in the far end of the land, too small to be counted. Beings pressed against each other in fear, petrified by the enormous power that had been unleashed in their land. In between fire and destruction, a small group of Leonty covered their faces, their eyes, trying to resist the unbearable, evil energy, screaming from uncontrollable terror; but one of them, a young of her species, had found the strength to resist. Driven by a sick desire and untouched by her kind's pain, she started to walk, moving dangerously close to the source of that power. Her look was Revelia's look. Her face was uncannily familiar, same body, same long hard hair, but somehow different, even more beautiful than we had seen before. She moved slowly amidst the destruction, her gaze fixed upon the one who raged across the lands.

'You do not fear?' A voice thundered from the raging heavens. 'You are unlike the others. What is this... anger I sense? No, it is more than anger. It is wrath, a desire for

380

annihilation.' Yet Una remained silent, her eyes fixed upon the malevolent entity above, a hint of a smile playing upon her lips. 'So you seek it from me... It was you I had seen...'

'Free me...' Una whispered, tears flowing on her green cheeks. 'Free me from this pain.'

'And so I will! You come to me in a time of need, as I do to you. I shall transform your fury into a power unlike any known to kind. You shall wield the might of this God and his dominion, bending it to your will, for as long as I require to fulfil my design!'

A haunting whistle pierced the air, as if every element of the dying planet were being drawn inexorably towards a singular point. In that instant, the one who had been fighting against the evil was reduced to nothing but a brilliant speck, cast into the abyss below a Temple. Amidst the swirling dust and flames, a Clepsydra descended, coming to rest within Una's outstretched hands.

'Others have come to me before, seeking the same power you now crave...' The voice echoed through the frozen expanse, holding the lands and sky in a dark, motionless tableau. In a world on the brink of death, one heart raced with anticipation; Una's eyes gleamed with a fierce desire. 'But your desire is of a different nature. They sought to conquer; you seek to obliterate...'

'I seek to end it,' the young Leonty declared, unflinching. 'I want to end it all! I have been enslaved, imprisoned by forces I have never even encountered. And for what? There is no reason, no justification at all!'

'You were wrought by the hand of one who shaped all existence. As you were not meant to be, so too is your anguish. This suffering is a... gift, a direct consequence of the rebellion against me. Should you wish, you can undo it all. Strip away everything. With the power I offer, you can erase all that exists. Future, present, past...'

'Who are you?' Una asked.

'I'm Nothing, and Nothing will always be.'

Few moments later, the light around us flashed, one, two, three times and then we were gone. Time had passed, places transformed. We were brought somewhere else but one thing remained the same. Una was alone. Waiting for someone by her tower, her hands firmly holding that same artefact. She had been summoned. Her face had changed, her beauty was now of a stranger making, darker, deeper.

'Your work here is not finished,' a familiar, incorporeal voice suddenly reverberated around the walls.

'It's almost done. Besides my own sisters, there is only one kind left on this planet,' Una replied, her gaze fixed on the bare stone wall. 'Five of the six stones are in my hands.'

'You better be finished when I'm done with my mission. His power is still crawling across these lands, his magic still lingers in the hands of your own kind. Take it and be done with it!' Nothing replied, disappointment evident in his tone. 'Nevertheless, you have given me time to destroy Creation's stupid Gods. However,' he resumed after a brief silence, 'these Gods are painfully stubborn. It seems I'm prevented from destroy them completely, but sure I can trap them indefinitely. The one you watch over, the one whose power lies in your hands now, might even try to come back to life, with the help of others. If anyone or anything crosses the gates of this world, you must use the power I've given you to tear them down! If necessary, take half of this planet with them, but do it!'

Once again, the space around us trembled, the light had flickered and dimmed till it eventually disappeared. We were brought back to our time, to the giant room, by the Mirrors. Treekan's eyes were wide open, rewinding in his mind the revelation we had received. For a brief moment, Anita and I looked at each other, our brains spinning fast. There was so much to understand, so much to recall. I had witnessed things for the first time but also things I had seen before. Una was holding something I had already seen in my vision.

'Treekan,' Anita finally interrupted our long silence, 'were we not the first ones to cross the gate?'

'My dear...I thought you were. This is why I had to go and see Aura...'

'Does this mean...we are here to free Time?' Anita had already connected the dots. Although I hadn't picked that up, at first, I soon realized what we had actually seen and heard, and how the latest event had put us in the spotlight.

'It looks like you are.' The Chomp turned his face away, his thoughts choking, sinking his heart to the ground.

'Are you OK?' I asked, moving closer. 'What's wrong?'

'Nothing, Human,' he said, brushing the moment away. 'Something unrelated came to my mind. I can look at it later. Don't worry.' But his lie came through naked, obvious. He was upset by something important, but he wouldn't let it out.

'So this is it. This is how it began,' Treekan continued. 'Now I know how the Crimson Queen got her power, and from who. She is still drawing her strength from him. 'And he looked at us, like we would easily understand.

'You didn't know?' I asked. 'Reela told me you knew more than anyone else, that you were the master of your history?'

'I knew only what I could remember, what I could bear. I always felt a great risk in trading my yacs with theirs.' And Treekan pointed at the mirrors.

'Trading? What does it mean?' Anita preceded me.

'For every rhoc and every yac I gained knowledge of, I must to give one of mine back. It's the spell's will. There is no other way.' And his face turned sad. Whatever he was worried about, it was still haunting him.

'You mean you need to give away the time you have left, in exchange for the one you are pulling from the mirrors?' I continued Anita's question.

'Yes, Human. But don't worry,' he added, noticing our shocked faces. 'There is no time for us, here in Runae. Whatever I have been deprived of, it doesn't affect me. Now,'—and his tone suddenly changed—'we know why you are here. You will put an end to our misery, you will free our God and protector!'

'Wait…OK, let's hold on. How are we supposed to do that?' Anita, like me, was unprepared to go and start any rescue mission.

'You have magic, and terrifying powers…we have nothing. Just a stupid box that doesn't do anything but put

384

us in trouble already,' I continued on the same line. My grandma's gift had come with no secret ability that we were aware of, no instructions, no hope.

'You have already performed miracles. You came here, you Humans. A kind we believed long gone and forgotten. You are the spark that will change our fate.' Treekan was putting an unbearable amount of faith in us. It was disheartening.

'Whatever that box has done, it can't be done again. Not without Noah, right?' Anita looked at me, giving me another reason to doubt.

'Treekan,' I said. 'We need to find Noah. If you really think we can help you, that can be done only if Noah is with me!' I omitted we had to still figure that piece out. We didn't know yet how to trigger our visions by being together, still less how to generate a far superior magic. But one thing was clear, Noah and I had to be close.

'This one has no power?' Treekan asked, pointing his finger at Anita. She wasn't pleased.

'She does,' I replied. 'But not of the kind you mean...'

'But Aura said only the Gods can cross the gates. You must be one of them!' Treekan pushed back on the idea Anita was just a victim of circumstance.

'We just saw someone crossing the gate, in that vision,' Anita replied. 'Didn't look like a God to me. Something is missing here.'

'Someone we thought had come to help.' And Treekan's face changed again, into an expression of sorrow and guilt.

385

A sound of rushing steps came to interrupt our conversation, Trusk hurried with updates we were not going to like.

'Fafher,' he started, panting. 'He is nof in fhe village any more. We looked everywhere.' And he put his hands on his chest. His heartbeat could nearly be heard.

'If this is the case,' Treekan replied, 'we need to know what happened. We might not know where he is now...but we might know where he was a few hocs ago.'

And he turned back again, moved to the mirror at the far left and launched the spell once more. This time there was no light, no vision coming to life. Treekan could see the past in his own mind and, after a few moments, he started to share his thoughts.

'He left from the west side and crossed the wall, where the Flare can't protect him. He was walking towards Broken Crown ruins when the spectres felt him.' My heart started to race. Noah was gone and between us were who knew how many miles. 'They have him. They asked him where the others were. He didn't answer. They penetrated his head. They are still there, trying to extort what they can.' And then Treekan took his hands from the mirror frame, his eyes wide open, staring at us, his voice shaking. 'They will bring him to her!'

'No!' Anita screamed. 'No! Daniel, we need to wake up, now!'

I was petrified. I could feel the fear dragging me down, trapping my body under the large black stones of the pavement. Anita had let go the full strength of her panic and begged me to let her free from the enchantment, as if I

386

were responsible for holding her prisoner. There was no way out. The wide-open doors to the far end of the room were growing smaller with every breath, the red light coming from the powerful star had left us; the darkness was swallowing me as fast as the blood was pulsing into my head.

What is this? Why are we here? This was a mistake. A mistake we are going to pay for with our lives. Why can't we go back? My thoughts twisted painfully in my mind. I could feel them mixing with something else, a noise reaching from below, like a beacon sending a message in between my ears. *'I feel it. He is one of them. I feel it. I have to set him free…he has been by my side since I was a child, since forever. I have to. We have to, Daniel, we have to!'*

'I can feel him!' I said aloud. 'Anita, I can hear Noah, in my head!'

'Oh my God, is he OK?' She rushed to me, holding my face with her hands, her panic leaving some space for hope.

'It's true,' I continued, my eyes lost in an invisible trail of thoughts. 'The one who's been kept prisoner, is the one who has been calling me…and calling him for all this time.'

'You mean Time is the one you've been seeing? Has he been sending you the visions?' Anita was trying to read through my words.

The two Chomps looked at us, disoriented by our conversation. There was so much we had learned from them and so little they had received in exchange. They knew their history but not ours, not mine.

'I believe he is, at least one of the three,' I finally replied. My head had come back under my will, Noah's mind had turned off. 'This must be the reason why everything has happened. I do know you got caught up in the middle, and I'm sorry. But I have to go and rescue Noah before I can even try to do anything else. 'But you are safe here… You should stay!'

'My fearcel would be happy to take care of you.' Treekan moved closer, his hands on us in a sign of comfort.

'No!' Anita firmly replied. 'This is not your fault, Daniel. The moment you left my backyard, the moment I put my hand on your shoulder, being carried here…I chose. I chose to be here with you, for you. I pushed you to hunt for the truth. I can't deny it now only because this truth worries me. We are going to do this together!' And a weak smile appeared on her face.

.

Chapter Twenty-Six
The Path Of The Lost Ones

∞

In a fight against time, in a world where there wasn't time at all, we all felt the risk and the hurry to rescue Noah. If we were going to attempt the biggest challenge of our lives, we had to save him first. It wasn't long since we had left the Ancient Mirrors behind us when we arrived at Treekan's home. The old Chomp had instructions to give us, a plan needed to be made. Anita was secretly happy to have someone who could think things through, plan accordingly and reduce the risks. Reela took us by surprise, hugging both of us at the front door. Despite her small size, she was holding us together, her tiny wings flapping slightly, as if they were showing her emotions.

'I'm really sorry for your friend! I wish I'd been here to stop him…' she said.

'Come on, Reela,' Treekan replied. 'The Humans have little to wait and very much to go.'

Trusk sat by the table as we followed his father inside. He pulled a few things from an old cabinet lying in the corner of the room and placed them on the table.

'Alright, we have no way to show you where to go. There is no map that goes as far as you need to go. We do know our way around, though. Trusk knows a good bit of what lies over the wall, but I'm the only one who knows the way to the Crimson Queen. We will lead you in. If we are fast enough, and lucky, we could get to your friend before the end of the road.'

Reela was quietly listening. My eyes had gone from Treekan to Trusk then to her. I felt sorry for putting them at that risk and seeing the worry in her eyes made me sick. She wasn't challenging his decision but I could feel she wanted to.

'The two of you will need mine and Trusk's invisibility power. We won't be able to use it in close proximity to the evil. The further away we are from our Flare, the less power we have. If your friend is still at the Broken Crown ruins, by the time we arrive, we might have a chance to take the spectres by surprise. They will sense us but won't be able to see where we are. After that…I don't think we will have much of an advantage.'

'How far is this place?' I asked.

'It's where the Humans' kingdom once stood,' Treekan replied. For a moment, I had forgotten we didn't have the same perception of time, or space.

'Will we fly?' Anita added.

'We will if if's safe,' Trusk stepped into the conversation. Like by the forest, he was happy to carry us with his tiny powerful wings.

'There are few things we need to count on. For one, we need to hope our only friend will be on our side, when the time comes,' Treekan continued, taking in his hands a bow that was hanging on the wall.

'That's not a weapon. That's help, if you need it,' Reela continued, noticing our worried faces. 'That's how Treekan calls the Leonty and lets her know we want to speak to her. He shoots it up in the sky, through the ceiling of our dome. And she knows she has been summoned.'

'We also need to hope the evil doesn't send the unexpected clouds over us. Like she had done the moment you arrived, she could do it again, if she knows where we are.'

So she has also that power, I thought. *That's why the Chomps were taken by surprise, that day.* Revelia had hinted at something like that, but only now I could make sense of it.

'Can we trust her? I mean, Revelia.' I was still stuck on that part.

'Since the Great Dawn, her kind has never been good to any other being on Runae. There is a reason why Una was chosen, I understand that now. After all this time, I still can't believe the Humans were right...' Treekan replied.

391

'But Revelia has always been different. She can see things ahead, before they happen, sometimes. I believe this has given her the ability to doubt her sister's intention. The ability to know everyone's intentions.' It didn't sound like a yes to me, nor to Anita who looked at me, not particularly convinced.

'There is one last thing,' he continued. 'On our way, we will cross lands that once belonged to other kinds, now in disrepair. Nobody was left alive, nowhere, except for a place we will try to fly over. It's the house of the dead. It's what once was the land of the Witches of Fárahal. I'll tell you more on our way, there is no time now to go through ghost stories but, please, don't ever leave our side, ever!'

And the old Chomp filled a bag made of a material similar to hemp with everything he had collected on the table. His bow on his shoulder and only one arrow in his hand, he was ready to walk us out. Reela called Trusk up to her side, hugged him, kissed him and gave him another similar bag to carry.

'I didn't manage to make much, but some of our friends have filled the bag with whatever they had ready. It should last long enough for you not to starve…'

'Thank you, Reela,' I said, and Anita hugged her.

'Be careful, all of you.' And, after holding us a little longer in her small arms, she let us go, worried.

A few Chomps had gathered close to the house, probably the same ones who had helped Reela put together the food we needed for the journey. They must have known what we were setting out to do; their troubled faces followed us while we walked towards the edge of the village. At the very end of the west side, where nothing else was left standing, we lost sight of that incredible group of beings. Looking back, our minds holding to the affection we had received, Anita and I felt like there wasn't going to be a way back.

'Dear,' Treekan said to Anita, 'Take my hand. We need to cross the wall side by side. My veil will cover your body too. We must be quiet. We don't know who is waiting on the other side...'

Anita immediately complied, her eyes on mine, as I took Trusk's hand before crossing the invisible border. The pressure on our bodies was as strong as we remembered, but this time there was no repelling force to fight against us. Instead, it felt as if the dome was pushing us out, unwanted. A moment later, we found ourselves in the unknown. The silence had come in as a demanding guest, none of the Chomps made a sound and we, like them, kept our thoughts to ourselves. There was no difference between before and after, everything looked like we had seen it from inside that magical protective power. No one was spying in the shadow of the large rocks scattered around, we could not see anyone ready to attack.

'Stay silent. I can't see them now but they could be nearby. Their form is of a pure evil spirit. Sometimes you see them shifting, but not always. Let's go now...'

Our steps went faster, we ran through the danger like little ninjas, invisible to naked eyes. In front of us, the fields were harsh, like rust had spilled all over the ground. To the left, hills kept the distance from the far sea, and to the right, massive grey mountains covered a good portion of the sky. Shortly after we had completely lost sight of where the

Chomp's village was supposed to be, the fields started to slope down, all pointing to a large mass of white buildings in ruins.

'That's the entry for Broken Crown,' Treekan whispered. 'That's where we are heading, but we need to cross that path below.'

Right where the field sloped down, a different one rose up, both crashing into each other, creating a dramatic mash of colours. In the middle, an old path in ruin snaked through from one part to another. Once arrived near its edge, we stopped.

'It looks like we are alone,' Treekan said again, his voice barely audible. 'There is something strange in the air, I feel like an oppressive force is playing here. I believe all the witched died a very long time ago, but still, I'm not confident we should fly yet. Let's keep walking. Stay close.'

I could not see him, I didn't know where Treekan and Anita were, but Trusk moved with no uncertainty. He could see his father through their magic and I could not help but wonder how long they could keep that power going.

We walked a very long distance, and my feet had started to complain. The landscape around us had undergone a complete transformation. The fields ascended steeply, and the rising lands resembled walls that enclosed us in a narrow, claustrophobic road. The ground we walked on was neatly paved, but large portions were missing here and there. It seemed like something great had been built somewhere nearby, at some point in the distant past.

Right when I was about to call for a stop, the world in front of us opened up. Large white columns scattered around, hundreds of them, some in pieces, others crashed down on their sides, some still standing. Further down, large buildings kept their balance on the few walls they had left. Everything was white, like a bright, clean marble had been shaped to form a vast, heavenly place. A heaven turned to hell it was, broken, in ruins. The long shadows of the buildings started to fade away as the sky got darker, wetter. *We must have already reached the Broken Crown ruins,* I thought.

'Fafher...' After being quiet for a very long time, Trusk finally spoke.

'I know...' Treekan replied. 'We won't make it on time to the other side and we won't be able to fly.' Something was about to happen. I had learned to read the signals, read through their words. 'This is not the sky's doing. Let's hurry! We need to hide you somewhere,' the Chomp continued.

A flash came out from an invisible spot ahead of me; a golden dart left the ground to reach the black sky. Trusk suddenly pulled my arm into a quick sprint. We sped up towards somewhere; I had no idea if we were running from something or somebody, but my mind had gone to Anita. I could not see her and I didn't want to lose her too.

'If we sleep, you will be see,' Trusk said, panting, his voice loud. Any fear of being detected, identified by the enemy, had lost relevance compared to what would come next.

The light dimmed at every step we made, darkness approaching from every corner. That feeling was familiar, we had faced the same threat before. It was going to rain soon. A moment later, my face was on the ground. As I had been pulled back from Trusk's heavy weight, his hand still in mine, he lay down like he had suddenly died, the heavy rain bouncing on his body.

With my lungs in convulsion, I looked around to find the others. There, Anita stood several steps away, just beside a cracked wall at the entrance of a house. I could barely see her through the lashing hell, her hands telling me to come over. With Trusk on my shoulder, I hurried into the house where Anita struggled to drag Treekan. The silence we had vowed to uphold still permeated the air. As our fear intensified, we grew even quieter. Treekan's words echoed in our minds. We had to remain invisible, devoid of magic or any form of protection. There was only a broken wall standing between us and the evil.

We spent some time hiding, staring outside in terror, praying for the rain to pass. Once our minds and our bodies had adjusted to a panic that was never going to leave, we started to talk. Our conversation wasn't through sound and voices, but pure gestures and expressions. If the situation hadn't been so worrying, we could have laughed at our newly discovered way of communicating. Anita opened up with the strong belief the rain was the queen's doing and I agreed. Somehow she could manipulate the weather and, according to what Treekan had said, she could decide where. She knew where we were, and that was terrible.

'We might actually be able to wait this out here,' Anita whispered. Her mouth close to my ear, our bodies squeezed against a corner as if we could merge with it.

'All we need is to resist, to go unnoticed till they wake up. Then Treekan will tell us what to do,' I answered. 'Let's stay quiet.'

But the rain fell mercilessly, matched by the night that had come with it, with its dark purpose. All we could hear was the crashing storm around us, the cry of the wind that had started to haunt that crippled house. It was as if whispers had come to keep us company; the history of that place was telling us about the atrocity it had witnessed.

'We were gone, but we never left,' someone was saying. 'Cast away from the Crown City, we fled to the whispering forest. The evil found us there and we had no other way but to come here... And we could not move further. Our only way was the heaven...but we were prevented from leaving...'

I could clearly hear the talk in my head. Anita lay down, her head resting at the wall; I was the only one listening to that cry.

'Time was held still, our souls ready to reach the Gods, but we could not go further. We were lost in between life and death...waiting...waiting for a prophecy that never came true.'

'You can still go...why are you not going?'

Multiple voices talked to me; they knew me and were telling me there was a way out, a way to end the madness we had fallen into. That was certainly what I wanted. I wanted to bring Anita home. I wanted to see John again, see his face, his silent smile.

'It's in your hands…you can, if you want. Just close your eyes and follow our voice. We can guide you out. Leave this place of eternal death. Don't join the lost ones, move further…'

It was indeed what I wanted. If I had left that place, I would have set free Anita and Noah. We could have gone back home in a snap. All I had to do was close my eyes and let my heart go. What would happen to Trusk…Treekan? My mind was holding to a sense of gratitude for everything they had done and tried to do still, to save us. I can't leave them here…they would die by the hand of the spectres…

'They belong here. They know how to survive…' The voices answered me. 'You don't belong here. Save your friends…go…'

I was split in between my will and my duty. We were brought there for a reason. We had believed in it. Now, I was cowardly willing to leave things unfinished. I had risked our lives and the Chomps' lives for nothing. But I wanted to go home, I wanted to be normal again. I could see the gates, the house, Daisy wagging her tail. John standing at the front door, arms out to greet me.

'Where have you been?' he said.

'I'm sorry, John, so many things have happened. I need to tell you so much! I want to tell you everything.'

'It's OK. You know you don't need to worry. I will always be here for you. You are home now.'

'You don't understand! I've been...I've been...' The words scrambled in my head. I wasn't thinking clearly. 'I've been in some places. I lost Anita and I lost Noah...'

'It doesn't matter, Daniel. All that matters is that you found your way back to me. All you need to do now is to close your eyes and hug me...'

John's love was more tangible than ever before. He wasn't asking questions, he didn't asked who Noah was. He was ready to put everything aside and move on. I had the chance to close that chapter forever, to forget what it was and live whatever was going to be...with him. My past could be left behind, the mysteries forgotten. I could do what Grandma had done. Wake up and find all my memories gone.

Grandma...she had protected me from my past. No, she had protected me in a vision of my future. She believed I had to come to terms with all of this. I had to stay. I wanted to stay. Her face was still impressed in my mind. I could see her smile when she had come back from the oblivion and had recognized me. How much love was in it? How much had she done for me all those years? Her fight to get back to me, to tell me the truth, wasn't something I could waste.

I was back to my senses. The wind was gone and the rain had nearly stopped. It was like I had fallen asleep, but I hadn't. I was completely sure now, all this time we weren't in one of my visions; what I had just experienced was. That was the difference between reality and dreams. We had left Earth physically, to reach Runae. John was only a beautiful but sad projection of my mind. Nothing more. It was as if my life had flipped into reverse. I was now in the world of my dreams and my visions were about the life I had. My fear was almost gone when it sharply turned to horror. Anita was gone. She wasn't there any more. I was alone, beside me, only the two motionless Chomps.

I could not breathe, my hands started to shake. That wasn't real, it wasn't possible. She had to be there, somewhere. I had to be brave and get out, find her anywhere she had gone.

So I left Treekan and Trusk behind, left the house and stepped outside. The rain was getting thinner and the space around me was coming back, visible. I was a tiny, powerless dot in an immense, dead city. As I ran randomly, with no clue of the surroundings, every corner looked the same, every wall had the same colour. I could feel the desperation mounting. We were lost. I had lost her, I had lost Noah and myself, I had lost my way back to the Chomps. So I crashed onto my knees, my face mixing tears with rain. My hands on the ground, I knew it was our hope coming to an end.

Chapter Twenty-Seven
A Traitor To Her Own Kind

∞

Victory was only moments away. Her smile was unnatural, her mind had long forgotten what satisfaction would look like, would feel like. But she was victorious again, like she had been before. All her sisters stood behind, looking at her back, waiting. Instructions had been given, commands moved from her to them, like whippings on their flesh. The only Leonty left alive were hers to move, direct to attack, to kill. All but one.

'Where is she?' the Crimson Queen asked. Her body still refusing to turn and look at her own kind, her own blood.

'She was coming with us, my queen,' one of them replied. 'But just before we reached the gates, she parted ways.'

'Demetra, I imagine you know why?' Una expected a devoted, truthful confession.

'She has learned to block my power, my queen. I tried; she can shield her thoughts now.'

That was unacceptable, an insult to the obedience due to her. She finally turned around. Her appearance was nothing like theirs. She was far more beautiful and far more terrifying.

'We will address this later,' she snapped. 'There is something far more important. The threat has been handled. As we speak, the spectres are bringing one of these...insignificant Humans...here, to me.'

'What about the others, my queen?' a Leonty asked.

'The others have been stopped too, Trasfigea. And those disgusting Chomps with them. A few more moments and they will be gone forever.' And the wicked smile came back on her face.

'What do you want us to do?' Like her sister Revelia, Demetra had no access to Una's mind. Her power was too great to overcome and any attempt would have been perceived and seen as a betrayal.

'When they bring the Human, I want you to extract every single piece of memory from his mind...and when you are done with it, kill him! You!' Una continued, briefly looking at Trasfigea. 'You and the others go to the ruins. Once there, I want you to take your sister's form.'

'My queen?' The Leonty couldn't follow her master's words.

'The one that seems to have a will of her own. I have been tolerating her insubordination for too long. Whatever she is doing while she disappears, has to come to an end. Go to the Ruins and be her. Let them see you as her. Set them free.'

'You are sending us all the way there to set them free?'

'No, you silly shapeshifter! You are going to prove me right. I know what she is up to. Once there, show me how Revelia has been betraying us, betraying her queen for all this time. Now go!'

There was no order that could be disobeyed and there was no Leonty who didn't love the evil. So Demetra left the room. As instructed, she was going to wait for the precious gift to be delivered while Trasfigea and the other sisters would go to Broken Crown to lay the trap before collecting the bodies of the new dead.

Alone again, the Crimson Queen engaged in a fight between the satisfaction of the upcoming victory and the feeling of a new danger arising. She was certain the final move had been made. The outcome was obvious and final. She had a power like no other, but someone else had proven differently. It was the idea of Revelia, who was now able to block Demetra's ability, watering down the sweet taste of victory. With the power she possessed already, she could become a menace. They all could. Her own sisters were not like her; they were nothing compared to her. Their Flare, their magic was not going to bring any advantage, unless she could use it herself. A new, toxic desire took root in her dark heart. It was time to consider the next move. It was time to absorb the last two remaining Flares, for good.

In between the deceitful ruins I was about to surrender. There wasn't much to fight for, any more. I was the only one left and I was sure the spectres would find me soon, there in the open. I gave a final look around before letting my final strengths leave, and there she was. Further ahead, Anita stood on the edge of a house built on a steep slope. My eyes struggled to adjust to the idea I had found her. She was still there, a few steps away. I rushed my feet to get to her; I was about to stretch my arm and grab her when someone spoke.

'Don't! She is about to trade her life with theirs.' Revelia appeared from nowhere, her eyes glowing red.

'Revelia? Please help me, she is going to fall down!' begged, with the fear she wasn't going to be the ally Treekan had described.

'Hold still. It's vital we let the future move ahead, just another bit. Their fingers hold tight on her mind. If we wake her now, she won't be your friend any more.' And she moved closer.

'What does it mean? Please do something!' I had no idea what was happening to her. If Revelia was telling the truth, I was about to lose Anita, this time for good.

'There is something strange in here, stranger than I thought.' And the Leonty scanned the space around Anita, her eyes glowing like tiny stars on fire. 'There is not only one future ahead. There are two. There is someone else beside her...what magic is this?'

Anita's face had lost colour. Her eyes were open but the light had left its place to a grey shadow. Her mouth was open, like she was screaming in terror. Her hands down, her body wasn't hers to possess any longer.

'Your scent mixes with the one we have seen...' a voice whispered. You have been close to him, the one we saw coming, before the end of us all...'

'You are long dead, there is no place for you to be. You can't come back!' Revelia replied, gazing all around Anita.

'Let us taste the power of a prophecy once more...' the unknown continued, ignoring the Leonty's demand. 'She shares a path with the one who will seat on the throne again. We must have her, to see our prediction come true...'

'She doesn't belong here. She is not yours. Let her go!' And Revelia's voice powerfully travelled in the far land, full of anger and determination. I was sure the evil had heard her and found us.

'We want to go further...' a whisper said. Whoever Revelia was talking to, it was engaging.

'You will! Time has come. You will be free again soon. Now, let her go!' she repeated, this time directly to Anita.

And then the silence came back. Anita's body moved for a moment, then she collapsed in Revelia's arms.

'What happened?' I asked, moving closer. She looked lifeless still, but the soft colour of her skin had started to come back. Her eyes closed, her mouth shut.

'You are lucky I saw the signal...few more minutes and I would have missed it.' And I knew what I had seen earlier was Treekan's arrow flying up to the sky. 'This place is cursed. Everywhere, spirits and witches are waiting for a spark of life.'

405

'Whose spirits?' Anita's hands were getting warmer again.

'The Humans my sister has killed! Their souls are trapped here, in this place…since time doesn't pass, their journey never began. Their only way further is to come back, in someone's body. And this body'—and looked at Anita with renewed interest—'this body seems to be already a good vessel.'

'This must be the place Treekan has warned us about…but we had no way of knowing it. Both he and Trusk are lying asleep somewhere here around.' And I looked back, hoping I could remember where I had left them.

'Don't worry. We'll get to them shortly. Your friend is about to wake up. We need to leave this place at once. The spectres are not the only ones looking for you any more.'

Anita opened her eyes. She was disoriented and confused. Her first attempt to stand up was a failure, but after regaining strength, she raised herself onto her feet.

'Daniel…' she said slowly. 'I had a very strange dream…we were in this strange, huge palace…'

'No, honey…it wasn't a dream. I had it too. It was a trap. Can you walk? We need to move.'

'Where are the Chomps?' she asked, looking around. 'How did I get here?'

'Let's leave the answers for later.' Revelia held her tight. I had misjudged her. She was indeed an ally. 'You'll feel better soon. Let's go.'

We made our way back to the Chomps; wherever they were, I had no idea how to get to them. Revelia seemed to know her way around as much as Treekan had earlier.

'The Chomp called you with the arrow, didn't he?' I asked, as we walked in between the large ruins.

'Yes. I was about to go and see Una, with the company of my sisters, when I saw the white trail passing through the sky. I left with no excuse, so I can imagine she has already sent someone after me.'

'You imagine or you have seen it?' I asked.

'I can't be sure...you have to understand, Una is very strong, I can't easily see her taking a decision, but I can still see a part of the future connected to it. I've seen Trasfigea, one of my sisters, coming to this place.' And she helped Anita to sit in a lonely corner to take a brief rest. Her strength lagged in its return from the other side, where the dead had her briefly in their hands.

Not too far away, by the crooked house, Trusk and his father were already waking up.

'Revelia...you came.' Treekan's eyes adjusted to the surprise.

'Where are the others?' the Leonty said, sharp.

'Una has sent the rain to stop us...we lost them somewhere.' And the Chomp stood up, his face locked to his son. Something wasn't right and Trusk was the only one he could think of in a time of danger.

'What's your plan?' Revelia said, her eyes on fire.

407

'What's *your* plan?' Treekan replied, his hands turning into fists. 'I know the Leonty's power. The red glow appears only when she is scanning the future.'

'And if never lasf fhis long!' Trusk added, moving closer to his father.

'Who are you?' the Chomp shouted.

'She is Trasfigea, my beloved sister.' Another Revelia appeared from the back of the home. Identical, like exact copies of one another, there was only one difference. The original, the real friend and ally, wasn't using any power, her eyes looked clean like quiet, crystal water.

'So our queen was right... You are a traitor!' Trasfigea said, as her mouth twitched, her hair, bones and her whole figure turned back to its original form. Anita and I moved away, petrified by her power.

'It appears there are two sides here...so yes, I'm a traitor in Una's eyes.' Revelia moved forward, unafraid. 'But am I to you, my sister?'

'You know her will is the only will.' Trasfigea moved back a little. Whatever their relationship was, it was clear she felt her sister's remarks like blades cutting through her skin.

'Her will has brought only destruction and sorrow. Look around you! There is nothing left, only them and a few of us.' Revelia was not conceding, putting space between us and her sister.

'She did it for us, to protect all of us!'

'Did she? And how many of us are left standing? Think about it, Trasfigea. We can't even extend our numbers any more. There is not a male of our kind left and only ten of us. Think about it.'

'She did what she had to!' Another Leonty had just appeared out of nowhere, followed by a few more. 'We were slaves to them and a danger to the Humans. They would have weeded us out from our own homes.'

'Perhaps…and she went so far into her quest for revenge that she is now taking their place. I know she is powerful, Ferhentia, but you can still read her emotions.'

'It doesn't matter,' another one chimed in, moving her steps forward, her eyes flickering with a purple flame. 'As you said, we are the only ones left. I can't lose another sister. Come here, I can help you, if you let me…'

'Obliviah, no!' Trasfigea said, putting her hand on her sister's arm, lowering it down. 'She is right. We can't reset our minds every time Una takes a piece of us. I'm done forgetting. I can't forget any longer. Go. Do what you have to.'

The enemy had suddenly given up. Somehow, Revelia had broken through their defences without using any power but the only true one they all shared, love. There was an invisible, strange bond between them, reaching across the two factions at war. Their sister the queen had changed them, pushed them to their limits in her rising victory, making them paying the price. They all had experienced the bitter taste of loss. Like all of us, like everybody else, they were pawns moved for a greater good and Revelia was soon going to be the next in line to be sacrificed.

'Go,' Trasfigea repeated, her face turned to the great mountain at her back. 'She has sent the spectres too. Our beloved queen doesn't trust any of us.'

'Do you know where our friend is?' I said, stepping into the unknown. I could have changed our fate just by talking to them, triggering another change of heart. But I didn't care. The only thing I had in mind was to rescue Noah.

'On his way to the keep. Demetra is waiting for him.'

And at those last words, the four Leonty moved away without adding any more detail. Their minds already projected to the wrath their sister would unleash on them once they had gone back without their prey, they left us at once, carrying the weight of Revelia's words in their hearts.

'You saved us!' I let out.

'The queen did. The clarity of her actions speaks of a great evil that can't be denied any longer,' Revelia added, looking at Treekan, his face in agreement to hers.

'Thank you,' Anita said, looking at Revelia. She had finally understood the risk she had faced back in the hands of the lost ones.

'It's OK. You feel well enough to go? We really have to be gone before they arrive.' Revelia looked behind us, scanning the world outside, scanning our future.

'Spectres!' Treekan let out.

'Not just them. The Crimson Queen will soon know my sisters have failed her. And I suspect she knows already about me. What was the reason for that whole trick with Trasfigea?'

'She knows what?' Anita was ready to leave that place at once.

'That I'm a traitor to my own kind.' At those words, we let Revelia take the lead. We left that place quickly, prudence long forgotten.

'Should we not become invisible again?' Anita was determined to not revisit that bad experience once more.

'We are far too deep in the dark power in here…their magic would not hold. Don't worry, I can tell if there is someone coming.' Revelia had her powers full on. Her mind was searching for others' intentions and no one seemed to be near, threatening us.

It felt like hours had gone by when we reached an open field at the bottom of a rocky hill. The white, large ruins had gotten small, but still visible. Some trees were grouped here and there, their ill look aggravated by some dead bushes scattered around. Revelia had decided to go around the large rocky mountains to avoid being seen by anyone. Treekan had put the time we spent walking to good use. He shared with her everything we had learned from the First Mirror and the intentions that came with it.

'If that's the case, the odds could be in our favour,' Revelia said. She walked ahead of us, her shoulders low; she looked like a lioness hunting for prey. 'My sisters are going back to the keep, leaving the temples unattended. We should find no one there, if we hurry.'

'Are you sure he's still there?' Treekan hinted at Time being kept prisoner under tons of rocks and soil.

411

'He is. I wouldn't be surprised if he is kept prisoner in his own temple, the temple of Time.' And she suddenly stopped. Her arms opened wide as a sign of caution.

'It's where the keep is?' I asked. Noah was still in need of rescue and we needed to succeed.

'No. Your friend will be brought to her. The keep is not too far from the temples. She will wait for Demetra to extract every bit of useful information, before taking his life.' An uncontrollable sigh came out of me.

'We need to get to him before trying anything else, right?' Anita knew saving Noah was our priority. Also, whatever magic I was supposed to attempt, I couldn't do it without him.

'I'm really sorry to say it, but I don't think there is anything we can do to rescue your friend,' Revelia replied. She made us crouch behind a large rock, hidden from malevolent eyes. 'Considering the odds, you should try and free Time. He will help you to go back home…but just the two of you, I'm afraid.'

'You don't understand,' I said, moving closer to Revelia, at the edge of our cover. 'Without Noah, there is no freeing anyone. I can't do it by myself!'

'Stay back,' Revelia lowered her voice, her head pointed ahead. 'There are spectres coming…'

The five of us hid in a precarious spot. In the middle of rough fields, the big rocks were the only cover we could rely on. Ahead of us, a narrow road ran in between two of the large, grey mountains. No features, no trees were left there to help us hide. We could not run further and we could not go back without being seen.

'We need to go that way,' Revelia continued. 'The temples and my sister fortress are just behind those mountains.'

'How do we cross the field without being seen?' I asked.

'Magic is nof working. I'm frying, buf won'f work.' Trusk's face went red. His clenched hands betrayed his determination to use his magic and disappear, unsuccessfully.

'They don't know... They don't know Una has sent my sisters looking for me. There might be a way, but you need to be quiet, invisible like you were actually using your power.'

'What's your plan?' Treekan whispered.

'I'll show myself to them. I'll tell them you are at the ruins. I'll try to send them over there. Now, stay still!' The Leonty moved away from her spot swiftly, fast.

The spectres were close, very close. We could hear Revelia engaging in a conversation with them.

'Finally! Where have you been?' she asked. Her voice was harsh, she was playing the part. 'They are at the ruins. You better hurry before they escape...'

'Where do you come from?' a spectre replied. 'Were you not supposed to answer our queen's call?'

'She knows I have more important business to attend to. She knows I'm watching them...now, go!'

'What is this hurry?' another spectre asked. Revelia's strategy was at risk. 'They won't go anywhere...the Lost ones will be minding them while we get there.'

413

'Yeah...why don't you tell us how it happens that you are not with your sisters?' someone else asked.

In between a slit in the rocks, I could see Revelia standing, looking around carefully. The audience she was engaging with was almost invisible. Like grey, intangible smoke, they moved slowly, appearing and disappearing. Their voices flickered, as they kept coming and going as they pleased.

'Why do we smell an awful scent of traitors on your skin?'

'Yeah,' another one added. 'You stink.'

'I've been there. I saw them, but I'm not a spectre, I could not fight them all by myself.' Her convincing performance was holding unchallenged.

'We already got one of them...he must be only moments away from our queen's hands...and he didn't have any power.'

'Yeah...how is it that you could not fight the rest of them? How many are there?' The spectres pushed forward. They could feel our presence, our bodies were hidden, but our smell travelled far, exposed.

'You are wasting my time and your queen's time!' Revelia's voice got louder. 'The rain has stopped. If the Chomps wake up, they will drive the Humans out of there, before you can get to them.'

'Chomps? Are there Chomps with them?' a spectre shouted.

'Yes. And they have powers too. Now go. I'll stay here at the Valahans' pass, watching carefully. If anybody tries to cross the bridge, I'll stop them.'

After a few moments of hesitation, the shifting ghosts finally decided to trust Revelia and move south. She was convincing beyond doubt. She had offered them the bait and they had swallowed it. When they all left, their minds set back to their bloody quest, the Leonty came back to us.

'It worked! I can see them reaching the ruins...they won't be happy to find out you are not there any more. I'm afraid they will soon get back to hunt us. I managed to convince them, but your odour will lead them back to you.'

'We need to get to Noah,' I repeated.

'It looks like the Humans have a collective power, Revelia.' Treekan was supporting my request. 'The power they own is triggered by them being together.'

'What is this power then?' she asked.

'We don't know yet. But everything we've managed to do so far, it's been possible only when Noah and I were together.'

'What about you?' Revelia looked at Anita. That was the second time someone had questioned her abilities.

'I have no power and no magic,' she replied. The group looked at her, making her feel uncomfortable. For some reason, Revelia wasn't convinced. The expression on her face spoke of a different opinion.

'Anita has helped me on the road so far. She might have no magic, but she is magic to me,' I said it again, loud and clear. 'So please, as far as we know, she has no power, I

415

have no power and neither does Noah. But if we have a chance, we need to get to him and finally…if we are lucky…we will find out what we can actually do.'

'OK, before we put your life, and my life at stake. Let's clarify this. You are asking me to lead you to Una, the most powerful being on Runae. With no power to even challenge her? When we could make our way to the five temples, free the God and have a chance to actually set you free?'

Revelia's sequence of questions could not be ignored. She was right. What we were pursuing was a leap of faith. A move based on intuition, based on a random collection of visions, history, unknown magic.

'Revelia.' Treekan's voice sounded the way it had before, when he showed us his full leadership and wisdom. 'The queen knows these Humans are a threat. We have seen it in the First Mirror. They are here, all of them, to free him. We might not know how, but she knows!'

'So we get there, we get caught and then we ask her: Oh, my queen, why are you so scared of these Humans? And I imagine she will tell us…' We went silent again. Revelia was right. Our plan was the worst plan we could have come up with. Then she continued. 'Hold on…maybe this is not a bad idea. Oh, it's stupid, believe me. But it could actually work.'

'What do you mean?' I asked, surprised by the quick turnaround.

'My sister is the only one that knows, right? She doesn't trust me, but she could, If I deliver you to her.' The plan she was laying down didn't sound any good.

'She will execute me and my son before we could even question her, and later she will do the same to them,' Treekan replied.

'Not if we come up with a strategy. Let's move. We will think of the details on foot.'

The troubled journey resumed. We had left the rocks behind and ran towards the narrow split between the mountains. If we wanted to go unseen, we had to move fast. There wasn't much around for us to get protected by, in case the danger would surprise us along the way, so we had to be quick, doubtless. The two large watched us speeding through their cracks, in silence.

Here and there black spots showed us the multitude of caves, spikes and lonely trees scattered over their hillsides. Halfway through, right by a very large cave, we turned right, close to a passage into the right mountain. Around us, the ground looked unstable, its edges visibly crumbling in the far below. We had no other way but to continue through a long, rocky pathway. At its end, a tall, old wooden bridge waited to lead us to the other side.

'This way…a few miles ahead, we will be able to cross the bridge.'

Under the Leonty's guide, we ran faster, our shadows clashing into the rocky side of the mountain we were about to pierce through. Just a few minutes later, Revelia stopped. Holding us in between the enemies and the path ahead, a sudden heat built up from beneath the surface. As if we were walking into hot steam, our eyes went blurry.

'Your friend is in the fortress. I can't see Una but Demetra is there. They brought him to her.'

'Is she going to hurt him?' Anita asked, her face terrified.

'My sister's power doesn't require brutal force. He will confess everything to her without even knowing,' she replied.

'Noah doesn't know anything. As I told you, we don't know anything!' I said out loud.

'OK, let's stop here. I need to see this through. Trusk, get to the bridge and let us know if the way ahead is free.' And he immediately complied. 'Treekan, watch over them. Take shelter in the shadow of that spike over there, by the dead Ollman tree.'

'What are you going to do?' Anita asked.

'I need to see what's their next move. We might be safe, for now. Trust me.'

So we hid in the dark of the mountain. Erion's light struggled to reach us in the depths of the mountains' feet and we had taken it as our advantage. If our hearts were in a hurry, our bodies were about to collapse. We had walked far, not slept for so long, so we took the chance to rest.

Chapter Twenty-Eight

Valahan Mogs

∞

In the suffocating embrace of the high mountains, Anita and I started to lose our strength. Even with the powerful sun hidden by the gigantic peaks, the heat increased by the minute. Worried by seeing us suffering the long wait, Treekan had gone to Revelia a few times, asking her to speed her magic up. His forehead sweating, he moved closer to the Leonty a third time.

'Revelia, we can't stay here much longer. Erion is going to bring us right to our death.'

'This is not the star's doing,' she said, her eyes locked on the roasting, rocky pathway. 'This is the work of the Valahan Mogs…'

'What are you talking about?,' the Chomp said, gazing around. 'They are long gone and so is their Flare.'

'They are indeed. But their work, the things they have done, the way they have turned these lands into pure Mog. That hasn't gone away.'

'What is it?' I chimed in, getting closer. Exhausted and weakened by the heat, my arm around Anita, I was trying to help her stand up.

'Trusk is coming back,' Revelia replied, her eyes shining. 'It's not good. The road that leads to the bridge is gone.'

'What now?' Anita asked, breathing heavily.

'Can't we fly over it?' I said.

'Not in these conditions. I can barely stand up,' Treekan replied, his hands on his sweaty face.

'No!' Revelia said sharp, out of nowhere. Her eyes fixed on the old Chomp.

'Leonty!' He raised his voice. 'At least let me speak my thoughts before reading my intentions!'

'Can someone tell us what's going on?' I let out.

'If we can't fly to the bridge, we have to take the path to the Valahans' caves.'

'No! There is a reason they are called Mogs,' Revelia was determined to oppose the Chomp's decision. 'I'd rather meet Una right now than walk in those caves.'

'What does Mogs mean?' Anita moved a little, her hands reaching out to Trusk who flew back in a confused manner, his wings losing their strength fast.

420

'It's when fire, metal and death meet for the end of the world.' Treekan replied, helping his son to get up from the dusty ground.

'Hell,' Anita whispered.

If we were to come to an agreement, we had to do it fast. As the heat was becoming unbearable, we had to choose whether to take the risk of entering the caves or take our chances with the jump to the bridge. Moving her attention to our near future, Revelia left Noah's fate behind and screened through the pages of our next hours. Unhappy, she complied with Treekan's request to turn back and enter the caves from the large entrance we had seen earlier.

Leaving behind the original route came with an immediate benefit. In the shadow of the large cave, the power of Erion had released the grip on our skins, leaving us fighting only the heat from the roots of that harsh land. In the dark of the way ahead, red sparks of light blinked randomly, moved by the fire spilling from the depths, projecting on the walls majestic shades of yellow and orange.

'These are enemies' lands still,' Revelia whispered.

'Who are they?' I asked, my shadow doubling in size from one spot to the next.

'The Valahans were expert miners and blacksmiths,' Treekan replied, his head lowered to allow him to squeeze in between the cracks of a wall standing in front of us as dead end. 'Before the war started, they used these mines to dig minerals. High in demand, they were indispensable for the Humans who had kept building and expanding their domain to the edge of the Leonty's hills. Later on, they thought these same caves would protect them from the Crimson Queen. Their Flare and so all Flares were forged by the same power you feel in your bones, right now. It was pure energy and fire. Their one specifically could melt rocks and metal as they pleased.'

'In the later days, way before Una had taken the Humans' kingdom, the Valahans met Time somewhere not far from where you stand now. Together they found the great Mother Flare and brought it in the open. Our Key master eventually parted it in six different Flares and handed them to inhabitants of our world,' Treekan added.

'What happened then?' Anita asked, fully immersed in their story.

'Time hoped that power would keep all beings in balance and allow them to fight the evil that was spreading fast from the Cloudy Mountains, in the very north,' Revelia continued.

'But by then the Great Dawn was very near. Time was eventually gone and Una had turned into the Crimson Queen.' And a sad expression appeared in the old Chomp's face. 'Once the Humans had been exterminated, her evil will moved against the Valahans. They had no choice but to hide in here, continuing to dig deep in the desperate attempt to reach the other side of the Mogs mountain. And so they dug too deep, reaching the core of Runae itself.'

Revelia moved slowly across a small room, her eyes carefully inspecting the ground and the red ceiling. As her hands searched for a passage in the walls, she vanished in a snap. Followed by Treekan, Anita and I held on to Trusk's hand, as he led us to a new, large opening. With large stairs going in three different directions, a few empty, enormous holes dived down to an infinite end.

'This is where the Valahans found their end.' Revelia continued. 'It's said Vasheer had gone mad, trapped in here with the enemy on one side and the unbreakable wall of the mountain on the other side. His kingdom and his people were trapped here. Not even his son Varuk was able to master the full power of their Flare and break them free. There was no way out.'

'But there is a way out...now,' I said. *If we took this road, we have to come out the other side*, I thought.

'There is,' Revelia replied, her face pointed at the stairs leading to the left. Here and there, entire parts of their foundations were gone. 'In the desperate attempt to get free, Vasheer and Varuk summoned the full power of their Flare, breaking the layer they had already made thin, between air and fire. The explosion created the same large cavity where the wooden bridge stands, today.'

'It was easy for the Crimson Queen to walk these lands and take their Flare away from them, once they were all dead,' Treekan continued, following the Leonty down the wobbling walkway.

As the Valahan before, we walked down the same slippery path, descending into the abyss, mixing air and smoke in our lungs. No matter how long since the events had unfolded, the place still showed the scars of their last act. Fire boiling in the planet's bowels, we had escaped the steaming ground to only choose a worse path.

'You hold your breath now,' Treekan added. 'We need to be silent and quiet. We don't know who's watching these dark places. If we are lucky, we will exit right at the bridge.'

'It won't take long,' the Leonty added. 'Please keep your senses sharp. I need to look beyond these walls again. My sister's voice is getting stronger...'

If our fate was still unwritten, Noah's was coming to an end. Few spectres had arrived at the fortress and were bringing him to the Crimson Queen. Revelia could see in her own eyes the decisions that were about to be made, by the spectres, by her sister. Demetra waited behind the gates of the fortress, alone. Most of the queen's emissaries had gone to the Broken Crown ruins, looking for the strangers. The guards at the top of the front wall floated silently; like a fog with many eyes, they had just seen Noah dragged onto the path to the stronghold. When the doors opened, Demetra went to greet the spectres who were holding him hostage.

'He is mine! The queen wants me to question him.'

'It's all yours,' one of them replied. His voice, like a whistle, hurt Noah's ears.

'You are coming with me!' And she fiercely pulled his arm, an anticipation of the pain she was going to inflict on him.

Pulled inside a cold, dark room, Noah was pushed towards the back wall. A rusty gate shut close, leaving no way to escape from his cell. Demetra started to walk back and forth in front of it, silently, looking right at his face, her eyes fixed on his. Then, a red flash wriggled from one eye to the other, as if her irises had caught on fire.

424

'The more you resist, the more painful it is going to be. You can't stop me and you can't escape. May I suggest you to just...let me in?'

'Why are you doing this to me?' Noah was in tears, his body showed the many tortures the spectres had inflicted on him.

'You have come here...uninvited, unwanted...what else would you expect? A pompous celebration? The evening flowers scattered along the welcoming path? Or maybe the king's thousand steps in all its majestic, sick solemnity?' Demetra laughed, her sarcasm hiding more than just an evil soul. She was distracting him while her mental claws pierced through his brain, uncovering the wanted secrets.

'Stop it! Stop it!' Noah screamed in pain.

'There are some...interesting facts in here. Oh don't get me wrong, I don't find your mind particularly fascinating, but there is something peculiar about it...' And she dug deeper, inflicting her will on him.

'Demetra. Her Majesty is looking for you.' The sadistic game was suddenly interrupted by a spectre who had been sent to deliver the queen's message.

'I'll go when I'm done with him. Tell her... Tell the queen I'll be coming shortly.' She gazed back to Noah who, in that brief moment of freedom, had hoped his friends would come to save him.

'Yes! There it is!' she continued. 'Your mind is...well beyond these walls. There is some sort of channel open between your mind and the world out there. No, actually between your mind and another.'

425

'Please, help me…' Noah cried out loud.

'I see it!' And Demetra's eyes widened, a vicious smile appeared on her face.

'Noah! I screamed, taking Anita by surprise.

'What's wrong? Are you OK?' she asked.

We had managed to arrive at the stony gates at the other side of the mountain. Right where the walls had collapsed, we could see the destruction brought by the Valahans' Flare. Everywhere we looked, tons of rocks amassed on top of each other. Underneath their silent weight, metal spoils of hundreds of beings spoke of a horrible past. Their fate had been eternally written in their burial monument. A piercing hole brought the outside light right in, making their ancient bones shine, sparkling like long dead stars.

From the same way Una had found her way in, we had walked outside, right where the wooden bridge swung slowly. Steam and smoke rose from the depth of the crater, hiding the other end of the bridge from sight. Waiting for Revelia to give us the order to go, Trusk flew over to the other side, looking for enemies. With my hand on the hot surface of the mountain, I suddenly stopped, held by the vision of Noah's face in my mind; his tears were running down on my own cheeks.

'It's OK, don't worry. I'm just worried about Noah. I wish he was with us,' I lied to the surprised group.

'Me too.' And Anita took my hand, putting up a weak smile to show me she knew what had just happened to me and that she cared.

'I know I've been hard on him...you know? With all his pushing, moving fast, regardless of the risk. I can't stop thinking... If I had listened more, understood...maybe he would be with us now.'

'Everything feels so stupid,' she said, capturing my attention. 'Oh, I wasn't referring to what you said, sorry. It just got me thinking. All the things we thought were important...the things that I thought were a deal breaker...'

'What are you saying?' I wasn't sure where she was going with that.

'Patrick left because I asked him to. I made him leave me.' And she looked at me, embarrassed.

Of all the moments I would have expected Anita's window to open, that was the least predictable. She had held so long to that thought, she could not keep it for herself any longer. Perhaps, as we stood at the edge of a cliff, our bodies a step away from falling, we were stripping ourselves from any excessive weight.

'What the hell happened?' I asked, after looking at Revelia. She was still wandering the multitude of steps ahead of us.

'Does it matter?' Anita replied, smiling. 'Look at us. I don't even know if we are going to make it back home. All the things we've seen, felt... Does it matter what happened to me and him? It's like another life now. A life I was stupidly living halfway.'

'Don't say that. I know what you mean, but it's because of that life, the way you are, that has made us come here. I know, I know,' I added before she could interrupt me, 'not

427

just because of you. Because of me, Noah…and them. Now, tell me, what happened? Before we get back on the road.'

'Well, I don't know when it started any more. I guessed we collected too many things left unsaid, too many broken dreams. Our lives started to part ways and the difference between what I wanted and what he wanted has grown wider.'

'Did you have a fight?' I asked.

'No, not really. I mean, we fought a few times, but it felt like we had lost interest in that too. You know Patrick. He doesn't know what he wants, he moves around like he has no intention to build something with me, to achieve anything in life. And I want more, I always wanted more.'

'And talking didn't help,' I said, nearly talking to myself.

'Right. And here and there he would come up with some weird plan, something unpractical, something random, and you know me…I'm all about calculating risks, digging, planning.'

'And here you are…I brought you into this place, the pure core of my madness. I know this isn't easy for you.' I had to admit it. Although I hadn't done it on purpose, I had done her wrong.

'It's not easy for you either. We are both reeling.'

'What should we do? What do we do once we…if we get there?'

'I don't know.' Anita turned away, her eyes pointing at the far sky trapped in between the mountain peaks. 'We walked miles and yet we are standing still on the same very

428

unknown spot. But something we saw in that mirror...I can't stop thinking about it.'

'What is it?' I said, looking up as if I could grasp the truth just by looking at the same spot she had her eyes on.

'We were the first ones to walk through the node...after, what do they call it? The Great Dawn. But we also saw someone else doing the same before the whole destruction happened. That man said he had come from Earth?'

'I wonder who he was...' I let out.

'I believe he was Noah. Think about it,' she continued before I could question her idea. 'We know he has been living for a long time. Who knows, maybe he tried to come here before?'

'So you think it could be him?'

'It wasn't your friend,' Treekan interrupted, taking us by surprise. 'He didn't look anything like him, not in his look, nor in his heart.'

'How do you know?' I said, standing up. 'Hold on, you said you were already alive when the war happened. You have met him?'

'I have indeed, briefly. And believe me, he was nothing like your friend. Oh, trust me, he sounded genuine and kind. He was able to gain the trust of all the Aqualymphs, the Humans, us. He was the one who suggested to get our Flares together to fight the enemy.'

'Treekan, what are you saying?' Anita asked.

'I can't stop thinking...the Aqualymphs became spectres not long after he arrived. They had never gone into any alliance before, but they did after he arrived. Providing

429

support to the Humans, they did terrible things. Things that turned them into the evil spirits they are today. We lost the war and lost ourselves after his suggestion to use our Flares. I know what I'm talking about. My father was one of the ten! I don't know why but something tells me, he was behind the whole thing.'

'It's time to move!' Revelia walked back to us, our next steps were already decided by someone who could see well beyond our reach. Treekan came closer, his face quietly telling us to hold our conversation for a better moment in the future. The time had come to continue our risky journey through the mountains.

'It looks like my sister Demetra has her hands on your friend. He is OK, for now,' Revelia quickly added, noticing our worried faces. 'But she will bring him to her…Demetra won't kill him.'

'Is it good news, right?' I asked. 'We might have time to get him out of there?'

'There is no good news as long as he is there, I'm afraid. But something has happened to Demetra. Somehow, her decisions have stalled. She must have seen something in your friend. Something that she didn't know before.'

'We should go then. We are not too far now. We better plan our next move while we continue ahead.' Treekan took the lead, walking towards the bridge.

Trusk had left his watch and came back us, taking the final spot of the queue, just behind Revelia. We were lined up on a very old, untrustworthy path, hundreds of feet from the distant ground, afraid that the bridge would collapse under our weight. The two mountains blocked the star behind, turning the entire place grey, in a flat, plain shadow. We held our breath as if a small amount of extra air in our lungs could make the difference between life and death. The top was as far as the bottom, the sky was out of sight, so was the end of the precarious construction.

'Is it late to tell you that I'm afraid of heights?' Anita said, her tone between fear and sarcasm.

'Why is everything so...quiet? There is no wind, no birds,' I said.

'Whaf is brids?' Trusk asked, his voice loud enough to reach my ears at the front of the queue. A strange echo bounced his words back and forth.

'Speak low, Chomp,' Revelia whispered. 'We don't know who might be around listening.'

'Birds, not brids,' I answered, smiling. 'Birds are creatures that we have in our world. They can fly like you and sing.'

'Exactly like him,' Anita added. 'Remember when we met him?' And to that I held myself back from laughing.

Our hands firmly gripped to a big rope on either side of the bridge, were slowly sliding on it, hurting our skin. Afraid of letting go, we looked straight ahead, avoiding checking how far we were from the black, deep ground, crossing the path.

'We should get to the end fairly quickly,' Revelia said. 'Once we are out of here, you will see a hill on your left with temples standing over the top. On your right, a slope downhill that leads to the queen's fortress. We won't be in

431

the open right away. There are many steps to go down. I need you to be careful. It's a steep way down.'

'Doesn't sound good, does it?' Anita asked, looking at me.

We had walked a long distance since the moment we had entered the slit in between the giant twins and an opening had grown wide right in front of us. The end of that dangerous walk was near, making the path ahead clearer and brighter. Suddenly, Revelia stopped.

'Hold on,' she said. 'Some of the spectres we met earlier have disputed my words. I think they are coming back!'

'What? Where are they?' I asked. We stopped and turned around, looking at her.

'When did they change their minds?' Treekan asked.

'I can't be sure. I wasn't looking for it. I heard my name in their heads, so I checked. It looks like they are already back where we met them.'

'They will be at the bridge soon!' Treekan responded.

'They might be there already!' And we all looked behind the Leonty.

Trusk held her hand, flapping his wings and rising above our heads. The side we had walked from was like a tiny white dot in a silvery ocean. We could not see anything but the bridge, dying at the centre of the horizon.

'You go ahead. I'll fly over and come back!' Trusk said.

'No, it's too dangerous!' Treekan replied. 'Let's keep walking, we are nearly there.'

'Don'f worry, Fafher! I'll fly very high. Fhey won'f see me. And if fhey do, fhey won'f cafch me.'

Treekan withheld his fear, quietly looking at Revelia. In the middle, Anita and I were afraid of saying anything. Eventually the Leonty agreed to Trusk's plan. It was going to be safe as long as he stayed out of reach. So the Chomp left the group, his wings bringing him so high we could barely see his body floating in the air.

'Let's move, fast. Don't worry, Chomp. I'll let you know if they see him.'

Driven by fear and guilt, Anita and I rushed our feet behind Treekan, who had seen his only son putting his life at stake for us, two strangers. Breathless and our hands cramped and burnt by the constant sliding and gripping on the rope, the four of us finally arrived at the end. The opening, the way out, was large enough to fit an entire army. If the spectres were there to surprise us, we would have no chance to survive.

'They know. They saw him flying back to us. He should be here in a few moments,' Revelia said, putting her hand on the small Chomp. And as she had predicted, came right towards us, his wings on full speed.

'Fhey are coming! Many of fhem! Fhey are coming!' His voice loud, the echo multiplied his words of warning, emphasizing his fear.

'We won't make it down! It will take too long to walk down the steps,' Revelia said to Treekan.

At the edge of the mountains we stood. The path was at its very end; right into the deep below, tiny steps went down in a steep spiral. We were trapped in between the

433

empty space ahead and the spectres sliding over the bridge with no resistance, no delay. In the rush of the risky moment, Trusk flew right beside us, his hands around my and Anita's arms. We were pushed ahead, into the profound nothing. Our feet swinging in the hot air, our hair wildly fluttering around, we descended fast, the ground enlarging rapidly.

Right above us, Treekan came down at the same speed, Revelia beside him, holding on to his arm, petrified. This time, with no rain to hinder the Chomps, we landed easily on the hard ground.

The space around us was made of a pure desolation. The soil was dry and cracks ran all over the surface. Like Revelia had told us, a few miles to the right, a large stronghold stood alone in the middle of a desert. The grey and red stones formed a large square defence all around and a few towers spiked up, unchallenged. If the queen lived there, there was no way in without being seen. The entire place was watched from the inside of the towers in each corner and a gigantic door at the front wall was closed shut.

All around there was nothing. Not a tree, a rock, nothing that could hide us on our way in. Revelia's plan to reach the temples seemed more feasible and less of a death sentence. The hill on which the Leonty's home stood was a sharp contrast to the arid landscape. Their land was green; trees gathered together, like small groves had been thrown randomly on the high ground.

'I understand now why you wanted to go to the temples,' I let out. All considered, going left seemed like a walk in a fairy tale.

434

'How are we going to cross all that space without being seen?' Anita shared our same concerns.

'There are few spectres left in the keep. But I can tell you already, they are watching the outside carefully,' Revelia said.

'Our power is gone...we can't even try to disappear,' Treekan added with the tone of an obvious defeat.

'But you can still fly,' Anita said. She was up to something.

'Of course... We are Chomps!'

'OK. Tell me if this is crazy or not.' And she continued, 'Let's say we fly very, very high. Erion, your star, would be right on top of our heads.' And Revelia gave a confident smile. She knew we were about to take a decision, and she liked it. 'They won't expect us to come from above, and even if they looked up, they wouldn't see us, right?'

'And we land down direcfly!' Trusk concluded Anita's plan.

'We can't land randomly anywhere,' I said. 'We need to know where the safest place is. Do you know it?' I asked Revelia.

'It's a big risk. As right now, I can't see that type of future. I can't see every spectre's move at any point in time.'

'Not every spectre,' Anita replied. 'Just Demetra. We need to get to Noah, right?'

'If that's the case, we need to hurry. She will bring him to her. Once there, well...there isn't much we can do.'

435

'We need to hurry anyway. We have guests coming!' And Treekan pointed at the very top of the stairway we had left behind.

'OK. Let's do this!' I shouted.

In the Chomps' embrace we found ourselves again. The sky was the limit. The higher they could bring us, the safer we would be. Like space shuttles, we cast ourselves into the star's rays, side by side. If there was something I would keep with me, in my dearest memories, it would be that incredible feeling. Flying like eagles, we were untouchable by any evil. Once we got as high as we could, the two Chomps stalled their position, their wings flapping fast. It was time for Revelia to tell us where to land. So her eyes turned red once more. She could see her sister a few steps away from Noah. Her scrutiny was about to end.

'So this is your biggest secret?' Demetra looked at him with genuine interest. 'You share his memories, his feelings? What are you? Part of the same soul?'

'I don't know what you are talking about...I told you! I don't know how we got here... I don't know why you are doing this to me!' Noah was still in pain but it wasn't Demetra's doing.

'You got the key of your world...well, half of it? And now you want the key of ours. But you don't even know what this key is. Well, let me tell you this. Even if you knew it... It's in our queen's hands. There is no power without that key. I'm afraid your quest is going to end soon.'

'Please...let me go!' Noah was begging for his life.

'I'm nearly done with you. I need to see our queen, but I'll be back to finish our little conversation...'

436

'Wait...' Noah whispered, exhausted by his torturer. 'You can clearly pull anything you want out of my head. Help me. Tell me what I can't see for myself...'

'You want what?' Demetra was taken by surprise. She had used her power many times before, but surely she had never been asked to continue inflicting it. 'You do...you are really asking...' And her eyes turned into pure blood. 'There is so much in your head. Impossible for a human to have lived so much and for so long!'

'Please...' And Noah closed his eyes, succumbing to the pain.

'Someone is holding the memories for you...not your memories, someone else's! It's not you resisting, there is another being shielding the past from me? How is this possible?'

But Demetra's questions were left hanging in the dark of that cell. Noah had collapsed under the grip of her deadly power. The diabolic duty had to be postponed so Demetra left Noah behind. A trapped prisoner in a small, cold cell was not of any use if not awake. The Leonty moved away, wondering why her queen had asked for audience. She left no spectre watching over Noah. After all, no one could come and rescue him.

"She's gone to the queen's tower! Noah is by himself, in a cell by the back side of the second floor, to the left corner!' Revelia shouted mid-air.

'Can we gef in?' Trusk asked.

'There is an opening, right on the second floor. A wide window for the guards. But I can't see anyone there. Yes, we will get in!'

And the Chomps' confidence in Revelia's prophecy was all they needed. Their wings stopped immediately and our fall went so fast that my eyes were forced wide open. In a few seconds we had almost reached the ground and started to slow down as we neared the indicated landing spot.

'Stay quiet,' Treekan whispered, after helping Revelia to get in through the large opening.

Anita and I hopped onto the floor right after Treekan, Trusk right at our back. The inside was all made in grey stones, reflecting the same cold austerity we had seen from outside, and long walls were running around, forming multiple squares, one inside the next, like smaller copies of themselves. At the centre, the floor opened onto a small staircase leading downwards. We stopped behind a wall, standing right in front of the large window, trying to not make a sound. Some of the perimetric walls had small cubicles with their fronts shut by rusty gates. Noah had to be in one of them. Quickly guessing which one could have made the difference between an easy rescue and an unpleasant encounter.

'Your friend is right there,' Revelia whispered, pointing at the wall right across the floor.

'There are also spectres right there,' Treekan replied, his voice barely audible.

'You don't move. Let me handle this.' And before he could object, Revelia walked into the middle of the floor, owning her right to be there, in that very place.

'Hey, you!' a spectre shouted. That was the first time we'd heard them with their voice being more than a hiss. 'When did you get here?'

438

'I came to see Demetra. But she said Her Majesty wants to talk to her, so she asked me to watch the prisoner.' Her voice was strong, her lies were well spoken.

'You weren't here earlier...when did you arrive?' the spectre asked, once more.

'Just before she went, I was sent to the Broken Crown ruins, with the rest of your kind. They are coming, by the way. Go and open the gates!' And the spectre looked to another one who stood a few steps away. With a simple whisper he asked the other to verify Revelia's words.

'I know my sister is quite good at what she does...but I'd like to question the Human myself... you know...to keep the pain going.' And Revelia put on the evillest smile she could come up with.

While the spectre waited on his spot, his shape shifting a little, the other one came back, confirming they had spotted the rest of their kind close to the gates. That verified news was like a granted pass for Revelia who, a few seconds later, held Noah's cell key in her hands.

After a brief smile, she said: 'Has he screamed yet?'

'Not enough.' And a creepy smile could be seen on the ghost's face.

Noah was still lying down on the floor, his head resting at the wall. His eyes were closed, the bags beneath them showing the pain he had felt in Demetra's hands. Revelia had just opened the gate, when he jumped from the fear of a new torment arriving. Before he could shout, Revelia put her hand on his mouth, telling him to stay quiet.

As far as Noah knew, she was a dubious friend, a friend of the same Chomps who had been so kind to him. Passing through the same indecision we previously had, he had to quickly decide to trust her or not.

'Daniel and Anita are here, just over there. We are here to save you,' Revelia whispered. Noah's face gained back some light. 'You can trust me. Treekan and Trusk are also here with them. We need to hurry. Demetra will be back soon...'

Demetra had no idea why her sister had called her over. Last time they spoke, she had received a clear command: *Get the information we need and kill him!* What had changed since then? Had it something to do with what Demetra had seen in Noah's head? Right at the top of the queen's tower, Demetra stopped for a moment. Being her sister didn't grant her immunity. Every time she had responded to her calls, she had no idea if she would make it out alive. Now, once again, the fear mounted. Incapable of reading her mind, all she could do was to enter the queen's room and hope for the best.

Una stood at the very end of the large room by her tower. The inside looked as cold and empty as the outside. An oppressive, flat red light ran all over the stony room. Candles flickered on top of a large bare locker, projecting dark shadows into the many cracks of the ruinous walls; a sense of emptiness invited Demetra in.

'Is he dead?' Una asked. She was looking at her own fingers. Surprised and disappointed, it was like she had seen someone else's hands instead of her own.

'Not yet. I'm done with him, but I wanted to know what you had for me, before finishing him.' Demetra's words were measured. The temptation of reading her sister's mind was an inviting risk too high to take.

'Good. There has been a slight change to my plans...I need him alive,' she added, still without looking at her sister.

'What has changed?'

'This is none of your business, is it?' Una finally looked at Demetra who was ready to abandon her plan of reading her sister's thoughts. 'Do you know where your sister is?' The queen's words clearly pushed away the idea of any possible relation between Revelia and herself. It was Demetra's sister, not hers.

'No, my queen. Should I send the spectres to find her?'

'That won't be necessary,' Una replied, leaving Demetra surprised. In other circumstances, that would have been for Revelia a death sentence on the spot. After all, they had lost most of their kind by her queen's hands for much less. 'I'll be visiting the temples shortly. It's time to eradicate those Chomps from my world.'

'My queen...' Demetra started. 'Their Flare won't let you see them or touch them. You have tried before. How are you going to fight them?'

'Again, this is none of your business!' Una snapped.

Demetra moved a few steps back, standing close to the door again. She could not understand how her queen could be so understanding of Revelia, who had always been not very compliant, but also be so harsh to her, who had always done her best to serve her.

'I can feel your mind spinning, Demetra.' And Una came closer to her, to reach an old cabinet beside the front door. After grabbing a key sitting in it, she continued, 'Come with me. I'll show you what I'm going to do...'

The Leonty had very little to hope for and very much fear. However, she could do nothing but obey. So Demetra started to walk behind her queen who left her room and walked close to the spiral stairs. Instead of walking down, she went up. A smaller set of stairs turned around a circular pillar. Few steps ahead, a strong metal door stood shut. Demetra had never been there before, nor even come close. As far as she knew, the world ended at her queen's room, on top of the tallest tower of the keep.

When Una opened the door, something unexpected came to light. The room was identical to the queen's room but smaller. It had no openings of any kind; everything inside was kept secret and safe from the outside world. At the edges of the circular room, six short columns stood still and, on top of them, Flares were burning. All except two were lit and bright. In the middle, an artefact stood on a silvery plate. All round, a magic spell made of whirling green lights revolved around its core.

'This is the secret of my power, Demetra.' And the Leonty quietly looked around, finally understanding where the entire power of Runae had gone, where the life of her world had been kept all that time. 'The flames you see lit, are the ones I rightfully conquered from the Humans, the Aqualymphs, the Garughals, and the Valahan

Mogs. This empty column is for the Chomps.' And Demetra finally knew what she was looking at.

Before the Crimson Queen could finish her speech, Demetra already knew. The last one, one of the two missing Flares, was their own. The Leonty's power was one of the two she hadn't collected yet. *Why? Why has she kept us alive, all this time? Is not like she has ever been considering us, her sisters,* she thought.

'Oh, well...it's not that hard to understand now, is it? Suddenly you don't feel the need to read my mind, do you?' the queen sarcastically continued. 'You see...I have been thinking about it. A few times I got closer to do it and finish it.'

'Finish it?' Demetra asked, in shock. 'You mean with us?'

'You see, when the Flares were given to the six, it didn't only enhance each race's power. Oh no, Demetra, it did also merge their lives, their souls with it. I did not kill for my pleasure only. I have to admit I enjoyed seeing the Humans die by my hand. But that was just...a collateral joy. The truth is that I did it so their Flare could finally come to me! When it was clear that the Chomps had a stronger power, when they opposed my attack, I decided to take yours for myself too...but you were my sisters. How could I ever do that?' And her expression was horrifying, in between fun and anger. 'So I did it. I took the life of our males the Humans had spared during the war. Fathers, brothers... When they were all finally gone, our Flare's magic got shared only between the ten of us.'

443

'You did that. Was not enough?' Demetra was petrified. Her mind could barely contain the idea of the upcoming peril.

'Oh, stop being so naive. I didn't collect all of you, didn't I?' And her tone got harsher. A personal hate came right through. 'I was happy to take them first. You don't know what they have done to us. What they have done to our mothers, our sisters... To me! *They deserved it!*'

There wasn't going to be any challenge to her words. Demetra could not stand her power, her cruelty, or her hate. Although she had learned about the atrocities her kind had gone through, everything before the Great Dawn was too far to reach, to grasp, to fully understand. She knew she had been evil herself too, but that type of maleficence was of a superior kind.

'I stand now, not with one threat any more, but two. I'm afraid the time has come, sister. I'm truly grateful for what you have done for me, but I need to take the reins of this situation, of my destiny and your power.'

Demetra's eyes widened. Her skin could have been made of the same stones of the room she was standing in as she felt the terror crawling on her flesh. She could not move, she could not run away from the horror she was about to witness. Her eyes went red for a brief moment, a last attempt to read her sister's mind. But it was too late. The petrifying fear had spilled over into reality, her moves gone, her last heartbeat had resounded in her ears. A last red flicker flashing through the room, Una's hand had moved swiftly, her deadly magic finding her victim unable to challenge back.

A moment before Demetra turned into a lifeless statue, her magic had left her eyes, dragged out from her soul, to finally reach the ones of her killer.

Chapter Twenty-Nine
Not Ours, Not Theirs

∞

Hand in hand, Noah was pulled right up by Revelia whose small smile was already of a great comfort to his pain. Something had flashed into Revelia's mind, but her focus was to free him from his cell and get to the others as quickly as possible. In the background, the spectres stirred, talking loudly. A larger group had just entered the fortress spreading the news of the latest events.

Noah and Revelia walked fast towards us, her face anticipating the worries she carried with her. My heart beat faster as Noah got closer and, impatiently, I left the hiding spot to hug him. My arms around his shoulder, my head beside his, I was happy to see him once again, to see him alive.

'Oh my God, Noah, I'm glad you are OK! I was so worried…'

'Thank you for saving me,' he replied, nearly in tears. 'I thought I had come to my end.'

'Noah! Please don't ever leave us again! You have no idea how worried we were,' Anita added, her hands on our heads, a smiling relief on her face.

'Yes, Yes,' Treekan interrupted. 'We are all happy. We need to leave this place at once. Let's go back home!'

'No,' Revelia whispered, preventing us from leaving. 'Something terrible is about to happen. We have to get to the temples.'

'What? What's happening?' he replied.

'I can't see Demetra's future any more. I was getting Noah out of there when her voice called my name in my head. But I can't see her any more. I can't see any of my sisters' futures either!'

My mind went back to the never-ending dilemma about Revelia. Our trust in her was strong, stronger than ever, but there she was, once again between two sides. If she had helped us to save Noah, it looked like she was now trying to save her sisters.

'What does it mean?' I asked.

'It means Una has finally made the decision…she is going to take our Flare!'

'You mean, your lives?' Anita asked, in shock.

447

'We need to finish what we have set to do. Revelia is right, we need to go to the temples. If we are lucky, we will be able to save you all and free Time at once!' I added.

'Hold on,' Noah said, before we could go and fly away from the keep. 'Demetra told me something about the key, the key of Runae. She confirmed, it's in her hands, she said. She has it… Without, we can't make it.'

We were all taken by surprise by a such confirmation. That detail was going to change our plan, whatever that plan was. We were proceeding by instinct, trying to assess the next move, step by step.

'Do you know where this key is?' Anita asked.

'She said she has it.'

'Does she have it *with her*? All the time?' Anita kept asking, this time to Revelia.

'I don't even know what this key looks like,' she replied.

'It's like a clepsydra. You know, an hourglass. A glassy object with something inside that shows the time passing by. I've seen it before. She had it the day she got her powers, the day she enslaved Time.' I jumped in.

'I've never seen anything like that. If she has it she must have it hidden somewhere,' Revelia replied.

'Something so valuable, she must be carrying it with her,' I said.

'I don't think so.' Anita was trying to think fast. 'She doesn't need it to be powerful, right? She needs it to keep Time where it is. If she was ever to be defeated, she wouldn't have the key next to her, to be taken from her.'

'If that's the case, she has it in her keep. If she is there, we have no way of facing her power and leaving unharmed.' Revelia replied.

'Where is it?' Treekan asked. He knew what we were trying to attempt.

'Above our heads. In the tall tower,' Revelia said. 'But don't think it's going to be as easy as it was to get here and fool few spectres.'

'Can we fly from oufside?' Trusk asked.

'The windows are too narrow, even for you, tiny Chomp.'

'There is no way we can get in from inside either,' I added.

The chattering of spectres at the other side of the fortress had gotten louder; the two groups had merged together and Revelia's betrayal was now known. The guards at the second floor had just received the news when they went back to Noah's cell to find it empty.

'They know. We need to move now!' Revelia said.

'Wait!' Treekan started, putting his hand on Revelia's arm. 'There is something we can do, but it's something I wished I would never to do. But you have to promise, *you have to promise* my people are not going to be in danger!'

'What are you saying?' Revelia asked, puzzled.

'Where are your sisters now? Are all the spectres in here?' he continued.

'Chomp, what are you saying?'

'Tell me!' he whispered. The danger was getting closer.

449

'The spectres should all be here,' she replied, after her eyes had glowed red. 'I can't see my sisters any more, I told you...'

'You said they were coming back here, right?' I added.

'I'll pull the Flare from our land. My people will be exposed, but if we are fast enough, we could make it!'

'What? No!' I shouted, forgetting we were a step away from being uncovered.

In a blink of the eye, we were exposed. The spectres had found us, hiding behind the large wall. There was no way out but flying outside. If we made it out there alive, we would still be identified and the Crimson Queen would know it. A large smoke extended in front of us, like a wavy cloud made of hundreds of evil beings; the spectres were ready to attack.

Treekan's hands opened up, his wings started to flap fast, his body rose few feet above the floor. Then a large, massive energy crashed onto us, with no warning, turning the space around bright and empty. The Flare we had seen back at the village appeared in front of our eyes, floating in the air like its master. Under the astonished watch of the spectres, we disappeared from sight, vanished into nothing. The fortress had lost its enemies in a snap.

'What did you do?' Revelia shouted.

'What I had to do! There was no other way,' Treekan replied, gliding down.

'Are we...invisible?' Noah asked.

'You said we could not get invisible...that we were too far from the village. What did you do? Leave your people unprotected to bring the Flare to us?' I was shocked by Treekan's action. We had taken advantage of his kind willingness to help us to another extreme. The debt we had to repay, was now impossible to overcome.

'We move fast, Humans. We move fast, we find this key and we get out of here. I'll send the Flare back before they can harm any of my fellows. Let's move now!'

With a mix of gratitude and pure guilt, we left that dangerous spot, unseen. The world around us was still the way we had left it. We could run up the stairs, passing through the shifting, ireful spectres without being touched. Led by Revelia, we put speed on our feet, as if we could feel the end of the other Chomps nearer at every step.

Close to the queen's room, something unexpected started to unfold. A very loud trembling spread across the floor accompanied by a strange, bright light. A sense of oppression rose from our hearts and our stomachs, as if lightning was about to strike right through our bodies. In our race against time, ignored the signs of an imminent surge of power. Our goal was to find that key.

'What's happening?' Anita asked, her feet keeping up the speed.

'This is Una. She is about to unleash her power!' Revelia shouted.

'Oh my God... Does she know about the Flare?' I asked, just before we reached the door of the queen's room.

'No. I can see the Chomps' future still. I can see Trusk's. But...wait! I can't see yours!' Revelia said, holding Treekan's arm.

451

'And that's a good sign,' he said, smiling. 'Let's get in!'

We were invisible but were not able to pass through walls and doors. Opening the door would have meant letting the queen know someone had got in. She would have seen where we were, the exact moment we had walked in. *Could she hit us anyway?* I thought. With my eyes closed, we entered. I was petrified to look, waiting for our lives to end in a burst of magic. But the room was empty. The Crimson Queen wasn't there. Her power was spreading fast from somewhere else, moving the air around us. We had reached the very queen's room alive.

'Something terrible is happening!' Revelia shouted again. Her face in agony, she could see her sisters' future vanishing right before her eyes. Whatever power Una had released, it had the Leonty as target.

'Where is she?' I asked.

'We need to look for the key,' Noah's voice was like a whisper. The rumbling noise around us dulled our ears.

'I need to see this! I need to see it!' Revelia's eyes went bright and red. Her power pushed to the limit, she was fighting her sister's will, uncovering her future and her own future. We stopped moving. Held by the Leonty's desperate attempt, we were forced to a halt, waiting for the vision of the crime she was about to witness.

'It's coming from above, to our right!' Treekan let out.

'Can we stop her? Can we do anything?' looked around, trying to find a strategy that would not come to mind.

I left the group and moved around the room, trying to find the artefact we were desperately looking for. There was not much to see. The tower was mostly empty; a large, old cabinet stood alone in a corner with a familiar, ornate mirror placed on the top. Close to it, a chaise longue waited for its owner to come back.

'Treekan!' I shouted across the room. 'Is this an Ancient Mirror? It looks very much like the ones you have.'

'Great Erion! Where is this coming from?' he asked, a surprised expression imprinted on his face.

'Guys... Something is wrong with Revelia,' Anita called our attention back to the Leonty. She looked in an extreme pain, her hands on her head, bent onto her knees.

'We need to look into it,' Treekan said, pointing at the mirror.

'Fafher, we need fo go!' Trusk said, pulling the Chomp's arm.

'Let's take it,' I let out, as I pulled the mirror away from the wall.

Its weight was imperceptible, like I had just taken a feather in my hands. Whatever magic it contained, the history kept secret underneath its surface had to be brief. We turned back to Revelia, sure the room had no more secrets for us to steal. Our next destination was unknown, but we knew we had to climb another bit, just few steps away from the source of that extreme power. Revelia barely walked, her breath getting shorter, so Noah and I held her in our arms, like she had done before with him, climbing the stairs to the second smaller tower.

At our arrival, through the open door, the nature of the Leonty's pain was right in front of us to see. The Crimson

453

Queen stood in the middle of the small room, surrounded by five flames, swirling fast around her body. Her hair was like hectic darts pointing at every corner; her hands open, she was reaching each and every Leonty left alive, dragging their spirits, their souls away from their bodies. The hot air had turned the room into a furnace, Una's power had become a fire that could not be tamed. We were left there in a horrifying amazement, unseen and uninvited, finally aware that we had come to fight someone well beyond our reach.

'Stay strong, my friend,' Treekan said to Revelia who was about to faint. Her eyes were closed, her magic had gone away 'You have the blessing of our Flare now!'

'We go look now, quick!' And Trusk left the group, undetected by the Crimson Queen. We had to find the artefact and that was probably going to be the only opportunity left.

With a rushing fear leeched to my body, I followed Trusk, getting closer to the destroying power. I could feel the heat penetrating into my skin, my bones getting on fire. Then, in between some small columns, I found it. The clepsydra was levitating inside a clear bubble. Red droplets moved all around, as if blood gravitated inside that emptiness.

'I found it, I found it!' I shouted.

'Hold on!' Treekan said, at my back. 'That's a spell. A strong one!' And his eyes closed, his hands waving around the evil magic.

It was like Treekan could speak to it, reading through the words of that spell. The more we waited, the less I could resist the extreme power pushing against our bodies. We had to act fast.

The Chomp then continued, 'It requires the blood of a human being…only a human can take it. I suppose she did it because she knew the Humans were all gone.'

'Treekan, please. The pain is getting stronger!' I shouted.

'You are human, But you are under my Flare, you are a magical being right now. You can't interact with it while inside the dome.'

'Oh God. We need to come out? She will see us!' I was terrified by the idea.

'Trusk!' Treekan called. 'Listen to me. Tell Mama I love her. Very much…'

'No! Treekan… What are you doing?' I asked. The idea he was about to risk his life was as painful as the fire catching at my skin.

'You don't understand. When you'll free Time, I'll be gone anyway. I've traded all my yacs with the mirrors. When Time comes back, I will die instantly!'

I couldn't believe my ears. He knew, he knew all this time. We had set out on our mission to free Time with him. He had been looking in the Ancient Mirrors, all the way back to their history, trading more years than he actually had. If we had succeeded, death would have taken him away.

'Trusk!' He looked back at his son. 'You are the Chomps' leader now. You know everything there is to know to help them, to help Mama and the others. When the Flare comes to you, put back its power on them.' And Trusk looked at his father, his small, dark eyes buzzing in disbelief.

'Fafher?' The only words he could say.

'Daniel,' Treekan looked back at me. 'When we exit the protection of the Flare, you will be exposed. Take the artefact and run! No hesitation! Do you understand me?' And his hands held my arms, shaking me from my pain.

'Treekan...' And tears started to flow down my cheeks.

It wasn't just the agony the queen had released on us, but the feelings I had started to have for the Chomps, for the ones who had guided us, saved us.

'Do you understand me?' he repeated.

'I do,' I finally replied, sobbing.

'Your friends will be safe. Revelia will be safe. I'm removing only you and me from our magic. You grab the artefact. I'll face *her*!'

And determination turned his face into anger. He had been living his life in fear, prisoner of an eternal life built on unlimited knowledge, responsibilities and sense of duty. A beautiful but sad sentence hung on his head since the moment he had used the Ancient Mirrors. Now he was up for a last fight, the biggest of all fights.

'Trusk! Remember! When this is all over, the Flare must come back home! Feher tu, son...'

And everything happened at once. The Flare went off for the two of us; in that small room, we popped out, as if from nowhere. My hands ready to grab the key, Treekan was ready to face the queen's wrath.

Chapter Thirty

The Five Temples

∞

Her eyes were on us. She had seen Treekan and she had seen me standing behind him. Her fury turned the room into an exploding sun. Her voice shouted an unbearable sound, in between the waves she sent against us. Pushed away, I fell on the ground, while Treekan resisted, hands placed in front of his face.

'I see you!' she shouted again. 'I remember you! You, the one who stopped me right when I was about to end it all. The one who held all six Flares for a brief moment... You come to claim them all for yourself?'

'Daniel, now!' Treekan moved closer to the Crimson Queen, his hair and wings quickly catching on fire.

'I'll destroy you! I'll destroy each and every one who tries to take it away from me!'

My clothes were about to reach a melting point, I could barely keep my eyes open when I stood back up and fearlessly placed my hands on the artefact, through the spell surrounding it. Droplets of blood left their spell and come down my arms turning into red, cold lines freezing my skin at its touch. My fingers were close to the key, when another wave of magic was thrown against me. This time I didn't move.

Treekan had stood in between, stopping the queen's rage from reaching me. His body turned into flames, his will was the only, final wall preventing her from getting to me. With my hands firmly holding the clepsydra, I gave a final look to where Treekan stood, his ashes falling on me like his final blessing to protect me. Awaking Trusk from the painful shock, I called his name, and in the space of a second, I was gone. Back in the invisible realm, I could see Anita and Noah again, holding Revelia up. She was coming back to consciousness but her eyes were still closed. Mine had gone to Trusk, my heart twisted in horror in seeing his tears flowing, his eyes greyed out.

'I'm really sorry, Trusk...I really am!' And he looked at me, empty. He had no anger towards me, no anger towards Una. The emptiness his heart had fallen into, was the only thing he showed.

'We need to go, before it's too late,' I said.

Fighting against the odds, we had come back at the door. Revelia had just started to stand on her feet when Anita noticed I had come back alone.

'Where is Treekan?' Her worries were coming to life.

'We need to go! Now!' I pushed with all my strength.

'Daniel?' Noah said.

'We need fo go!' Trusk repeated. His first words focused on us, protecting our lives was still his main goal.

'You can't escape from me! Where is my Key?' the queen shouted. 'I can still reach you, wherever you are. You can't escape from me!'

Her power moved the space, shaking the foundations we stood on. Determined to destroy us, her magic went beyond her own safety. In a shattering move, a pulsing power expanded mighty and wide, pulling the floor from its foundations, scattering the walls in flying stones. The top of the tower fell to dust, no wall was left standing; she was the only thing left.

Pushed by the elements, we flew outside the crumbling tower, like darts shot into the sky. My hands on Trusk, we managed to grab Anita, Noah and Revelia on our way down. Although strong, the little Chomp struggled to keep us up, so we quickly reached the bare sandy desert at the fortress's feet. On the ground, we scattered around like old toys nobody wants. The mirror I had taken with me was stuck in the sand, unbroken, saved by the soft touch of the desert. But our minds were crushed, our hearts in pieces, we could not help ourselves rewinding the events that had just happened. We had come in to save Noah and we had lost Treekan, Revelia had lost her sisters.

'Daniel,' Noah repeated. 'Where is Treekan?'

'Treekan is gone,' I replied, the shock on my face mixing with the dark sand. 'He traded his life with mine...to allow me to take this.' And I showed the artefact resting in my hand.

'*No!*' Anita let out.

'Treekan is not the only one,' Revelia said. She finally talked again. 'Una has taken my sisters' lives. That magic we witnessed, it was hers, taking their souls, their powers for herself.'

'But you are OK, right? She didn't take you?' Anita asked, her hands on Revelia's shoulders.

'Dad's Flare...fhe Flare has profecfed her,' Trusk replied. He looked at his hands, like he had his father's blood on him; Treekan's sacrifice had moved the Flare and its responsibility onto him.

'If I weren't under the Chomp's magic, I'd be gone. She would have taken me too...' And the Leonty stood up, looking up to the sky.

Half of the queen's tower was gone. Parts were still falling under their weight and a tiny figure was visible from far away. Una floated into the air, her power supporting her. She scanned the landscape looking for us, trying to catch us. She could not see the group of thieves, but she knew where we were heading next. So she quickly left her tower in ruins and reached the spectres who were waiting for her, down below.

'We need to finish this fast.' I said to everybody. 'She knows we have the key and she also knows we have the Flare and that we used it. We can't free Time and protect the Chomps at the same time.'

'What do we do?' Noah asked, standing up.

'If we set Time free, will this end your sister's power?' Anita asked Revelia.

'Don't call her that. She is nothing to me. She has never been and she will never be! Yes, Time might be able to stop her.' In her mind, Revelia was fighting the truth she had just come to know, the evil that had struck her sisters, making her the only one left, beside Una. She started to walk towards the other side of the fortress. Right across the front gates, the way to the temples was calling us.

'We can't risk any more lives. We don't know who this Time is and what he is capable of. We don't even know if he is still alive. Should we not give the Flare back to the Chomps?' I asked.

'If we don't go now, soon the spectres will be roaming the temples, hundreds of them,' Revelia pushed us ahead.

'OK. We travel fast. Once there, we let Trusk go. He must place the Flare back at the village.' And the silence that came after my decision, proved that the group agreed.

We ran fast, under the protection of the Flare. From the side walls we could hear the Crimson Queen storming loudly. Her wrath had been unleashed on the spectres who had let us in, who had failed to protect her and protect her treasures. Trying to speed our escape, Trusk pulled us into the air once more, allowing us to fly for a brief length. A few times we put our feet on the ground, giving him the chance to rest, then to go again, floating in the air. Halfway through the hill, on our way to the five temples, the far back gates of the stronghold opened. From its mouth, the fortress spewed a multitude of spectres, all piled up like a

461

war machine. At the top, the Queen of the slayers was riding the carriage of death.

'She's coming!' Anita shouted, looking back.

'We are close. Once we get there, we need to enter the Temple of Time. It's the big one at the top.' Revelia let go of Trusk's hand and landed a few feet below, on the soft grass now starting to break through the yellow sand downhill. 'Fly now, faster. I'll be just behind you.

The awful feeling she was going to stay behind bounced in my head. She could be looking for revenge, for a quick end and I could not allow it. So I shouted:

'Don't leave us! We need you!'

'I'll be just right behind you, I promise.' And she ran fast, keeping up pace with us.

Right at the large temples, the three of us landed on the green grass, followed by Trusk. The structures were astonishingly similar to the sort of temples we knew. Large, tall columns ran all around the buildings and inside, walls enclosed the space inside into a large box. At the centre, at the very top of the hill, surrounded by purple, wide trees, a bigger temple held the core of the Leonty's homeland.

'Must be that one.' Noah pointed right at its entrance.

'Trusk, you need to go now,' Anita pushed him to go back to the Chomps' village and place the Flare on its rightful spot.

'I can'f leave you here! No!' He said, challenging our plan, fighting against the promise made to his father.

'Trusk, she knows. She might have sent the spectres to your village already...' I wasn't going to have Reela's and

462

the others Chomps' deaths on my conscience, tormenting me for the rest of my life, no matter how short it was going to be.

'If I go, you'll lose your invisibilify!'

'It doesn't matter any more. You need to go now!' And I hugged him hard, hoping he could feel I knew how much I owed him.

Trusk eventually complied. Unsure that was the right thing to do, he finally flew away, bringing his magic power with him. The three of us were left alone, alone as we had started our journey in that eventful place. It felt like weeks had passed since the day we had met Aura, since the day, like a storm, we had entered the Chomps' lives.

'What do we do? We get in?' Anita asked, her eyes locked at the bottom of the hill; Una's figure was growing bigger.

'Where is Revelia?' Noah asked. She was behind us a moment earlier and now she was gone out of sight.

'She knows where we are going. Let's go!' And I took their arms and pulled them inside the temple.

Past the colonnade, a large, bronzy dish stood in the middle of the front opening. Shiny rocks sat inside, motionless. Once we walked in, we found ourselves in a deep dark place. There were no openings, no windows. Runae's star was left behind, its rays lighting up only the entrance, at the very centre of the room.

'I can't see anything...where are we supposed to go?' Anita asked, her hand searching for me.

'We need to think something, quick.' And my thoughts went to Anita's home, where our smartphones and their flashlights had been left behind.

'Here, I knew we were going to need this.' Revelia's voice came to give us the comforting news.

She had stopped at the first temple and brought what it looked like a wooden stick. She had put the top into the dish we had found outside and a bright flame had come right out of it. Our run into the deepest level of the temple was now possible. Behind a small stony room, white stairs went right down, well below the surface.

The imposing walls engulfed us, plunging us into the depths of Runae. With little time remaining, we dashed recklessly forward. A long, dark corridor unfolded before us, extending from the base of the stairs. Lit by a bright torch, we became fugitives in pursuit of freedom. Just moments after we had begun our sprint along the passage, a sudden tremor startled us. The walls shook with intensity, and a cascade of white dust rained down, filling the air around us.

'Una is using her best tricks against us,' Revelia said.

'She will bury us alive, if she has to…' I added.

'Look, a door, there!' Anita let out, pointing at what looked like the end of the tunnel.

A few feet from us, a carved door closed the way further. A large ring was placed at the top and a strangely familiar cavity sat right beneath. Coming close to it, I could easily recall its shape. Narrow at its centre, widening at each end, that was the exact copy of the clepsydra we had taken away from the queen's hands.

'This is the place, look!' I said. The dust was getting denser and our eyes started to struggle. 'This symbol... It's the artefact.' And I took it out in my hands, showing it to them.

Cracks had started to appear in the walls around and through the ceiling. Our heads had turned white, our lungs fighting for fresh air. The loud sound of destruction struck our hearts at once. It was a warning of what was coming next. With the hope we were only a step away from our target, I pulled the ring, trying to open the door, but with no success. We had no magic, no spell to get through. We had to find a way in, or face the Crimson queen's rage, under tons of stones and columns soon crashing onto our powerless bodies. And then the silence came. The place had stopped moving frenetically; the last few cracks had found their balance in between life and death. It was like the evil queen had lost her grip on us, mercifully giving us the time to think.

'What is happening?' Noah asked, looking at the ceiling.

Then a loud scream ran through the air, flying across the temple, all the way down to where we stood. A familiar voice screamed of a terrible pain, above our petrified minds.

'Trusk!' I shouted. 'That is Trusk's voice!'

'He is somewhere over the temple!' Revelia added. 'He is using his Flare to cover the entire place against Una!'

'She can still reach him. I almost got skinned by the fire she released in the tower!' And my feet were already pointing at the way back.

'No! You find your way in. It's my time to intervene.' Revelia pulled me back, her body fighting against my will. 'I'll buy us some time, as much as I can. I can guarantee you, she will be surprised to see there is still another Leonty left standing!'

And she left us, with no hesitation. Desperate and not ready to lose our friends, we started to pull the door together, push it, kick it. Nothing was working.

'Daniel,' Anita suddenly said. 'The shape, the hole in the door. It's not a symbol, it's a cavity. The clepsydra needs to go right in it!'

Many feet above us, on the surface, Revelia walked out the Temple of Time, ready to cross over the protection of the Flare. The small Chomp held the Flare on the roof, in agony, against the fire sent to destroy him. His wings were about to catch on fire. When Revelia's figure came out from the invisible shield, Una's face was stunned. The multitude of spectres went silent at once. Whatever power their queen had, it didn't have an effect on that small Leonty who now stood in front of her, challenging her unlimited power.

'You!' the Crimson Queen said, horrified. Her magic had momentarily lowered. 'How?'

'How am I alive?' Revelia shouted. Her sister floated above the ground, many feet away. 'How did I manage to survive when you ripped the lives of my sisters out of their bodies?'

'I should have known better! You were with them all along!' And her rage rose up again.

'Did Demetra ask you why? Did Trasfigea and all my other sisters ask you why? Before you turned them into

466

nothing. Did you tell them why?' Revelia wasn't only buying time, her voice was filled with disgust and anger.

'Where is my key? Where are they?' the queen asked, ignoring her questions.

'I have the key, here with me. And I'm about to give it to them. So, sister, weigh your answer carefully. Why did you do it?'

'I'm done with you! I'm done with *all of you*! You want to know why?' she asked, her wrath mounting. 'Because I'm done with the pain. Because this world has given me nothing! And I'm giving nothing in return! Like everything that was taken away from me, I've taken everything away from them! Now...' she said slowly, '...before I turn your friends into dust, hand me my key!'

'I've been seeing your future, sister...but I can't see it any more.' And Revelia showed a smile of revenge on her face.

My hands had just placed the artefact into its cavity when the door started to pulse. A golden glow spread from the clepsydra to the edge of the wall, filling the space, digging its roots below the ground we stood on. When the place had absorbed its last drop of power, the yellow, bright light disappeared, leaving us in a dull silence.

'That's it?' Anita asked.

But a renewed, horrifying scream came back again from above. The Crimson Queen had released the full extent of her power on the dome Trusk held with his bare hands. Our bodies shifted away from the invisible realm and the temple started to tremble again. Trusk had protected the spot with every inch of power he had, but his hair had

467

started to melt and his burnt wings were about to leave his skin exposed. With tears and sweat, he pushed the Flare out of his hands and raised it up in the sky. His last attempt at delaying our miserable end was about to fail.

Una pushed forward, the long-awaited victory in her hands, her final blow was aiming at Revelia who had closed her eyes and was ready to greet the future she was still mysteriously smiling at. A roaring energy pushed its way out of the Temple of Time, bringing Trusk with it. The dome was gone, the Flare was dead.

At the cracked columns, we appeared, surging out of the hole of death. As we walked to Revelia, Una's power felt like a soft breeze on our skin. Behind us, a strong renewed being protected us from evil. The Crimson Queen looked terrified. She knew we had succeeded and her will was nothing compared to the power we had summoned. The spectres started to move back, dispersing through the land, leaving their master alone.

'Come back, you miserable cowards!' she shouted. 'This is not how it ends!'

'No, this is how it begins!' Noah and I replied together, our hands joined.

The magic we had brought with us had grown bigger and wider. At our back, the shape of a tall, large man formed, as he walked slowly, a golden aura covering his face. In front of him, the clepsydra floated in the air, pulsing with an intense light. Led by that protective power, Trusk softly landed on the ground, beside us, and Anita took him in her arms, his wings gone, his body showing the marks of his sufferings.

Chapter Thirty-One

Time

∞

If the final fight was about to break out, this time both sides had brought an evenly matched power, the same magic, but with different motives. The Crimson Queen was determined to bring desolation to every land of Runae, but we had unearthed a long-forgotten power from the very roots of that planet, bringing it back to life. He who had been calling us from far away, was finally back to protect it; he was going to save Revelia, Trusk and all the Chomps from her diabolical intentions.

'I own the Flares!' she shouted, desperately. 'There is no power that can match mine! Whoever you have brought to life, it's my duty and will to keep my promise. You will not prevail. *You are nothing!*' And she lined up the five sacred flames in front of her.

Her body became the centre of their gravitational spin. The Flares, large and pulsing, wrapped her up in a cocoon of pure magic. Red and bright, waves expanded away from her, moving around the land, burning everything they touched. The temples started to crumble on their own feet and the purple trees were turned in a long-gone memory. Faster than the spectres running away, Una's fury turned against her own slaves, turning them into dust, vaporizing their corrupted souls in a blink. Horrified by her final act, I held Noah's hand in a silent call for action. My mind and his were one; entangled to our saviour's will, we were clashing his energy against hers, pushing her back.

'Noah,' I said. 'We need to let him!'

'Yes, let's set him free!'

And the surge of our defence turned in attack. Time's power exploded in a blinding, pure light. Stretching over our shoulders, in between our legs, the magic left us untouched, like beholders of a supreme will. Time was everything and everywhere around, crashing his golden essence on Una's magic. Unwilling to accept the coming defeat, she pushed her strength to their limits, her power turning against her, pushed backwards, like a betrayer to her own mind, she was trapped in a pure, benevolent light.

The Chomp's flare had left the temples under its master's desire, darting in the far sky above. Una's last opportunity to prevail flashed before her eyes. As she stretched her hands forward, the five Flares resounded at the sight of their last, lost sibling. Their hovering, magnetizing force reached across the space, pulling the stone back.

In the exact moment the Sháten Déil reached the others, a stunning blast unleashed from the Crimson Queen's spot. Pushed back by the gigantic explosion, we fell on our backs and rolled a few feet downhill. As Anita helped Trusk in her arms, she pulled him close to her chest, her eyes closed, terrified by the fall.

Everything around us suddenly froze. Una stood still, her eyes shut, as she floated in the sky. Her skin and hair wobbled as if melting under the raging fire of the stones. A deep sound waved in quick succession, the omen of a greater power reached our ears, making them dull. When Una opened her eyes back, death itself manifested.

In the fraction of a second, the entire landscape exploded. The ground broke and lifted in the air, the matter of every existing element pulled apart, shredded into myriads of particles. We followed through, our bodies and hearts exposed, weak, powerless.

I gazed at Noah and Anita as we were pushed further away, my eyes unable to focus. I knew it was them I had seen last with the only power of my heart as my sight failed me, my bones and flesh left behind as my soul was stripped out of my body.

Whatever happened in that moment, it's something only Time knows. For a brief moment, we had died. There hadn't been any understanding; the consciousness of being greeted by death lasted an instant. And yet, as we were gone, so we were brought back. The only thing we witnessed was a quick rewinding of time and space, Runae's God standing right in front of Una.

471

He glowed bright, reaching the power of the same star that shone on our heads. Without hesitation, Time extended his arms and engulfed the Crimson Queen in his pure, unchallenged magic, trapping her within the power of the six Flares.

'Nothing! Nothing!' were the only last words she said.

Then, the Crimson Queen collapsed under her own power. A power that had moved against its owner, crushed by the immense goodness Time's energy had released. The space around became empty, the queen's cruelty dissipating in the air, her malicious domain was over.

The four of us stood back at the edge of the temple in ruins, looking at what we had just accomplished. Something that looked impossible to achieve was now, against the odds, a reality. Noah and I smiled at each other and found ourselves in a meaningful hug. Our joy at the end of our peril was multiplied by Anita's and Revelia's hands, placed on our heads, tears flowing on everyone's cheeks. Trusk was still in between life and death; his scars marking his body, he was attempting a weak smile. He had put his life at risk for us, for his people, for their future.

'Daniel,' Anita started, sobbing. 'I don't think he is going to make it.' And she placed Trusk on the ground, his head on a cracked stone.

'Thank you, Trusk, thank you!' That was all I could say. His tiny hands in mine, he tried to smile at me.

'Revelia?' I asked, hoping she could help him, somehow. But her face was sad, silent.

'It's not too late,' a voice said. 'Actually, *I'm* not too late.'

The powerful being we had set free moved closer, his body taking the full shape of a man, his face finally visible. He had the look of an angel, a golden fluid moved in his eyes, a long cloth covered his shoulder, his hips and his legs. On his neck, a pendant in the shape of a moved with his walk, from side to side like it had a will of its own, like a pendulum ticking the seconds. Once close to Anita, he bent on his knees, his hands moving forward to Trusk who struggled to breathe.

'You have given me a great gift. It's time for you to come back. I can't give you life, but I can give you time to heal.'

And a glowing magic left his hands to reach the Chomp's body, enclosing him in a protective shield. We stood by his side, witnessing Trusk's life being paused, frozen in an ethereal casket. Then, he turned to us.

'Thank you, my friends. You have fulfilled the first and most important task of my and your existence.'

'What are you?' Revelia asked.

'I'm Time, one of the protectors,' he replied, his voice soft, nearly ethereal. 'One of the Gods left standing. Thanks to your help, I'll be able to help you back, to move forward.'

'Can you take us home?' I asked, glad to hear those words.

'I can. I can take you home, but I'm afraid that is not the home you are destined to get to. And Time moved away, looking at the vastity in front of us, now a testament to what the Crimson Queen had turned Runae into. 'We are late to our quest…there is so much to do. But me being back, it's what matters, for now.'

473

'What is going to happen? To them, to this world?' Anita was still looking at Trusk.

'Yes. Them...' Time turned around, his hands on the precious artefact now back its the rightful owner. 'The day will pass, the night will come. And so more will be. Let's bring him home. Let's give them back what belongs to them, their hero.'

The clepsydra shone again, its magic turning the never-ending day into motion. Erion was unlocked from its position and the night stars were going to give it some rest, soon. Time moved his hands ahead, inviting us to follow him. And so we did. Embraced by his kind power, we dissolved into thin air, travelling through space, over the desert and the mountains. We appeared in a known, friendly place. Our feet stepped right where the Chomps' Flare used to be, the crooked building looking right at us, welcoming us back. Trusk's body floated and moved downhill, locked on its own destination. Time spoke again.

'His heart knows where he belongs. Please,' he continued, looking at Revelia, 'Make sure they know he will be alright. You are welcome here, they will trust your words.'

'We are not going too? Can we see them once more, before we go home?' Anita was not rushing to go back home any more. Too much had happened, we had experienced too much to simply let go.

'You are not going home, just yet. I need to speak to you. There is more coming, for you.' And he nodded to Revelia, telling her she was free to go. 'Now, follow me.'

Time could have easily been Treekan in a new body. His moves, his way of leading us, and the place he was leading us to, everything looked like a flashback. We walked to the Ancient Mirrors, inside that place we knew well. Once inside, our gaze shifted to the First Mirror. It remained untouched, just as we had left it on the day we summoned its magic to show us the past. Treekan's sacrifice still lingered within me, leaving behind the bitter taste of loss

'I'm confident you know these artefacts. These mirrors were created by me, in the attempt to build the path we were all destined to take. Only few in the early days, when my power was gone from me, when I was cast away into the depth of this world, I became one with its very essence, producing more and more of those. Every kind in Runae were given mirrors to remember what had happened when I got enslaved. With their history, I hoped I had given them the truth, preventing their end, stopping the evil from taking their hearts. But a stronger hand was at play here. With the centuries, the wars and the atrocities, many of the mirrors had gone, destroyed by a wicked will. Only three beings have them still. The Aqualymphs, the Chomps and the Leonty.'

Listening to his words was like putting all the pieces back together. We had been running around, taking decisions, taking risks knowing just as much as we needed, to continue our journey. But finally, we were getting the whole truth. He continued.

'The first ones were eventually taken by the queen and, with them, their mirrors were turned to dust. All but one. Survivor of the war between the Leonty and the Aqualymphs, Aura has been protecting theirs since the beginning of their dark ages, since how they called it, the Great Dawn. The Chomps instead, protected by their Flare, were able to master the use of my gifts. They were my way through to you. And last, the Leonty. The queen had destroyed all the ones given to her kind. For her, remembering was like looking back at all the evil she had done, the true, wicked nature of her soul. However, she kept one. The one about her life, the one able to tell how she came to be. Somehow, she fed her anger by it.'

'We have seen it. We took it from her, but I'm afraid we left it behind, in the desert, by the fortress.' I said, sad.

'My friend, there is no memory lost, if I'm here to recall it.' And the mirror just appeared out of nowhere, right in front of our eyes. It was the exact same mirror we had stolen from the Crimson Queen. The same one we had left intact, partially buried in the sand. 'I'll let you see inside, eventually. It's important to understand why she did what she did. But there is a far more important matter to discuss. For now, we need to talk about the future, not the past!' And Time placed the Mirror at the wall, replacing a broken one, beside the First.

'Our future?' Noah had paid with severe pain for rushing into his destiny, into the answers we both craved. Now, that fragile spark was igniting again.

'Yes, your future, our future.' Time moved his hands up into the air, flaring up an incorporeal vision around the room. Stars floated, their lights faint. Then he continued.

'In the beginning, when no matter existed, when no *Soul* had walked any land, *Nothing* was. He was violent and forceful, king of the vast nowhere, Nothing was the only power allowed to be. Then, before *Time* could even be, a power started to become. Energy of the cosmos found its way to grow and *Creation* came to life. Creation was the first God, the most powerful of the Gods that would eventually come after her. But her strength had yet to become a threat. Her energy was pure desire of making and so, when she was ready, she created the first world. Three more came soon after. Beings were made to walk the lands, stars were ignited to sustain their life.' The space in the whole room had become brighter. His words turned into a transparent reality. The three of us were enchanted by his voice and his magic becoming real.

'This is the moment of creation. The big bang?' Anita exclaimed, her head up, the stars reflecting in her eyes.

'I believe this goes beyond what we have learned in school,' I replied. After a brief pause, Time continued.

'Looking at all she had done, Creation felt her first feeling. She felt Love. This is how the Second God came to be. *Love* was strong, as strong as his creator. Wanting to give more to the existence, Creation and Love produced *Health*. The third God could now give all the beings in the universe the immortality they deserved. Then I came to be. I was the fourth God who had given the worlds their memories, a past, present and future. And at last, Soul, the fifth God, came to be, so that the cosmos could have its own destiny. Irate by the existence of the vastity as it was, Nothing's wrath surged against us. An immensely powerful war between Nothing and us Gods started. It was violent and yet eternal. No one could defeat the other. So Nothing moved to destroy the beings and their worlds.'

477

'Standing in defence of one of those worlds, Health was the first God to be defeated. Her power was great, but not enough to prevail, so Nothing cast her away into the emptiness. The universe had lost its immortality and started to perish. In that exact moment, to protect the creatures of Runae, I froze this universe in a never-ending frame. Erion was brought to still, the day lasting for millennia. A foolish attempt to buy more time mine was...' And Time turned his face away. Whatever history he withheld in his memory, it was painful. 'Creation, who was determined to stop Nothing and to protect her children, had made her final move. Something of an immense magic was released when the two powers clashed. Soul, Love and I were bound to a spell of immortality. In exchange to that precious gift, we had lost our mother and creator. At the same time, in the opposite corner of the universe, Soul had been fighting long and fiercely. His magic was holding Nothing to the stand. So the evil trapped him under a powerful spell, in the depths of nowhere.'

The vision suddenly paused and so did the tale, giving us a moment to indulge in our discovery. Time's face showed sadness and pain.

'We know what happened to you. We have seen it in the First Mirror,' I said, thinking that was the reason why he had stopped talking.

'It's not what happened to me that saddens me. It's what happened to you that does,' he replied.

I was puzzled. *When did we come to be in that tale?* Time's prolonged silence worried me. I glanced at Anita and Noah, and they returned the same uncertain look.

478

Whatever awaited us in the unfolding narrative, there was a lingering question: could it truly be connected with us?

'Love was the God protector of Earth, your world. He protected it for centuries and centuries, till the day Nothing came to face him in battle. Knowing that Creation's spell could not be broken, it turned its power on the Humans, forcing Love to engage in a terrible fight. Despite the odds, he was very close to casting Nothing away for eternity, but the evil could not give up. On Love's final blow, a spell was released against him. On its way to annihilation, Nothing had reached the God with the wickedest of all spells. It broke Love in two, ceasing his existence.'

And Time paused again. His eyes pointed to me, like he wanted to make sure I could understand the meaning of all of that. Then, he resumed.

'Being immortal, Love could not just die. His essence was parted in two halves, but indeed he was still alive. So, for some mysterious reasons, he was reborn in two of the gentlest souls that have walked the Earth. Sleeping, inside their hearts, Love has been waiting to be reunited and become one once more.'

And that fascinating storyteller stopped again. The three of us struggled to put all the pieces together. The things we had learned from the Ancient Mirrors, from Revelia, Treekan and now, Time. I couldn't go beyond that. My visions before Runae, my dreams, were not part of it. My heart was telling me I had to, but my mind could not make sense of it. Eventually, Noah asked the question that would bring everything together.

'Is it you? One of the three entities I have seen all my life?' But Time didn't answer. Gazing at his virtual masterpiece moving slowly in the space above us, he kept silent. 'Your voice, your face is so familiar. I've seen you before. How is it possible?'

'What about you two?' Time finally directed his attention back to us, Anita and me. 'Have you seen me?' Anita put on a weird face, feeling as if she had been pulled into an improvised exam in school.

'She hasn't,' I answered. 'I have.'

'Very well. My mind was seeing right. You are both here.'

'What does it mean?' I asked.

'Remember what we saw in the First Mirror, right here, in this room?' Anita asked, stepping back, taking a distance from us. 'The queen was told that only one of them could set him free.'

'What's wrong? What are you saying?' I moved closer to her, trying to understand why she was looking at me like I was suddenly a stranger, a dangerous enemy. I knew Anita had grasped the whole truth before me. She had always been faster, smarter. I was well late to the party, and being emotionally involved in that situation didn't help at all.

'She knows,' Time replied. 'Very well. I knew there was something special in her, regardless. You two, my friends, you two are the two halves. The two parts of Love that have yet to be reunited.'

And the worlds on our heads disappeared, the magic dissolved. The history lesson was over. It was time for us to take it in, digest the impossible truth. I could not speak, I was trapped in a sequence of past events flashing before my eyes. I was not one of them. I had no powers, I had no memory of it. My past was blurred, but it certainly couldn't be that. Anita's eyes were on me, she could see my struggle, my bouncing back and forth accepting and denying the idea I could be a God. Scared, but still wanting to be by my side, she came closer and took my arm in her hands.

'I think this is it, Daniel. You have been looking for the truth, a reason why all that madness happened to you. Think about it. You have no father, you have no mother. You and Noah have been dreaming about each other and you have been dreaming of *him*. This is your history, your real history.' And a brief smile appeared on her face.

Carefully listening to her words, I looked at Noah who stood still, in silence, his eyes on me. He was a step ahead as he had always been. He was ready to embrace the revelation of our lives, glad everything had a meaning. So he crossed the room and came to my side. His hands on my face, he was holding me and holding my thoughts, making sure they would sink in.

'What happens now?' Anita asked, looking at Time.

'We have laid down only the first stone. I'm free, but the road stretches far, very far. There is much more you both need to know… But we can't move further before we get the others.'

'The others?' I asked. *Is he hinting at the Chomps? Who else needs to be rescued?*

481

'We need to find Soul and bring him back. I'll make sure you get home safe, before I leave this world and go, looking for him.'

'Hold on,' I struggled to keep up. 'Are you saying there is another one of you to be rescued? Where?'

'Not here, not in your world. Soul is trapped in his own version of slavery. There is no way to reach him or to find him. But I will look further. I'll find a way.'

'Time?' Noah interjected. 'Was it you, all these years? Was it you coming to me, to Daniel?'

'No, my friend. I could not leave these lands without crossing the node. Actually, I could not leave at all. My spirit and my power were under someone else's control.'

'How is it possible then? Us finding you? Getting here?' Noah pushed his question once more, this time he looked at me as if I could help him with an answer.'

'It wasn't him. It wasn't them,' Anita let out, preceding the God. 'It was your memory. Both of you were called by your inner soul, by your past...'

As I said, there is something special about you," Time remarked, casting Anita a brief smile before turning away. Without further explanation, he strode towards the large door, casting a meaningful glance at us and silently inviting us to follow.

Chapter Thirty-Two

The Making Of A Greater Evil

∞

If a journey was about to end, a greater one was wating to begin. Like Noah, I had awaited understanding of why I was chosen to face such challenges, and recently, why we were chosen to save Runae from the encroaching evil. 'There is another one,' Grandma had said. *Was she talking about Noah? Time? Another God, she meant? Did she know I am…we are forgotten Gods, waiting to be awoken?*

'Let's give our farewell to the Chomps,' Time said.

Without affording us the chance to pose more questions or to contemplate all we had just learned, Time whisked us through space. In the blink of an eye, we vanished and reappeared in the Chomps' village, standing before Trusk's home. The enchantment that had held the village in an eternal day was dissipating; the sun had shifted, and the evening was drawing near. Dozens of Chomps bustled about, engaged in conversation and movement, while a few lingered by Reela's side on her porch. Just emerging from the house, after having ensured Trusk's well-being, Revelia approached us with a smile lighting up her face.

'This is the first time I see the dark coming in the outside world. It's the first time I feel the pleasure of the fresh breeze. The Chomps have been worried. Since the dome disappeared, they have been waiting in fear. I told them what I could. They are still processing it.'

'Did you tell her?' I asked, referring to what had happened to Reela's fearcel.

'No. But I think she guessed. She was too worried seeing Trusk in those conditions.'

I swiftly broke away from the group and approached Reela, who abruptly stopped her conversation with the other Chomps as I drew near. Tears welled in her eyes, yet a faint smile emerged amidst her sorrow.

'Reela...' I started, my eyes getting wet. I was sorry and felt terribly responsible for the pain I had caused.

'I know,' she interrupted me. 'He knew what he was going to risk.'

'You are not talking about Trusk...'

'No child. I'm not. It's OK, don't cry. I know he had to do what he had to do. He is now part of the history. And history was what he truly loved, more than anything else in this world.'

484

'He loved you and loved Trusk more than anything else,' I said. 'It's because of his sacrifice that we made it here. But before pushing himself into the fight, he gave Trusk a message for you. You were in his mind, till the end. He asked to let you know.'

And that precious, small Chomp put her tiny arms around me, crying desperately. Anita ran towards us, her tears joining ours. So did Noah a few moments later.

'Dear friends!' Time loudly started. 'You have fought hard and for a very, very long time. You are free from your prison. Now, you are free from evil. The protector of your world stands before you. You won't be suffering any more pain. This is my promise to you... The queen *is gone!*'

A clamour of wonder, happiness and joy spread across the entire land. Everywhere Chomps hugged, smiled, and cried. Their fate had been constantly at stake but they were now free to live their lives without fear.

'Reela,' I continued. 'Trusk is going to be alright. He only needs time to heal. The Flare is gone, all Flares are. But don't worry, you won't need them any more. Chomps are the only beings left alive. They will need yours and Trusk's lead to adjust to their new life.'

'Did you see?' Anita added. 'Erion is moving again! You will have nights and days, like Treekan used to tell you. His memory will stay with you, with them, with your star forever...'

'Thank you for lending us a hand when we needed it the most. Thank you for welcoming us,' Noah said.

'No, thank you for bringing my Trusk back to me!' Reela said, hugging the three of us again.

485

The long-awaited night had eventually come. We asked Time to let us stay in Runae one more day. We wanted to be close to Trusk and Reela a little bit longer. Knowing the Chomps would set a great ceremony in memory of Treekan's life and sacrifice, we promised them to help in organizing it. So that night, we were ready to spend our last few hours in that small home we had learned to love and care for.

Sitting outside, enjoying the chill air of the night, Anita and Noah talked about all the things their hearts and their minds had gone through. I spent a few hours sitting beside Trusk as he slept in bed, no longer in need of Time's magic to protect him. His wounds were still hard to look at, but, to my relief, his face showed no pain any more. After a while, I left him in his tiny room, Reela asleep close to his bed on an old chair by the low window, on the second floor and moved outside. Before closing the door, I gave her another look, thinking how beautiful it would have been to have a mother just like her.

'How is he?' Anita asked, as I sat down beside her.

'Looks better. Whatever Time has done to him, seems like it's working fast. Reela is still there, asleep beside him.'

'Must be very confusing for them,' Noah said. 'I mean, this whole day and night routine.'

'Let me check,' Anita replied, standing up. 'If Reela wants to, I'll take her place for a little while. She might need it.'

Noah and I were left alone, in between the inside and the outside of that strange, welcoming home. An uncomfortable distance held the invisible partition

486

between the two of us. Like an indication of what our journey had turned to be, we still moved at different speeds. Afraid of getting closer, we held our thoughts to ourselves. My eyes went to his few times. He wasn't shying away from my attempt to read his mind and, eventually, he smiled, making the marks left by Demetra's torture even more visible.

'What about you?' I said, sliding closer to him, my hands already moving towards his face. 'We didn't get the chance to make sure you were alright.'

'I'm fine, really.' And he let me touch him, slowly pushing his cheek against my right hand. 'It was terrible, there in the moment, but it's just a bad memory now...that's all.'

'I heard your voice in my head, you know? As we were running to save you, I heard you inside my mind.'

'It must have been when Demetra found out we were connected. She said something about me containing more than my own soul. I'm sure she was talking about you.' And Noah moved his hand to find mine.

'I wish we didn't have to do this,' I replied, my head moving closer to his. I could see the deepest pits of his soul right through his eyes. I could have counted all his freckles, if I wanted to. 'I wish we didn't have to endure this pain.'

'If it meant us feeling the way we feel now, the way I feel in this very moment...I'd do it again.'

In my heart, I knew what Noah was trying to tell me. We had come closer and closer. Despite the risks, losing him and finding him again had only brought us to the undeniable truth. We were destined to be together, in a way

487

or another. But I could not release myself from the oppressive idea that something was still wrong. Instead of steering my mind towards my life, my feelings for John, I had taken the deceiving path of denial. Whatever Noah said, it referred to something else, to Runae and the defeat of the Chomps' oppressor. Few moments later, with us still frozen in an intimate frame, Anita came back. No judgement in her face this time, we had gone a long way from that night in Noah's Bridge. Instead, she put her hands on our shoulders and smiled.

'He is back,' she said, looking at the far end of the village. Time had appeared out of nowhere, his cloak shining in the dark. His golden eyes were like the ones of a cat lurking in the shadow. In his hands, he held something familiar.

'I see you can't rest. How's our little friend?'

'He is getting better,' I said. 'Pain has left his body, but he's still unconscious. We can't sleep. There is so much in our heads, we might be staying awake for weeks!'

'Then maybe…you want to look at this?' And he pushed Una's mirror through the air, right in front of us. 'I know you wanted to see.'

'Shall we?' Anita asked, after looking at the both of us. If that was our last trip into their past, we had to do it before leaving.

The same night we lived in, waited in Una's past. We saw the world changing; the large was sun shone brightly but an unnatural dark floated in the memory of that past. The Chomps' village had left its place to a different land. The five temples had multiplied in number; the ones we had seen in our reality were only few compared to the multitude of the new ones scattered across the landscape. Within one of these houses, candles burned brightly, casting warm flickers against the stark surroundings. A loud voice thundered from inside. A Leonty lay on the floor, by the corner, beside a large bed.

Her look resembled Una's and Revelia's, but she wasn't either one of them. Crying, her hands were raised at protection of her own face; she had been hit by someone else, much taller than her. What appeared to be another Leonty stood next to her, distinguishable by broader shoulders, dark and tangled hair, and a thick beard framing the neck. It was the first time we had encountered a male of their kind.

'You disgust me!' he shouted. 'You swore she had no blood shared with the evil! You swore she wasn't like you... But here you are, given birth to a monster. She is a monster, as much as you are!'

The 'monster' lay on the bed, near the corner of the room. The baby was a Leonty, with pale skin and red eyes. She stared at the ceiling, unaware of the vicious words her father yelled.

'I did not mean to lie to you.' She cried desperately. 'Something has taken over my power. Since our daughter was born, I have been looking at her seeing only a normal creature, like you...'

'You lied to me, Vertatis, *you lied!*' And he kicked her face harder, spilling a purple blood all over the floor. 'Do you want to go to war against them again? Do you? Don't you know how hard is for me to protect you, to make sure they

489

won't know? I had to bribe the last Valahan that came to do business with me. When he realized that I was consulting you to verify his words, I had to pay him to stay silent!'

Whatever we looked at, it wasn't right. Anger welled up inside me, mounting with each passing moment. I clenched my hands tightly as the desire to punch him screamed in my head. Anita, unable to bear witnessing the brutal scene, covered her face with her hands.

'You know what the Humans' law says... *She must die!*' he shouted.

'No! No!' Noah screamed. Yet nobody could hear him. We were ghosts passing through the past.

'Don't worry,' Time said, putting his hands on Noah's shoulders. 'Look at that baby...you know who she is.'

A moment later, we jumped into another memory. Vertatis engaged with a small group of Leonty. For what we had just learned, no male was present during that secret gathering. The scared Leonty held her baby in her arms, hidden in many layers of fabric.

'You need to help me, sisters! This is my baby!' she was begging them, desperately. 'I can't let them do her any harm!'

'Sister,' one said. 'This is the law. One of our kind carrying magic in her veins...that's evil!'

'She is one of us, Mementhya! If she is evil, so are we!' another one answered.

'She won't survive,' an old Leonty said. For the first time, we witnessed time passing by on the skin of that strange kind. 'You know this disease is upon females of our

490

kind only. They won't come to any agreement. They treat all of us like nothing. Imagine if one of us has that magic inside!'

'She needs to die…' a third one interrupted. 'Don't be alarmed. The Humans don't need to know she has ever existed. We can give her to the Gods at the temples. The Runers will raise her like one of their own.'

'But I won't be able to see her again, to see my baby!' Vertatis cried.

'It's the only way. The Runers will turn her into a priestess. If she really has no magic, one day you might tell her the truth.'

'Why do I have to do something so terrible? Why do we have to endure all this pain?'

'It's the law. The same law that protects us from the enemy who's trying to destroy us, all of us. There is no other way!'

If that baby was Una, she was no different than me and Noah. Vertatis was forced to give her up, for her own baby's sake. I could not help but thinking if my real mother had faced the same terrible fate. Trapped in my thoughts, I was taken by surprise when the scene changed. Una was now older; her body resembled the one we knew. She wore a red robe with silver edges and golden marks all over. Her mouth was shut, her face covered and locked by a disturbing mask. Another Leonty, a male of their kind, was talking to her, while watching her bending on her knees, cleaning the floor.

'When you are done with this, you can go to the Temple of Grace. Stand there away from the others. I don't want to

491

see you resting or lying down. You don't deserve rest...' he said, his hands holding a heavy stick he had just used against her. 'Turning the others against their masters? Is this how you repay us? Your words slip through your mouth like snakes, lying through your teeth, manipulating, turning people's thoughts at command!'

Una looked at him in anger. Her eyes glowed red, a terrible premonition of what she would become.

'Do your evil magic... Your eyes won't help you. Your mouth is shut. You can't speak spells any more, monster!' And after striking her once more, he left the place. And so did we.

We were brought into a moment we had seen before, in the middle of a raging war between the Gods. The skies were on fire and the lands were shaking.

Una was much older but her look was still stunning. She had struck a priest with a heavy tool and he was lying dead on the white crumbling floor of a temple. With blood still on her hands, she took a key from the priest's rope and freed herself from the heavy mask, running away before the temple collapsed. On her way to the long-desired freedom, a chance for revenge waited for her, in the path ahead.

As Time was losing strength, crushed by an evil too strong to be defeated, the Leonty stopped right in front of the vast magnitude of their collision, her eyes wide open in disbelief. She was witnessing the full power she was craving. The ground was breaking apart, trees dying at the touch of the evil's power, their roots ripped from their rightful homes. Yet, the protector of the dying world was not giving up. Despite the enemy waves of power coming against him, Time rewound his own form, briefly escaping the horrifying destiny. The more he fought to hold his position, the wider the destruction ran wild, subverting the law of matter, turning the burning world into nothing.

As her kind ran away in fear, Una was drawn by it instead. Unaware of who she really was, some of them tried to stop her, convince her to run for her life, but Una's will was as strong as her desire to break free. As her wish of vengeance got stronger, the evil saw her fearless move towards him. And so Nothing had quickly found a better way to end the eternal fight by diverting from its original plan. Found its ideal jailer, the one who could comply to its maleficent will, the dark entity spoke.

'You are not afraid?' a thundering, deep voice spread from the raging sky. Although we were sneaking in the vision of a remote past, we felt its voice shaking our hearts. 'You are not like the others. What is this...anger I feel? No...it's not just anger. It's wrath, desire for annihilation.' But Una didn't talk. Her face locked into the depth of the enemy above, she was almost smiling.

'So you come to me to ask for it? Very well! I'll turn your rage into a power that no kind has ever seen. You will be taming this...God and its power to make it yours. For now and as long as I need to complete my plan!'

Shocked by what we had seen, we finally realized we were not the only ones who had witnessed her first murder, her first act of revenge that would pave the road to her red dominion. Something had seen it too, something who had cursed Time into a never-ending slavery, caged by the one who soon would be called the Crimson Queen.

So the pages of time moved forward, the landscape and places quickly changed again. We were brought back to the Broken Ruins where fire and death mixed fiercely in the aftermath of a different war. In one of the few large buildings left standing, Una walked slowly into a circular room. In a corner, a few Humans were left in between life and dead, terror imprinted on their faces. A young man held his left hip with his hand, trying to stop the blood running down his leg. Beside him, someone we had seen before was about to speak.

'You don't understand,' he said. His words, counted and slow, were slipping through his silvery white beard. 'We are on the same side here...we both belong to the same master.'

'There has never been a side that was the same,' Una replied, her eyes on fire. 'I've never been on the same side with any other living being.'

'But we are...you and I were sent by the same one.' And he slowly moved backwards, trying to put distance between himself and death.

'Your magic is not working...why do you keep trying?' Una mocked. 'Keep your lies in your defiant mouth. You have been plotting in the shadows for a long time. You have corrupted the souls of the many who lived in these lands, turning one kind against another. You are the one who started the hunt against my people, convincing the Humans we were the enemy. Convincing our own kind to strike the ones like me who had magic in their veins.'

494

'Leonty…' the young man interrupted, taking his crown off his head. 'If it's our Flare you want, you can have it. But please, spare my family and the few left alive.'

'I was never given any chance, why would I now be the one who gives it? I don't want your crown. I want you to witness the true nature of the evil you and everybody else made me become.'

And Una's face turned back to the old man. Her eyes fixed on the ones of her enemy, he was enchanted by the Leonty's power. Her will becoming his, she moved him like a pawn, dragging his feet against his own command. He moved to the largest opening of the room, stepped onto the windowsill and jumped to his death. Determined to accomplish her mission, she showed no hesitation, and with the bare swing of her left arm, she cut through the king's throat, making him fall on the cold floor, his crown slipping from his hand, rolling towards the new queen. And so the history had been told. We were back at the village, in the quiet of the night, our minds puzzled, bewildered.

'So this is how it started?' Noah asked.

'Yes. This is how the Crimson Queen became the evil we know,' Time replied, looking at the far horizon.

'If we had known all of this,' I said, 'I don't know if we would have fought so hard against her.'

'She did horrible things, Daniel.' Anita could not understand how strongly I had connected to that story.

Una's life had been way different than mine, but a few elements had brought up in me the pain I had felt too. The scars I secretly carried were similar. I had been taken away

495

from my origins, raised in the fear of a religion that kept telling me I was a monster. I was a sinner against God's will.

'What would I have become, if I had her power?' I said, thinking out loud.

'You would have never done something like that... No matter what!' Anita said.

'Listen to your friend, Daniel,' Time added. 'Love is your true nature, the very essence of who you are. And this is also why you feel so considerate of her, the evillest being that walked these lands.'

'I feel the same,' Noah said, sitting in the exact same spot he sat the first day we had walked into Trusk's home. 'She was a victim too. This is what is all about. Evil brings only evil.'

'In the ages watching over this world, I've witnessed many attempts from the evil to tear this planet apart from within. Many diabolic souls were appearing everywhere. I did my best to eradicate it, but it kept spreading. The hate Humans had for the Leonty and their power was not justified. They had done no evil. The Humans had. Their fear had turned into war. Eventually, they all came to the agreement that the females of their kind would not use their magic, ever. But prohibition soon became hunting, from the Humans and from the Leonty themselves who soon turned against their own kind.'

'We have no magic in our world,' Anita interrupted. 'But we do know hate and discrimination. This is uncomfortably familiar.'

'So the hunt begun with the Humans going after the Leonty?' Noah asked, looking at the far-off land, his eyes remembering his troubled moments in the queen's keep.

'It begun with the death of King Lohan first and intensified with the death of his son, Romohan, the very father of the young king you just saw. Romohan was taken by the hand of a Leonty with no magic. A male of their kind,' Time answered, triggering our curiosity. 'Protheux was his name. He was Vertatis's brother, the brother of the very one you saw in Una's mirror.'

'Why did he do that?' Noah asked.

'Because the Humans were convinced the true evil lived inside those kinds who had magic. And the Leonty with such power were high in number and their magic was dangerously effective.'

'I imagine it was that old man who persuaded them,' Anita let out. 'The same one who came here from Earth, if we believe what he said. The same one who convinced the Aqualymphs to leave their true nature.'

'Once again, you are correct,' Time replied. 'Vertatis, Una's mother, was brought to the Humans and executed right because of her power. Oh, believe me, her power was not offensive, but was of a different kind of danger to the one who had manipulated too many minds. Although all Leonty with magic were afraid to use their powers, after Una's mother died, Vertatis had risen to a peculiar popularity. She became well known for her ability to determine if someone was telling the truth or lying. And that was a threat too big to ignore. The old man who guided the old and the new king's action had her captured and brought to his presence. She was executed before she could manage to tell the truth about who was behind all that hate and lies, before her magic could reach the king and the other Humans. Her death was the initial spark of the greatest war ever fought in Runae. Not long after, her brother Protheux managed to infiltrate the palace and, avenging his sister, killed king Romohan in his sleep. From that moment, the history of this world was written... I have to go now.' Time turned around, looking at the edge of the village, towards the dead sea. 'I have to speak to Aura. I need to tell her you are crossing the gateway, tomorrow.'

'You are not coming with us?' Anita asked.

'Not for now. They need me. I'll need to think what will come next, for all of us. But don't worry, I'll be here when Erion rises.' And Time vanished into the dark night.

We sat at the porch for a little while, in silence. Our minds changed, we had come to an end and were about to start a new beginning. Leaving Runae wasn't a necessity any more. The impending threat was gone, but we were not ready to say goodbye. Yes, our minds had changed indeed.

Not long after being left alone, the soothing embrace of silence welcomed us in a soft, long-desired sleep. Noah and Anita fell asleep in the tiny dining room, in between the inside and the outside. Not too far from them, I lay on the wooden floor, my eyes closing in a blurry, inviting vision. As if I could dream before falling asleep, a glowing star guided the beginning of my oneiric walk. In the deepest dark of my heart and sight, Una's mirror shone still, gravitating in the air, slowly spinning on its own core. As if she could still talk to me, use her magic through space

498

and time, she asked me to get closer again, touch her memories, feel her truth as it was mine.

Fighting the need to let it go, I stood up, briefly challenged by the idea of waking Anita and Noah up. Somehow, the queen was telling me to come and meet her alone. Whatever conversation she was waiting to have, it was for my ears only. As if it had saved the most important vision for me alone, something new formed right before my eyes. The grey, bare walls, the almost empty room that formed was familiar. That was the same room where the mirror was left alone, unattended, before I had stolen it from Una. I was brought back to her keep, I was brought back to be reprehended for what I had done, I thought. But Una didn't acknowledge my presence. Her beauty was as powerful as her evil soul. Her eyes enchanted by the artefact she held in her hand, she was engulfed in a green light moving all over her skin.

'What is this power I feel? It's more than he owned. It's more than time itself... Even without all the Flares in my hands yet, I can feel more power coming through this...whatever this is.' And Una carelessly threw the clepsydra on the purple sheets covering her bed and moved to a little opening of the high tower.

'My queen.' A Leonty walked in, accompanied by her sister. The two of them stared at the cold floor, their skin showing a petrifying tension. 'You called?'

'Demetra, Ferhentia,' Una said, without turning around. Whatever she felt for her own sisters, I could not understand why she had kept them alive, allowing them to withhold their own Flare but never hiding the deep hate towards them. 'I need you to...extend your powers beyond their boundaries. I know your magic works only on beings with a mind and a soul. But I need you to look at something apparently dead, a mere, insignificant object as if it were alive.'

'My queen?' Demetra could not bring herself to try reading her sister's mind. Just the attempt would have brought her to her immediate death.

'Look over my bed. The green object you see. It's a key, just a key, but I keep feeling like there is more than a function behind it.'

'I do too,' Ferhentia said, without moving from her spot. Her eyes red, she was still staring at the floor. 'I felt it entering the room. I feel it now. There is like a flowing of thoughts, emotions coming from that thing. What is it?'

'Demetra?' Una went, ignoring her sister's question.

'I can't really tell. It does not feel like it has a mind of its own. It's more a powerful echo of a will passing through.'

'Just one?' The queen finally turned around, her face showing some interest.

'No, more than one. Many. Four? No maybe five. This object is not the only one of its kind… It has a shared memory, a mind existing way beyond those walls. This one is one of four. A stronger one, a fifth one holds all the whispers you hear, my Queen. '

I was listening carefully. Squeezed in the shadow of the walls, I was intrigued by the entire conversation and, at the same time, petrified by Una's presence. What had she seen in Time's artefact? *Why is she showing it to me?* I thought. The Crimson Queen was proving worthy of the duty she

500

had been given. After all, her magic was so powerful, she had detected something beyond Time's energy. Somehow, she saw through it, finding more than the eye could see. Destined to stay in the dark, like the owner of that same vision, I was brought back to my reality, in the dark of a long, quiet night.

The next morning came by fast. I had fallen asleep next to Anita, my face still pointed towards Noah. Slowing, I had entered my dreams carrying the worry Noah would disappear again. My hand on the floor, a few inches from his arm, showed my fear to the early, rising sun. Reela came downstairs to make sure we were ready to get up and get some food. The star might have gone back to its old cycle, but the Chomps had only started to live the night and day experience, and most of the inhabitants were already up and about. Reela's soft touch woke me up.

'My dear, Trusk is awake.' And a smile appeared on her face. 'The others have already set everything for the ceremony. We are going to the river, over the dome. Well, the dome is gone now, but you know? Over the edges of our village. It's right in this way. My fearcel had always dreamt of a life without boundaries.'

'I'm going to check on him, if you don't mind,' I said, standing up. My legs felt like wooden sticks.

Leaving to Reela the hard duty of waking the others up, I went upstairs, through the narrow stairs. Trusk was awake; his back against a soft, rustic pillow, he was up, sitting on the bed.

'Hey... I'm so happy to see you awake!'

'Daniel!' he exclaimed, his bright face showing improvements. 'I'm nof sure whaf happened... Mama says fhe queen is gone?'

'Yes, my dear friend, we made it. We made it, because of you!' And I sat on the floor, my arms on his bed.

'Fhis is good. Because I fhink we have no Flare any more...' And to that, I smiled.

'You are going to be OK, Trusk. Time will take care of you, all of you. And, while I'm here, let me thank you. Thank you for trusting us when we met in the forest. Thank you for bringing us to your father. Thank you for saving us, many times! I owe you my life.'

'I knew you were special, when you passed fhe wall! Nobody ever, EVER done fhaf! Yes, I knew you were special!'

'We are going to have a special ceremony for your father, down the river. Do you feel strong enough to come with me?' I asked.

'Yes,' he replied, determined. 'My fafher is a hero...'

'Yes, he is, indeed!' And I stood up, leaving Trusk to rest a bit longer.

Downstairs I found Anita and Noah ready at the table. Reela once again had put aside her emotions, her thoughts, to feed us with what she could provide. I hadn't touched food in so long, that I just realized I was starving, by looking at them with their hands on those heavy plates.

Soon enough, we left the house, crossed the line where the wall once stood, and walked towards the river. A large crowd moved down at once. Every single Chomp was there, to celebrate their saviour, the one who had set them free. Not well enough to walk, Trusk held on to my shoulders, happy to be with us, one beside the other. At the far end, Time stood beside the riverbed, right where Noah, Anita and I had stopped to rest what felt like months prior, on our way to the Chomps' village. The same signs Noah could not read were silently waiting for us. A large wooden chest floated on the water, anchored with a rope to the side of the river. Inside, pink petals filled the otherwise empty box.

It was upsetting not having a body to say goodbye to. I could feel the one I had called Key master's ashes still on my skin, that final act impressed in my eyes. A large, rounded shape made of little stones lay on the grass. The Chomps had painted them with the colours of the rainbow. At its centre, Revelia held a long wooden stick. A cloth was attached to it and the soft breeze moved it slowly. On it, two wings had been painted on it and a brief sentence appeared written just below:

Flioch tu, Laoch.

The running water of the river started to move upwards, from the sea to the far distant mountains. A crystal shape rose above its surface and eventually stopped beside the wooden chest. Aura emerged, bright and transparent.

'To the kind that has witnessed the evil and defeated it...better days are coming!' she started, her body slowly taking shape from the ground. She stepped out of the water under the Chomps' shocked faces. 'Treekan's act of courage had made it possible! Our protector is back with us, thanks to his kindness and his rightful sense of justice!'

503

'Flioch Tu, Laoch!, Thank you, hero!' Time said loudly.

'Flioch Tu, Laoch!' the entire group of Chomps repeated.

It was like the entire place had one mind and one body. They were all paying respect to the one who had helped us in our quest. We joined them in their praise. 'Flioch Tu, Laoch!' we repeated. A few minutes later, the crowd mixed in conversations, smiles and tears. Noah, Anita, Trusk and I moved close to Aura and Time. That was the first time we saw the gatekeeper since the moment we had landed on that small island over the grey fog.

'Are you ready?' Time asked.

'Will we ever be?' Noah replied, smiling.

'You have done something incredible! Time, the grey wall at the dead sea is now gone. You can cross the node, when you want,' Aura said.

'It's time to go home,' I said, resisting the idea.

It was like I had forgotten my real life, the things I left unattended, the people I had left behind. Whatever length of time we had been away, it didn't matter any more. Somewhere in my heart, I was still craving to see John, Daisy, Harry, but it was like listening to someone else's desires, a distant voice in the far land.

'Time,' I continued. 'My grandma was a Praetorian. She had been keeping this for me, till the moment I was ready.' And I showed him the box with a shell carved into it. 'What is it?'

'This is just a box, my friend. What is inside it's more important.' And he took it from my hands and opened it. 'This shell, lying here…it's waiting for another artefact.

504

Both of you carry one. This means, protection, creation and secret.'

'Where is the other one?' I asked, puzzled.

'I believe your other half has it?' Time looked at Noah, waiting.

'I'm afraid I have no idea what you are referring to? I don't have anything like that.' Noah felt like he had suddenly lost his pass to our future.

'It's like a heart...with a crown on top of it. Like in the paintings you saw at John's show, remember?' Anita said out loud. She had put together many of the details I had shared with her. Time's eyes shone briefly.

'Once more, my friend, you are incredibly smart!' Time smiled. 'Yes, it's exactly it. Somewhere, in your world, the artefact is waiting for you, and for its other half.'

'My heroes,' Aura interrupted. 'I need to get back to the dead sea. I imagine we can give back his name, now? The Aqualymphs' sea?' She looked at Time who nodded to her request. 'I'll see you soon!' And she turned into pure water, swept away by the flowing of the river.

'Your world and its creatures are very different from this one,' Time continued, looking back at me. 'But I know that much that is needed. Whoever kept your key, and you alive, is indeed a Praetorian, but if your...grandma you called it? I assume she was human...?' And to that question I nodded in agreement. 'This type of power reminds me of Health making. She would have been the one able to do something like that.' And Time looked into the empty space ahead, thinking. 'Anyway, a Human alone cannot be a Praetorian. Someone else must have been with her,

505

sharing her duty. Someone close to your true nature. Pretty much like it is happening with your friend.'

To those last words, Noah and I looked at Anita, who made a puzzled face. Time spoke in riddles, adding more questions as he had just responded to some, old ones. With his strength not fully back, Trusk had started to get weak. His little voice sounded in my left ear while I was still carrying him on my shoulders. He wanted to go back home, so Time offered to take him instead. In that way, it would be only a matter of seconds.

'I might not see you for a while, little fella,' I said to Trusk, now wrapped in Time's arms.

'Thank you. We will never forget you!' Anita gave him a kiss on his cheek and Trusk blushed.

'I will always remember you...all of you,' Trusk let out.

'You can head south; Aura is waiting for you. I'll see you at the node. Don't cross it before I get there!'

After Noah hugged Trusk a last time and I took his little hand once more, Time disappeared, taking our tiny saviour away.

Chapter Thirty-Three
Same Home, Different Me

∞

We were leaving with our hearts lagging behind. Our wills were dragged by our duty to leave that place and go home. We had come to Runae as Daniel, Noah and Anita but we were now leaving being other people entirely. We had changed sometime during our adventure. I was going back home reborn as a new man.

How will I ever explain all of this to John? What can I say that would make him understand? Before leaving Earth, I had got used to lying about the things I wasn't ready to share, the things I didn't know how to explain. But not any more. I could not find a lie that I could possibly make peace with it. Whatever conversation I was going to have with him, it was going to be the exciting, confusing, painful truth.

We crossed the land where the rain had taken us unprepared before, making us crash on the ground, and entered the forest where we had met Trusk for the first time. Walking freely, without the fear of being found by the spectres, without the rush of running away from them, we finally had the chance to enjoy the beauty of the surroundings.

'I know it sounds crazy, but I wish we were staying a bit longer...this place is incredible...when you actually have the time, and the peace, to look at it,' Anita said.

'Very true,' Noah replied. 'I barely remember running through these woods.'

'What was that song that Trusk was singing?' I asked, smiling.

'And remember his face, when I could not say his name correctly?' Anita asked, and we found ourselves laughing again, after so long.

'God...do you also feel like it has been ages since then?' Noah asked.

We all felt the same. The star wasn't moving then, but the time had flown by. Our clocks ticked the same, maybe even faster. Eventually we left the forest behind and arrived at the top of the hill; we could see the vast sea at the bottom of the other side, right in front of us. Speeding up on the steep way down, few minutes later we were already at the shoreline. Aura emerged the same moment we arrived and her voice was calling us.

'There is two too many,' she said, smiling. Those were the exact words she had said to us, the day we had arrived.

'But now we know why!' Noah replied.

'Aura,' I said. 'We saw you, a past version of you, in the Ancient Mirrors. I'm really sorry you had to see the end of your kind and sacrifice everything to protect this place.'

'We have seen someone walking through this node,' Anita added. 'Someone who said he had come from Earth?'

'Someone the evil sent to defy us.' Aura's face turned away. Sorrow and guilt had been long-lasting companions for her. 'Someone Queen Eah trusted when she should have never. Yet, It was my fault all this started. Every painful event started the moment we brought that human to our queen!'

'No Aura,' I replied, moving closer to her. 'The evil was here and everywhere well before that. He was just one of the many ways it could reach you. Don't let the sadness of the past make you forget what you have done now, for us.'

'Trusk is resting.' Time had just appeared out of nowhere. 'Reela wanted you to know, you are always welcome to her home, now and forever.'

'Shall we?' Aura asked, her spirit renewed by Time's presence. After turning around towards the calm water she disappeared, swallowed by the sea.

'Give me your hands,' Time said.

'No crazy diving, this time?' I asked, smiling.

'Not this time,' he replied.

In a split second stood on the small island in the middle of the crystal surface. Aura moved from side to side pretty fast and few seconds later she re-emerged into the clear air.

'With my key and Aura's help, you will be able to cross the node now and go back home...but before you go,' Time said, 'let me say something. First and foremost, thank you! I believe you know already how much your brave, courageous act means to me, so I won't bother you with that any longer. Of the Gods left standing, beside me and you, Soul is still out there, somewhere. I can feel it, and I'm sure you have been feeling it too.'

'Time?' I interrupted him. 'Both Noah and I have been seeing...entities before. I believe one was you. Your clepsydra has been popping into my head since then. But someone else has been there too. An old woman, with golden eyes like yours. Sometimes I've seen her like a grey shadow, a shadow holding on to a long stick, a rod with a snake twisting on it.' And Time showed a glimpse of surprise. 'But also a third one, wearing a tiara on his head.'

'Yes, my friend,' he replied, after a moment of hesitation. 'The tiara is Soul's artefact. He has been reaching out too.'

'So it wasn't simply their memories calling from afar?' Anita asked.

'Although different to one another, the Gods share the same power, the same mind. They are made out of the same spark. But yes, like I was, Soul is still caged. He can't fully reach you. It was you who were echoing his voice in your head.'

'What do we do if and when we find him?' Noah asked.

'We'd better not go so fast. Our paths will part ways for little bit. Your task is to find the Crowned Heart. Mine is to find Soul.'

'What then?' I interrupted. 'What happens then?'

510

'As I said, it's better we don't go too fast. You need time to process your real nature. Don't worry,' he added, noticing we felt a little disappointed. 'We are going to meet again, soon. It's important that you understand we must find Soul and your artefact, before we do anything else.'

'OK,' I replied. 'Noah and I will try our best.'

'Not just you two! As I said, this girl has much more than meets the eye. Make sure she knows and remembers!' And Time smiled at her. 'Now, before you go, I believe someone wants to say goodbye.'

And Time glowed quickly, teleporting Revelia just beside him. I had hoped we could see her again, once more. She moved towards us as soon as she arrived, hugging me, Noah and Anita.

'I know I've lost my sisters,' she said, holding her tears back. 'But I gained a new family. A family of a better kind!'

'We are sorry for what happened to them,' Noah said. Despite the suffering Demetra had inflicted on his mind and on his soul, he could feel Revelia's loss as if it was his.

'It's OK. We didn't share much, our hearts were beating differently, but they were still my sisters, you know? Anyway, please don't forget about me. I will always be waiting for you. My Flare is gone and so it seems is my power, so please, don't let me guess the future for too long...'

'We'll see you again. I promise,' I said.

'Aura.' Time called. 'Be strong, be fast. I'll be seeing you soon!' And Time's clepsydra pulsed, three times.

We left as we had arrived. The space around us flipping upside down, darkness and light mixing fast, twisting our eyes and our minds. Our bodies were back on the ground of Anita's backyard, getting wet in the little rain that came down from the afternoon sky. We were home.

'What…what happened?' Anita said, worried. She was looking around, upset, watching us getting up.

The place had changed. Anita's backyard was empty. Table and chairs had been moved to the side. The broken cups were gone, and so were our personal items. In our world, time had moved ahead. Someone else had been there while we were gone.

'How long have we been gone?' I asked.

'Gone where? What the hell happened?' looked at us in shock.

'What do you mean?' Noah was puzzled.

'We were getting back in the house…just a few moments ago… Something happened and now everything looks changed!'

'Anita, we must have spent weeks in Runae,' I said, my hands on her shoulders.

'Where? What is Runae?' she asked, leaving us astonished.

Anita's memories were gone. She had no recollection of anything we had gone through. Somehow she had left her greatest experience behind, at the node. I was speechless.

'Let's get inside,' she said, pulling the patio doors.

'She doesn't remember?' Noah whispered to me.

I didn't know what to say. 'Make sure she knows'…*that's what Time said. Did he mean he knew she would forget and it is up to us to bring her memories back to her?*

The patio doors were closed shut. Someone had closed them up for some strange reason. If that someone had been there, they must have found the place empty. We were physically gone for all that time. Anita walked to the front door going around the side of the house, pulled away one of the old, squeaky chairs and took a key that was hidden under a vase. Once inside, Anita started to roam around, looking for other strange, inexplicable changes. Her phone was on the worktop, in the kitchen, beside the tons of books piled one on top of the other. There was no sign of my stuff, nor of Noah's.

'Someone was here. But I don't understand…were we like…in one of your visions?' It was like we had gone back weeks. She had no idea of what it had happened to us.

'Anita,' I said loudly, getting her attention. 'Let's sit for a moment. We need to talk to you.'

And so we spent a few hours trying to pull her memories back. Although resistant, she eventually started to accept the idea we had been gone for a good while. When she had calmed down and come to reason, we agreed we would continue that conversation another time. There were more urgent matters. If we had been gone for that long, there would have been people worried sick. I had to go home to John. She had to get back to Patrick, see if he had been looking for her. If they had sent people, maybe even the Gardaí, looking for us, we had a long explanation to give.

'I do remember being scared, crying, laughing...but I can't remember why... I do believe you, Daniel. I just can't understand why I can feel it but I can't see it in my mind,' she said.

'It will come back to you, trust me. Now, we need to make sure the rest of our world hasn't collapsed,' I answered.

'Sure, sure!' she replied. 'Your car is gone; we can use mine. I'll bring you home to John. Afterwards I'll go and see Patrick. What about you, Noah?'

'Well...' He didn't know what to say. He didn't have anybody to go back to and he was now in the middle of a crisis. The entire development of our relationship, his with her, with me, was blurred in the background. 'I think it's best if I go back home. We have to find the Crowned Heart and we need to start from somewhere... Can you bring me to the train station, after leaving Daniel at home?'

'Of course. Let's go!' she answered.

Keys in hand, we hopped into the car. Again, a sense of urgency ran through our bodies. If the end of the world had come, we had been fighting abroad, away from our loved ones.

Ten minutes later, we had arrived at my place. The gates were open but the front door was shut. I knew John was home; the outdoor lights were on. Close to the house, I got out of the car just as John's face appeared at the front door. He looked different. An unusually long, dishevelled beard outlined a white face, under his eyes were two dark shadows. Before I could come closer, he stormed out of the house, in tears.

514

'Oh my God, Daniel!' And he hugged me with all the strength he had. Daisy followed him outside, jumping all over our feet. Anita had come out of the car too, but Noah stayed inside, his heart slightly cracked by that scene.

'John!' she said. 'I don't know what happened… We…' But she couldn't continue. She could not confess a truth she could not even remember.

'What happened to you? Who is that man?' And he looked briefly at Noah.

'It's a long story, John. I'm OK. We are all OK. I'm sorry if I worried you sick. We had no idea we had been gone for so long,' I said.

'What do you mean?' John struggled to grasp the magnitude of what he was going to learn, soon.

'I'll tell you everything, I promise! Anita needs to find Patrick, make sure everything is OK.'

'Patrick and I were at your place,' John said to her. 'Several times. The Gardaí was there too...for a while. We filled a missing person report, but they had no lead to follow. You have been gone for three weeks!'

'A missing person? Three bloody weeks?' Anita said out loud. 'I need to fix this right away! John, Daniel will explain everything to you. I need to take Noah to the station and get to Patrick…or maybe I should go to the Gardaí Station first?' She panicked.

'Anita…Anita…' I was trying to calm her down, again. 'Bring Noah to the train station first. It's getting late, I'm not sure there is a train for Galway this late. Then go to Patrick and to the Gardaí. Tell them I'm home too, safe and sound. I'm sure they will pay us a visit.' And I hugged her, whispering: 'Skip the magic details, please, and come back here when you are ready.'

Anita got back in the car in a flash and drove away, speeding up. I had no chance to say goodbye to Noah, nor to look at him before he was gone. But it was better that way. A long conversation with John was waiting and Noah was one of the most difficult parts I had to go through. With his arm still on my shoulder, his head close to mine, we turned around and walked in, Daisy stuck to our feet. I looked at the far gates for a brief moment, my mind moving from Anita and Noah to Trusk, Revelia, Treekan, Time…and I let out a deep, loud breath.

'You better be ready for what I'm about to tell you. You will hardly believe it. But before I start'—and John was looking at me closely, his face locked to mine—'I missed you, and I love you…very much!'

A long-awaited kiss introduced the tale of my life. Closing the door to the dark of the evening, I started to share my incredible, magical truth.

∞

The End

The Power of Love
The One

Epilogue

A Tale of Time

∞

Since the early moments after Daniel, Noah, and Anita had gone back home, a question infiltrated their minds, moving right at the top of their pressing need for answers: What did Treekan discuss with Aura that made him change his mind? What did she show him that could have turned his mind around? If he had finally found a reason to help those three Humans lost in their journey, risking his life and the lives of those he loved the most, that reason must be in Aura's hands.

It is said that Time owns all the answers. He has seen, he keeps seeing and he foresees the eternal flow of every moment. *What if my brother could tell? What if he could show*

*me what the Aqualymphs' mirror had stored deep within its
ancient wisdom... What would we know?*

One Yac had passed since the creation of the six Flares,
and the God of Runae had disappeared from sight once
again. Hidden in between space and reality, he was
desperately attempting to see the myriad of possible
futures, searching for the one where Nothing would be
defeated. Too many versions of the same end were
repeating right in front of him. The universe was
succumbing to the same destiny over and over again. In
most of those multiplying opportunities, one thing
remained the same: Time wasn't the one bringing the long-
desired victory. In each variant of his future, he was
defeated and enslaved by the evil in an eternal, magical
prison. But as his eyes were focused on the only thing that
mattered, much more had slipped through the cracks of his
infinite mind.

In the lands at the southwest, the Humans roared in an
unstoppable demand for conquest. Their rightful portion
of Time's magic, their own Flare, seemed to be less
powerful than the others. As they were the only ones on the
entire planet without magic of their own, Time's decision
to provide them with an ineffective power was impossible
to digest—a further insult to everything they had
produced, to what they had become. They had been
discriminated against once more. Growing tired of being
confined within the same walls they had built against the
Leonty, the edges of the Crown domain were seething
restlessly. Eager to legitimize their position as victims of an
evil power growing in the Leonty's hills, King Lohan and
his only son had demanded a hearing with the

Aqualymphs, who had first spoken about an emerging threat from the cloudy mountains.

In the Yac hundred of the third millennium, at the turn of the warm Fohalt season, the two Humans had entered the pass to the coast on the south side, in between the Aqualymphs' Sea and the Chomps' land. Moving quickly down the hills, the two had kept quiet, as their mission was a secret, not speaking of it to anyone they met along the way. Unannounced and earlier than expected, King Lohan and his son Romohan arrived at the edge of the sea, their boots squashing in the sacred waters as if they wanted to be heard by the deep water inhabitants. A few moments later, a large wave moved from part to part, bringing the blue of the sea and the purple sky to a virtual touch. In the vortex of the boiling water, the protector of the node showed herself to the trespassers.

'I'm Aura, the gatekeeper and guardian of the passage,' she stated as if she was merely pronouncing a ritual prayer. Then she suddenly changed her tone. 'King Lohan! We were not expecting you for another rhoc. Why do you enter our lands as if they were yours to command?'

'I'm here for an urgent business. A business that cannot wait another rhoc! Bring me to your queen, please.'

'I'm sure that can be arranged, but you know our lands are not made for your kind. There is work that needs to be done so we can allow your presence in the depths of our kingdom.' And in the snap of a finger, the Aqualymph disappeared, exchanging her spot with two more of her kind.

Made of the same crystal water they were standing in, they didn't changed form and avoided any engagement with their guests. Instead, they joined their liquid arms together and moved them in a circle, performing an ancient ceremonial spell, giving form to a clear, shiny bubble. As it wasn't the first time the king and his son had entered the sea, the Humans promptly moved ahead, with the warm water rising to their chests as they entered the space created by their hosts. With both visitors trapped in a sphere filled with pure air, the Aqualymphs submerged into the deep blue sea, carrying them along, and disappeared from sight.

Their vessel pulled fast by the two powerful creatures of the sea, the Humans sprinted through the many layers of deep water, following the trail left by the Aqualymphs. As every detail faded away, diving into a dense, blue matter, the guests' carriage broke through an invisible wall of magic and entered the hosts' dominion. Made of corals and stones, several large buildings were scattered across the submerged land. Vegetation danced from part to part with the silent whistle of the many Aqualymphs diving in every direction. At the centre of a large area, a red, shining tower conquered the blue space, like a spike for its flag—it was clearly the queen's residence.

As they approached its entrance, Aura presented herself to the king and Romohan once more. Her hands moved towards the inside of the palace, she silently invited them to enter. Once the bubble protecting the Humans touched the still-shut doors, the surface wobbled a little, becoming intangible to the existing reality. The king and his son penetrated the hard, pinkish coral as if it was a pure illusion of the mind. Once they reached the other side, the

521

incredible mass of water filling the vast space collapsed on the ground. As if it has suddenly lost its matter, the sea had disappeared from the entire room, draining away to an imperceptible depth, leaving only a large puddle slowly moving on the stone pavement. The space filled with air, it was time for the Humans to leave their vessel and walk freely.

Fierce and determined to speak to the queen, King Lohan quickly moved ahead, leaving the long corridor behind. At the top of a large set of stairs, an empty throne awaited his disappointment.

'The queen is not here?' Romohan asked, looking around, his eyes in disbelief in front of the magic he was witnessing for the very first time.

'Oh, she is here,' Lohan replied, his eyes zipping to the left of the empty chair. 'Queen of the Seas. I have an urgent matter to discuss. I could not wait for our agreed meeting. I hope you understand,' he said, slightly bending his shoulders, enough to show respect but little enough to let his ego go unchallenged.

'And tell me, Lohan, King of the Humans, does Time know of your request for an audience with the guardian of the passage?' Queen Eah materialized before her guests, her feet seemingly anchored in the gently undulating water on the ground. Her legs took on the colours of the surrounding corals and stones, followed by her body and arms. Finally, her face emerged, her cerulean eyes framed by golden sand, a crown fashioned from shells adorning her regal visage as the Queen of the Aqualymphs.

522

'Time is nowhere near our lands, my Queen,' Romohan said, his gaze fixed on the ground, hesitant to meet her eyes. At the mention of my Queen, King Lohan gave his son a disapproving glare.

'I know why you are here, and I cannot assist you with what you are about to request,' Queen Eah's words were measured. With a slow pace, she advanced towards the front of her throne. The gentle rustling of her gown's elaborate train crafted from pebbles and shells added an air of tension to the room, unsettling her guests.

'I know you have witnessed the growing threat of evil in the west. It is no coincidence that it has chosen that particular place amidst all the lands in our world. It festers, feeding on those who conceal dark magic in their veins!' the King declared.

'There is no evil within the heart of the Leonty. And you too possess magic, thanks to our God,' Queen Eah replied, settling onto her throne. Her eyes briefly flickered as if sensing another presence approaching from afar.

'Magic? Is that what we've been granted? With the Flare, their powers have only grown stronger! The Valahans have been endowed with strength. The Chomps have been gifted with invisibility. They elude us at every turn. Even the Garughals now possess the ability to transmute matter permanently. They can shape the world at will!'

'And we have been granted little more than you, King,' the Queen exclaimed. 'Our ability to venture beyond the sacred waters is merely extended, but not to a life-altering degree. Isn't that so? You, on the other hand, have been bestowed with the power of a new science. Some might call that magic.'

'Bending the laws of matter and harnessing pure energy. But what good is such a gift if we cannot defend ourselves? It is time to wield it in defence of our lands and eradicate this threat,' Lohan asserted.

'So, what exactly have you come here to request? To seek validation of your stance? Perhaps an alliance with my people against them?' The Queen swiftly descended from her throne, closing the distance between herself and her guests. In their minds, the sudden shift in her manner hinted at an impending confrontation. King Lohan was poised to speak once more when another Aqualymph materialized beside them.

'My Queen, someone has entered our lands, through the node!' Aura's eyes conveyed fear as she addressed her Queen. The other two fell silent, stunned by the revelation. In their minds, threats loomed large and fast.

How? Only the Gods possess the ability to pass through. Act swiftly. Take the guards with you and escort this unwelcome guest to my presence. They can join the other two here. As for you, you are strongly urged to remain here; our discussion is not yet concluded.' The Queen pivoted and knelt upon the water's surface, her crystal fingers dipping into the liquid. Unseen by the King and his son, she initiated her magic, conjuring a formidable defensive barrier along the shorelines above. Stretching from left to right, as far as the eye could discern, a dense grey fog enveloped the node, obscuring the midlands from view.

Shortly after, Aura and several more Aqualymphs emerged on the surface. On the small, rounded island, a human with white hair and a white beard stood motionless, his eyes fixed on the emerging barrier.

'I am Aura,' she introduced herself as soon as she took form. 'The God of this world has tasked me as Gatekeeper. We did not anticipate any visitors. This gateway is open only to the Gods. Who are you?'

'My name is Lëogan,' the man replied, attempting a wry smile amidst his unkempt beard. 'I am here because my world is in danger. I have come to seek help.'

'What world do you speak of?' the Aqualymph regarded her guest suspiciously. Something felt wrong.

'Earth. We are under attack! We require your assistance, your power, your magic to combat the enemy...'

'If his words hold truth, we must bring him before the council!' another Aqualymph suggested.

'Yes, please. I must speak with them!'

Like King Lohan and Romohan before him, the new guest plunged into the seas with haste, guided swiftly by the Aqualymphs toward the Queen's home. In their urgency, all security measures seemed to be overlooked. To the King's surprise, the stranger was ushered to the Queen's domain with considerably less resistance than they had encountered earlier. Before he could voice his objection, Eah spoke.

'Who are you, and how did you enter Runae?' she inquired.

'I am Lëogan, and I come from Earth. I approach you all bearing news of a looming threat in the distant skies—an enemy of our God is waging war against us. The evil had deployed a formidable army with the intent of erase us all. I have come seeking help,' the stranger replied.

'Tell me, Lëogan...' The Queen hurried her walk along the corridor, her steps quickening. The King, observing the unequal treatment, bristled with indignation. 'You appear human, yet you are not. What are you?'

'Our kind differs from yours. Do not be deceived by appearances. Listen closely to my words,' Lëogan cautioned, his eyes gleaming with a dark energy. An invisible, magnetizing force emanated from his presence. 'A grave danger approaches not only over my world but yours as well. Something malevolent is coming...'

'It is already here, you fool!' The King erupted, weary of being treated as inferior. 'The enemy has already infiltrated our lands, amassing strength in the west and spreading fast!'

'It is...' Lëogan's expression betrayed a hint of satisfaction. He had acquired the knowledge he sought. To lend credibility to his fabrications, he needed to quickly find something that could resonate with the fears of those beings. 'I fear my arrival may be too late then. If his forces are already among your people, there is little you can do.'

'If there is a threat, we will meet it head-on!' The Queen's response was sharp, igniting Lohan's fury.

'So you are prepared to heed the counsel of a stranger in matters of conflict, yet you hesitated when I, King of the

526

Humans, sought your aid in driving back the Leonty from the Cloudy Mountains!' he accused.

'Do not give in to anger, my King,' Lëogan interjected smoothly, his voice carrying an unusual authority. 'Your wisdom in seeking alliances in times of crisis is commendable. I trust you are all in agreement. Action must be taken!'

'And action shall be taken!' The Queen's declaration caught Aura off guard. Aqualymphs rarely engaged in disputes, let alone discussed the prospect of war with the inhabitants of Runae. Feeling the weight of the Queen's sudden shift in behaviour, she felt compelled to deviate from protocol.

'My Queen, this is madness! It is neither wise nor our duty to entertain thoughts of conflict and warfare. Perhaps we should consult our God before making any decisions?' Aura asked, earning a disapproving glare from Queen Eah.

'It is natural to feel the burden of a such responsibility...' the stranger began, before the Queen could speak. Whatever influence he wielded, it seemed not as effective against a simple Aqualymph like Aura. 'There will be a time to report to your God, just as there is a time to act. That time is now.'

'Agreed,' King Lohan exclaimed. 'We shall march to the northwest hills. We assume we have your approval and support?'

'Indeed, you do!' the sovereign affirmed, leaving Aura stunned. 'Prepare for war. With the power of our Flare, we will depart these lands for as long as necessary to aid our ally in need!' Queen Eah turned around and extended her right hand towards Lëogan. 'Come with me,' she invited. 'I'm truly eager to know any additional details you can provide.'

As the stranger took her hand, the two vanished in an instant, leaving a trail of vapor in the room. The king and his son exchanged resentful glances. Though they had achieved their objective, the Queen's behaviour felt disrespectful. In the depths of their minds, they both acknowledged her as an ally, albeit one whose commitment was destined to be short-lived.

∞

The Power of Love
A Tale of Time

The Power of Love
The One

R.J. Kinnaird

About the Author

Ross Joseph Kinnaird was born in a far land something like 1000 years ago. He moved to Italy as an infant and grew up in the deep south, shaped by the sun and the wildness of the sea. After moving to Ireland in 2010, he began collecting and organizing the many stories he had written. They all seemed to have one theme, one soul. With the Celtic magic that his new home brought to him, Ross finally saw his novel taking shape through the mystical eyes of his mind. And so, *"The Power of Love"* became the journey of a lifetime, perhaps spanning many lifetimes.

In the realm between reality and fantasy, he fused together the diverse ways life presented itself to him. Through a literary roller-coaster of emotions and feelings — pain, sorrow, happiness, friendship, and love — Ross J. Kinnaird wrote the many stories we tell ourselves in our never-ending search for greater meaning.

"Art, feelings, music, emotions have always been the strongest part of me. I was only a young teenager when I started transferring my busy mind onto paper.
As the years passed, life and experiences enriched my soul to a point where The Power of Love finally took form.
With the strongest connection to what I saw life as, the story of Daniel, Noah and Anita became an extension of who I am, of who many of us are."

R. J. Kinnaird

ISBN: 978-1-7394634-1-0

For more info on The Power of Love Series®
www.thepoweofloveseries.com

The adventures of Daniel, Noah and Anita continue in:

The Power of Love – The Two
The Power of Love – The Three

Made in the USA
Monee, IL
25 June 2024

60609500R00308